ROYAL BLOOD

A FOUR STORY PARANORMAL ROMANCE
COLLECTION

AJ TIPTON

Illustrated by
CIRCECORP

Copyright © AJ Tipton 2015 The right of AJ Tipton to be identified as the author of this work has been asserted by her in accordance with the Copyright, Designs and Patents Act 1988 (or other similar law, depending on your country). All rights reserved. No part of this book may be reproduced, stored in a retrieval system, or transmitted, in any form, or by any means (electronic, mechanical, photocopying, recording or otherwise) without the prior written permission of the author, except in cases of brief quotations embodied in reviews or articles. It may not be edited, amended, lent, resold, hired out, distributed or otherwise circulated without the publisher's written permission. Permission can be obtained from a.j.tipton.author@gmail.com

This book is for sale to adult audiences only. It contains substantial sexually explicit scenes and graphic language which may be considered offensive by some readers.

This is a work of fiction. All characters, names, places and incidents appearing in this work are fictitious. Any resemblance to real persons, living or dead, organizations, events or locales is purely coincidental.

All sexually active characters in this work are 18 years of age or older.

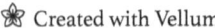 Created with Vellum

THE VAMPIRE'S THRONE

A lice Jones stifled a gag as she entered the perfume-saturated air of the high-end art gallery. Everything about the daunting gallery's decor was first-class rough chic, from the staggering large rooms with artistically exposed pipes in the ceiling to the intimate nooks of brick and glass.

Alice's borrowed stilettos threatened to dump her on her ass with every step, but she was determined to keep her head up. *Classy. Remember you're supposed to be classy,* she thought. With each nervous step, Alice half-expected someone to shout "plebeian intruder!" in her direction and tear her photographs off the wall. But, so far, the wealthy guests were nodding at her work politely and smiling as widely as their Botox allowed.

A heavy glass of wine materialized in her hand, and Alice looked up into the flashing grin of the gallery's owner, Margot Dal.

"You looked like you needed a drink." Margot nodded towards the glass, which was filled so high Alice was sure a slight breeze would spill it down her front.

"To wear?" Alice asked. She made a show of carefully craning down to sip at the brimming drink without moving her hand, while still sending Margot a grateful smile. Alice had been working closely with Margot over the last few weeks to prepare for the opening, but the tall, statuesque woman still intimidated the crap out of Alice.

"What can I say? A good friend pushes your boundaries." Margot seemed to only be paying half attention to what she was saying, her eyes already roaming the crowd like she was looking for someone.

Alice forced herself not to fidget. She'd give anything for even *half* of Margot's composure. Margot looked effortlessly comfortable wherever she was, but within her gallery she was striking. Her dark skin glowed golden in the light, and her black dress was simple, tasteful, and probably cost more than twice Alice's rent. For her photographs' first big debut, Alice had scraped together every spare penny to get a new dress. She caught her own reflection and frowned. Her red hair was coming undone from her tightly-wound braid, sending out stray tendrils, and her bright blue eyes looked unnaturally wide between the thick lines of eye makeup. The strapless green dress wasn't too bad. It hugged her body, emphasizing the curve of her waist, with elaborate white beading along the top drawing the eye to her peeking cleavage. A purple shawl covered her shoulders and across her neck, the same color as her chandelier-beaded earrings. She resisted the urge to hide herself in the folds of her shawl. The longer she was here, the more she wished she'd taken up Margot's offer to borrow one of her many designer gowns.

"So, do you know if there have been any sales yet?" Alice sipped her drink cautiously, keeping her voice casual like she didn't particularly care about the answer.

Margot chuckled, not fooled at all. "Don't you worry, sweetie. Little red dots indicating finalized sales are going up all over the place." She raised her eyebrows at Alice. "But you know what would help those sales?"

"What?" Alice's stomach sank. She already knew what Margot was going to say.

"You need to *talk* to people. Help them get to know you, the stories behind your work." Margot flicked her wrist, the small gesture taking in the rest of the people in the gallery. "You know these rich folks; it's not just the art they want, it's the *secrets* behind the art." Margot gave Alice a stern look. "Sip down at least an inch of that wine and then shoo from this corner before I prod you out with a broom." Her tone was joking, but Alice had no doubt Margot would actually do it.

A woman who looked like she'd stepped off the cover of a magazine walked by and winked at Margot. The gallery owner grabbed a new glass of wine from a passing waiter and smiled.

"Duty calls." Margot licked her lips and then gave Alice's hand a squeeze. "You can do this. This is your big night! Enjoy it." And then she was gone. Alice blinked and Margot was already on the other side of the room, smiling wide and standing intimately close to the cover girl.

Alice stared down at her drink. A couple more sips and it would be at a manageable height for mingling. She contemplated hiding in the corner for another hour just to be contrary, but she knew Margot was right. This show was her big chance to make the connections and cash to launch her photography career and escape her crappy day job as an administrative assistant. She took a deep gulp of the wine.

No more paperwork.

No more endless commutes.

No more wedging in photo shoots during thirty-minute lunch breaks.

Talking to strangers was downright palatable if it meant she could quit her soul-sucking corporate job. Her hand tightened around the stem of her wine glass. A well-dressed couple Alice vaguely recognized from a reality TV show were staring at her. The woman played with the edge of her leopard-print jacket while the man kept fiddling with his phone.

"It's all so derivative and prosaic." The woman sniffed loudly. "Rhys will have a good laugh over Margot's descent from good taste. What's with all the..." The woman pointed at Alice's closest photo, a high-contrast image of the bolts on the side of a trashcan at dusk.

Alice fought to keep a blush from creeping up her face. The man looked up from his phone. "What's that, snookums?"

"The title of the show, *Detail Wonders*. What's *wondrous* about a stupid trash can?"

The man shrugged. "Some rock star just bought the one with the hairbrush for five figures. He said it was urban or something."

"*Humans*, am I right? Such bullshit." She rubbed her nose, mumbling something about having to go to the bathroom, and the man nodded and followed.

Alice fought the urge to bury herself deeper into the corner. *Bullshit?* Getting the perfect photo required understanding the precise angle of the light, or catching the exact moment when the sun hit the--

Alice shook her head.

You can do this. You don't need their respect or their understanding. Someone just bought one of my photos for five figures! They can't all be shallow jerks. Just step up.

She managed to push forward one foot, then the next, until momentum pulled the rest of her toward the center of the room.

No day job.

No day job.

The words were a steady chant in her head as she smiled and nodded her way around the room. The folks who recognized her from the program's bio called out a few generic congratulations about her first big show. It was all very nice, but by the fiftieth time Alice told someone, "Yes, it's a real honor to be here," she worried her strain was starting to show.

Alice dabbed at the sweat behind her neck, looking around for Margot. *Will she skin me if I just pretend to have a headache and leave?* Alice wondered.

"I didn't think it could be possible for the artist to be more beautiful than the artwork," a smooth voice said from behind her.

Alice whipped around. Her glass tilted in her hand and she watched in what felt like slow motion as wine flew out of her glass in an arc toward a tall man with a trim beard standing a few feet away. The wine sprayed across him like a murder scene.

Noooooo. She reached out a hand like she could grab the liquid back from the air, but it was too late. The stain was already seeping through his crisp, white shirt like a blobby map of Asia across his chest.

"Oh my god! I'm so sorry!" Alice cried, jumping forward to dab the end of her shawl on the stain.

"It's quite all right." The man's voice was low and musical, sending little shivers down her spine. "This shirt needed a splash of color anyway."

Alice snuck a glance at his face, and his smile beamed at her like she was caught in a spotlight. She wanted to photograph his face from every angle. The Golden Ratio perfection of his features, the scruff of beard along the slope of his chin, the slight laugh lines around his mouth, and the care furrows on his forehead all demanded a zoom-in lens and the brightest light she could muster. She'd never been much for taking portraits, but this man--with the smile growing wider the longer she stared at him--was one she wanted to make into an intense study. *Preferably nude*.

"Um, hi. I'm Alice, and, uh, I take photos." Her words rushed out in a semi-incoherent string. She took a slow breath, forced herself to straighten up and stop staring at the sculpted muscles she could see through his wet shirt. "I'm usually more eloquent, I swear."

He laughed. "I believe it. Margot told me a lot about you; she's an old friend." He held out a hand. "Christopher Dal."

"Christopher Dal?" Alice shook his hand, feeling callouses along his palm that she didn't expect from somebody in a bespoke suit. "You and Margot have the same last name. Are you related?" They didn't look at all alike, but families came in all shapes and sizes.

He smiled. "No relation, but we've known each other so long she feels like family."

Alice felt a brief pang. She'd left behind all her hometown friends when she moved to the big city and had lost touch with everyone over the years. Between her job and her art, it was hard to find the time to make new friends. The warmth and familiarity in Christopher's voice when he said Margot's name sent a spike of loneliness through her. She forced a smile.

Christopher pointed at the picture behind her. "Your photos are remarkable."

"Thanks." She moved a wild strand of hair behind her ear, shifting her weight from one foot to the other.

"No, I mean it." Christopher stepped a little closer. "They're extraordinary. The way you honed in on such tiny details within mundane objects to find the hidden beauty is amazing. You have a remarkable eye."

Alice's repeated, "Thanks" was much more sincere this time. A happy warmth suffused her chest, flowing outward. *Finally!*

"Of all the people I've talked to tonight, you're the first one to understand that," Alice said. "I really appreciate it. I wanted people to walk away from this show with a new appreciation for the small details all around us."

Christopher smiled. "Isn't it fascinating how art can do that? It can present something that we look at every day in a different light to put the object into a new context."

Alice wanted to hug him. "That's exactly what I think! Beauty isn't just a sunset over the mountains." Her words picked up speed as she warmed to her topic. "Beauty can be the rim of a mailbox and how it complements the home behind it, or the construction of an anthill."

Christopher touched her hand and she felt the coolness of his skin like a soothing balm all the way down her arm. "You're an amazing artist, Alice. Do you realize how rare it is that you can see that, and then capture it so that others can see it too? You should be doing this full time."

Alice blushed. "You're being kind. I wish I had more time to really embrace my art." She pointed to a red dot next to the photo of a split tree. "I'm hoping the sales from tonight can help with that. I was lucky the light happened to be right a few minutes after I found that tree, but I almost missed it because of a meeting at work that ran late. There's never enough time to find every beautiful moment that's out there, but I'd sure like the chance to try."

Alice glanced accusingly at her wine, surprised she'd shared so much with a total stranger. From his small nods and understanding expression, Christopher seemed to know exactly what she meant.

"The world is so big," she said, "I wish I had the time to capture everything."

Christopher's grin broadened. "You never know. From what I've seen, tonight has been even more successful than even Margot anticipated." He held out his arm. "I've kept you too long from the rest of your guests. Do you feel like braving them together?"

Alice nodded, looping her arm through his and feeling

the cords of muscles through his coat. Perhaps talking with strangers wasn't so bad, after all.

CHRISTOPHER BREATHED in Alice's scent, intoxicating in its beauty: soap, a light touch of a vanilla perfume, and her blood pumping through the delicate skin of her neck. Suggestions of her mood sang from her blood: hesitation, anxiety, and...he really hoped he was interpreting it right...*longing*. Longing for him? Or just longing for a successful show? He would have to drink her blood to know for sure, and he was enjoying his time with her far too much to break the mood. As far as he could tell, she didn't have the Sight to recognize him as a vampire, or any of the other supernatural beings drinking wine and sniffing each other at the show.

His pulse raced at the gentle touch of Alice's hand against his forearm as they meandered through the gallery. Everything about her fascinated him. Her movements held a grace that hearkened back to refined royalty of centuries past, while her gentle spirit was like that of a magical, woodland nymph.

Her beauty shone like a beacon among the stilted bourgeois milling about the art gallery. As they walked arm and arm through the gallery, Alice's brilliant glow drew everyone they passed. Christopher settled into the role of the strong and silent companion, only jumping into the conversation to support Alice's lively explanation of her work. A tiger shifter flanked by her lovers came up to compliment a photo, and Alice launched into a charming, although somewhat rambling, description of why she photographed the cabinet in just that way. The tigress smiled, showing rows of perfect teeth, and Christopher felt himself stiffening up, protective instincts roaring to the surface which he clamped down before Alice noticed.

"I'm glad we dove back in." Alice's voice was steadier after the first lap around the room, but her grip on his arm was still tight with nerves.

"As am I." Christopher stared deeply into her bright, blue eyes.

I want to look into her eyes forever.

The thought flashed through him, stunning him with its certainty. He didn't sire other vampires often, but he always knew who he wanted within the first moments of meeting them. He pushed the thought down.

Not her. Please not her.

"Have you seen the rest of the exhibit?" He asked, actively distracting himself from his own thoughts.

Alice fiddled with the fringe on her wine-stained shawl. "I've seen it, but I'll be happy to view it again." She smiled at him. "There's so many wonderful pieces." Her joy was infectious and he held her hand against his arm, covering the back of her hand with his palm. Her skin was warm, her pulse beating fast as they moved into one of the side galleries of the other showcased artists.

She stopped short a little way into the room, pulling him with her.

"This one's my favorite," she said.

The photographer had captured the instant a champagne flute shattered. Glass shards flew in all directions, sparkling against a jet black background, forming perfectly symmetrical outlines like wings surrounding the remains of the glass.

"Absolutely stunning," Christopher said, not taking his eyes off of Alice.

A pink blush overtook Alice's cheeks. "You're not even looking at the art."

"Aren't I?" Christopher asked.

Alice blushed, turning quickly back towards the photograph. "Don't you just love this? An instant, captured forever. Something we'd never truly be able to appreciate if it wasn't frozen in time for us to see."

Christopher regarded the photo. "Being frozen in time is not all it is cracked up to be." He frowned.

"But, don't you see? Even if the image is frozen, what the viewer perceives isn't." Alice's entire face lit up. "It doesn't change over time, but time changes *it*." She pointed at the glass's stem in the picture. "You and I see a champagne flute, but in years to come, glass may be out of use and unrecognizable to people. Wouldn't that be magical? Seeing glass shatter for the first time, capturing what's a mundane moment for us in a way that translates across time?"

She'd make an amazing vampire. The tantalizing thought penetrated him again. "I see why Margot insisted you participate in this show. You have a unique perspective. Grounded, yet passionate," Christopher said.

"It's not usually an asset." Alice guided Christopher into a leisurely lap back to the main gallery. "I can't tell you how many school assignments I flunked because I got too carried away with the specifics."

He chuckled, noticing with a start that the art gallery had mostly emptied out, with only a few stragglers left. The gallery would be closing soon, and she would disappear from his life.

I should let her go. She would continue on her natural course: age and change and love and die like everybody else. And perhaps in a few hundred years he might forget the way light danced off of the curls of her hair, and how even the edge of a trashcan was lovely in her eyes.

"Would you mind if I call you sometime?" The words slipped out before Christopher could stop them, and yet he felt selfishly grateful they were out there. "I have had such an enchanting evening with you. I would love to continue our conversation."

Alice smiled, handing him a small, white card from her handbag. "I would love that. The 'business number' on there is my cell." She played with the edge of her shawl. "I had these made up for the show and thought it would look more professional."

"I'm sorry I completely monopolized you tonight." He didn't feel in the least bit sorry. "I hope you still had a good time."

Alice laughed. "Don't worry, I mingled as much as I could stand. You saved me from hiding in the corner all night. Besides..." She directed her gaze at her feet. "I enjoyed being monopolized." She rose onto her toes to give him a quick kiss on the cheek before hastily gathering her things and heading out the gallery door.

Christopher touched his face, the shadow of her kiss on his skin like a blazing brand. The last patrons stumbled together out the door, giggling into their last complimentary glass of wine, and then he was alone in the echoing room.

"Well done, Christopher." He hadn't heard Margot approach, but she could be as silent as a cat when she wanted to. She stood in front of one of Alice's photos which captured a small portion of a building's facade. The five-foot tall print showcased the intricate designs painstakingly crafted in a section of the cement.

"Alice told me this photo was taken seventy-two stories up. Can you believe it?" Margot asked. "She had to bribe a window washer to let her use his rig, but she didn't have the right harness. The wind at that height was so wild and strong, it nearly blew her off the side. It was a hell of a risk to take, but look at what she did with it." Margot sipped her glass of champagne thoughtfully, rising an eyebrow in his direction. "That kind of persistence, over centuries... I think we'd all be *very* impressed with what she could do."

Damn it, not Margot too. "Oh, hush," Christopher said. "That's not why I was talking to her, she's special and..." His voice trailed off when he looked over at Margot.

She was opening and closing her mouth like she was trying to speak, but no words came out. With an annoyed grimace, Margot pointed at her throat and then at Christopher.

Christopher's stomach churned. "Shit! I do *not* compel you to hush." His words reversed the compulsion of his inadvertent sire command, and Margot massaged her now unlocked jaw.

"Ugh. I'll never get used to that damn *hortari*." Margot took an impressively-large swig out of the champagne glass she was holding.

"Me neither." Christopher sighed, running his fingers roughly through his hair. *This* was why he didn't see Margot or his other sirelings as often as he wanted. He'd gotten out of the habit of carefully choosing his words to avoid even the hint of a command. As the vampire who turned Margot from human to vampire-kind, his words were impossible for her to resist and he *hated* it. The sire command, called a *hortari,* was the one part of being a vampire that Christopher deeply resented.

This is why you cannot turn Alice, the rational voice in his mind reminded the part of him that still wanted to run after her.

He followed Margot back to a door marked "Staff Only" at the back of the gallery. She glanced at him and finished off her champagne like a shot.

"I'm sorry," he said.

She waved away his words, pressing a code into a keypad by the door. "Just watch it with the definitive sentences, okay?" She set down her glass. "I'm glad you were able to come tonight." The door slid open and the lights switched on to reveal a high-ceilinged room. Art covered every inch of the walls and up onto the ceiling, most of it hundreds of years old: masks from Nigeria and Mali, paintings from Parisian masters who never got their big breaks, headdresses from Native American cultures so old that their names were lost to time. The effect was chaotic and a little mad, but still gorgeous, much like the room's decorator. Christopher never regretted giving Margot the chance at immortality, and she'd used her time well.

"Tell me, how have you been?" He asked.

Margot poured another glass of champagne. "Fine as things go. Roxanne the succubus passed through town a few weeks ago and we had some fun before she moved on." Margot waved the bottle in his direction. "Want any of this?"

"No thanks. I never understood why you drink that human stuff. It's not like you're able to get drunk."

"I like the bubbles." Margot walked over to the wall and tilted a stunning portrait of a naked woman to the side until Christopher heard a *click*. "But you have the look of someone who needs to get drunk for real, and I have some excellent options in here." A panel in the wall opened up, revealing a bar set and wine fridge filled with hanging bags of blood.

"Anything 'A positive' would be great, thanks." Christopher stretched his arms behind his back and sat down on one of the low couches in the middle of the room.

Margot handed him a crystal glass filled with blood. "Cheers." She sipped deeply from her own glass. "I have an instinct about you and Alice."

Christopher sat up straight, nearly spilling the blood down his wine-sprayed shirt. "What are you talking about?"

She laughed. "You, her, the way you just jumped at the sound of her name like you got poked by a unicorn in the ass." She swirled the blood in her glass slightly. "I'm not wrong. You like her."

He leaned back. "She's magnificent, what's not to like?" Christopher sipped from his own glass. Emotions from the blood's donor washed over him as the crimson liquid necessary for his survival coursed down his throat. The male donor had been drunk and in love when he donated, his emotions rich and rolling within his blood. With each sip of the man's heady happiness, Christopher wondered more about what Alice was doing right now. He eyed his glass, then Margot. With her choice of vintage, she was definitely trying to play matchmaker.

"Alice has a profoundly passionate worldview and a good eye." Margot pointed an accusatory finger at Christopher. "Perception like that is worth preserving for the centuries."

He groaned. Margot's words matched so closely how he'd felt when he first met Alice.

"That's true." Christopher took a long gulp of blood. "The way she thinks, her passion, her kindness..." He turned away. "...her immense beauty. It would be a crime to let all she is wither and fade away."

Margot frowned. "Then why are you hesitating?"

"I'm not." He was. "If she agrees to be turned, I *will* do it, but..."

"But you have your *rules*," Margot smiled, her expression wicked. "You must want her *bad* if you're this conflicted about turning her. Poor sire. You can bang her, *or* turn her." Margot kicked off her high heels with a happy sigh, settling next to him on the couch.

"You know why I have my rules. It would be monstrous to sleep with somebody I have such *absolute* control over." Christopher sighed. "I can barely spend time with you or the rest of my sirelings as it is. But you're right, I need to put my attraction to her aside." He nodded, sure in his decision. "She'll be a tremendous asset to my sire line, to our family."

"Good. I'll be glad to have her. You're a good sire. Even if we're sad we don't get to see you often, we're all grateful you're so careful with avoiding the sire compulsion."

Christopher shrugged. His brother, Rhys, had a distinctly different view of how a sire should treat his turned vamps. In his twisted way, he thought he was actually *helping* his sirelings by taking away their will. As the last sirelings of the Vampire King, Christopher and Rhys were the only heirs, and their conflicting approaches to sireing made presenting a unified example for their people impossible. Christopher had spent centuries trying to convince the king to set laws for how sirelings should be treated, with no success.

"I'll offer Alice the transition, explain how it all works, and let her decide." Christopher said.

"I'll drink to that." Margot lifted her glass.

"To Alice."

ALICE RECHECKED her phone to confirm she had come to the right place. When Christopher texted her where they were going to meet, she hadn't been sure what to expect, but a smoky dive bar with a pink, neon sign reading "AUDREY'S", was not what she had pictured. AUDREY'S was a lone building several stories tall surrounded by dark forest, with a parking lot mostly filled with motorcycles and beat-up sedans. Frost on the front windows made it difficult to see much inside, but Alice liked the feel of the place. Music curled out of the entrance's double doors, with laughter and light creating the welcoming glow of a lighthouse's beacon.

Her phone beeped with a text from Christopher confirming that he'd arrived and was waiting for her at the bar. He must have arrived right before she did. *Punctual and polite. Two more points for the hot guy.* She smiled. After her last few disappointing dates, tonight was looking very promising.

Alice stepped through the doors and was immediately hit with the strongest allergic reaction she'd ever had. Her vision misted, her eyes itched, and her headache felt like something large was pounding to escape her forehead. She pressed her fingers to the bridge of her nose and held her breath, hoping the feeling would pass.

Crap. Not now. She'd had this kind of allergy attack before, but it usually only lasted a couple of seconds. She was hiking the last time this happened. Her headache flared up just as she'd passed a group of folks watching a track and field event. It was only after she'd climbed a ways away and stopped even *thinking* about what she'd seen that the feeling cleared.

Through what felt like a cloudy film over her eyes, Alice scanned the crowd around the bar for Christopher. She found him in intense discussion with the bartender, a pale woman with a mane of black braids sticking up from her head and an intricate rose tattoo that took up most of her chest.

Christopher looked so gorgeous Alice had to stop and collect herself. He filled out his jeans, sneakers, and t-shirt so perfectly, it was like they were tailored to show off the tapered lines of his waist, the curve of his shoulders, and the tight cording of his biceps. His hands were clenched so tightly around his glass, the skin on his fingers was almost white, and his eyebrows were furrowed with stress. The bartender kept mixing and handing out drinks to other patrons, but her expression of patient compassion didn't waver from Christopher's face. Neither seemed to have noticed Alice yet as she made her way carefully through the crowd, her headache getting worse the further she waded into the bar.

To her left, four big guys with mohawks were grunting loudly as they egged on a furious arm wrestling competition taking place at the next table between a petite, teenage girl in a floral dress and a looming beast of a man with skin so pale, he looked almost blue. Alice blinked, her headache spiking as she looked at them, and for a second it almost appeared like the men with mohawks had green skin and the teenager had flowers growing out of her hair. Alice shook her head. *That's impossible.* Alice's headache faded for a second and the flower woman was once more just a girl, the men were biker dudes, and the big guy was just being nice by pretending to strain against the girl's strength.

A bird flew across the rafters, nearly hitting Alice in the face and she let out a small squeal of alarm. *What's a bird doing in here?*

A hand gently cradled her elbow, and Alice recognized the callouses against her skin even before she turned to confirm Christopher had found her. His skin felt even colder than she remembered from the gallery, but it was strangely soothing in contrast to the hot roar of her headache.

Christopher smiled at her. "I'm glad you made it. Sorry, this place can be a bit much."

Alice didn't mind leaning on him a bit for balance as they made their way over to the bar. "It's okay. I think someone must be wearing a perfume or something that's aggravating my allergies. I was hoping you wouldn't mind if we went someplace else?"

Christopher shared a glance with the bartender. The woman leaned over the bar, stretching out a hand to Alice.

"Hi, I'm Lola. It's been a while since we had some fresh blood in here." Lola smiled, flashing white teeth. "That headache is your perception of reality getting threatened, and your body trying to fight it off. Ignore everything except me and Christopher and you'll feel a lot better."

What the hell? My perception of reality? Alice shook the bartender's hand automatically and her headache disappeared like turning off a light.

Alice sunk onto one of the padded barstools. The misty feeling still hung over her eyes and Alice tried to blink it away. *What's happening?* A sensible, quiet voice inside her head was screaming at her to run away from this place as quickly as possible, but she was too curious to leave. She glanced at Christopher. He was looking at her with an expression of hope that warmed her down to her toes.

Christopher's handsomeness was almost unreal in its perfection. His features were perfectly symmetrical, the only imperfection a tiny scar along one cheek above the line of his beard, and his tousled hair which seemed to fly in whatever direction it wanted. The bartender slid a pink drink across the bar and Alice grabbed it before it slid off the ledge.

"Good save." Lola winked and turned away to serve something bright green to a stocky man whose head barely reached the top of the counter.

Alice flinched as the bird flew past, barely missing her head. It landed on the shoulder of the young girl who was still arm wrestling.

"That poor bird." Alice blinked rapidly. The whole room looked like it was swimming behind a misty veil. "We should try to help it out of here, shouldn't we? I bet that bartender has something we could use."

Christopher settled on the stool next to Alice, looking at her with concern in his deep, brown eyes.

"That's not a bird. We can still go if you want. If we continue to stay here, I suspect your worldview is going to be changed forever. I know of another place where we could go if you're not up for that."

Alice took a sip of the drink. It tasted divine, with an initial sweetness which gave way to a spicy aftertaste that nipped at the back of her throat all the way down. Alice shook her head. All this talk of challenging reality was a little weird, but she wasn't leaving the best cocktail she'd had in years.

"It's okay. I like it here. It's just not where I would have pictured our first date."

Christopher leaned back from her quickly, all trace of humor erased from his face. "Ms. Jones, I invited you here because there's a business arrangement I would like to discuss with you.

Alice felt a blush surge up into her cheeks. *I'm such an idiot! Of course, this isn't a date.* "Oh, right. I hadn't realized." She frantically scrambled for a shred of dignity. "What an interesting venue for a business meeting. What can I do for you?"

"I invited you here because I think the world would be a better place if you continued to live in it beyond your natural lifespan." Christopher's tone was serious.

"What?" Her headache was brewing again behind her temple.

"I'm a vampire. And I think you would make a great vampire too."

The headache was back in full force, building like a wave of heat. She took a long gulp of her drink, but all she could taste now was the burn. Alice peered at Christopher, waiting for him to smile and admit that it was all just a big joke.

"Vampires don't exist." *Of course I end up on a non-date with a crazy person.* "You're certainly welcome to believe in whatever you want, but I think I'll be going now," she said slowly.

Christopher reached forward to gently lay his hand on top of hers on the bar. "Wait just a moment. Look around. Look *closer*. Most humans ignore the supernatural with a stubbornness that lasts a lifetime, but you're an artist. You've been discovering beauty your whole life." His fingers rubbed along the top of her hand, sending little shivers of want up her arm. *Why is it the hot ones are always unhinged?* She shifted in her chair, trying to ignore what he was saying, but the misty feeling in front of her eyes was *fading* like an opaque veil becoming more transparent by the moment.

How is this possible? There was no denying that something was definitely happening.

Christopher's voice dropped to a low hum, sexy and strong. "It's up to you. You can go back to your old life. You can forget all of this, write me off as some nut you met at a gallery. But you have to decide."

"Decide what?" The headache pounded like a desert rave. What had Lola said? That the headache was the challenge to her perception? If Alice wanted it to stop, she knew what she had to do: focus on the grains of wood on the bar, look at her glass, look at what was sane.

Maybe it's time for a little crazy. She remembered at the art gallery, shyly tucking herself away. If she hadn't taken a risk, she would never have met Christopher, wouldn't be here now. If there was something *more* to the world which she hadn't been able to see, didn't she owe it to herself to find the truth? Even if everything about this was utterly insane.

She straightened in her chair and looked out into the room, concentrating on every detail she could spot.

"That's it." She could hear the smile in Christopher's voice, even though she wasn't looking at him. "See the truth. There are more wonders in the world than we could see in twenty lifetimes."

She clutched his hand like a lifeline. The misty look of the room shimmered, and then ripped apart like a curtain tearing at the seams. Every memory when she'd thought she was having an allergic reaction flooded in all at once, with new vision.

Months ago she'd looked up to see low-flying airplanes and gotten a massive headache. *Those weren't planes.* They'd been brightly-scaled dragons flying together across the sky. The track and field event she'd seen had been an elaborate obstacle course of men and women transforming back and forth between animal and human forms as they overcame magical barriers.

"Ms. Jones?" Christopher gave her shoulder a little shake.

Alice blinked, frozen by fear and awe fighting each other under her skin. *Everything I know about the world is wrong.*

"Alice, are you okay?"

At the table less than ten feet away, the men with the mohawks looked like trolls from storybooks, their skin swamp green and their brightly-colored hair actually rocks sprouting from the top of their heads. A blue-skinned man with marble-white skin and hands like claws was arm wrestling with all his might against a woman with golden skin, flowers sprouting from her forehead, and rainbow wings fluttering from her back. On her shoulder sat a tiny brown-skinned man riding an oversized butterfly, a bow and arrow strapped to his shoulders.

"Alice?" Christopher's voice had been calling to her for the last minute, but she'd barely heard.

"There's so much." Her voice sounded like it was coming from far away.

Dragons, magic, vampires, *everything* was real.

"It's a lot," Christopher said. "Are you okay?"

Alice nodded. "I never knew the world was so..." She waved vaguely at the woman with wings. "That there are so many *amazing* things all around us. Will I always be able to see things this way?"

Christopher nodded. "Yes. Once you see this world, you can almost never un-see it. If you were really determined, you could probably convince yourself that this was just a dream, but if you want to continue seeing the truth, you'll see it forever."

A roar went up from behind them. The woman--"a pixie," Christopher whispered in her ear, his breath brushing against her neck spreading goosebumps down her back--had defeated the blue-skinned man in the arm wrestling contest. The pixie jumped up on the table, sending the tiny man riding the butterfly on her shoulder rocketing up into the air.

"Suck it, yeti boy!" the pixie squeaked in a high-pitched voice. "Suck it, everyone!" She threw up both middle fingers, and the yeti laughed. He scooped her up off the table and deposited her into his lap, where they started making out with loud slurping noises and groans. Everyone in the bar clapped and cheered, and Alice found herself clapping along.

"Let's get some air," Christopher said, holding out his arm for her.

She grabbed hold, appreciating Christopher's help dismounting her bar stool. She turned to pay her tab, but Lola waved her off.

"Come back here after you and Chris have your talk." Lola smiled. "Good luck."

Alice nodded, smiling her thanks as she followed Christopher out the back door to the wide field behind the bar. The field was littered with a series of hay bales and low hurdles like at a horse riding competition. The sound of traffic from the street was almost a whisper, and the low murmur of voices from the bar and the roar of the wind through the trees were the only sounds Alice could hear in the still night.

The moon was bright and beamed down, highlighting Christopher's face into stark contrasts of black and white. He grinned and walked forward, effortlessly hopping onto the top of a ten-foot stack of bales; it was so high his feet swung level with Alice's head. He spread his hands out wide like a magician completing a trick and grinned. Alice noticed for the first time his front canines were two sharp points. A shiver ran down her spine.

Vampire.

He hadn't been lying. The ramifications struck her like a train.

Christopher Dal really is a vampire.

She'd spilled her wine on a vampire the first time she saw him.

She'd given her number to a vampire.

"This is crazy," she said, her voice barely louder than a whisper.

Christopher jumped down, landing effortlessly with barely a sound. "I know. Not everybody can handle the truth the way I believe you can. The fact that you're not running away is further evidence that I am right about you." He stepped closer. The scent from his body was woody with a slight musk, and it made her long to snuggle up against him and lick along his neck.

This isn't a date, he'd said.

It was hard for Alice to remember why he'd invited her here. With Christopher standing so close, the fabric of her dress brushed against his t-shirt when she breathed in and out. He leaned down and, for a second, she was sure he was going to kiss her. His fingertips caressed along her shoulders, brushing against a few tendrils of red hair which had come loose from her braid.

"You have the flexibility of mind to be a great vampire," he said. "And, believe me, the condition comes with some major advantages."

That's right! He wants me to be a vampire!

Alice stepped back from him, distancing herself from the intoxication of his scent and the temptation of rubbing her cheek against the scruff of his beard. In the days since her photographs were displayed at Margot's gallery, she'd barely gotten her head around the idea that she might actually be able to leave her crappy job and be a full time photographer. But becoming a vampire? That was a life change beyond her wildest dreams.

"Immortality is just the beginning," Christopher continued. He leaned back against the hay bale and crossed his arms like a chiseled model at a cover shoot. "You'll be able to smell emotions. With other vampires, they'd have to be cut and their blood exposed to the air, or you'll have to drink it directly, but with non-vampires, you can sense their feelings through their skin just by being close to them." He nodded to her. "Like right now, I can smell your amazement, and a tinge of fear at what I'm offering you."

Alice blushed scarlet. He could smell her emotions?

Christopher smiled. "You don't have to be embarrassed."

He stepped forward and she instinctively pressed closer. He cupped her face between his hands and leaned down until his breath brushed across her lips.

"That desire you feel?" He was so close. The strength of him, the power of him, was a pull stronger than she'd ever felt before. A thrill shot down spine, pooling in wetness between her legs. "I feel it too." His voice was like a purr. "You're so beautiful, I can barely stand it."

Kiss me! Kiss me! Alice hoped her blood was screaming it to him as strongly as she screamed in her own head. She reached forward to grab his waist, but he released her, withdrawing fast like her emotions burned him.

"But there's a few downsides to being a vampire." Christopher turned away, jumping back to the top of the hale bale, far from her. "The most important one is the sire compulsion. The vampire who turns you has absolute command over you. We call it *hortari*. The origin of the *hortari* was to protect the population from the strength and hunger of newly-turned vampires. A sire's will is binding no matter what the command, even if the sire didn't mean to issue a command."

"I would have to do whatever you tell me?"

Christopher nodded. "It's not a power to be taken lightly. You'll have supernatural strength, speed, and live forever, looking exactly as you are now, unless someone takes off your head or sets you on fire. You'll only receive nourishment from blood, although you can still enjoy the taste of food and drink. And knowing the emotional states of those around you is helpful in more situations than you'd think."

Alice felt lightheaded with all of the possibilities. *Am I really considering becoming a vampire?*

Christopher stood up on the top of the hay bale and flipped through the air in a tight somersault to land on tip-toe on the top of the narrow wall ten feet from him. Her heart leapt into her throat, sure he was going to break his neck before she remembered, *Right. Vampire.* He made another jump, this time landing on his hands and flipping back upright a few yards away with a smooth grace that would put the most experienced acrobat to shame.

That could be me.

The thought was more tempting than she'd anticipated. She'd live forever without aging. Forever with Christopher. She'd never felt so attuned to a man before, his kindness and attention at the gallery like a scene from her dearest dreams. The memory of his breath on her lips, the brush of his chest against her dress, teasing her breasts with that brief flutter of contact, sent new shivers of want coursing through her body. What would sex be like as a vampire? With all that strength and speed, it had to be super intense. If she drank Christopher's blood while they were making love, she'd be able to feel everything he was feeling, enjoy the pleasure she was giving him. She swallowed to keep from drooling.

"Alice." Christopher's voice had an edge. "Your longing is calling to me. You must know, if I'm going to sire you, we can never be together. Not like that." His words splashed against her skin like a burst of cold water.

What?

"The sire compulsion is too strong. I could never make love to you knowing that if I phrased my words in the wrong way, you would lose your free will to choose."

"But, I *want* to be with you..."

He shook his head. "I take my responsibility as a sire seriously. Once I sire you, no matter how we might feel for each other, we would have to go our separate ways. My other sirelings would be your mentors to guide you through this life without robbing you of your agency. They're good people. I chose them the same way I chose you: I knew that they could make the world a better place if they had more time."

"But--"

Christopher stepped farther away from her. "There's a lot for you to think about. You know how to contact me when you have your answer. Take your time." He winked at her. "We have all the time in the world."

He turned away and disappeared around the corner of the bar before Alice could put the puzzle of her thoughts into something resembling a complete picture. *Vampires are real. Dragons, pixies, what else was real out there? Witches? Werewolves? Ghosts?* All those magical creatures were really out there. *I could be one.* She pressed her fingers against her forehead. *I have time to decide.*

Remembering that she still had to pay for her tab at the

bar, Alice walked back into AUDREY's feeling like she was still half in a dream.

The sense of unreality strengthened when she arrived inside. The pixie and yeti had gone off to finish off their evening and the four trolls were singing a drinking song that was off-key, didn't rhyme, and seemed to have four different tunes at once.

At the bar, with her legs crossed to reveal an impressive amount of skin through a slit in her red dress, perched Margot Dal. The gallery owner raised a flute of champagne in Alice's direction and patted the empty stool next to her.

"Hey, hon. I heard Christopher gave you the pitch," Margot said. She smiled, revealing pointed canines.

"Holy shit, you're a..." Alice swallowed the word before she said it.

Margot licked her lips. "Yep, I'm a vampire. Actually, I'm Christopher's first sireling. He turned me centuries ago, back when being black, a woman, and a lesbian was immediately worthy of capital punishment." She wrinkled her nose. "The world is...better now. Accepting an offer of near-invincibility was an easy choice for me." Margot eyed Alice. "But you have other choices. And there are costs to being what I am."

"Christopher mentioned the *hortari* whatsit. Does Christopher... has he ever made you do anything?"

Margot shook her head. "Never on purpose. He's always been very careful, but it's ridiculously easy to slip up. He's a good sire that way; a lot of other vamps get off on the power to make sirelings dance to their tune. Christopher's brother, Rhys, is a piece of work that way. If you accept Christopher's offer, you'll definitely have to meet that ass-wipe, although you won't be compelled to obey him." She set down her glass. "I don't mean to throw all of this at you at once, but you should have all the details." She held up her hand and counted off the points on each finger. "Becoming a vampire means you'll never get pregnant, *but* you'll never have your period again so that's a win. You'll be able to eat all the food you want and never absorb any of it, so you'll never gain a pound. Picture eating fudge non-stop for the rest of eternity and still looking as delightfully trim as you are right now. The only thing you'll *need* to consume is blood."

Alice had never really thought about kids. She'd vaguely assumed it might happen eventually, but she'd never really pursued it. She'd always figured it was one of those things that just *happened* over time.

But I'd be able to see the world, explore all its beauties forever.

"You really drink blood?" Alice asked.

"Yeah, it takes some getting used to. Some old-school vamps drink directly from the neck, and during sex it's stupid fun, but mostly we have arrangements with blood banks where they give us the old bags that are no longer viable for humans."

"So, let's just say that I decide to become a vampire..." Alice said. It was surprisingly easy to consider once she'd wrapped her head around it. The sire compulsion was worrying, but if Christopher kept his word--and every instinct she had declared that he would--then he would stay away to allow her autonomy. Vampirism was a chance to have the *time* to accomplish everything she ever wanted. She would be an idiot to turn down this chance. But then...there was Christopher.

"Yes?" Margot sat forward, looking excited.

"Um, would *you* turn me? We're already friends and I trust you. And, uh, if Christopher's not my sire, then maybe..."

"Then he'd consider a relationship?" Margot chuckled at

Alice's blush. "Sweetie, your hormones have been screaming at him since I pointed him in your direction at the gallery. But, sorry, I don't sire people. I'm happy to train other vamps' sirelings, and be a good friend to the rest of Christopher's sire line, but having my own sire line isn't something I've ever wanted. Sorry, hon, if you want all of this..." She gestured around at the hubbub of supernatural beings having fun around them. "Then Christopher's your best chance." Margot swung off of her bar stool. "It's all up to you." She pushed some cash across the bar at Lola. "I got your tab. Whatever you decide, definitely hit me up when you're ready for your next show."

Alice nodded, the gallery and her previous life feeling far away. At the end of the bar, a woman with bright red hair and horns coming out of her head cursed at the trolls to "shut the fuck up, or I will wish you into deep space!", and the trolls quieted down with minimal grumbles. A wolf was sleeping under one of the tables, a dish of what looked like beer cradled between his paws. Curled up against the wolf's back was an immense lioness who was chewing on the wolf's ear in a way that looked simultaneously intimate and annoying, but the wolf only grunted in his sleep and kicked his back legs.

"I want this," Alice said. She thought she said it too quietly for anyone to hear, but Lola's silky voice replied behind her,

"Then go get it."

Alice grinned and jumped off her stool. The future looked like it was going to be magical. She just had to find a way to keep Christopher in it.

〜

CHRISTOPHER SIPPED from his crystal glass of blood and leaned back against his long Chesterfield couch, the rounded back cushioning his head as he let out a long breath. He'd chosen blood donated by a yoga master to try and drink up a little calm, but it wasn't working.

He set his glass down before his grip threatened to shatter the antique and closed his eyes, willing himself to think about anything but Alice. Or the way the light hit her hair. Or the way the smell of her intense longing had so perfectly mirrored his own that it had taken centuries of self-control to not pull her to him and kiss her until her knees shook.

The world will benefit from her as a vampire, he told his cock, which was already half-hard at the mere memory of her. That growing part of him was hoping she'd turn down his offer, that she'd decide to stay human. It would mean only a few brief decades with her before he and the world lost that light in her eyes, but he'd be able to carry the memory of her touch, the feeling of her lips, with him through all the long years to come.

"It's her choice," he told his empty living room. He'd decorated his home in the 1920s during what Margot laughingly referred to as his Gatsby phase, and never bothered to change anything beyond the crucial updates for electricity, plumbing, and Wi-Fi. All the chairs and sofas were wide and cushioned, grand Oriental rugs covered bold black and white-checkered tiles, and paintings from forgotten masters took up most of the walls. Tiffany lamps blazed color along the Art Deco lines up the wall to the tall ceiling dripping with chandeliers.

Christopher picked up his glass, took a long gulp of the blood, and waited for the yogi's serenity to wash through him. He propped his slippered feet up on the couch and closed his eyes.

Rhys was growing bolder. Christopher's brother was beginning to make public claims that he was going to "clean up" the vampire community and "deal with dissenters", whatever that meant. Christopher had come home to a note scrawled on his fridge from his sireling, Danny, that Christopher's lieutenants-- the four vampires Christopher had turned directly--were going to be gathering the next day to discuss Rhys's hateful rhetoric and what they were going to do about it. It wasn't as if the king would ever do anything. Christopher took a long sip of blood. His sire's leadership style of using *hortari* on his sirelings when needed and then apathetic neglect the rest of the time meant Rhys could get away with *actual* murder so long as his actions didn't impact the king's immediate comfort. Christopher would just have to be careful. As the eldest of the king's turned, Christopher was his sire's heir apparent, but vampire tradition allowed for a challenge.

Perhaps now isn't the right time for siring a new vampire.

Christopher pushed down the selfish thought before he began to believe it. There was always trouble, in one form or another; if Alice wanted to become a vampire, his own wish for romance shouldn't hold her back.

The sound of his doorbell startled him so badly he spilled a splatter of blood down his shirt.

"Damn." He tried to brush it away, smearing the drops into gruesome finger painting across his chest.

The doorbell rang again and he called out, "Coming!" as he grabbed a jacket hanging by the door to hide the stains.

He checked the view-hole in the door, and his hand shook slightly as he opened the door.

"Alice," he said.

She looked amazing. Her eyes sparkled in the moonlight, and she'd changed into the green dress she'd worn at the gallery which hugged her lean curves. Excitement and fear came off of her skin in waves. He knew what she was going to say before she opened her mouth.

"I'm in. I want to be like you." As soon as she said the words, the smell of excitement in her blood spiked, and she shifted her weight to her toes like a little dance. She was so lovely it hurt.

A small, petty voice in his head reminded him that Alice's choice meant that she wanted to be a vampire more than she wanted to be with him. He pushed down the feeling.

"That's wonderful news! Come on in." Christopher stepped back to allow Alice inside, savoring the sweet scent of her as she walked by. The excitement rolling off her still warred with her fear, but under those, he could smell a thrilled arousal in Alice's blood that gave him pause.

"You have such a beautiful home!" Alice twirled in the foyer, a wide, circular room lined with alternating panels of cherrywood and floor-to-ceiling windows. The moonlight spilled in, bathing Alice in a warm glow. She pointed to the windows. "I thought daylight was a no-no for your kind." She stopped short. "Our kind?"

"Curtains." Christopher pressed a code into his cell phone and reams of dark fabric lowered over the windows. Without the moonlight, the space felt darker, more intimate.

"This I like even more." Alice's voice was low. She stepped forward, her fingertips tracing the lines of his jacket. The slight brush of her touch made him bite back a groan. Everything about her called to him. She was so close, he could feel the heat radiating off her body, hear the blood coursing through her veins, and smell her desire. He tensed up, balling his fists, desperately trying to stop himself from leaning forward and capturing her lips. He couldn't bring himself to move away, but he managed to not move any closer either.

She opened his jacket, her eyes widening at the splatter of blood across his shirt. She laughed, the sound so light and enchanting Christopher's fists clenched white.

"I'm glad I'm not the only one who has trouble keeping your shirt clean."

He laughed too, then cut himself off. *I'm toast, we already have inside jokes*. He shifted his weight so he stood infinitesimally closer and the beaded top of her dress brushed against his shirt.

"You know I can smell your emotions, Alice." Christopher spoke, regretting each word as he formed it. He reached up to brush a fingertip along her face, her skin smooth and perfect. "We cannot be together, not in that way."

"Actually," Alice reached up to hold his hand against her face, leaning her cheek into his palm. "You said we couldn't be together *after* I've been turned." She turned her head, placing a kiss on his skin that sent lines of fire down his arm and through his torso.

Yessss! Every cell in his body demanded.

Alice ran her other hand down his chest, her fingers tracing the pattern of red, making little circles. "Right now, I'm still human. And I want to have one, last, purely human experience before I'm changed forever. And I want it to be with you, Christopher."

Her blood smelled of a primal desire boiling deeper than just saying farewell to her humanity. Christopher couldn't resist running his hands through her hair, caressing the back of her neck and watching the goosebumps rise along the trail of his fingers. *This is such a bad idea*. He was already half in love with her. Knowing what it would be like to really be with her, and then denying himself her touch for the rest of eternity, would be excruciating. *Is a lifetime of pain worth it for just one night?*

"I can see you thinking it over, weighing the pros and cons." Alice smiled. "You may have vampire senses, but sometimes I can tell what *you're* thinking."

Alice stared up at him, questioning. She raised a hand to mirror his touch on her face, her nimble fingers tracing along the sharp edge of Christopher's jawline, then dancing down to the sensitive surface of his mouth, and teasing across his bottom lip. He groaned, biting down gently on her fingertips.

But-- He was a man at war with himself, and each side was losing.

Alice pushed onto her tiptoes to align her mouth with his. "Don't you want this?" She asked, before capturing his lips with her own.

All resistance, all composure fled Christopher's being as he responded to Alice's kiss, his passion flaring up to match hers. His hands roamed her body, discovering new territory, mapping the hills and valleys of her form.

"Gods, I want you so much," he groaned.

"Good, because if this is only going to be the one night..." Her voice hitched slightly. "Then we need to make it count."

Alice unbuttoned Christopher's shirt, her mouth following her hands in a sensuous trail down his torso. He leaned his head back, reveling in the sensations from her lips, her tongue, her teeth. She lightly traced her tongue along the grooves of his six-pack, pleasure tickling down along every nerve ending.

In a sudden movement, Alice loosened Christopher's

belt and swept Christopher's pants and boxers to the ground. She raked her nails up his calves, winding her way up to where he needed her most.

"You don't need to do this." He was panting now, the sight of her sultry smile the most gorgeous thing he'd seen in five hundred years.

"Oh yes, I do." She licked her lips. "I'm going to bring you, my handsome vampire, to your knees."

He let out a groan of pleasure as she licked a line up his swollen shaft, teasing him with her mouth as her hands wound around to grasp his ass.

Her red hair spilled over her green dress in a sensuous wave, and he knew he wouldn't be able to resist unwrapping her for much longer. She looked up, and her shockingly blue eyes pierced him as she finally took him into her mouth. She moaned around his hard length, sending waves of pleasure through Christopher's body as he reveled in the feel of her lips and tongue dancing along his cock. He twined his fingers through her hair and watched, entranced, as she bobbed along his length.

Alice smiled as she released him with a pop, and Christopher struggled against his release. He wanted their first time together--their *only* time--to last.

Christopher pulled Alice to her feet, spinning her so her back was flat against his chest. He looked around the stark foyer. They'd barely moved four feet from the door since she arrived. He grabbed her under her knees and swung her up into his arms.

"We need the proper setting for this," he said.

She squealed and hugged his neck as he ran up the stairs two at a time, not caring about his crumpled pants lying in the middle of the foyer. The roaring desire in her veins smelled glorious.

"Christo--" He ran so fast, he kicked his bedroom door open and deposited Alice on the bed before she could finish the word. Her voice changed to a cooing, "ooo" when she saw the room. The ceiling was draped with hanging silk, the enormous four-poster bed piled high with pillows, and the crystal chandelier sparkled the light into rainbow prisms.

"This is amazing," she said, her hands still around his neck.

Christopher slid his hands around the contours of her dress, finding a single, long zipper that ran from her neck to her ass.

"*This* is far more so." With a low growl, he slowly unzipped her, following the zipper with a long trail of nips and kisses down her back. The dress slid easily off her body, and Christopher's arousal grew when he realized she wasn't wearing anything underneath her dress.

He stood back in awe of her. Her breasts were everything he'd dreamed they would be, round and pert, her nipples already pebbled in arousal, and the slight indentations of her muscled core lean and perfect.

Alice raised an eyebrow at him, her stance confident in her nudity, and kissed him gently on the lips. She stroked his erect cock, her touch feeling so good a drop of pre-cum beaded at his tip.

Christopher scooped Alice up with one arm, and deposited the giggling temptress onto the bed. He peppered the sensitive skin of her inner thighs with kisses, moving closer and closer to her core. Alice sighed happily and bucked her hips, every emotion he could smell off her skin begging him for more. His fingers played with the sensitive skin along her stomach and sides, stroking under her knees and along her arms.

"Don't be a tease." Alice's hands roamed her own body, grasping at the nipples of her exposed breasts.

"How can I not? You look so beautiful when I keep you waiting." Christopher winked.

Christopher's skilled tongue moved to Alice's soaked core, gently running laps around her sensitive flesh. He flicked the very tip of his tongue at her clit, and bit back a smile as she melted underneath him. He covered her mound with his mouth, sucking and kissing her as Alice moaned.

"Holy fuck, that feels good," Alice whimpered. "Christopher, I'm so close."

The scent of her arousal intoxicated him. The emotions flowing from her: excitement, trust, and something more, something deeper, called to him. Christopher latched onto Alice's clit with his mouth and pounded two fingers into her sopping core, moving inside her with a merciless rhythm. Alice shouted out in pleasure as she pulsed around his fingers. He kept moving inside of her until he felt a second orgasm rip through her body, and she shuddered around him once more. Her pleasure overwhelmed him until he felt like he was drowning in it.

Alice pulled Christopher onto the bed and he was helpless to resist. She pushed him onto his back and pulled off his shirt so he was naked before her. Her admiration of his hard muscles, well-defined pecs, and abs flowed off her in waves, her pulse increasing with the strong scent of anticipation.

He felt exposed for the first time, every want and dream for her, for them, laid bare. She licked her lips as she moved over him. Her hair was wild with red strands stuck with sweat to her face and neck. She was absolutely stunning.

"I want you," he said, *with me forever*, he didn't finish.

"Then come take me." With a wicked grin, Alice positioned her core over Christopher's length, her face tensing up and then relaxing as she took his entire length inside of her. She fit so perfectly tight around him, Christopher had to actively resist thrusting inside of her, letting her set the pace.

Slowly, Alice began moving, sliding along his length as she braced herself by leaning back onto his thighs. Christopher clasped her firm ass with both hands as she writhed on top of him. Alice rotated her hips in small circles, shooting pleasure up his body. He closed his eyes, his head falling back, a moan of delight escaping his lips.

Alice's legs shook as she continued pumping on him, and Christopher leaned forward to rub her swollen clit. She moaned at his touch, now moving faster on top of him. Christopher was enchanted, almost mesmerized at the sight of her on the brink. Alice's breath came quickly, and her entire body pulsed with anticipation.

With a scream, Alice came shuddering around him, pulsing against his hard cock with her inner walls. It took everything Christopher had not to follow her over the edge.

Alice laid her head on Christopher's chest, panting. "It may be a stupid question but..." she turned away. "Don't vampires, when they have sex..." She trailed off.

"It's okay, you can ask me anything." Christopher cradled Alice's head in his hands.

"Isn't there biting involved?" Alice turned bright red, a blush that trailed all the way down to her chest.

"Sometimes." Christopher grinned. "It's a way for us to connect, for a vampire to feel their partner's emotions with more intensity." He gently kissed Alice's neck. He could hear her pulse roaring at such a close distance and could smell her wanting. "I don't want to hurt you."

She shook her head. "I know, I trust you."

She lifted off of his cock to sit beside him on the bed. Before he could respond, her hand encircled his length, playing with the underside of the shaft and making a ring with her fingers around the tip, squeezing just enough for his back to arch and he fought with centuries of self-control to hold onto this release.

"Woman, you're going to kill me." He moaned.

"Well, I did promise you I was going to bring you to your knees."

Alice grinned at him, lying down and pulling Christopher so he crouched on his knees on top of her. She bucked her hips, raising her legs to hook over his shoulders, her core lifting to make brief contact with Christopher's length.

"I want this," she said. "All of this."

With a low growl, Christopher thrust into Alice, reveling in each sweet inch of her passage. She gasped as he moved within her, harder and faster than before. He could smell her blood as it ran excited laps around her body. Christopher's hands roamed her skin, and his canines elongated from his gums into their fully primal state. He looked Alice in the eye and she spoke a single word.

"Yes."

Christopher bit down into the flesh of Alice's shoulder, feeling her tense beneath him at the brief moment of pain. He drank deep and Alice's essence streamed into him as he continued moving inside of her. Her compassion tasted like sunlight, her enchanting view of the world, her joy, her excitement, her arousal all flowed through him. He tasted her past loneliness, her longing for a community which she couldn't quite articulate. Her dreams of endless time to learn, to explore, to see wonders washed over him. Everything about his world fascinated her, and the glimpse she'd seen into the larger supernatural community beckoned with a promise of fun, excitement, and something new.

He broke away quickly, but he had drank enough to know that he'd fallen head over heels in love with Alice. With a few stuttered thrusts he spilled his seed in her, calling out her name as she came once more in a screaming, writhing surge of humanity. He collapsed back against the pillows.

They held each other in silence for a few long heartbeats, grinning as they each caught their breath. Christopher tasted the words on the tip of his tongue. *I love you, I want us to be together. Please stay human.*

Alice spoke first.

"This would be the perfect time for you to turn me." She snuggled into his arms a little further.

Christopher pushed down his selfish disappointment before it showed on his face. *This is her choice.* Christopher used his teeth to cut a small gash in his forearm and offered it to Alice.

"Only if you're *sure.*"

Without hesitation, Alice's lips found Christopher's arm, and she drank, the crimson liquid dripping over her lips and down her chin. Christopher felt his power passing into her, his past, his future, all irrevocably connecting him to this incredible woman. *At least now the world will have her preserved for the ages, even if I can never be with her.*

Alice looked up and delicately wiped away the blood trailing down from her mouth. "Is that enough? I'm beginning to feel a little woozy."

"Yes. It's done. You should rest now." Christopher wrapped Alice in his arms, savoring the memory of the first and last time they would ever be together.

ALICE BLINKED AWAKE. A note on the pillow next to her said, "Back Soon" in sweeping, old-fashioned handwriting. She smiled and stretched out on the soft silk sheets. She'd woken up a few times in the last few hours, woozy and feeling like every muscle weighed a hundred pounds, but upon waking this time she felt strong enough to lift up Christopher's four poster bed and throw it across the room.

The curtains were thrown open, revealing the sparkling brightness of the moon. Even though the room was fairly dim, everything looked brighter. Her senses were alive, the sounds of branches groaning in the wind and squirrels scratching at bark louder and more distinct than she'd ever heard before. She inhaled, and she could smell Christopher's scent imbedded in the sheets, as well as the faint burning of filament in the light bulbs of the chandelier above her. Every detail of everything around her was clearer, more beautiful than anything in her previous life.

Even her memories were sharper; the frame by frame replay of Christopher's skin, his lips, his tongue sliding and writhing with her, made her pulse race. She shifted beneath the covers, enjoying the slide of the silk against her skin. *Margot was right. Sex as a vampire will be amazing.*

She heard Christopher's footsteps approaching the top of the stairs, and she propped herself up in bed as attractively as possible. He opened the door slowly, like he was being careful of waking her, and nudged the door open with his hip while balancing a large tray between his hands.

The smell of orange juice, warm bread, and blood hit her nostrils like a wave. She'd smelled blood before once when she cut her hand cooking, the scent metallic like old pennies, but the row of red-filled shot glasses across the back of the tray Christopher carried gave off a confusing combination of scents, like she was smelling *feelings*.

Christopher smiled. "Excellent. You're awake. I brought you breakfast." He set down the tray on the end of the bed and walked over to give her a gentle kiss on the forehead.

"Thank you." She realized that she still wasn't wearing any clothes, and looked around to see a robe sitting on the bedside table beside her.

"Not a problem, it's just the beginning of getting you accustomed to all this." He settled next to the tray, keeping it between them, and averting his eyes as she pulled on the robe. Once she was relatively dressed, she crawled across the bed to join him.

"Are you regretting last night?" she asked.

His head popped up. "No! Last night was incredible, one of the best nights of my life. But it can't happen again, not now that I'm your sire."

Alice pushed down her disappointment. She'd known this was going to be the price of becoming a vampire, but that didn't make it feel any less like a rejection. The sex last night had been so much more intense than she'd anticipated, the feeling of being really *one* with him had been more than she'd ever felt with anyone else. *Had he felt the same?* She tried to distract herself by studying the tray he'd brought.

The man knew how to make a breakfast, she had to give him that. The tray was laden with a three-cheese omelet, warm cinnamon rolls dripping with icing, fresh-squeezed orange and mango juice, and a bowl of freshly-cut fruit. Across the back of the tray were six shot glasses filled with blood. The blood's intense pull sent nervous shivers of desire down her spine. *I'm a vampire. Holy shit.*

She picked up the tray. With her enhanced vampire muscles, the tray felt like it weighed almost nothing at all.

"This is way too much food," she said.

Christopher grinned. "Think of it as my welcome to your new life. Nobody should start a fresh existence on an empty stomach, especially when your body is still adjusting."

Alice took a bite of the omelet and let out a moan. Each individual ingredient and spice was amplified beyond her imagination. Every morsel tasted divine.

"Do you want some? There's enough here for at least three people," Alice said.

Christopher shook his head. "I already ate."

Alice didn't need any further encouragement. She tucked in, each bite better than the last. And yet, there was a sense of emptiness that grew the more she ate, her hunger roaring at her even as she polished off the last strawberry from the fruit salad and licked the plates clean.

"Thanks, that was amazing," she said.

"You're very welcome. There's a lot to love about this life, I hope you enjoy it." Christopher ran a hand up and down her arm. Alice relaxed into his touch.

"No broody vampires on your watch?" She smiled at him, feeling the warmth of his gaze all the way down to her toes.

Christopher laughed. "Exactly." His face lit up when he laughed. He was truly the most handsome man she'd ever seen.

"Have you ever regretted becoming a vampire?" she asked.

Christopher sat back on his elbows so he was lounging next to her on the bed with his legs hanging off the side.

"I suppose every decision comes with certain downsides. I'll never know what it feels like to grow old. The turn of the seasons doesn't have the same relief it used to; the arrival of spring loses its joy when winter seemed to pass in a moment." He touched her hand softly. "I've met so many extraordinary people only to witness them age and die in what feels like the blink of an eye. It's part of what draws me to art: it's how thoughts are preserved after the artists are gone." He sat back, his smile shaky but still there. "But I've never seen the point in focusing on the downsides of my chosen path. Life is just too long to dwell on regrets." He put his hand over hers. "Are you having doubts already?"

"No! I just woke up, and everything is amazing. You've been so kind. I'll remember fondly my first moments as a vampire forever."

Christopher looked away. "I'm very glad."

Alice put down the tray to curl up next to him. "What is it?"

"Just remembering something."

She brushed a stray lock of hair behind his ear. "Tell me." He suddenly looked so sad, so tired that she wanted to wrap him in her arms.

"I was thinking about my brother, Rhys. He and I were turned at the same time, by the same sire. Rhys wasn't a big fan of humanity. Within an hour of being turned, he slaughtered an *entire* village. Our sire didn't care. Humans were basically ants in his eyes. My first moments as a vampire were spent trying to save Rhys's victims, and I've been doing it ever since." He sat up. "But I refuse to be defined by that." He nudged the tray toward her.

He grinned again, and Alice could see the effort behind it. *Damn, I could fall in love with this man.* Her stomach sank. That wasn't an option. But everything about him called to her: his optimism and hope in the face of centuries of conflict, his kindness, and his smile. The way the moonlight hit his face transformed him into an angel, and she hungered to climb on top of him and ride his cock until she screamed.

Christopher had been talking for a couple of seconds. Alice shook herself to stop staring at his lips and actually pay attention to his words.

"--shot glasses are all blood from different types of supernaturals. You'll learn in time how to tell the difference between each kind, and how to interpret what they were feeling when they donated. For right now, let's just start with the basics."

Alice lifted one of the shot glasses and took a sniff. It smelled like soaring skies and fire, like cold scales and strength. She took a deep breath and drank down the shot in one go. A huge sense of power surged through her, and under all that, a sense of peace, joy, and contentment.

"A dragon?" Alice asked. She could barely believe that such things actually existed, and yet she loved how *full* the world was now since she gained her Sight.

Christopher clapped his hands. "Yes! That's the blood of a dragon shifter friend of mine who agreed to donate a bit for training purposes. She just got married a few weeks ago, and you should be able to smell her state of mind in addition to her species."

"We can really tell all that?" Alice asked. She tried to lean into the feelings that washed over her when she drank, but she couldn't hold onto them. She sniffed at Christopher. "Why can't I smell your emotions now that I'm a vampire?"

He tapped his nose. "That would work only if I'm human. As a vampire, my blood would have to be in the open air for you to smell it."

"I can barely believe this is really real."

"This and more." He held out another glass. "Here, try this."

Alice felt her whole body go rigid. Fear pulsed through her. She tried to say something, but her jaw was locked. Her hand lashed out, moving against her will toward the shot glass. Every cell in her body demanded that she take the glass from Christopher and consume its contents.

What is happening? She yelled the words in her head, but nothing came out. Her body wasn't her own, her hand moving against her will even as she tried with all her might to force it away from the glass. Her fingers clutched around the shot and she downed the blood in one gulp. A surge of sweetness and flowers and light and sun passed over her tongue, but Alice couldn't savor anything in her terror. As soon as she swallowed, her body returned to her in a rush, and she fell back limp against the bed.

"What was that?" Her voice sounded small and scared. "What just happened to me? I couldn't stop."

"Oh gods, Alice, I'm so sorry." Christopher's words came in an anguished rush. "I didn't mean to. It's the *hortari*. Even when I don't mean to give you a command, my words require you to do what I say." He scrambled off the bed. "This is why I stay away from the vampires I sire. You deserve your free will, to learn and grow and be your own person."

A knock at the door made them both jump.

"Christopher?" A woman's voice said from the other side of the door.

"Yes, Valerie, I'm in here." He sounded relieved.

A lovely Latina woman with black hair pulled back into a long braid that reached down to her waist opened the door. Her brow was furrowed and her tight-lipped smile looked forced. *Something's wrong.*

"Christopher, you need to get to the castle immediately." She glanced at Alice. "We'll look after the new recruit."

Christopher's face paled. He turned to lay a hand on Alice's shoulder. "I'm so sorry that things can't be different. Please feel free to explore as you wish the rest of the house and get to know the lieutenants in my sire line." He spoke slowly, like he was carefully choosing each word to make sure that nothing could be interpreted as a demand. He touched her face gently, like a farewell, and before Alice could say anything, he was gone. Valerie gave her a tight smile and followed after, leaving Alice alone.

Alice lay back against the soft sheets. Her heartbeat still raced. Both Christopher and Margot had warned her about the sire compulsion, but she hadn't realized how scary it would be to lose control of her body. It was terrifying to be *forced* to act against her will, even for something as mundane as tasting a drink she was planning on drinking anyway. Christopher's sorrow at having mistakenly used his sire power on her was sincere, but could she ever really be comfortable with him knowing that the slightest turn of phrase could strip her of her free will?

For the first time since meeting him, she understood fully why she wouldn't be able to have him in her life.

Alice shook herself. Christopher was right. There was no sense in concentrating on the negative. *Life is just too long to dwell on regrets.* She had heightened senses and super strength, and could tell how any human was feeling just by their scent.

I'm a vampire!

She certainly wasn't going to spend her first day as a vampire in bed, moping about how the one guy she wanted to be with was the one guy she couldn't have. Alice quickly got dressed in the outfit someone--probably Margot from the designer labels--had laid out for her and headed out into the rest of the house. She followed the sound of voices through the foyer and down a hallway to a door opening up to the backyard.

She couldn't believe how *bright* the night looked. With her new vampire eyes, every detail looked as clear as if the sun shone overhead. The wide lawn looked like a set for a training montage in a Robin Hood movie. Straw dummies stuffed into vaguely humanoid shapes lined the side of the walled compound, their stuffing sticking out from knife and arrow holes all over their bodies. Padded columns serving as punching bags stood in various clumps across the space, along with various beams and gymnastics equipment for balance training.

In the middle of a marked, padded space, Margot and two men Alice didn't recognize bantered as they attacked each other in a flurry of strikes with five-foot tall staffs. They jumped and weaved around each other, the staffs almost invisible blurs, as they twirled and struck with hard cracks. Alice stared, her mouth open. She'd known Margot was a vampire, but Alice wasn't prepared to see her suave, gallery-owning friend jumping six feet in the air to aim a kick at a guy's head like an anime heroine.

Margot blocked a particularly vicious head strike and Alice squeaked in alarm. One of the men—a wiry Asian man in tight, leather pants—turned to look in the direction of the noise. It was all the distraction the other two needed to hit him simultaneously on the back and under his knees. He flew sprawling onto the pads.

"No fair!" The fallen man shouted. "Chris's newest sireling is awake."

Margot leaned on her staff, her smile wicked. "Yeah, and enemies are going to do everything they can to distract you too."

The man shrugged and jumped to his feet in a single,

fluid movement. "Whatever, I'll just have to kick your ass *twice* as hard next time."

The other man, taller with dark skin and chest armor made from overlapping metal gears, laughed. "Danny, that logic makes absolutely no sense."

"It does in my head, shut up!" Danny said, smiling. He took a running leap which propelled him across the twenty-foot space between the group and Alice. He held out a hand to her. "I'm Danny. Adventurer and lover and forever at your service."

"Lay off. She's barely hours old," Margot said. She walked over to join them, with the gear-plated man close behind. "You'll make her regret joining our motley crew."

"Please ignore them." The taller man said. His voice was deep, with a measured, calm quality that radiated a sense of peace around him. He nodded to Alice, but kept his distance. "I'm Ben." He shrugged. "I'm the mad scientist of the group."

Alice stared. Except for the overlapping gears criss-crossing his chest, she would have believed he was a monk before she would ever label him as mad.

Margot punched his shoulder. "Don't call yourself that!" She winked at him. "You're the mad *genius* of the group, get it right."

"Hey, I thought I was the mad genius?" Danny said.

Margot shook her head. "No, you're just insane."

"Oh yeah, that makes more sense." Danny laughed. "Come on, let's see what you've got." In one motion, he drew a knife from a thigh holster and threw it directly at Alice's chest.

Time slowed.

Alice watched the knife coming at her, moon glinting off the metal, the movement so slow it was an easy dance to step away from the point's path and grab the knife from the air.

The group applauded. "She's a natural!" Margot cried.

Alice looked down at the knife in her hand, still amazed at what had just happened. She'd *snatched a knife from midair*. She looked back at Danny.

"You...that could have..."

Danny grinned. "You're immortal. Even if you *were* too slow, a knife wound to the chest wouldn't kill you; it would only hurt like hell. Although, for the record, you should stay away from beheading or fire; those will keep you down permanently." He walked over to a table covered with swords, axes, knives of several sizes, and a machete. He grabbed the axe and hurled it like a Frisbee at one of the straw dummies against the wall. It chopped the head straight off, the stuffing landing with a soft thump on the ground.

Alice's stomach plummeted. It might have just been a dummy's head this time, but what had she signed up for? Did they really expect her to kill someone? She was a photographer!

"I'm not so sure about all this," Alice said. The table of weapons was intimidating in itself. She pointed at a pile of acorn-sized cylinders that, with her enhanced vampire senses, smelled like harsh chemicals and something else, elusive and tantalizing. "I don't even know what half of these things are."

Ben picked up one of the cylinders. "These are my UV flash bombs. Sunlight can weaken us, so I've duplicated the effects of the sun's rays on whatever vampire they hit. These are non-fatal rounds; they just hurt like crazy. With enough exposure, they can knock an enemy unconscious long enough to make a hasty retreat." He tossed it in the air and

Alice fought the instinct to jump away from it. "I'm very proud of these babies." He handed one to her. "Check it out!"

Alice recoiled away from it. "I don't know…"

Margot walked up to give Alice a gentle pat on the shoulder. "I know it's a lot all at once." She gave Ben a hard stare. "Let's start off easy before we move up to the pyrotechnics, shall we?" Margot picked up a sword from the table and handed it to Alice. "Try this. You've got a swordmaiden look about you."

"Who do you expect me to fight?" Alice's hands were shaking.

"Right now? Nobody. But living a life that lasts centuries pretty much guarantees you'll come across one danger or another. The only expectation we have is for you to be able to defend yourself."

Alice had to admit, the sword felt good in her hand. The handle was a simple grip with a metal hemisphere protecting her hand and wrist like she'd seen in old Three Musketeer movies. Although it was a solid, three-foot metal blade, she held the weight easily. She whipped the sword around the air a few times, enjoying the swishing sound as it cut the air.

"Hold on there, little vamp, you're not chopping wood," Danny said. He came up to stand next to her, rearranging her grip so that her thumb guided the blade like it was an extension of her arm.

Margot picked up another of the blades, standing opposite Alice. "All right, I'm going to show you a couple of attacks."

Margot was patient with Alice's many questions as she explained footwork, how to parry, and how to attack, with Danny and Ben giving a running commentary of their various run-ins with past foes. Danny especially seemed to run into confrontations at least once a week, a fact which Ben gently scolded him about.

They both cheered when Alice managed to clumsily recreate a feint, and she swelled with pride. Alice looked between Margot, Danny, and Ben. The connection of their family was so strong, it was like an invisible force joining them together.

This is the best part of being a vampire, she realized. *I'm a part of this.*

"Oh good, you found them."

Alice turned toward the voice, and the Latina woman, Valerie, who had called Christopher away joined them in the courtyard. Something in Valerie's expression made Margot's shoulders immediately tense. Margot always played it so cool, Alice found it unnerving to see the gallery owner looking unsure.

Valerie smiled warily at Alice. "Christopher wanted to make sure you made it out okay."

"He thought she couldn't make it down a flight of stairs?" Danny asked.

Valerie's smile widened. "I think our sire just wanted to make sure our newest member was *satisfied* with her transition." She leaned hard enough on the word to make everybody chuckle and Alice blush.

"It's not like that--" Alice started to say.

"Not anymore it's not," Margot said. "Christopher's just too good a guy to bang somebody he has absolute control over. We all know that would be a recipe for disaster." Her tone indicated the topic was closed, and it was Ben who changed the subject, turning to Valerie.

"What's the news from the palace? What has Christopher out of here so early?"

Valerie's grin died. "It's the king. He's dead."

They all started talking at once, their questions overlapping on top of one another.

"What?"

"How?"

"When?"

"You couldn't have led with that?" Danny cried.

"What are we going to do?" Margot said last.

Alice looked between them, her heart beginning to beat faster in alarm. *The king?*

Valerie held up her hands for silence. "We just got word an hour ago. It was a freak accident at the palace. We told him time and time again not to decorate his walls with ceremonial blades, but the king never bothered to listen to the opinions of others." Valerie rolled her eyes. "Christopher is headed there now to investigate and confirm the plan for succession."

"He's going *right now* with no backup?" Margot sounded outraged. She buckled the sword to her waist and grabbed a couple of UV bombs from the table. She pointed at Danny. "Come on!"

Danny nodded, and the two raced away.

Alice watched them disappear with a growing sense of alarm.

"What's going on?" She asked the rest.

Valerie looked at her sadly. "I'm sorry this is happening today of all days. As the king's last remaining sirelings, Christopher and Rhys are the heirs. It's really a matter of who claims the throne and who can hold it. Christopher is the oldest so he'll get priority, but..." Valerie paused. "If Rhys becomes king, we're all *very* fucked."

"The king's death means there's going to be a war," Ben said.

Valerie jumped in. "There *might* be a war."

"War?" The sword suddenly felt heavy in Alice's hand. She looked down at the decapitated dummy head. "Now?"

Valerie shook her head. "No, there will be a lot of negotiations and diplomacy first, but the king..." Her voice trailed off. Ben laid a hand on her shoulder. "He was an ornery old bastard who held onto outdated traditions. But he's been the king for as long as I've been alive. It's hard to believe he's really gone."

Ben twirled a small dagger in his hand, over and over like he couldn't stop. "It will be all right, you'll see. Margot and Danny were the first vampires Christopher turned, they're the strongest of us all. With them as backup, Christopher should be fine."

"But can't we help in some way?" Alice asked.

Valerie bit her lip. "Any more than those two would look like an attack, and might put all of them in danger." She sounded like she was mostly trying to convince herself. "We can help by staying here and rallying the troops. Let's call our sirelings, and they'll call *their* sirelings and we'll all get ready, in case the worse should happen."

Alice looked between them. "What's the worst that could happen?"

Valerie and Ben shared a loaded look. "Rhys being Rhys."

MOURNERS STOOD dozens thick outside the looming iron gates of the ancient royal castle as Christopher's car approached. Black flags bearing the family crest hung from the castle's Gothic turrets at half-mast, and the grounds felt strangely quiet, like even the birds who lived in the gardens knew death hung in the air.

Christopher had passed through these same gates regularly for centuries, and it never felt like this. He instinctively began to rehearse what to say to the king to try and knock him from the dark ages, but then Christopher remembered that there would be no arguments this time. His sire was dead.

Christopher rubbed a hand across his forehead. There hadn't been a new vampire king in over two millennia, but his sire's advisors would probably insist on following the rarely-used ancient rituals for mourning a monarch: months of dark clothing and plodding ceremonies as the advisors handled any business pending from the former king's rule. After that, the eldest prince would be educated at great length on trade deals, treaties, and taxes. The pomp would be endless, and Christopher already dreaded every minute of it.

The only upside he saw in the coming months was that he could finally start building a new, progressive future for his people. He drummed his fingers against the car's window. With a slow transition, Christopher hoped he could convince the remaining traditionally-minded folks to start thinking more inclusively, and he could give his people the prosperous future they deserved.

Twin motorcycles gunned down the drive at breakneck speed as Christopher got out of the car, and he tensed until he recognized Danny and Margot's helmets. They jumped off their motorcycles, grabbing weapons out of duffle bags and arming themselves to the teeth with swords and machetes lashed to their sides for easy reach.

"What are you doing here?" Christopher asked as Margot strapped a second knife to her forearm. "This visit is just a formality to see my sire's body and start planning for the transition." He looked at the bulges along her belt. "Are those grenades?"

Margot raised an eyebrow at him. "Didn't you hear? Grenades are the new black--"

"Except with a lot more fire," Danny finished, securing a machete to his thigh.

"This really isn't necessary--" Christopher started to say.

"Just think of us as your backup plan. You will be damned happy to see these grenades if your brother tries some shit," Margot said.

Christopher threw up his hands as he started up the stairs towards the castle. Margot and Danny walked on each side of him. The rhythmic tattoo of metal hitting metal as their weapons struck against armor sounded more comforting than Christopher wanted to admit. The castle, usually bustling with activity, was too quiet. *Where are the funeral planners and staff to set up the castle for mourners?*

Christopher's unease only grew as they approached the throne room. Strikingly large guards he didn't recognize stood along both sides of the hallway, easily three times as many than were necessary. Four of them blocked the double-doors to the throne room. Margot and Danny tensed on either side of him and Christopher's hand itched to grab for weapons he hadn't thought he'd need.

"Who are you?" The guard who stepped forward from the door had muscles the size of basketballs, no neck, and lips so thin his sharp canines dipped down outside his mouth like a stray dog.

Danny slid forward before Christopher got the chance to speak, stepping in between him and the guard. "This is Prince Christopher, you disrespectful, no-neck--"

"There's no need for that." Christopher moved forward.

He eyed the guard. The vampire had the unsteady look of the newly turned. With all that muscle mass, he'd be a challenge to take down, but Christopher had no doubt that he, Margot, and Danny would be more than a match for the goons blocking the door. The other thirty vamps behind them would be a bigger problem.

He placed a calming hand on Danny's shoulder. "I am here to speak with my brother and pay my respects to my sire. Let us pass."

The guard shared a smirk with the others at the door and the one nearest the handle pulled the mighty-oak door open with a loud groan.

"Yeah, sure, your highness," the guard chuckled. "The king has been looking forward to this."

Christopher's unease transformed into dread. *The king?*

The throne room was the same as Christopher remembered it: gray, echoing, and cold with arched ceilings and stone gargoyles snarling from every corner. Dust hung in the air, and Christopher heard the sound of weeping from down another hallway.

Christopher's longing for a weapon grew with each second. His sire's advisors knelt on the floor along one side of the wall, their hands chained together. Guards stood over the advisors, brandishing axes and frigid expressions. There was no sign of Christopher's sire's coffin, and the royal throne was already occupied.

Rhys sneered down at his brother, one leg slung over the side of the throne's golden arm, his boots swinging with glee. Rhys's short, blonde hair lay slicked back on his head, the grease reflecting off the candlelight beside him. Christopher ground his teeth, fighting for a civil tone.

"What are you doing on our sire's throne?" Christopher eyed his brother's heavily-armed cadre of guards as he spoke. He could see Margot and Danny move closer out of the corner of his eye to guard his back, weapons at the ready.

Rhys wriggled where he sat. "It's quite a comfortable perch. I can see why he liked it so much." His jocular tone had an edge like a sabre.

He's insane. Dread and fear coiled in Christopher's chest. He looked toward the chained advisors. They had been his sire's friends for centuries, men and women who had helped *raise* them both. *What could Rhys possibly be thinking*?

"Let them go." His fists clenched in an effort to appear calm. "Even if you will not listen to their counsel, you cannot leave them like this for the funeral."

"There isn't going to be a funeral." Rhys's foot swung back and forth, his voice smooth like he was commenting on the weather. "Our dear sire's body was already burned this morning, his ashes scattered in the garden. We're done with him."

Shock hit Christopher like a petrification spell. Margot and Danny made small noises of concern behind him, but the world seemed unstable around him and he couldn't move to comfort them. Christopher's mouth gaped open and he fought to find words.

"What? But...you can't...you..."

"I think you'll find I can. My coronation is in three days, and I don't need that old bag of bones just lying around."

"I am the rightful heir to that throne," Christopher said. "Our sire is dead. In response to news of such a tragedy, you do not mourn him, you do not comfort your sire line. You instead seek to usurp my position with this..." Christopher gestured at Rhys's guards, "attempt at intimidation."

Rhys blew a bubble with his gum, a bright pink orb that

expanded out six inches before snapping. He picked the bits off his nose with a manic grin.

"Who do I need to intimidate? You? Those freaks you've turned? You've spent your centuries turning poets and outcasts." He gestured at a large man with tattoos of barbed wire circling his bald head and neck. "This big bastard here was a champion powerlifter before I made him part of my sire line. Now his will is mine. What chance do your ballerinas have against a force like him?"

Rhys hopped off the throne and strode toward him. Margot and Danny moved to block him, but Christopher extended his hand to stop them from interfering. Rhys's eyes were crazy, his long fingers taking Christopher's chin in a tight grip.

"All of your little, artsy farsty, riff raff sirelings," Rhys said in a sing-song tone, "are *ruining* what it means to be a vampire." He shouted the last words, spit flecking out in all directions.

Christopher pried Rhys's hand from his face. "My sirelings are none of your business."

Rhys tsked as he jumped back to delicately perch on the throne once more. "They're my business when you refuse to hold them to your will. You let your pets run around with no leash." He spat on the stone floor. "It's an *embarrassment*. How could a sire like you rule our people? You can't even rule your own line." He pointed to the guards poised next to the kneeling advisors. They weren't quite as beefcake as Rhys's new personal guards, but they all had the same vacant expressions. "Do you see my new sirelings? I selected these lucky bastards into my command because those old farts at their feet are their drinking buddies and mentors." He raised his hand and brought down like a falling guillotine. "Kill them."

Before Christopher could move, the guards' swords chopped off the heads of the kneeling advisors. The decapitated bodies of his sire's most trusted confidants fell to the stone floor with sickening, wet thumps. Rhys's hold broken the moment they fulfilled the command, the guards holding the swords immediately started to shake and sputter in shock. One started to vomit, another fell to the ground, sobbing.

"Fucking hell," Danny cursed behind Christopher, his voice small with shock and horror.

"I can take them," Margot said, quiet enough that only Christopher could hear.

"I'm so sorry! I'm so sorry! I'm so sorry!" One guard wailed over and over.

"Shut up!" Rhys yelled and his guards all froze silently in place, tears and horror cemented on their faces. Rhys leaned back onto his throne and crossed his legs. "Anyone who disagrees with me is going to face the same consequences."

Rage and shame circled in a whirlwind inside Christopher.

"This isn't over." If they stayed in the room any longer, Christopher knew he wouldn't be able to stop Margot, Danny, or himself from attacking Rhys, and they were hopelessly outnumbered. They needed a plan. Christopher pulled Margot and Danny out of the throne room, their footsteps echoing against the empty stone walls.

They didn't speak until they'd gotten outside and the moonlit sky was a welcome relief from the castle's weight.

"Well...that's not great." Margot's voice broke the silence.

Danny ran a hand through his short, black hair. "I don't know why we didn't just kill him right there."

"We will stop him." Christopher stood tall now, steady in his conviction. "But first, we need to get out of here. Now."

. . .

CHRISTOPHER BARELY REMEMBERED the car ride back. Danny and Margot drove their motorcycles in front and behind of his car to keep watch in case Rhys sent one of his mind-wiped minions to run Christopher off the road. Rhys had always been reckless with his use of the *hortari*, but Christopher had never believed his brother would go this far. The sound of the heads hitting the floor, immediately followed by the anguished cries of their friends who couldn't resist Rhys's command, was a miserable loop repeating in his memory.

Rhys has to be stopped.

As soon as they arrived home, Christopher asked an anxious-looking Danny and Margot to gather the lieutenants in the dining room. Shouts of horror reverberated throughout the house as his sirelings learned of Rhys's actions. Christopher ransacked his rooms, dumped boxes out of storage and gathered as many floor plans and charts of the castle that he could find. He was about to ask his sirelings, his family, to engage in a full-scale assault against a fortified castle, and he couldn't leave anything to chance.

Christopher was in the midst of unrolling each map along the long, wooden dining table, and weighing down the edges with coasters and candlesticks when his sirelings filed in. Margot came first, taking her place at his right hand, and nodding to Danny, Ben, and Valerie as they ringed the rest of the table, their expressions grave. The dining room wasn't outfitted as a war room--the pastoral paintings of hillsides weren't exactly the scenes to inspire battle--but it was the only room with a big enough table for all the maps scattered across its surface.

I'm not outfitted for war, Christopher thought with a nervous twinge.

A moment later, Alice slipped in behind them. Christopher's heart skipped a beat in terror. He left the table to pull her aside.

"I don't want you anywhere near this," he said. "Whatever we decide here today, you shouldn't be a part of it." He tried to push down images of Alice mangled on the battlefield. Alice being torn to shreds by Rhys's men. Alice broken and dying all because Christopher wanted to be king.

She raised her chin and pulled her arm out of his grip. "If you didn't want me to be a part of this, then you shouldn't have made me one of you. I have a right to be here."

Christopher looked at his other sirelings. Margot, Danny, Ben, and Valerie had spent decades learning to fight. At one time or another, they'd had to defend themselves or someone else, but they'd never seen real war. Thinking of any of them hurt was like a stabbing pain through his heart. But if Rhys became king, his choices would harm them too. They deserved the right to choose their fate. He touched Alice's hand, needing the comforting contact of her touch.

"You're right," he said in a quiet voice.

He took a deep breath and stepped back to the front of the table. Christopher's sirelings were already pouring over the blueprints and maps spread across the table. He tried to keep his eyes off of Alice as she took an open space between Margot and Ben, looking down at the plans.

"Thank you all for joining me." He straightened his spine and raised his voice to be easily heard throughout the room. "I'm sure by now that you've all heard that my sire, your king, has died."

Somber murmurs made small laps around the room. Margot banged her fist down on the table for silence.

"As his eldest sireling, I am the rightful heir to that throne. As vampires, we can never age, but that does not mean we cannot grow." Christopher calmly clasped his hands in front of him. "We must ensure our values of freedom, independent expression, and respect for all are protected. The vampire community must know that, although the *hortari* is a reality of our existence, it does not give anyone the right to enslave others." Christopher smiled a thin smile, dreading what he must ask of them all. "Rhys has seized the throne as his own, muscling his way to sovereignty. He threatens to make legions of *hortari*-locked slaves to carry out his whims. We must prove that our way is stronger."

"And how do we do that?" Valerie asked.

"We are going to take back the castle."

"Okaaayyy," Danny said slowly. "How?"

Christopher smiled. "That's the point. The ability of each of us to think for ourselves is what will preserve our ideals." He outstretched his hands to encompass the table of maps and drawings of the castle. "We're going to combine our skills to build a plan *together*. Rhys's coronation is in three days. I need you to bring in everyone you need, and consult with every contact you have. We are stronger because we are together, and we *will* win."

The whole table broke out into cheers and applause. Christopher's heart swelled with pride at their loyalty, but his gaze was irrevocably drawn back to Alice, her head bowed in intense conversation with Ben at the far end of the room.

He walked along the length of the table watching the others jump into action. Margot and Valerie pulled maps toward themselves and started to point out weaknesses in the outer structure, while Danny scanned the lists of castle employees and made notes on his tablet. Christopher cared for all of them, but Alice looked so vulnerable next to his years-hardened sirelings, his chest ached with worry.

"Alice, what do you think about checking out my dark room?" Christopher told Alice once he'd reached her side. "You can start to develop some new photos. We're safe here for now, you don't have to stick around for all the planning." He pressed his hand to the small of her back, guiding her towards the exit.

"Are you going to use your UV flash bombs?" Alice slid out of Christopher's grasp, returning to the table next to Ben, taking a device about the size of a roll of quarters out of the inventor's hand. She seemed to be studiously ignoring Christopher, her gaze fixed on the delicate glass and steel structure.

Christopher couldn't smell her emotions now that she was a vampire the way he'd been able to when she was a human, but he recognized the tightness in her jaw and the hunch in her shoulders as signs of fear.

She shouldn't be doing this. Alice was an artist. She didn't have the training for war. Of all his sirelings, she was the most likely to get hurt, and the thought terrified him more than he thought was possible.

Ben smiled at Alice. "You don't have to be so gentle with it, this one's inactive." Ben pointed down at the blueprints of the royal throne room. "If we set them up to blast here, here, and here." He pointed to three different sections of the page. "We should be able to knock 'em back a bit."

"Hmmm." Alice bit on her thumb, then pulled some loose change out of her pocket and placed the coins down onto the map. "You've got a really good strategy, *but* there's an opportunity to miss some of Rhys's men in the shadows you've created here and here. If you install the UV flash bombs where I've put these coins, they will overlap so every inch of the throne room will be covered."

Ben tilted his head to examine the new placement of the coins. "That's brilliant!" Ben clapped Alice on the shoulder proudly. "How did you know to do that?"

Alice smiled. "When I first started taking pictures, learning proper lighting was rough. But now I'm a bit of an expert."

"A lighting expert! Good thinking, bringing this one in, Christopher." Ben laughed heartily. "They'll never see it comin'."

Margot leaned over, "What's this? Our photo prodigy is going to help us UV the crap out of these douchebags?"

"Just in the initial planning," Christopher growled. "She's not trained for battle."

Ben shrugged and Alice opened her mouth like she was about to say something, but Margot tapped her arm and shook her head. Alice glanced at Christopher and blushed, then went back to studying the blueprints, moving the coins slightly on the map and edging around the table to look at the picture from a different angle. The light from the chandelier elongated the shadows under her eyes like she was already dead.

No, not her. Never her. Christopher circled the room to put some distance between himself and Alice, knowing he was being selfish trying to minimize her involvement. He couldn't stop thinking that making her a vampire had been supposed to preserve Alice and keep her from harm. Now she was helping them plan for battle.

Danny looked up from a debate with Valerie about whether it was worth trying to proactively turn some of Rhys's sirelings to their cause before the battle when he saw

Christopher approach. Danny lightheartedly elbowed Christopher in the ribs.

"Hey there, Chris. It's nice having us all together, admit it."

"Even if I'm marching you to your probable deaths?" Christopher asked.

"Even if."

"I do enjoy seeing you all, being together as a family but..." Christopher sighed, "Just the other day I accidentally rendered Margot mute, just from a careless word. This damn *hortari* makes me a danger to all of you."

"I'm not sure if shutting up Margot for a moment is *such* a bad thing." Danny ducked out of the way of a flying candlestick thrown with impressive speed. "Just kidding." He waved his hands in surrender. "It doesn't *have* to be this way. I've heard stories of vamps breaking the *hortari*."

"That's what they are, stories." Christopher ran his hand through his short, dark hair and gripped at the ends in frustration. "The *hortari* bond is unbreakable, and Rhys is going to use it to enslave everyone around him." Christopher looked around the room. How many would still be alive when all of this was over? "We will have to call on everybody we can trust, every ally."

"My sirelings have sirelings," Danny said. "Gotta love that exponential growth."

Christopher plunged a knife into the nearest blueprint. "We're going to need every advantage we can get."

ALICE STARED at the knife wedged deep into the table. It cut through the throne. *Not a comforting image.* Christopher and his sirelings were still discussing battle strategies and how to ensure safe avenues of retreat. For all that Christopher turned people he respected as artisans, they were also all trained warriors and had lived long enough to learn a few things about strategy.

I want to join the battle.

She wasn't sure when she'd come to the realization. Sure, Alice had always wanted to help, but actually being part of a physical assault? It was almost unthinkable. It might have been seeing Christopher pace around the room with fear etched in the lines around his eyes. Or hearing him stand amidst his people and *request* support in a room full of vampires who would have no choice but to help if he had been less careful in his wording. Christopher was a good man, and the sirelings he'd created were some of the most fun and clever people she'd ever known. The thought of any of them getting hurt made her feel sick.

Alice slid her coins on the map of the throne room, adjusting it slightly. She bit her lip. There were so many variables that would come into play when positioning the flash bombs. The blueprints showed how tall the room was and where the windows were positioned, but there could be any number of factors that might impact the reach of the UV rays.

"I have to go with you," Alice said.

Danny and Margot were in a loud argument about the comparative merit of spears in the coronation room versus their uselessness in the tight castle corridors.

Alice raised her voice to be heard. "I'm going to come with you to the coronation."

"That's ridiculous," Christopher said.

Danny and Margot stopped arguing. Margot turned to Alice and pursed her lips.

"You're barely turned, Alice," Margot said. "That makes

you weaker than every vampire there. You might be good with that sword with a few more years of training, but you're nowhere near ready, hon."

"I didn't turn you so you could die a week later." Christopher's voice sounded final.

"You don't get it," Alice said. "Those UV bombs. You're going to need me there to maximize their reach."

"Ben can handle it. He invented them," Christopher said.

Ben raised his hand. "Actually, Ben can't." Christopher scowled at him. "Look, I just make the contraptions. I leave it up to you guys to use them to the best of your abilities. My expertise is in chemical reactions and mechanics, not light distribution."

"It's not happening," Christopher said. He looked around the room. "And that's final."

"But--" Alice started to say.

Christopher held up a hand. "Stop."

Alice's entire body locked in place, her mouth clicking shut as Christopher's sire compulsion took control.

She struggled to move, sweat beading on her forehead at the effort. She concentrated on the specific command. *He said 'stop', not 'stop talking'.*

"My liege, can I talk to you a second?" The words took effort to leave her mouth, but since his command had been so unspecific, Alice managed to form the words.

Christopher pulled his fingers through his hair. He let out a long breath. "Yes, sorry. We can talk outside." He looked at the others. "All of you, you know what to do. We'll meet again tomorrow to compare numbers and continue to fine-tune the plan."

The sirelings all shared significant looks and filed out. Christopher held open the door for Alice and walked beside her until they were outside on the front porch. Her car from the day before--which felt like a million years ago--was still parked at the end of the driveway.

Alice waited until she heard the last of the other sirelings leave and they were alone before turning back to Christopher.

"You need me there. Not bringing me puts the others at risk."

Christopher shook his head. "Are you so determined to die?" His voice grew louder with each word.

Alice stepped toward him, determined to calm him down. "You gave me immortality so that I could have more chances to do *good* in this world. Helping stop your brother is exactly that."

"Rhys is my problem, not yours. Your death is Not. An. Option." Christopher stepped so close, his breath brushed against her face. Everything in her body felt charged being near him. Her muscles practically vibrated with a need to touch him: to comfort or slap him, she wasn't sure.

She pressed her palm against his cheek. "This is my choice. I'm going with you."

He pulled her closer, his mouth pressing against hers in sudden desperation. His tongue pushed into her mouth, and she opened to him, grabbing his shoulders to pull herself close. His fingers laced through her hair, tangling in the strands, while his other hand cupped her ass. She shivered with pleasure.

He felt so *right*, so perfect against her body. All day she'd been trying to not think about their night together, but it all rushed back at the feel of his hands, the scent of him surrounding her, her enhanced vampire senses making every detail of him more intense.

He broke away from the kiss, still holding her close. "Don't you understand? I can't lose you. You mean so much to me, more than anyone ever has. I need you to be safe." She started to protest, but he looked deep into her eyes. "Get in your car, Alice. Drive away and live your life the way you choose, but never look for me. I will never come near you again. This is my last command to you. Go." He stepped away from her.

"No!" But it was too late, the *hortari* had already taken control. Every muscle in her body forced her towards her car. "Christopher, stop this!" She pushed back against the compulsion with everything she could, her mind screaming as she tried to gain control of a body that kept putting one foot in front of another in an irrevocable march.

Christopher stood behind her, tears in his eyes and grief etched in every line of his face, but he didn't come any closer.

Nightmare images flashed through her mind. The bright light of the UV bombs missing key areas of the room, Rhys's faceless evil minions descending on Christopher and his sire line, their fangs dripping with blood like some B horror movie. All because she wasn't there. Danny dead. Valerie dead. Ben dead. Margot dead.

Christopher dead.

"No! I need to stay!" She looped her arms around one of the lamp posts that lined the side of the driveway and held on with all her might. With every second she tried to resist the *hortari*'s pull, the pain increased. Her shoulders ached as her lower body pulled towards the car. A hot heaviness was forcing itself up from her feet through her legs and into her stomach, magma filling her limbs. She locked her arms around the pole as her legs throbbed in pain as they tried to walk away. She lowered herself to the ground, one hand under the other, until she lay flat on her stomach and her feet could only kick spasmodically behind her.

"What are you doing?" Christopher asked. He came closer, his expression a mix of curiosity and awe.

She closed her eyes, shutting out the pain, letting a growing fury push back against the weight of hot magma burning up her chest and into her neck. Alice screamed, the sound breaking through the agony.

"This is such *bullshit*!" Fury like she'd never felt pulsed through her. This was her body. This was her *will*. She had to *break* this.

Memories swirled. Christopher kissing her. Christopher carrying her to his bed. The pleasure shooting through her as she came over and over against at the feel of his mouth. Christopher's face when he told her they could never be together because it was his blood that made her a vampire. Everything about her new existence was perfect, could be perfect, if she could only break through this.

The pain was agonizing, but she leaned into it now. Somewhere inside herself, Alice looked straight at the pain, acknowledged it, welcomed it. This was a goddamn staring contest from hell and there was no way she was about to blink.

I can do this.

One in a million broke the sire bond, but there was always that one.

The pain tried to take over, pain spiking into her. She screamed again, a mindless wail of agony that was nowhere near accepting defeat.

I can do this.

Blackness tinged her vision, and Alice felt like she was passing out. *No, that's the hortari.* She fought against it, looking up into Christopher's face. He was smiling now, laughing almost, tears rolling down his face.

"I can't believe it," he said. "You're amazing."

She held on, pushing against the blackness, focusing on his smile.

The *hortari* shattered.

She collapsed limp against the ground.

The pain disappeared, leaving only a dull ache in her limbs from all the strain and the kicking. The pull to leave was gone.

She shakily got to her feet, dusting off the gravel that stuck to her arms and side.

"Tell me to do something," she said, her voice breathless with hope and anticipation.

Christopher shook off his shock. "Um, I don't know. Touch your nose."

She waited a second to see if she felt anything, but there was nothing. Alice wiggled her fingers freely in front of Christopher's face.

"Nope! Not gonna do it!" She laughed and jumped forward into his arms, kissing him furiously. He kissed her back, pulling her closer and carrying her to the house, her legs straddling his waist and her arms wrapped around his shoulders.

"No one..." He said in between kisses to her mouth, her neck, her cheek. "No one has ever fought so hard for me. I didn't think it was possible."

She roughly pulled a fistful of his hair, forcing his head back, while pressing her chest closer so her hard nipples rubbed against the front of his jacket.

"It wasn't all for you. I was fighting for my freedom." She pressed her lips against his, moaning when his mouth opened for her and her tongue battled against his for dominance. "And for this." She reached down to stroke his erect cock pressing against her stomach.

He looked around. They were still in the middle of the

driveway. The others would be returning at any time with their reinforcements.

"Race you to the bedroom," she said, dropping to her feet and running with her enhanced vampire speed back into the house.

"No fair! You got a head start!"

She was already so far in front of him, she could barely hear his words. Alice raced up the stairs and down the hallway at a speed that reduced the house's carefully-curated decorations into a tasteful blur. She kicked open the bedroom door and spun in time to grab hold of Christopher and use his momentum to toss him onto the bed. He sprawled against the headboard and she jumped onto him, tearing off her shirt and bra in a single rip and pressing her nipple against his mouth. He sucked and licked at her command, the shuddering pleasure running through her not stopping as he managed to pull apart his shirt without breaking contact. He switched his attention from one breast to another, licking and sucking her nipples to tight points.

She could feel every indent on his tongue, every hair on his arms where they wrapped around her back. His aroused scent made wetness pool between her legs, demanding she become closer to him. Enhanced strength made ripping off his pants, the fabric tearing like paper, all the easier. Her own pants came next until they were both bare.

"Alice, you're---"

"Shut up." She pressed him down against the bed, positioning her pussy above his mouth. "I'm still pissed at you for *commanding* me to leave."

"I'm at your command now. Whatever you want, I'm yours. Forever." He grabbed her hips, pulling her wet mound towards him so he could lick her clit, his tongue making wide sweeps along her slit, exploring all her folds.

Spikes of pleasure rushed through her every time his tongue flicked her bud.

"Yes, that," she panted.

He flicked her clit again, and Alice couldn't help but thrust until she was riding his face in wild gyrations, her clit rubbing against his nose, his mouth, his lips. The intensity of the sensations was more than she'd ever felt before; every place they touched thrilled her, drove her on.

"Oh gods, I'm coming!" she screamed, just as he thrust his tongue deep into her, fucking her deep, as his fingers danced against her clit. She came in waves, lights flashing behind her eyes as she spasmed on top of his face. When the waves slowed, she sat back. His face glistened with her cum and he licked his lips. She leaned forward and tasted herself on his mouth. Behind her, his enormous cock strained upwards, brushing against her ass.

It felt too gorgeous to resist. She turned to lean down and lick along his shaft, wrapping her lips around his tip. Christopher gripped the sheets so tight, the fabric threatened to tear.

"Careful, I'm so close," he said.

She grabbed his cock with her hand, using his pre-cum to lubricate her palm as she stroked him up and down with fast, measured strokes. His cock jumped and she licked along the tip, putting gentle pressure on the underside and licking upward. His chest vibrated with tension between her thighs. She lifted her head, letting go of his shaft just before he came. She jumped off to kneel beside him. He looked so gorgeous laying there. He was the most exquisite being she'd ever seen. *And he's mine.*

He reached for her. "Tell me, what do you need?" he asked.

She crawled closer, straddling his cock. She locked eyes

with him as she lowered herself down onto his shaft. He was so big, his cock stretched at her walls.

"You. I need all of you."

He moaned, his hands massaging her breasts as he thrust up into her wet heat.

She leaned down and bit his lip, rolling her hips so his stomach brushed against her clit with each movement. His cock felt amazing buried deep inside her, every part of them connected. She remembered her last night as a human, the perfection of him inside her. And this time, it wasn't their final chance, it was just the beginning.

She came screaming Christopher's name, bliss infusing every limb as she let the pleasure wash over her. Christopher's thrusts under her became more urgent until he was groaning loudly and she felt him spill inside of her.

"Yesssss." She curled up on top of him, feeling him slowly go soft while still inside her. She touched his face. "This is worth everything."

He kissed her gently. "I wish I could keep you safe."

Alice smiled, kissing his nose. "I appreciate that, but if protecting me means taking away my choices, then we're going to have problems."

He grinned. "Well, even if the *hortari* isn't working, I could still tie you up to keep you from joining the battle."

"Haha, by that logic, I should tie *you* up so you don't get hurt either." She wiggled her hips a little.

"*That* image I don't mind at all." His hands started to roam her back. "Taking turns with the cuffs..." His hands found her wrists, pulled them together and back behind her so her chest arched back and he could lean up to kiss her breasts.

She laughed. "Keep that up, and neither of us will ever leave."

He licked her nipple. "Perhaps that's the best option." Christopher's smile dimmed and he leaned back against the pillows, releasing her wrists. "Unfortunately, Rhys is a problem that I have to fix."

"Why does it have to be you?" She dismounted his cock and curled up next to him, spooning against him. She pulled up the sheet so its smooth fabric cocooned them both.

"Rhys and I are more than just sired by the same vampire, we were born brothers. He's always been selfish and power-mad, and I've always tried to protect others from him. We weren't born rich, our family herded sheep, and Rhys always seemed to resent it. One of the few memories I still have from when I was human is from when I was sixteen or seventeen and Rhys was fifteen or so. There was this girl in our town born with a cleft lip that partially deformed her face. Really nice girl, amazing weaver." Christopher took a deep breath. "Rhys convinced the other boys in the village that she was evil, that they could prove their strength as men if they hurt her. I did everything I could to protect her, but once the idea circulated far enough through town, there was no stopping the attacks. I managed to safely smuggle her out of town and place her with some distant aunts. But it always haunted me, how Rhys's cruelty managed to alter somebody's life so drastically. It was the first time I saw something like that, but definitely not the last." Christopher leaned back against the bed's headrest, closing his eyes. "With our sire's death, Rhys and I are the oldest vampires still alive. I can't let him have influence over the direction of our people and I'm the only one with a strength that equals his own." His breath stirred Alice's hair and she cuddled closer to him. She ached at the pain in his voice.

"Then you need all the help you can get to stop him."
She pulled at his hand so it reached around her and rested
on her stomach.

He gripped her hand. "I do. I was scared and selfish and
tried to keep you safe at the expense of the success of the
battle. You're right, though. You have a talent that will be
invaluable in battle. Without you, my sirelings could end up
hurt or worse." Christopher's fingers caressed her stomach.
"I just... I'm terrified at the thought of you getting harmed."

"Why is that?"

He sat up on one arm so he could look down at her face.
"You want me to say it, don't you?"

"We're going into battle," she reminded him, turning so
their eyes were level. "If there's anything you want off your
chest, you should say it now."

He kissed her, his lips attacking hers as he pulled her
closer. He pulled her leg up over him so they were wrapped
together on their sides in the bed. His cock was hard against
her opening, and all it took was just a slightly different angle
of his hips and he slid inside her from behind in one
smooth stroke. He started to thrust gently into her, holding
her so close his cock barely had to move to slide against her
clit.

"I love you, Alice. I love you more than my own immortality, more than the beauty in the world, more than
anything else I've ever encountered in a thousand years."
Each swipe of his cock drove her higher and she rolled so
she was on her stomach. He grabbed her ass and pulled her
hips high to change the angle and thrust into her even
deeper.

Her breath came in desperate gasps. "I love you too. So
much."

Their orgasms hit faster than Alice believed possible,

their moans intermingled with one another as they both went over the edge together.

Christopher leaned his forehead against hers, his breath slowly evening out. "Whatever happens, we're together."

Alice nodded. "Forever."

CHRISTOPHER LAY on his stomach on the castle's peaked roof and checked his watch, counting down the seconds before the explosives were set to demolish the building's entrance. Margot and her forces were harnessed up along the top of the roofline, ropes attached to the castle's stone gargoyles already hooked into the straps on their waists. They'd spooked the security cameras with looping footage to hide their position, but Christopher didn't like how exposed they were out in the open. Margot caught his eye and nodded in encouragement, her expression alight with anticipation. He wished he shared her thrill.

They'd separated their forces among Christopher's four lieutenants, each with a specific timed mission: Ben's team would infiltrate the castle's hallways and throne room ahead of the coronation to position as many UV flash bombs as possible. Danny's team was in charge of diverting as many of Rhys's forces as possible to the furthest reaches of the castle grounds, away from the power of Rhys's voice. Valerie and Margot's two teams would crash through the ancient, stained, glass windows of the throne room attacking from both sides to clear the room and get innocents out of the way before Christopher swept in to defeat Rhys. It depended on their key advantages over Rhys' forces: their trust in one another, and their ability to improvise.

This plan also positioned Alice on Ben's team, helping

the inventor set up his devices to their best advantage. There was no denying Alice's expertise was needed there, but Christopher's hands shook thinking about how the only confirmation he had that she was okay were the hourly group texts with updates about the number and placements of the bombs. With every passing moment in between texts, he fought to push away the nightmares of Rhys catching her, stringing her up on his throne room wall, and making Christopher watch as he tore her to pieces. *If he has her, Rhys would damn sure let me know.* Christopher held onto that not-so-comforting thought as he steadied himself.

Three...two...one.

An explosion burning so hot its flames licked blue and white blasted open the front doors of the castle. Screams rang out from within the castle, the sound of stampeding feet thumping down the hallways as staff and guests of the coronation searched for safe exits. Christopher could almost imagine he heard Rhys's voice through the chaos screaming orders at people.

A second explosion thundered from the East side of the castle where Margot's team and Christopher waited. It was smaller than the explosion at the front gate, but the heat was intense enough Christopher could feel it against his face even seventy feet up.

The group text to all the lieutenants' phones came through at once from Alice, still hidden in the throne room: *"Half of Rhys's forces gone 2 investigate. Most guests cleared."*

Margot didn't hesitate. She made the arranged signal with her fist and her twenty vampires and Christopher all descended the side of the building, kicking out the stained glass windows of the throne room and bursting into the immense room.

The coronation was already underway. The main room

was filled with rows of long, wooden benches and Rhys stood at the top of the room's dais wearing a sly smirk and their sire's finest regalia. A priest, who looked a lot like Rhys's barbed-wire-tattooed sireling in a hood, stood poised with his hand raised in blessing and a vacant, mind-controlled expression on his face. The crown of their vampire kingdom was still on its ceremonial pedestal, gleaming dangerously.

"This man is not your rightful king," Christopher bellowed.

The remaining coronation guests who hadn't fled all turned to watch Christopher advance down the central aisle of the throne room. Christopher recognized many of the faces, vampires who had known the royal family for centuries.

Margot's forces stood protectively in a semicircle around Christopher, keeping his path to Rhys clear. As he advanced, Ben's forces emerged from the room's alcoves to fill in gaps from the ranks. He caught a glimpse of Alice, dressed in black and armed with a sword and UV grenades strapped crossways down her torso, joining the group surrounding him. He pushed aside the worry gnawing at his insides. *If she is a casualty of this battle, I will never forgive myself.*

"Now, brother," Rhys tutted from his chair. "Jealousy is not a good color on you."

"I will not stand by and let your thirst for power destroy our people." Worried gasps sprung out among the coronation's attendees. Some were still trying to flee, but many of the older ones had stayed, curious to see how this played out.

"So dramatic, Christopher." Rhys spoke calmly. He picked up the crown from its resting place, placing the ring of gold filigree onto his head. He sat back in his throne, smiling. "I only seek to be what you can never be: a strong leader."

A click from the rafters let Christopher know the cameras Ben had installed throughout the room were switched on, broadcasting what was happening in the throne room to all the vampire television stations worldwide.

"A leader is someone who people *choose* to follow. You seek to rule solely through *hortari*, intimidation, and fear."

"You only want the throne for yourself." Rhys snarled. "You've been after our sire's power for *centuries*, always badgering him to change what makes us vampires."

Through the open windows, Christopher could hear the sounds of clashing metal and shouting. One of his teams was fighting against Rhys's goons. He sent up a quick prayer to any gods who were listening that none of them would be hurt.

"And what is it that makes us vampires, brother?" Christopher asked.

Rhys rose from the throne, standing tall with his hands above his head. "Blood and strength!"

Many of the guests roared in support, along with a sprinkling of cheers and assents from Rhys's guards around the walls.

"Yet you stand there, shedding no blood," Christopher said. "My sirelings fight for me of their own free will because they know me, they've worked with me, and they know the vision I have for our kingdom comes from a sincere desire to see us progress and grow. Can you say the same, brother?"

"You question my honorable intentions?" Rhys held his empty hands out like a saintly benediction. The crowd was lapping it up, looking between Rhys, secure on his throne, and Christopher surrounded by armed guards. Christopher knew who looked like the usurper. *This isn't going to work.*

"You can prove it." Alice had snuck closer in the cluster of guards surrounding him. Her voice was only a whisper, but it cut through the sound of blood pumping in Christopher's ears.

"No, I can't," Christopher said.

"You can." Alice pulled a dagger from her boot and sliced a cut along Christopher's arm.

He jumped back, startled and surprised that she of all people would be the one to attack him. The blood gleamed red in the candlelight of the throne room, and the smell of it tickled his nose as it wafted past. Beside him, Margot grabbed a fan from her belt, each rib edged with a razor-sharp talon, and started waving it behind him, the breeze pushing the scent of Christopher's blood across the room.

That's it.

Christopher held his bleeding arm aloft, addressing the people. "You wish to know my intentions? Here they are. The blood doesn't lie." He turned to Rhys. "If your would-be king has nothing to hide, then surely he will join me in proving so."

The crowd murmured approvingly. A few of the older vampires moved towards Christopher, bowing slightly with respect. Others too far away to smell Christopher's blood spread the word to their neighbors until the whole room was alight with speculative looks toward Rhys. Christopher's blood clearly spelled out his intentions for the throne and his people. It was an unbeatable campaign.

"You want to *cut* me? I believe that's a direct threat against your future king," Rhys growled. "How *dare* you and your rabble disrespect me in such a manner. GUARDS!" He shrieked, a shrill, echoing wail that bounced across the high ceilings of the throne room. "Kill them! Cut off their heads and bring them to me in SACKS!"

Screams rose from the remaining crowd as most of them bolted in all directions, shoving each other in an undignified attempt to get away from Rhys's soldiers.

Rhys's muscled guards couldn't resist the *hortari* in Rhys's command and ran at Christopher and his people, their arms poised overhead for neck strikes. Christopher's heart twisted for them. Many of their eyes were wide and scared. Christopher didn't want to think how many atrocities Rhys had forced them to commit since becoming vampires.

"Now!" Christopher shouted, and Ben and Margot's teams surrounding him whipped heavy cloaks and sunglasses from their packs and covered all their exposed skin.

Alice didn't hesitate. She withdrew the detonator from her sleeve and pressed the button with a magnificent glow of satisfaction on her face. Rhys's guards nearly made it to Christopher before brilliant flashes of light detonated across the room. Christopher adjusted his sunglasses, proud that Alice's calculations had been correct. There wasn't a single inch of the throne room unaffected by the UV's flashes.

Rhys and his guards screamed and grunted in the light, their skin smoking slightly as the UV rays burned their sensitive flesh. Many of those surrounding Rhys who got the worst of the blast fell to the ground unconscious.

"Get up! I command you to kill them all! As your sire, I demand it of you!" Rhys screeched from where he thrashed on the floor. "Kill them for your king!"

The guards who could still move pulled themselves from the ground like marionettes on strings. Many had expressions of complete terror frozen on their faces. Their arms chopped the air in front of them like wind-up toys, moving in spasming, wild thrusts toward Christopher and his followers.

"Spread out!" Margot bellowed, yelling the commands she and Christopher had arranged earlier so that in the heat of battle he didn't accidentally use *hortari* against his people. "Try and avoid killing them, they didn't choose this!"

The cluster of sirelings surrounding Christopher broke into smaller groups, Margot staying close to Christopher while the rest ran toward the corners of the room, breaking Rhys's men into isolated groups who Ben's team hiding in the room's rafters could shoot with paralytic-tipped arrows. They fell in swaths, Rhys's soldiers' expressions filled with relief as the arrows stopped their movements. Margot and Ben's teams on the ground immediately chained up the unmoving and unconscious guards before the shock of the UV rays or the arrows wore off.

"Get reinforcements!" Rhys bellowed, pointing to one of his guards cowering behind the throne. "Tell them I will eat their sirelings if they disobey me!" Rhys bellowed.

"Brother, think about what you're doing!" Christopher shouted. "You are only harming your own people!"

Margot was hard at work defending herself against one of Rhys's better soldiers, a six-foot tall muscled woman with a shock of bright pink hair. They moved so fast, Christopher didn't dare interfere for fear of hurting Margot. Their sparing cleared the area around them, their clashing axes sending sparks into the air.

"My people exist to serve me!" Rhys yelled.

His shout distracted Margot's opponent and Margot laughed triumphantly as she launched a flying kick through the air that sent the woman sprawling to the ground. Margot planted her knee firmly in the back of Rhys's minion as she clanked heavy manacles around the woman's wrists.

"I always wanted to use these outside of the bedroom," Margot said with a wink.

"Is this really the time for--" Christopher started to say, but was cut short by the sight of Alice across the room.

Alice stood in the middle of the battle, beautiful as she shouted orders to the team repositioning another wave of the UV flash bombs. Christopher sprinted forward to help as Alice ducked under a minion's swinging axe and continued her work undeterred. The soldier facing her couldn't have been older than twenty when he was turned, acne blotching his face for eternity.

My brother is evil.

"Stay away from her." Christopher stepped in between the boy and Alice.

"Can't, sir," the boy said through clenched teeth. "Must kill."

"You can fight it!" Alice cried, still prudently standing behind Christopher. "I broke the *hortari*, so can you."

The boy gasped, and for a second, his axe hesitated on the downswing. Christopher held his breath, hoping for a miracle, then the blade continued down and Christopher dodged out of the way, missing getting an axe dug into his shoulder by a hair.

"I'm sorry!" the boy wailed. "I can't stop it!"

Alice unhooked one of the grenades from her holster and pulled the pin, throwing it at the boy just as she raised the edge of her cloak to cover herself and Christopher. The dangerous light blazed around the corner of her cloak and the boy fell screaming, his axe skidding away. Christopher jumped forward, slapping cuffs on the boy before he could grab his weapon.

"Thank you," the boy gasped as he lay curled on the ground.

The sounds of battle outside the throne room were dimming, replaced with victorious chanting of Christopher's name. Reinforcements streamed in as Valerie's team finished securing the last door and flooded the ballroom to help take down those still-standing among Rhys's forces.

Danny's was the last team to swarm in wearing triumphant expressions.

"We tricked thirty of them into a storage container!" he yelled.

"That's great!" Christopher replied. "Why don't we--" He didn't finish when an axe sliced so close to his ear, Christopher felt the breeze of it on his cheek.

Rhys stood an arm's length away, his mouth twisted into a snarl, an axe twirling in each hand so fast they blurred in silver circles on either side of him.

"You think you've won? You're nothing!" Rhys bellowed. His arms flashed forward with deadly speed, the twin axes spinning for Christopher's neck.

"I've got a shot, I can take him down," Ben's voice yelled down from the rafters, light glinting off the tip of his arrow.

"He's mine!" Christopher called up. In a fluid motion, he withdrew a knife from his belt, diving to grab the fallen teenager's axe still at Alice's feet. Christopher circled his brother warily, looking for the twitching tell of when he was going to strike.

"Watch your words, brother," Rhys smirked. "You might actually show some balls and give an order to one of your precious sirelings." He attacked without warning in a flurry of jabs, each axe swipe perilously close to Christopher's neck.

Christopher blocked and dodged, knowing that when it

came to hand to hand combat, his brother was always willing to cheat.

Unless..."Do you hear the cameras rolling, brother?" Christopher ducked just before one of the axes connected with his head and he rolled through Rhys's wide stance. "Everyone will know what happened here."

"What are you talking about?"

Christopher sprung to his feet, kicking Rhys hard in the back, surprising his brother and knocking him off balance. "You're a greedy liar who uses *hortari* to treat your sirelings as cannon fodder."

Rhys dodged out of the way, rolling under Christopher's swing with his awes twirling. "I *saved* them. You have no idea how broken these people were when I found them, how much they regretted the choices they'd made." He feinted to the right with one axe, the left striking out so fast Christopher couldn't duck away quick enough. The axe's fine edge sliced a long cut down Christopher's forearm, dripping blood.

"I gave them *immortality*," Rhys yelled. "And then I took away their burden of choice."

"They're *killing* people." Christopher flexed his injured arm. The cut burned and would need stitches, but adrenaline made it easy to shake off.

Rhys rolled his eyes. "You just don't get it. They *want* this. They're free from consequences. They're just following orders. No guilt. No repercussions."

"Then you've promised them an illusion." Christopher advanced on his brother, his axe and knife flying in a complex sequence of swings and stabs which had Rhys retreating backward to dodge out of the way. "Everything we do has consequences." He swung his knife for Rhys's stomach as he kicked out for Rhys's knees. Rhys jumped away, but for the first time, he showed fear. "Everything else is just excuses."

Distantly he heard their audience murmuring to themselves, nodding heads of agreement and tones of consideration surround them.

Christopher smiled. "The entire kingdom sees you for what you are."

"I am a *king*! I'm the savior of our people!"

"You're a weak, terrified coward."

Rhys screamed in mindless fury, swinging his axe in a wild arc. Christopher raised one arm, blocking the downswing of Rhys's axe on his metal arm-guard while he leapt in a roundhouse kick, connecting with Rhys's head.

The sound of Rhys's body hitting the ground was the most satisfying thud Christopher had heard in ages. Christopher snapped cuffs on his brother's hands and stepped back. Rhys lay sprawled across the red carpet like a broken doll.

"Long live the vampire king," Margot's impressed voice rang out uncomfortably loud in the now-silent throne room.

"Is that it?" Danny asked from his perch atop a guard's back.

"We did it!" Alice ran to Christopher, wrapping her arms around his neck. She stood on tiptoe and brought her lips to his.

He smiled against Alice's lips as he pressed into her, his tongue roaming her mouth with the same ferocity his hands roamed her body.

"Let's go take the former-prince and the other prisoners to the dungeon." Margot shouted across the hall with a laugh. "Our new king is busy making out."

ALICE DECIDED she liked sitting on a throne. The throne room was absolutely stunning now that Margot had insisted on redecorating. Alice never thought she'd ever feel so at home. Ruling had taken a few months to get used to, especially as Christopher and his sire line were busy writing new policies, ferreting out Rhys's remaining supporters, and building up new allies to solidify their rule. It still boggled Alice's mind that when Christopher talked about his rule, he meant *centuries*. There were moments when she still couldn't quite believe only a few months ago she'd been a photographer whose most ambitious dream was to financially support herself with her art. Now she was the acting *Queen of the Vampires*. Submitting her resignation letter at her old day job had been nearly as satisfying as helping defeat Rhys.

A group of vampires knelt below her in the throne room, heads bowed. A female vampire who looked like she was in her mid-twenties, but was probably older than Alice's great-grandmother, stepped forward. She made a small cut on her finger, raising the blood toward Alice. Since Alice's impromptu move during the coronation that betrayed Rhys's malicious intentions, small gestures of bloodletting when making a request to the court had become standard practice.

"We have come to make a formal petition to the court to break our *hortari*." The woman's blood stank of terror, long-held grudges, and a spirit nearly broken to pieces. The others huddled behind the leader made small cuts as well. *All women*, Alice noticed, with a sense of unease. Since it was known that Alice wasn't bound to Christopher any more, vampire women coming forward and asking her to break their own bonds was distressingly common.

"Unfortunately, the *hortari* isn't something that I or

anyone else has the power to lift," Alice said. "I broke mine because I was desperate to save the people I loved. With sufficient will and training, you can do the same."

"Please, *teach us*," the woman in front said. "Our sire is a sadistic bastard. We were only able to get away by tricking and gagging him. We must break our bond to him before he finds us." The others behind her nodded.

A sinking feeling filled Alice's chest. There was so much still to do, so much left to fix. Having no accountability for sires for so long had kept so many awful practices in the dark. Regulating how sires treated their sirelings was the first step towards trying to make things right. *It's a good thing we have time.*

"You have sanctuary here for as long as you need," Alice said. "And I will teach you as best I can." She beckoned to one of the stewards to take them to the wing they were refurnishing specifically for guests. "Take them to clean rooms and collect statements about their sire and who else might still be under his thrall. We'll send out Danny to lead a team to question and detain the sire."

Alice kept an expression of royal serenity on her face until the last woman left the room, then sunk against the back of the door.

"That was well done," Margot said, approaching from the side of the room where she'd been watching the proceedings.

Alice rubbed her forehead. "I still don't know why it's me who has to do this. I'm not the one who fought my evil brother in order to become the ruler." *An evil brother pouting in the dungeon for at least the next millennia*, Alice thought. It was only Christopher's belief that Rhys could someday change that had stayed his execution for treason.

Margot gave Alice a pat on the shoulder that would have been heavy enough to bruise if Alice had still been human.

"You're a natural. And you're learning the rest. Christopher is out getting to know the people and enforcing the rules, which only he has the centuries of experience to do. And you're new to being a vampire, so you don't have all the baggage that the rest of us carry."

"I guess." Alice looked at Margot and saw a wealth of understanding in the woman's brown eyes. "I just miss him."

"Anyone who told you that ruling a scattered nation of blood-sucking immortals was going to be easy was having you on."

"Haha. Funny."

"And I happen to know that a certain king arrived a few minutes ago through the side entrance and might be hogging up the hot water to make himself look presentable for his queen."

"Christopher is home?" Alice jumped off the throne and started to run toward the stairs before turning back around to look at Margot. "Why didn't you say something earlier?"

Margot grinned. "It's my prerogative as your Princess of Intelligence. I get to decide when and how you know things. Trust me, you wanted to give him a few minutes to wash off before you saw him."

"You're the *Head* of Intelligence," Alice said, confused.

"Yes, and my sire is king, so I'm a princess." Margot waved a hand at Alice, effectively dismissing her.

Alice didn't bother to chastise her. Margot was usually right. And Christopher was waiting.

Alice raced up the stairs, memories of the first time Christopher and she raced to the bedroom as vampires flashing through her mind, warming her insides. She kicked open their bedroom door.

Christopher stood in the middle of the room wearing only a towel. His smile when he turned to face her was radiant. He held out her arms, the towel fell, and Alice jumped into his arms with so much enthusiasm, her crown fell off her head and rolled under the bed.

His kiss devoured her, as passionate as the first time he ever held her. He murmured into her mouth. "You look beautiful, your majesty. Are you wearing anything too precious to tear off of you right now? Because I really need you naked."

"Hmm, go slow, I want to savor this." Her hands slid across his skin, still slightly wet from his shower. "You look far too sexy to be king." She gripped his bare ass, amazed again that she'd somehow ended up with the perfect man. "Are you sure you're not some roguish, activist prince trying to change the world?"

"That was last year. What did you tell me the first time we met? Even those frozen in time can get redefined by context."

She laughed. "That doesn't sound like me."

He kissed her soundly as he unzipped the back of her dress, caressing along her spine. "It sounds eloquent, so it sounds *exactly* like you." His hands against the cool skin of her back felt divine.

Alice leaned back to look at her face. "I love you more than anything in this world, Christopher."

His hands paused. "There's something I've been meaning to talk to you about, Alice."

"Oh? Does this mean I have to stop getting undressed?" She pushed down the spray of nerves that jingled in her stomach.

He chuckled. "Heavens, no. Are you mad, woman? I would never stop you from getting undressed." As he spoke, he helped pull down her dress, unclasping her bra, and standing in awe for a long moment at her naked breasts. He walked her to the bed and lifted her up, sitting beside her with a grave expression on his face as he played one of her nipples into an erect point.

"Alice," he breathed the word like a prayer, leaning over to latch his mouth around her breast as his fingers traced lines down her stomach to cup her mound. She arched her back into the exquisiteness of his touch, grabbing his hair to pull him closer. "You've been acting as queen in my stead for months now, but you've been the queen of my heart since we met." He lifted his mouth from her nipple to capture her mouth. "Please, make me the happiest being in all of time and space by agreeing to be my queen, my wife, in truth. Marry me."

Joy erupted through Alice's chest and up through her head in a rush. She rolled on top of Christopher's naked body, latching onto his mouth and then moving to his neck.

"I broke the *hortari* to be with you." She licked the musky sweat from his skin, savoring everything about her perfect king. "I want you as my husband."

He tilted his neck, baring his throat to her elongating teeth. "Then take me. Take me, my love." At his words, she sunk her teeth into his flesh, drinking deep. Christopher's essence flowed through her as she sucked his blood: his joy her joy, his love her love. His cock slid into her warmth as they moved together. She gasped with happiness as he bit deep into her shoulder, their feelings combined as they drank and rode each other in waves of pleasure that built like oncoming storms.

They came together, Alice feeling like she was floating on their shared ecstasy. She lay panting against his chest. Out there in the world, there would be many battles left to face. Injustice didn't end with the installation of one just monarch. Years of work lay ahead, as well as moments of wonder and awe and captured moments.

Her hand found the camera beside the bed and she snapped a picture of Christopher's sleeping face. She glanced at the frozen image in the viewfinder and sighed with contentment. Perhaps the context of the picture would change over time, but one thing would never change: she loved Christopher, and would love Christopher, for as long as immortality allowed.

THE VAMPIRE'S LAIR

"Y ou chicken?" Danny called out across the bar. *What am I getting myself into?* The eight-foot tall troll lumbered up to Danny's table and Danny sipped at his glass of O positive blood, focusing on looking casual even as his stomach churned.

The troll bristled, the rocks protruding from his skull standing at their peak.

"What did you say to me?" With each word came a punctuation of spit, sending chunks of saliva and what looked like tree bark splattering across the surface of Danny's table.

Trolls were huge creatures, rarely under seven-feet tall, but this one was well over nine, his head dusting the roof of the bar. Blagfor had an impressive biome of lichen running along his left side, starting at his shoulders and traveling down to his waist, and looked like he'd been chiseled off the side of a mountain.

Danny flexed his hands, steeling his nerves. *You've gone up against worse than this*, he reminded himself. As an investigator for the vampire king, and a vampire prince himself, he had taken down vampire crime lords, wrestled the vampire kingdom away from an evil tyrant, and once even stole the last fry off of his sire's plate. But somehow, none of those felt quite as perilous as the walking mountain staring down at him.

"I *said*..." Danny downed the rest of his drink in a single gulp and banged the glass down for emphasis. "Wanna arm wrestle?"

All eyes turned toward them and, for a long moment, everything was silent. AUDREY'S bar wasn't much to look at: a tall, wooden shack in the middle of nowhere with beaten up furniture and no ambiance to speak of, but it was *the* spot for supernaturals. Tonight it was stuffed to the brim with pixies, yetis, witches, werewolves, and some folks with spikes Danny couldn't even identify. All of them drooled in their excitement to see a drunk, rich clown get taken down by a troll.

Which was precisely the idea.

"Do you really think you can take *me* down, little man?" The troll sneered with what few teeth he had left. "I am Blagfor the mighty!" His posse of trolls all roared in support, shaking the rafters.

"I know I can. In fact..." Danny pulled a stack of hundred-dollar bills from the interior pocket of his leather jacket and slapped them down on the table. "I'll bet on it." Danny let the muscles in his face sag, swaying in his seat for effect.

Dumb, drunk, and rich. Danny repeated the mantra in his head. *I need them to believe I'm dumb, drunk, and rich.* He never considered himself much of an actor, but the investigation hinged on him calling on his inner trust-fund brat to put on a good show.

Blagfor opened his arms and called out to his friends. "This'll be the easiest money I ever made." He cracked his knuckles and shook, his joints all snapping at once in a horrible chorus.

Danny placed his elbow down onto the table and slipped for good measure, nearly smacking his face on the table before catching himself at the last moment with his free hand and righting himself. The trolls laughed and slapped each other on their backs, their focus never leaving the pile of cash.

Blagfor planted his elbow across from Danny's and took his hand. Danny stifled a laugh at how surprisingly soft the troll's palm was.

"Three," Blagfor said.

"Two." Danny's hand closed tightly around Blagfor's palm in a crushing grip.

"One!" They shouted in unison, both pushing against each other with all their might.

Blagfor's right side bulged, the muscles in his rock-hard arms straining for dominance.

But he didn't know Danny was a vampire.

To the trolls, Danny appeared as a tall, Asian human in his twenties, fit but not muscular. It made it easy to miss that it wasn't a fair fight.

Danny feigned a struggle, his vampire strength keeping Blagfor's hand dangerously close to the surface of the table. *Stick to the plan*, Danny chastised himself. Slowly, Danny allowed his arm to be pushed backwards by the troll's strength, pressing just enough to show he wasn't giving the game away. He bit back a sigh of relief as his fist smashed down under Blagfor's. The slam echoed through the bar, overpowered by the cheer ringing out from the spectating patrons.

Small flashes of light came from the raised cell phones all around him. *Perfect,* Danny thought, hiding a triumphant smile. Social media was a blessing in so many ways for the intrepid private investigator.

Blagfor let out a roar, raising his arms to the ceiling and painting the bar with his impressive stench. More cameras flashed.

Danny, closest to the troll's armpits, stifled a gag as he slid over the stack of cash. He made sure to smile gamely. "Not too bad, troll."

Blagfor leaned in to whisper, "You almost had me there, vampire. Maybe next time you'll give me a *real* match."

"Next time," Danny said with a wink. Blagfor smiled, pocketed the cash, and lumbered back to his friends.

Time to take this up a notch.

Danny jumped on top of his barstool, balancing easily on the shaky wood. "Never let it be said that Prince Danny Dal is a poor loser. The next round is on me!" He pointed over to the bartender, whose long black braids were hypnotically floating above her head in a rhythmic dance. "Make sure to give 'em the good stuff, Lola!"

Further bursts of photos flashed in Danny's direction and the suddenly infamous vampire prince hopped to the ground. Bear and dragon shifters slapped him on the back, a couple witches gave him thumbs up, as the crowd surged toward the bar for their round.

Drinks flowed, Blagfor bought a round, loudly proclaiming it was with Danny's money, and Danny checked his watch for the second time that hour. *I couldn't be making more of a scene if I wanted to. Where are they?*

If they didn't show up soon, he feared he was going to have to start up the karaoke machine. Usually his private eye gigs resulted in him chasing around adulterers and embezzlers. But this time was different. His sire, the Vampire King Christopher Dal, had sent him to investigate rumors of abuse at a vampire pleasure palace, the Blood Oasis. The rumors were little more than gossip, and Danny wasn't expecting to find anything, but it still felt good to be on an official mission for the palace.

But *finding* the place to investigate was tricky. The Blood Oasis's location was secret and invite-only. Danny tried not to fidget in his seat. Surely, the club had somebody on their payroll scoping out social media for easy marks?

"I've got a thousand bucks for whoever can beat me at darts!" He called out to the room, grabbing a pile of them off the board next to him.

Warm fingers closed around Danny's hand, encapsulating the dart.

"Throwing sharp objects in your state is probably not the best idea." The woman's voice came from behind him. "Especially with so many people taking video."

The human female's scent hit him like all the hidden notes of a complex wine coming together at once. It wasn't just her skin--the sweetness of vanilla with an underlying deep scent of earth and moss--but her emotions singing to him from her blood. Smelling the emotions of non-vampires was one of his favorite advantages of being a vampire, although sometimes the insights were less than flattering. She was excited and scared, but mostly annoyed. *At me, probably,* Danny thought. Knowing he was being a jackass on purpose didn't make her frustration any more enjoyable.

She was stunning: a tall brunette with pale skin and brown eyes flecked with gold. Just looking at her, Danny felt like he'd missed a step in the dark and gotten the breath knocked out of him. He froze, grasping for his mask of indifferent rich boy that kept slipping under her penetrating gaze.

"Prince Dal?" The woman released his hand from her grip, placing the captive dart back onto the pub table. "My name is Robin Ballard. There's something I'd like to discuss with you." She guided him to a secluded table in the back of the bar, away from the ruckus of the crowd.

Danny resisted the urge to pull away from her, to go back to his plan of conspicuous money-losing. But there was something about her that intrigued him. *The Blood Oasis needs time to marshal their contacts anyway,* he told himself.

He glanced around and there was no one in earshot. "Ms. Ballard," he said, dropping his drunken act. "I only have a few moments to spare. How can I help you?" She sat straight in her chair, her poise and the cut of her black suit all business. Danny pressed down his disappointment. She likely had a case to report to the vampire king. Since Danny's sire was crowned king, Christopher's sirelings had been busy uncovering the scandals which the former king hadn't bothered to police.

A blood cocktail slid into place beside his elbow and Danny nodded thanks to the bartender, Lola, as she also placed a whiskey on the rocks next to Robin. The beautiful woman thanked Lola before turning her gold-flecked gaze back onto Danny's face. Anxiety churned in Robin's blood. He fought the instinct to lay a reassuring hand on her arm.

"I appreciate your time. Feel free to call me Robin." She sipped at her drink and smiled. "I *thought* that drunk act you were pulling out there was a bit on the nose. I'm glad to see you can handle your blood." She splayed her fingers out onto the table. "Since you're in a rush, I'll be blunt. I need you to turn me into a vampire."

What? Danny resisted the urge to laugh incredulously. "I appreciate your gumption. But, to be equally blunt, no." He moved to stand. Danny had decided a long time ago he was done with siring.

Robin placed her hand over his, freezing him in place. "It does sound ridiculous, I agree. Please sit, there's a lot of information you don't have."

Danny raised an eyebrow, but took his seat. As she spoke, Danny sniffed out a scent he hated to pick up from her: fear.

"I can't say I'm not curious." He took a generous swig of his drink. "You have until I'm done with this cocktail."

Robin's words tumbled out, chasing each other in her haste to explain. "I'm a conservationist, working to protect the endangered Scarred Vultrich. It's a fascinating bird, but isn't very attractive." She chuckled. "It basically looks like an ostrich and a vulture got smashed together. It's also nocturnal, which makes it even harder for people to sympathize with. There's not a lot of support to save animals that aren't cute."

"I imagine there isn't." Danny didn't know much about wildlife and tried not to smirk at his hideous mental approximation of what the vultrich might look like.

"These birds can breed and thrive in a very small habitat. Today, I lost a fight to a developer that would pave over *half* of what's left. I need to be able to defend these incredible creatures. I need the *time* to make sure they're safe." She pounded a fist down onto the table, shaking the glassware.

"So you figured you'd just swing down to the local pub and grab yourself some immortality?" Danny leaned back in his chair. "How would a human like you even know how to find a vampire?"

"My college roommate, Samantha, is a witch. She comes from a big family of witches, and I spend my holidays with them." Sadness washed the air around her and Danny fought to keep his expression casual. Centuries living among short-lived humans had taught him a thing or two about mourning. The woman was hurting, and the pain of it had driven her here.

Robin smiled and Danny's heart cracked a little. To smile through her grief like that, it took an admirable amount of strength.

"Samantha's aunts' gossip told me more about the supernatural world than I could have discovered from years of research."

"There's a lot more to being a vampire than you could

possibly understand just from idle chit-chat." Danny looked down into the thick, red liquid in his glass.

"I know some vampires turn their sirelings and then never see them again. This barely has to inconvenience you at all." Robin placed her hand over Danny's. Her touch sent fissions of lightning along his skin and he shivered. *Who is this woman?* Her expression was grave. "I've been thinking about this for a very long time and I did my research."

How can some birds be so important? Danny's curiosity threatened to get the better of him. "No." He downed his glass in a single gulp. "Siring a new vampire is a tremendous responsibility, and it's not one I take lightly anymore." Burned once, he didn't need that again. "You'll have to find somebody else to help you on your quest." He stood, throwing some cash on the table. "The drinks are on me."

Robin's face turned bright red. "You *selfish* sonofa..." She screamed, but he hurried out of earshot. Walking away from her felt like pulling against a riptide.

"Prince Dal, your majesty." A sleek gentleman in a pinstripe suit stepped in Danny's path, giving a small bow. "I heard you were...entertaining yourself here."

A quick whiff revealed the man as a cheetah shifter. Danny couldn't smell the man's emotions, though, a clear sign the messenger was also a vampire. Shifters rarely decided to become vampires, but immortality could be tempting to all types. He handed Danny a silver card, with the words "Blood Oasis" embossed in a deep red on the front.

Danny resisted the urge to sigh in relief. The Blood Oasis must have sent their fastest employee once they heard of Danny's whereabouts. He could stop acting like a drunken fool and finally get to work.

The cheetah shifter raised an eyebrow at Danny, leering

a little. "If you are seeking a more *stimulating* environment, I would like to extend an invitation to the Blood Oasis. It's a vampiric pleasure palace beyond your wildest dreams, and only available to an *exclusive* clientele." He flipped the card over, his thumbprint pressing a rune imbedded in the paper. Small lights on the card flared to life. "This card is spelled to lead you to the Oasis."

Danny turned the card over in his hand. The address flashed along the back of the heavy card stock, followed by an arrow pointing in the direction of the Blood Oasis.

"That sounds delightful. I'll be sure to stop by," Danny said.

The cheetah shifter bowed and spotted fur rippled in a wave over his skin, enveloping him as his form shrunk and transformed before Danny's eyes until a large cat with a long, swishing tail stood in a pool of pinstripe suit. The cat carefully folded the clothes away and darted out of the bar.

Danny glanced over at the corner where Robin had been fuming, but she was gone. *It's for the best*, he told himself, not quite believing it.

THE BLOOD OASIS business card twisted and twirled on his dashboard as he drove deeper into the woods, the paper lighting up with arrows and instructions that would probably have been more impressive if Danny didn't recognize a simple GPS spell knock-off.

As he drove, Danny kept catching a glimpse of a dented, red sedan in his rear view mirror. *Was the club keeping tabs on him?* A shiver of unease rippled through him. *Perhaps there is something to these rumors.* He cut his lights, turned off to the side of the road, letting the red sedan fly past him so he could get a better look at the driver.

Robin.

He chuckled. *Nice try.* The woman really was determined to find a vampire sire. Even with his own past disappointments with sireing, he might be tempted to help find her a suitable sire. But the mission called.

The Blood Oasis card chirped at him, the spell frustrated he had gone off route. He backed out and sped away. Behind him, the road was clear.

ROBIN'S HANDS tightened around her steering wheel as she watched Danny Dal's brake lights disappear around a corner. She figured he must still be headed in the direction of the Blood Oasis.

Excellent. She'd managed to get a quick glance at the Blood Oasis card back at AUDREY'S, and had jotted down the address. It was lucky, since she'd never been great at following people. The one time she'd tried to track down a construction foreman to show him pictures of baby vultrich, she'd gotten the cops called on her. Looking at Danny's final destination, she took the long way around to avoid having to be stealthy. Danny would have to reconsider turning her once he realized she wasn't going to leave him in peace until she got what she needed.

Robin followed her GPS out of the city and up into the hills, the road narrowing from four lanes, to two, down to one narrow strip of asphalt with trees clustered close on either side. The moonlight transformed the trees' bare branches into skeletal arms reaching across the road toward one another, ready to join forces to submerge the road entirely. When the road curved around a cliff, the lights from the city below were laid out like a kid's toy, but the slim crescent of moon did little to illuminate anything beyond her car's beams.

Her phone buzzed, a picture of her college roommate, Samantha, giving the finger to the camera popping up across the screen. Robin clicked it onto speaker, keeping her eyes on the road.

"Hey Samantha, I'm--"

Samantha cut her off. "I know exactly what you're doing, and you need to cut this shit out."

"You don't understand." Robin concentrated on sounding logical. Earlier that day, she'd driven by the construction site. Broken eggshells lay caught in the spokes of a tractor's bucket, fragments of baby birds mashed up among the rocks and dirt. Vultrich slept during the day, so Robin hadn't expected to see any, but she could have sworn she heard one's little squawks of distress. So many dead, all because she hadn't gotten there soon enough, hadn't done enough. Her jaw tightened.

"I'm the only one who cares enough about these birds to keep them safe. And if becoming a blood-guzzling immortal is what I need to do, then--"

"It isn't worth it," Samantha said. "Do you really want to never age, never have kids, and be *totally* beholden to your sire's will? Because that's what their *hortari* sire compulsion is, sweetie. You will *have* to do everything your sire says. You didn't like following instructions to build that bookshelf because you thought the directions were too constricting. How the hell are you going to feel when your sire tells you to smile because it makes you look pretty, and your lips move against your will? Are your birds worth that?"

Robin didn't hesitate. "Yes."

Somewhere out there, the vultrich were beginning to wake up. Did they already know half of their nesting ground was demolished? Would their screams when they found their broken nests be loud enough for neighboring businesses to hear what they'd done?

"Danny Dal isn't the responsible type," Robin continued. "He'll just sire me and then let me go do what I want, as long as I'm out of his hair. Everything he's done tonight makes him a perfect sire: wealthy, irresponsible, and a little stupid." *And ridiculously hot,* she didn't say.

When the bartender, Lola, first pointed him out at AUDREY'S, Robin's breath had burst out of her body and her nipples immediately tightened in the most extreme reaction of horniness she'd ever experienced. It was a good thing he was cocky and dumb. Having a clever sire would ruin her plans. She couldn't get distracted from her mission.

Samantha sighed. "Just tell me that you're going to be smart about this. Spend some time with him, make sure that your impression from watching him for a few hours is enough to make a decision that will impact you *for eternity.*"

A mansion loomed on top of the next hill. The Blood Oasis's sign was small, barely a plaque set inside a stone column next to a long driveway that curved off into the dark woods.

"Samantha, I have to go. I just arrived."

"Where?" Her voice dripped with suspicion.

"At home." Parked cars lined the edge of the drive and she pulled into an open spot. Robin opened her door and a gust of cold air stabbed at her bare legs and arms. Looking down, she was grateful she'd packed a spare outfit in addition to the suit she'd worn at the bar.

"You're a bad liar." Samantha sighed. "You're going to a vampire bar, aren't you? Those are basically brothels, Robin. That is so not your scene. Please, tell me you're not still doing this."

"I have to. Goodbye, Sam."

"Wait! Tell me where you are and I'll come get you. Robin--"

Robin hung up the phone, and then turned it off before Samantha could barrage her with more calls.

Yesterday, she'd been so sure she was going to be able to halt construction of that damn mini-mall. The local wildlife offices were on her side and were ready to come out and conduct inspections. She'd reached out to the U.S. Fish and Wildlife Service for assistance in enforcing the Endangered Species Act, and to the U.S. Army Corps of Engineers about classifying the nesting grounds as protected wetlands. She'd sent cease and desist letters to the construction company, and written over a hundred letters to her local Congressman to help advocate for the protection of an endangered species in his district. She'd finally gotten a member of his staff on the phone, and they'd seemed open to putting out a press release calling for the protection of their unique wildlife.

But all the construction company had to do was roll their tractors a week earlier than planned and it was all over. They would pay a fine that would barely put a dent in their overall profits, and they were busy publishing statements congratulating themselves on "cleaning out the disease-carrying vermin infesting the area."

Robin held her purse close to her chest and concentrated on not wobbling on the uneven cobblestone walkway up to the Blood Oasis.

Her steps slowed as she neared. It looked like a state mansion from a Jane Austen novel, at least six stories tall of white stone, with graceful, Grecian columns, and two curving stone staircases winding up to a fifteen-foot arched doorway. Pulsing colored lights and pumping bass music blared from the first floor, while the upper floor windows lay quiet.

If Samantha was right and this place was a brothel, then having a private upstairs for guests to enjoy themselves made sense. Her pulse quickened.

Perhaps Danny will want to have some fun before he turns me?

She shook off the thought before the fantasy of Danny's hands teasing her breasts and his mouth pressing against her neck became too vivid.

She wasn't here for *that*.

Robin was here to become a vampire.

Get strength to break their tractors before they can destroy nests.

Get *time* to build advocacy and teach others to appreciate the vultrich's rare beauty and wonder.

Danny Dal was just a means to an end.

A slot in the front door slid open and a pair of steely eyes looked over her outfit, which was less a dress and more a small piece of fabric wound around her. Her favorite part was the pink banded choker drawing attention to the long line of her neck and pulled-up brunette locks. Blood Oasis might be officially "invite only," but Robin had been to enough clubs in college to know that sometimes skin was its own all-access pass.

The enormous bouncer in a black suit held the door open wide.

"Welcome to the Blood Oasis. Let us cater to your fantasies." His voice was deep and musical, but the words were flat like he was reading them off cue cards.

Working the door at a vampire bar can't be the most glamorous job, Robin guessed. *All the fun happens inside.* She smiled at him in thanks and he gave her a stiff nod in reply before closing the door and sliding in the lock with a loud click.

Robin shivered.

Just find Danny. Considering the out-of-the-way route she took to get here, he had to have arrived before her. Looking around, she couldn't help but notice the interior was as gorgeous as the exterior. The foyer opened up into entrances for two different rooms: the one off to the right looked like an intimate library with dark-paneled wood, low light, walls covered in rows of book spines, and the sound of a live jazz band playing. Something about the cloistered, safe space made her think of the vultrich sanctuaries she visited at night with her parents.

The room to the left was wide open with glass windows covering the wall looking out into the swaying trees. Fun dance music and flashing colored lights filled the space while waiters circled with colorful cocktails filled to the brim. It was exactly the kind of place she'd spent too much time in during her college years, the lights and sounds making her wish she'd thought to pack her old goth clubbing gear. *Whatever happened to my knee-high boots? They'd be perfect for this place.*

Everywhere, pairs and trios danced and talked, black leather and flesh pressed against one another, makeup thick and smeared, hands roaming. Hormones and lust saturated the air. Blood flooded Robin's cheeks, wetness pooling between her legs as she looked around.

In the darkened library to the right, on a low couch, a man's head was buried deep between a woman's spread legs, her fingers clutching at his hair, and her head thrown back into an open-mouthed, silent scream of pleasure. A staff member caught the woman's eye, handed her a key, and pointed toward the stairs. The woman nodded, grabbed the kneeling man's hand, and the two ran towards the rooms upstairs.

I think I love this place, Robin thought.

Over in the dance room, a pair of men wearing skin-tight leather chaps and nothing else grinded a scantily-clad woman between them, one kissing her neck while the other's hands roamed over her shirt and down to caress her thighs. Two other men were heartedly making out against the window, their hips thrusting fast in time to the music as their hands wandered under each other's shirts. Robin felt surrounded by life and sex and fun. If this was the vampire lifestyle Samantha was so worried about, Robin was *in*.

Robin found the bar in the back of the dance room and ordered a cranberry juice so it would look like she was drinking a cocktail while still keeping her head clear. At some point, she wanted to come back and enjoy this place properly, but tonight she was going to find a sire.

"Hello, beautiful." The man's voice to her right was kind, but with the same flatness as the bouncer at the door. "I just *had* to come talk to you. Sweetness is my weakness."

Her eyes widened. The man was *definitely* a vampire. His canines were so elongated, they poked out to dig into his lower lip. He was taller than her by at least a foot and well-built, but his posture was slumped and his arms wrapped around himself in a protective gesture that made him look small and vulnerable. He wore jeans and a white shirt unbuttoned nearly to his navel so it flapped open, showing rows of hard muscles. The effect was supposed to be sexy, but mostly she just thought he looked cold.

"Are you okay?" she asked.

He straightened, his eyes darting around the room. "Of course!" Something about his voice was too jolly, forced. "I'm just so happy to be talking with the sexiest woman here. I mean, just look at you. Roses are red, violets are blue, but I didn't know perfect until I met you." He sounded like he was miserable about every word.

"What's your name?" she asked, hoping some friendliness would help ease the sadness in his shoulders. "Do you come here often?"

"I'm Seyah." He smiled, the edges pinched. "I'm here every night." He glanced upward and Robin spotted a camera's eye blinking red from the corner of the ceiling.

"You work here?" she whispered. When he nodded, still smiling the non-smile, she asked, "Are you okay?"

Seyah stepped away from her. "You know, I can see you're not really into this. You have a lovely evening. I know you'll find someone here who will cater to your fantasies." He disappeared into the throng of dancers.

Robin considered going after him, but he was obviously scared of something. She glanced around the room again, feeling unsettled. The music felt too loud now. The flashing lights made her head pound. The movements of some of the dancers looked too jerky, like marionettes being pulled around on strings, with their expression hard masks as their partners danced on top of them. Cradling her juice, Robin made her way around the outside of the room.

Just find Danny, and get out of here.

Could he have already found someone and gone upstairs? The thought made her even more uncomfortable.

The darkened library was quiet with the band on break sipping drinks in the corner. Fewer people milled around the dim space, most of the pairs gone. Robin assumed they had gone to dance, or upstairs to complete their evening. One woman lay draped across the back of a padded sofa playing with the long, red hair of a large man sitting near her. She was smiling and giggling at something he was saying, but she flinched when he touched her hand.

Maybe Samantha was right. I made a mistake coming here.

A petite, blond woman chatting with the musicians burst into a twinkling bell-like laughter so loud it filled the room. The sound was so happy, so purely joyous, Robin felt herself drawn toward the small woman like a magnet. She wore more clothes than most of the other women there combined, although the tightness of the red dress hugging her curves left nothing to the imagination. When she caught Robin looking her, the woman smiled and beckoned Robin forward.

"Hi there, you look a little lost." The woman's voice was as light and pretty as her laugh.

"I guess I am," Robin said. She searched the woman's features for any of Seyah's flatness or flinching, but the woman's bright smile lit up her eyes like twin glowing lamps. "I came here looking for someone, but I haven't seen him around."

"Stood up on a date? I'm so sorry, honey." She rested a hand lightly on Robin's arm. "You know the best way to get over a guy? Get under a new one." She laughed and pointed to a couple of the musicians who were sizing up Robin like she was a steak.

Robin stepped back hurriedly. "No, that's not it." *Although if Danny looked at me that way, I wouldn't be saying no.* The thought flashed by too fast for her to clamp it down. Robin continued on, talking quickly. "I'm actually looking for a vampire."

The woman smiled and Robin noticed for the first time how long her canines dipped in her mouth.

"Well, you found one." She held out a hand. "My name is Nia Ashmore."

Robin shook Nia's hand, appreciating the brisk strength in the woman's grip. "Robin Ballard. It's nice to meet you."

"Have you seen the gardens? They're not as stunning at night as I'm told they are during the day, but they're still lovely."

"Fresh air sounds amazing. Thanks."

Nia's stunning smile flashed again and Robin felt herself relaxing into the woman's company. They chatted easily as they walked through the mansion about music, the last movie they saw in theaters, where they went to college, and bad dates they'd been on recently. By the time they made it outside, Robin knew she'd found an amazing new friend. Nia was articulate, funny, and kind, with a positive viewpoint Robin knew to be all too rare.

"I'm so glad I came tonight," Robin said, wrapping an arm around Nia's diminutive shoulders.

"Me too." Nia smiled. She brushed her fingers along the back of Robin's hand. "I think you're exactly the kind of friend I've been looking for."

The gardens were just as stunning as Nia claimed: a landscaped vista of crisscrossing rocky streams, with a gazebo and roses that curled into each other in rich, romantic bouquets. Robin smiled, settling down on one of the stone benches that looked out onto the gardens.

"This is beautiful. You know, this place would be a great nesting place for vultrich." Robin sighed and leaned back against the bench. "With all these rocks and little nooks, it would be perfect."

"Vultrich? Those nocturnal vulture-looking birds that live around here?"

"Yes!" Robin grabbed Nia's hands and pulled her into a tight hug. "Nobody ever seems to know them, and they're amazing."

"Really?" Nia studied Robin's face. "I wouldn't have ever guessed I'd see someone so worked up over vultrich." She smiled, tilting her head to the side. "But then, I spent six months after college living in the rainforest helping save tropical frogs, so I know what it's like to feel passionately about a creature nobody else seems to care about."

"You worked with tropical frogs? That's so great!" Robin wanted to never stop hugging Nia, this extraordinary woman who seemed to understand every part of her completely. "Protecting the vultrich is my life's work. It's why I came here tonight, why I wanted to find a vampire."

"Oh?" Nia's smile was as curious as a kitten.

"Yes, I was looking to be turned into a vampire so that I can have a fighting chance of saving their habitat. I need time to convince others to love them as much as I do."

"Well, *I* could turn you," Nia said slowly. She smiled at Robin. "In fact, I would love to be your sire. I always have a good instinct about people, and I knew I would like you from the second we met. I have a vast family of vampires I've turned, and I've never regretted any for a moment."

Could it be that easy? Robin's heart started to beat fast. "You'd really turn me? Tonight?"

"Why not? There's no reason to delay." Nia stood up and held out her hand to Robin. "I can set everything up for the ritual upstairs right now."

Robin took Nia's hand and got to her feet.

"There's a ritual?" Samantha had never mentioned a ritual, but Robin supposed even witches wouldn't know every detail about how vampires were turned. She followed Nia back into the house, turning right and going up a flight of stairs so narrow and unadorned Robin doubted they were usually used by guests.

"Of course we have a ritual! We're not savages," Nia said

over her shoulder as she pulled Robin up the stairs. "Welcoming a new vampire to eternity is a big deal, we want to make sure it has the proper amount of ceremony."

Nia's grip on Robin's hand was tight and confident as she led her down a long corridor lined with numbered doors like at a hotel. Groaning, screams of "yes! more!" and the sound of slapping flesh coming from the doorways left Robin with no suspicion about what was happening on this floor. She blushed, feeling arousal pooling again in her lower stomach.

Would I recognize Danny's voice if I heard it? She wondered, but pushed the thought away. She didn't need Danny anymore. She had Nia: lovely, environmentally-active Nia who saved tree frogs and loved comic book movies.

Nia opened the last door on the hallway, this one marked "Private" and held it open for Robin to step through.

Robin paused.

When did Nia set all this up?

The entire room was lit with candles that surrounded the room on all sides, drawing attention to a huge, golden altar that took up one of the walls. Two hooded figures stood on either side of the altar, their robes blood red, and their hands clasped in front of them. Robin guessed they were men from the breadth of their shoulders, but it was hard to tell. On the altar were only two items: a silver knife with ornate filigree on the handle, and a chalice larger than Robin's head.

"This is---" Robin couldn't find the right word. *Ridiculous? Cheesy? Over-the-top? B-movie level dramatic?* "All for the ritual?"

Nia pulled her into the room and led her to a small pillow at the base of the altar. "Kneel here."

Nia whispered something to the hooded men and the

three of them huddled together around the knife and the cup. They chanted together softly, their words indistinguishable.

Holy shit, this is actually happening.

"What about the *hortari*? We never even talked about that," Robin said. "Do you, um, force the vampires you sire to do things?"

Nia turned, holding the chalice. It was now filled an inch-deep with thick, red blood. "I'm your friend, Robin. I would never make you do anything you didn't want to do." She took Robin's hands and wrapped them around the cup, pushing the lip toward Robin's mouth.

Everything's happening so fast.

"Now, drink this before it gets cold," Nia instructed. "Be the protector your birds deserve."

Yes. I will be their protector. Robin brought the cup to her lips and took a long gulp of the blood. It tasted like tap water run through rusty pipes, with a thick texture like cream that choked her all the way down.

"Was that it?" Robin asked. Her head felt she was floating, or uncomfortably high. She tried to raise a hand to wipe a bead of sweat off of her forehead and her arm felt so heavy, she could barely lift it. The room wobbled in front of her, everything going off kilter.

"Yeah, it's done, sweet cheeks," said a rough voice from the figure on the right.

Through a haze, she saw the two robed men shake off their hoods. Even with very different features, they had the same hard expressions, the same cruel glints in their eyes. The one on the right who had spoken had a long scar down his cheek, which carved his lips into a grimace.

"Who are you?" Robin's mouth felt like it was stuffed with cotton, her thoughts churning at a slow chug.

Nia ignored her, nodding to the one with the scarred face. "Seth, test her." Her voice was unrecognizable now. It had dropped an octave, each word clipped and sharp.

Something is very wrong. Fear bit like frozen spikes into Robin's chest. She tried to rise to her feet, every muscle feeling like it weighed fifty pounds.

"Sit down," Seth said.

Every muscle demanded that Robin sit down. Her body froze. Her knees bent and then gave out, sending her spilling to the floor. She fought against it, trying to stand, but it was no use. Her body was no longer under her command.

"Now, slap yourself across the face." Seth chuckled.

Robin watched with horror as her own hand rose against her command, drew back, and hit her hard across the face. She screamed out in pain and surprise.

"What's happening?" Robin yelled. She looked back and forth between Nia and Seth. *Nia* was supposed to be the only one whose sire command could compel her to do anything.

Seth pulled back the sleeve of his robe, revealing a long cut down his forearm. "You're mine, bitch."

"No!" Robin yelled, fighting to get to her feet.

"Sit down and stay there until I say so," Seth said.

Robin collapsed back onto the floor, her legs locked into a seated position. She tried to grab at her foot to pull it up using her hands, but it felt like it was welded to the floor.

Oh my god. This isn't happening. This isn't happening. The room was still hazy. *What have I done?*

Robin stared at Nia. "Why?"

Nia's angelic face now twisted into a sneer. "I'm not about to waste my time on every fool human that walks in this place. I have a few choice sirelings," She ran a finger down Seth's jaw, "who serve as my... middle management. You and the other underlings answer to them and stay out of my hair. It's all very simple."

"But--" Robin started to say.

"Shut up," Seth said. Robin wanted to scream, but her tongue wouldn't move. The only sound she could make was a low gurgle in the back of her throat.

Nia tapped Seth's chest. "You are *very* lucky that this one happened to wander in tonight after you lost your last one."

Robin stared at the two of them, horror and terror warring in her stomach. *Lost the last one?*

Seth shrugged. "It's not my fault the clients like it rough."

Nia caressed the side of Seth's face and then down to his neck in a gesture that might have been intimate, but looked threatening. "Remember to take better care of your toys, because I'm not always going to keep replacing them."

Seth bowed his head. "Yes, my sire."

Nia pointed to the other robed figure and snapped her fingers. "Rick, you're with me. You're driving me to the spa. I have a facial that starts in an hour." She glanced down at Robin and clicked her tongue. "Have fun with this one. She may need some breaking before she's fit for company." And with that, Nia sashayed out the door.

Seth let out a long breath the moment the door closed behind Nia.

"My sire demands that we have some fun." He loosened his belt and Nia felt the blood drain from her face. "So we're going to have fun."

No, no, no, no, no. Her mouth wouldn't move to make the words. Her heartbeat was so loud, she was sure Seth could hear it.

"What the fuck is it?" Seth shouted towards the door.

The banging wasn't just in her chest, it was also coming from outside.

A hard kick to the door sent it crashing inward, the lock exploding and showering both Seth and Robin with splinters.

Danny Dal burst in, his eyes taking in Robin crouched on the floor, Seth over her.

"What's going on here?" Danny asked, his voice hard.

Robin stared at him. This wasn't the same drunk, irresponsible vampire from the bar, this was someone totally different: Danny's voice was confident, strong, and he held himself straight.

"None of this is your business, Prince," Seth said. "This is between me and my new sireling."

"Sireling?" Danny looked at Robin, his eyes wide with horror. He turned to Robin. "You asked *him*?"

She tried to reply, but the words choked in her throat. She found Danny's eyes and shook her head, grateful Seth had told her to *stay down*, not *don't move*.

She mouthed the words, "Help!" and Danny's mouth compressed into a hard line.

"In the name of King Christopher, and in my capacity as enforcer of his majesty's laws against *hortari* abuse, I command you to release whatever demand you have holding this woman."

Seth smiled. "You have no command over me. My sire is the only one who matters, and her will trumps yours every time."

"All vampires answer to the king." Danny moved further into the room, stepping between Robin and Seth.

"Don't come any closer, or else you'll be responsible for what happens next," Seth said. "Bitch, pick up the knife."

Terror gripped her as his command worked its way into

her body. The silver knife Seth had used to cut his arm still lay on the floor next to the altar. Robin's hand moved forward, her fingers grasping the hilt. She kept her eyes on Danny's face, mouthing,

"Stop him. Please, stop him."

"This is your last warning, stop this right now." Danny growled.

Seth smiled wide. "I'm just having fun. Bitch, slice your--"

He didn't finish the word.

Robin blinked. She could move. She still felt woozy and heavy, but she got to her feet on shaking legs.

"What..." her voice trailed off.

A wet mound lay at Seth's feet. A second later, his body tumbled to the ground.

Danny re-holstered a machete against his thigh, the edge covered in blood.

"You cut off his head." Her voice seemed to be coming from far away.

"I stopped him from commanding you to hurt yourself. Robin, I'm so sorry I didn't get here sooner. Are you okay?"

"Yes, I'm..." The room tilted and everything went dark as she fainted away.

DANNY HADN'T TAKEN a complete breath in the three hour-drive back to his safe house with Robin stretched out as comfortably as she could in the back seat. It had been centuries since he'd first been turned, but Danny still remembered the total exhaustion that wracked his body as it transitioned from human to vampire. Robin's turning was certainly more disorienting than most.

I can't believe I let everything get so out of control. Danny couldn't remember the last time he'd blundered an investigation so badly. *This is what I get for dismissing those rumors out of hand.*

Danny pulled into his garage, then delicately carried Robin into the house. He laid her on his bed, taking off her shoes, leaving out clothes for her to change into once she'd woken up, and tucking the blankets around her. *What else can I do?* He went down to the kitchen, pouring himself a glass of blood and leaning his head against the cold counter surface.

He hated how close he'd been to losing her. When Danny first arrived at the Blood Oasis, he'd been amazed by the place. The lights, the music, and the exhilaration that flooded from the human guests were like finding a place he hadn't realized he'd been searching for. The vampire working the bar had been a little hesitant to answer Danny's questions, but she had also been busy serving drinks and doing her job. Before he could thoroughly investigate, Danny found himself surrounded by requests to dance, to check out the upstairs, and was herded into a party room for a horse shifter's bachelorette party of ladies so excited to be in the same room as a vampire; their brays rattled the mirrors on the walls. The horses had been so good-natured with their questions about vampire strength; Danny had barely noticed nearly an hour had passed until he heard Robin's scream from down the hall.

Danny squeezed his eyes shut to try and push away the memory, and the terror, which pricked at the back of his throat when he recognized her voice. *She should be awake by now*, he thought, glancing at the clock. She'd slept an entire day. He grabbed some blood from the fridge, arranging glasses on a tray. *Please, please let her be okay*. He padded up the stairs, wincing at each creak underfoot.

"Shit!" Danny whispered as the tray of glasses clinked against one another. Sometimes it felt like the quieter he tried to be, the louder he ended up being.

"It's okay, I'm awake!" A voice called out from the other side of the heavy wooden door.

Danny grinned. At least she didn't *sound* traumatized. He pushed open the door with one hand and proudly held out the tray in the other. "Breakfast is served."

Robin was at the window, radiant in the moonlight. She had changed into the clothes Danny bought her: jeans and a forest green cable knit sweater that dipped in a tantalizing crescent at her neck.

"How are you?" he asked.

"Better. That smells really good." Robin sniffed the air. "I knew vampires could smell a donor's emotions through their blood, but this is *extraordinary*." She plopped down onto the bed, eyeing the tray.

Danny grinned and set breakfast down on the table next to the bed. When he was first turned, he was a grumpy mess for a week. But of course Robin would be downright *agreeable*. She was a very special brand of tenacious.

"I managed to scrape together a flight of samples for you." He pulled a thin, orange piece of plastic from his pocket. "And a crazy straw."

Robin laughed, and the sound softened the knots of tension along Danny's shoulders. She took the straw delicately from his hand, tracing her fingers along the loops and twists.

"This is perfect." She took his hand in her own and felt her touch all the way up his arm. "Thank you so much for...for everything. I can't believe I was so *stupid*."

He placed his hand over hers. "It's not your fault, it sounds like a lot of people have been drawn in by the Blood Oasis. I was actually there to investigate rumors of *hortari* coercion. I'm just glad I showed up when I did." Danny nudged the tray towards Robin. He fought to keep his expression casual. The memory of what Robin had looked like curled on the floor, her body as still as a corpse, eyes wide with terror, made him want to pull her tight to his chest. Seth's head on the ground wasn't enough. Danny was going to slice through the Blood Oasis like jungle grasses.

Robin dipped her straw into the closest glass and drank deep, her face wrinkled in trepidation. As the liquid disappeared through the loops of the straw, Robin's face lit up, her eyes wide as a slow smile moved its way across her cheeks.

"This tastes like..." She pressed her fingertips against her lips. "Peace."

Danny nodded approvingly. "That donor was meditating when he gave blood. His serene calm is captured in the very cells of what you're drinking." He remembered fondly the first time his sire, Christopher, had presented him a very similar array of blood samples to teach Danny how to enjoy a wide variety of emotions. Danny pushed down a pang of regret. *If only I was as good a sire as Christopher.*

"Peace was a good choice for today. I still can't believe what happened last night." Robin sat back against the stacked pillows on the bed, rolling the glass of blood back and forth between her palms. "I was so naive to go in on my own."

"What *is* going on at that place?" Danny asked.

"The staff there, their movements were so unnatural, their smiles forced. Something just felt...off. It seemed like they didn't want to work there." Robin deposited her now-empty glass back onto the tray. "But when I met Nia

Ashmore," Robin shuddered, "and she agreed to turn me, I didn't even *think* about how creepy the staff was acting. From the way she and Seth spoke about their sirelings...they talked about them like disposable toys. I can't believe what could have happened..." Her voice trailed off, her face losing color.

Danny pulled her close, her body fitting against his perfectly. She laid her head on his shoulder.

"We are going to get those sons of bitches," he said into her hair. "We'll stop them from using the *hortari* to make any more slaves."

"Sex slaves." Robin shuddered. "We have to help them, get all of them out of there."

"We will." Danny pulled his phone out of his pocket. "We're going to need help if we're going to take on the entire Blood Oasis. Who knows how many vampires Nia has under her control?"

Danny was shocked when Christopher picked up his phone after only one ring. The king was usually bogged down by endless meetings and audiences.

"Danny, what's the news?" Christopher sounded anxious.

"Everything we've heard about the Blood Oasis is true." Danny's words flew out in a rush. "The brothel is run by vampires who use *hortari* to force their sirelings to prostitute themselves. I've texted you the address and some photos I managed to take while undercover."

"I feared that might be your report, although I desperately hoped to be wrong this time. Hold on." Christopher's voice muffled as he pulled away from the phone to talk with a female voice Danny recognized as his sireling sister and Christopher's head of security, Margot. "We can send you one hundred of our best soldiers. Because you're so remote, they'll get to your location in forty-eight hours."

"Thank you, Christopher." Danny hung up the phone and turned back to Robin. "We're all set. The king is sending soldiers to break up the Blood Oasis. In two days, the nightmare those vampires are living will be over."

"Just like that?" Robin dunked her straw into another glass of blood and drank deep.

"Christopher is my sire and my king. I trust him."

"I wish *my* sire had been that trustworthy." Robin started giggling, a delicate laugh that trickled its way down a whole octave.

"Robin?" *Is she having some kind of breakdown?*

"Sorry, I'm not laughing at you, it's the blood." She took another sip. "It's so bubbly and happy."

Danny relaxed. "That'll be the pixie, then." Danny laughed. "They're almost always in a great mood. I've never asked why." Danny settled on the bed, looking around the opulent bedroom of high ceilings and modern art Margot had designed for him over the years. The decorations usually brought him comfort, but not today. His mind kept looping back to what Robin had gone through.

"Robin, you deserve an explanation." He took a deep breath. "For why I didn't turn you when you asked the first time."

"No," she put a hand over his. "You don't have to explain yourself to me. I see that you're very upset by what happened, but, with all due respect, how I became a vampire isn't about you. I knew I was taking a risk, and I made the best decision I could with the information I had."

Robin finished the blood and stretched out, her long, lean legs curling past the end of the bed frame. Danny looked at her in amazement. She was one of the strongest women he'd ever met in three hundred years. Danny moved towards the door. If he didn't get out now, he was afraid he would do something rash, like kiss her.

"It's been a long night. You'll need your rest. Christopher's men will bring Nia to justice for what she's done to you. You can relax."

Robin jumped to her feet. "Are you crazy? I'm a *vampire* for goodness sake. I've already rested plenty. Let's have some fun."

"Anxious to try out your new super senses?" Danny asked with a laugh.

"Actually I've got something *much* more interesting in mind." Robin said as she pulled Danny out the door.

ROBIN HOPED she never got over the wonder of her vampire senses. The night had never been so bright, or the smells and sounds so distinct. The breeze against her skin felt like it cocooned her in a whirlwind.

The forest teemed with noise and colors she'd never noticed before, her vampire senses making the night seem as clear as day. She could spot every vultrich pecking in the underbrush in perfect detail.

At her first glance, being able to see them more clearly didn't enhance the vultrich's beauty. They still resembled raptors more than eagles. Their red, scaly heads with oversized, beady eyes and razor-sharp beaks didn't grow more charming now that she could see the detail of every scale and feather. Greater perception couldn't make their long, talon-pointed feet and fluffy wings more graceful.

And yet... the longer she studied them with her vampire senses, she could see details she'd never been able to spot before. So many small beauties she'd missed, like the gloss on their feathers shining with an emerald sheen in the moonlight. The sounds they made to each other had a nuanced complexity she hadn't heard before, with squeaks and squawks outside the range of human hearing, which sounded almost like speech.

She hadn't thought it was possible to love them more.

"So these are what you became a vampire for." Danny shifted his weight beside her. "What's the appeal?"

"Sure, they're not *traditionally* beautiful, but that doesn't mean they don't deserve the chance to live." The words surged forward automatically, too many arguments with contractors and real estate developers bringing the well-rehearsed script to her tongue.

Danny turned to her, eyebrows raised. "That's not what I meant. Why do you fight for *this* particular species? Why aren't you fighting for the rights of the centipede, for example? You had no problem stepping on one when we were hiking up here."

Blood rushed to Robin's face in embarrassment. Centipedes had always creeped her out on a primal level. When a three-inch one had crossed in front of them on the trail, stomping on it was instinctual.

"I *exist* because of these birds, so I feel a sort of responsibility to make sure that they continue to exist too."

"You don't *look* part bird to me." Danny chuckled and stared at Robin, turning his head from side to side. "You're going to have to explain that one." He sat down, leaning against an oak tree and patting the ground for her to join him. "If vultrich have magical life-creation abilities, that's something I'd like to know about."

She chuckled, walked over, and settled beside him on the ground, curling up against his side. On the other side of the nesting area, one of the adults made a warning caw and three of the adults converged to herd the nestlings--balls of grey fluff, feathers, and sharp beaks--into an alcove while the other adults attacked a snake creeping through the grass with sharp efficiency.

"Nothing like that. My mother was a birdwatcher. Well, she was a math teacher, but birdwatching was her love. She took it very seriously, brought a camera with her everywhere she went, and kept detailed logs of every bird she spotted." As Robin talked, the memories unfolded like a video recording, complete with the crinkling sound of the watermarked pages of her mother's journal as they turned, and the rich scent of earth that saturated both the notebook and her mother's hands.

Robin crossed her arms tight against her chest, wondering for the first time since her parents died what had happened to that notebook. It hadn't seemed significant at the time, just a list of bird names next to dates and locations. It had probably been trashed along with everything else that couldn't be donated. Robin inhaled deeply, drinking in the individual fragrances of the moss on the trees, the mushroom at her hip, and each separate leaf on the ground. None of them were quite a match for the smell of her mother's hands.

"And she taught you to like vultrich?" Danny's words brought her back to the present.

"Sort of. That's how she met my dad. He owned a couple vegan restaurants in town and was an avid jogger. He'd joke that he loved being out in the forest because he'd never heard a tree complain that tofu didn't taste like bacon. Dad was out running when my Mom waved a sky worm in the air and accidentally drew a flock of vultrich down on herself."

Robin smiled at the memory. She could almost feel the

weight and smoothness of the plastic container in her hands from when her mother first showed Robin her stash of sky worms.

Be careful with these, my Robin, she'd said as she carefully lifted the edge of the lid off, making the tiniest of holes for the scent of the sky worm to escape. *They may not seem tasty to you and me, but sometimes the most potent obsessions come in the smallest packages.*

The day Robin's parents met, her mother was still new to nocturnal birds and had only read about how vultrich were drawn to sky worms. To try and find one, she'd waved a sky worm in the air above her head like a tiny flag. When the swarm descended on her, it was all Robin's mother could do to drop the worm and run like hell as the sharp-beaked carnivores raced after the lingering scent of the worms on her fingertips. With her focus mostly on the enormous birds racing after her, she'd smashed into Robin's father running at full tilt.

At her scream for him to "Run!", they'd grabbed hands and sprinted out of the trees and to the safety of his truck parked nearby. Once the flock departed, Robin's dad had asked for the birdwatcher's number, and they'd never stopped running hand in hand together through the world, even up to the very end.

Robin smiled. "Mom always said she would have fallen head over heels for him no matter the circumstances, but it was the vultrich who gave her the right incentive."

"What do your parents think about your vultrich crusade?" Danny asked.

"I don't know, but I hope they're proud of me, wherever they are." The car crash that took them away five years ago felt just as raw as when she'd first gotten the phone call from the hospital.

We're so sorry to tell you this, miss, but we have some bad news...

She blinked away tears, hoping Danny hadn't seen.

"They took me on birdwatching trips every summer to look at the vultrich. Between Mom's teaching during the day and Dad having to man the restaurants in the evening, making time to go vultrich watching together are my favorite memories of when we were all together."

She fought against the flood of memories crashing down on her. Year after year of sitting against trees just like this one, her head nestled under her mother's arm as her father kissed her hair, all of them watching the slow pecking of the birds, pointing out when one made a particular cry, or a baby vultrich got loose underfoot. Robin once left an open container of sky worms in the family car, and a flock had broken every window and totaled the exterior trying to get in. Her parents just laughed, telling Robin it was a small price to pay for the vultrich's happiness.

Danny put his hand over hers. "Remembering everything like you're reliving it, it gets easier over time."

"How? It's all so much." And there, just lurking behind all the memories of her parents, were the more recent, ugly memories she never wanted to relive again. Nia's hands pushing the cup of Seth's blood toward her mouth. The smooth handle of the knife in her hand, her helpless terror seeing her own hand drawing the blade closer to her neck with no way to stop it. The thump of Seth's head landing on the floor, the sound of each drop of blood dripping off of Danny's machete.

"Robin? It's going to be okay." Danny's hands were on her shoulders, his grip loose and soothing. His touch brought her back to the present, sights and sounds around her coming into focus. One male vultrich pecked tentatively on the wing feathers of the female vultrich next to him, making small, plaintive noises.

"Exactly *how* is this going to be okay?" Robin gazed into his deep, brown eyes. "My birds' habitat is shrinking by the day. There are people being tortured and stripped of their will and we're just sitting here--"

He got to his feet, holding out a hand to help her up. "We move forward, that's what we do."

Robin fought the urge to roll her eyes. *As if it's that easy.* He didn't let go of her hand as they walked together away from the birds and back toward where they'd parked the car.

"We save your birds, we get justice for the assholes who hurt you, and you'll learn to live in the moment." He shrugged. "It's hard for a lot of us. But Christopher's wife, Alice, was turned recently too. She's an artist, always looking at the world around her, living pretty much perpetually in the present. The temptation to relive memories doesn't call to her. I'd forgotten how hard it is in the beginning to push the reveries away."

"It was hard for you too?"

Danny chuckled. "Yes, but that's mostly because I didn't try. I thought that the ability to pull up such clear memories all of the time was one of the prime perks of being a vamp. When I was turned about three hundred years or so ago, I wanted to map out the whole world. Christopher found me when I'd already been living in the deep jungle of what's now India for five years, and he thought I had the potential to make the world a better place if I had more time to live in it. Considering I was a hard-drinking and self-acknowledged rogue in those days, he saw a lot more potential in myself than I ever did."

He grinned at Robin and she blushed to her hair. Danny was a little too easy to visualize as a nineteenth century

Indiana Jones-type, cutting a swath through the under-growth with his machete. Getting sweaty. Maybe taking a skinny dip in a stream...

She shook herself. *What was it about Danny that was so completely distracting?* As they walked through the woods, she was hyper-aware of every place their bodies brushed, his palm pressed against hers. The smallest jostle of their hips against each other aroused her past anything she'd ever felt before.

His smile dropped a little. "The thing about being an explorer is that it isn't just being on the hunt for something that's never been found before, it's about comparing everything you see to what you've already experienced." He chuckled and shrugged. "I was making a hand-drawn map of the whole world, but it took me so long to get anywhere, by the time I'd looped back to a place I'd already been, it had changed completely. And for a long time, I loved that. Every time I swung by Constantinople, it was like a totally different city, with new temples and then churches and then temples again, the streets and people all changed and I gave up trying to keep track." He glanced at Robin. "I also realized how much of the present I was missing. Always thinking about the past was like living in a dream."

She nodded, remembering the strange disconnect of sitting against the tree watching the vultrich beside Danny while also living a dozen other memories of being beside her parents. How easy would it be, in the centuries to come, to simply relive past moments rather than making new memories?

No. I can't fall down that trap.

She didn't look back at the forest when they reached Danny's truck, concentrating on what was in front of her. His truck needed a thorough cleaning--the rubber mat on the floor was impacted with mud and fast food crumbs, with tissues crammed into the side pockets along with what looked like a plastic army toy--but smelled overwhelmingly like Danny. It was a pleasant smell, one that made it easy for her to rest her head back in the seat and let her body curve into the cushions.

Danny glanced at her as he maneuvered the truck into gear, his mouth thinning. "Are you going to be okay alone at my place? I can take you back to your house if you want."

"Where will you be?" she asked.

"I know the cavalry isn't coming in until the day after tomorrow, but I was thinking of heading back to the Blood Oasis. Christopher will need more information before they go in. I'm going to map out all the possible entry points and exits, the dimensions of the hallways, and plan an effective route in and out."

"I want to come too." The thought of going back to that place filled her with a chest-chilling terror, but if Danny was going back there, then she was too. The thought of him sleuthing around that hellhole while she relaxed in his Jacuzzi wasn't an option.

"You don't have the training. I've been doing this kind of investigating for hundreds of years."

"I need to do this. You know what they did to me. If there's *any* way I can help take them down, I'm going to do it."

He sighed, looking over at her. Robin kept her face carefully calm, with a determined set of her jaw so he would know she meant business. His hands clenched and unclenched around the steering wheel.

"Fine. I could use some backup." He looked her over again, his expression speculative. "But you can't go back there looking like that."

Robin looked down at herself. The jeans and sweater that Danny had provided when she woke up didn't exactly blend into a vampire club. Nia would definitely be out for Robin and Danny's blood after Seth's beheading.

"What did you have in mind?"

LOOKING into Danny's closet was like walking onto the set of a Mission Impossible porn parody. Rows of leather chaps and wicked-looking ribbon-laced corsets in men and women's sizes lined both sides, along with enough toys to fill two Amsterdam sex shops.

"How many whips does one man need?" Robin asked.

Danny grinned. "Most of these were gifts. My friends know I'm a collector."

"So, not *just* a world explorer, then?" Robin raised her eyebrows at him.

"Is anyone ever just one thing?"

Danny grabbed a black bra off a rack and held it up in front of Robin, tilting his head before putting it back and tossing her one with slightly larger cups. She didn't need to glance at the label to know the new one would fit perfectly.

"Let's say that I'm always down to try new things." He winked at her.

Hot damn. The man's winks were nuclear-powered. Just the movement of his eyelid had arousal surge between her legs. Heat filled her to her toes.

He strolled deeper into the closet, making little noises like he was running into old friends as he pulled back one hanger to take a better look at a pair of chaps with three-inch fringe on the side, and then caress a pair of blood-red knee-high boots with four-inch sparkling heels. For a second, she could picture him wearing the entire rig and the effect was irresistible.

Everything he does is sexy, Robin thought. *Good thing he's not my sire*. But she shut down that line of thought before she could think too hard on sires. Despite how awful the moment of her turning had been, she was grateful her sire was dead. She was free. Utterly free.

If she wanted to walk away from helping Danny take down Nia and the Blood Oasis, she could.

If she wanted to go explore the deep jungles of the world and forget the vultrich and every heartbreaking and warming memory she had...she could.

She was a vampire: a strong, fast, emotion-reading, blood-drinking immortal. Everything had been so crazy since she was turned she hadn't had a chance to sit back and appreciate that she'd *done* it. She'd gotten a vampire to turn her! Now she had all the time in the world to figure out what to do with herself.

Robin stalked forward into the closet, grabbing every costume piece that caught her eye. She remembered her joy when she first walked into the Blood Oasis, how the place promised a fantasy of freedom and fun. No matter how Nia had perverted that promise, Robin could live the life she chose.

Black corset that pushed her breasts sky-high? *Check*. Fishnet stockings held up by a garter belt? *Check*. Lace gloves inset with rubies that stretched up past her elbows? *Check*. A dab of body glitter between her breasts to draw the eye, along with eye liner drawn on so thick and bold it would make her mother tremble in her grave? *Check and check*.

Robin inspected her reflection. Nia definitely wouldn't recognize her. *Robin* barely recognized the sexy and confident woman in the mirror. She bared her fangs, tossing back her hair and letting her canines extend to dip into her lower lip. The vampire in the mirror looked ready to tear Nia's throat out, and anyone else who tried to stand in her way. She growled, smiling at the effect. The next time a contractor called her a "tree-hugging hippie" to get her to move from where she blocked his access to a nest, he was going to get quite a shock.

"Hot damn," Danny said behind her. His eyes roamed up and down her body like he couldn't get enough.

"Hot damn yourself."

Danny hadn't been idle while she was getting dressed. His leather pants were so tight they could have been painted on, and he wore a silk vest with nothing underneath, open to display acres of tight muscles and a truly drool-worthy set of abs. He caught her eye and raised one perfect eyebrow, his grin turning smug.

"Like what you see?" he asked.

She stalked forward, running her fingernails along the side of the fabric, tickling the soft skin along his pecs and down to his stomach. "I'm an environmentalist. I can always appreciate a fine natural specimen."

"Uh huh." He skimmed his fingers along her shoulders, caressing the top of her gloves where the fabric met the sensitive skin on the inside of her arm. To her enhanced senses, every brush of his fingers electrified, sizzling across her skin. He kissed her neck and she heated like a furnace burned in her lower belly, radiating out.

"As a former explorer, I just love discovering..." Danny's hands skated down her spine over her corset to land squarely on her ass. "New territories."

He dropped to his knees, nudging her legs apart and kissing a trail of nips and licks up her inner thigh, unhooking the garter belt to trace the edge of her fishnet stockings with his tongue.

"Oh yes," she panted. Danny grinned, his dimples filled with mischief as his fingers played with the ticklish skin behind her knees and along the back of her thigh. She grabbed the wall beside her for balance as her legs threatened to give way, her hand closing around a vibrator along a shelf. It was shaped like an egg, the buttons along the side alerting it to buzzing life as she picked it up.

"Ooo, good thought," Danny's fingers probed under the lace panties fully on display to caress down the crease between her ass. He plucked the egg from her fingers and tucked it into her panties so the elastic would hold it against her clit as his tongue traced tantalizing circles along her inner thighs so close, yet never close enough, to her core.

"More." Her breath came in rapid pants. "I need more."

The warm buzzing of the vibrator sent shooting pleasure down her legs.

"Holy crap!" she yelped as he pulled aside the piece of lace between her legs and plunged his tongue inside of her.

"Delicious," he murmured, tapping the egg so its force increased to maximum.

Her first orgasm hit so suddenly, her upper body convulsed against the wall, her head knocking aside a stack of harnesses and her scream echoing around the closet. She sagged against the clothes, already lightheaded.

He carefully withdrew the egg. "Having fun yet?"

"Oh, we're just starting." She grabbed his shirt, pulling it over his head and throwing it on the floor. Her lips fastened around his nipples, loving their pert tautness and his guttural groan as she lightly nibbled along the tips. Everything from his rugged smell, to the smoothness of his skin was more incredible than anything she'd ever felt before.

Feathers on the shelf next to her brushed against her face and it was so unexpected, she startled away, leaning instinctively closer into Danny. His arm closed around her. She tilted her head back in invitation and he dove for her lips, devouring her with abandon, sucking and fucking her mouth with his tongue. Still sensitive after her last orgasm, the sensations were too much and not enough, her hips desperately pushing closer to his until she felt the hard iron of his erection pressing against her stomach.

He bit a trail of kisses along her chin up to her ear, nibbling along the lobe. She hadn't thought anything so gentle could send her hormones racing again so fast, but her knees were on the verge of giving out under her. She grasped his shoulders with one hand to stay upright, the other beginning to unfasten his belt, her fingers clumsy in her speed to get all of his clothes off.

He yanked down his pants, his massive cock begging to be licked and caressed.

Robin slid seductively to the ground, letting her hands run down the length of Danny's chest. Her fingers played in the grooves of his abs until she reached her destination.

"My turn," she murmured.

She stared down at the hard length pulsing with desire for her, and Robin smiled at his enthusiastic response. She closed her hand around him, making Danny buck forward, eager for her touch. Robin licked a winding road along his shaft, taking her time with him, growing ever wetter as she tasted the precum that glistened on his tip.

Robin slid him inside her mouth and Danny let out a low groan as she teased his cock with her tongue, bobbing relentlessly. She slid her hands along his thighs, his ass, his balls. Everything about him felt right in her hands, each new sound of pleasure he made increasing the arousal surging between her legs and along her limbs.

Danny tensed, about to cum, and Robin released him with a pop. *No need to end the fun quite yet.*

"Is it too corny to tell you that you're the most beautiful and amazing being I've seen in centuries and I--"

Robin yanked down her panties, putting her hand over his mouth. "Show me. Fuck me right now."

She needed him: dirty, urgent, and surrounded by costumes, sex toys, and reminders of the whole new world she'd joined. She leaned over the top of a wooden trunk in the bottom of the closet, spreading her legs wide.

"Thank fuck," he cried.

"Yes!" She thrust her hips back just in time to feel his hands on her ass and the head of his cock slip between her wet folds. He was so big, he stretched her channel, and she moaned at the perfection of it. He slid in slow, giving her time to accommodate his size.

"I don't want you to be delicate," Robin commanded. "I'm a fucking vampire. Pound me, Danny."

"Yes, my love." He said the last so low she wasn't sure he heard him right, but by then, she couldn't think straight. He'd lifted her up so her feet no longer touched the ground, changing the angle so he could pull her forward with each stroke, withdrawing nearly all the way out before slamming back in over and over.

Danny pounded into her mercilessly and she loved every second of it. He hit every amazing spot inside, sending thrills of fireworks and building pulsing heat down to her curling toes.

Her breasts pressed against the hard top of the chest, the friction of the wood against the silken inside of the corset she still wore playing gentle havoc with her breasts and nipples. He shifted his weight so his arm held up her hips and he could use one hand to reach under her and play with her clit, squeezing and rubbing it just enough to send her over the edge.

"Yes! Yes, yes, yes, yes," she screamed over and over as she rode the wave of pleasure erupting through her. Fireworks of pleasure burst along her spine, her toes curled, and her fingers clenched tight around the edge of the chest so hard the wood splintered in between her knuckles. A second later, she felt his cock expand inside her as he shuddered over her, moaning low.

She collapsed against the top of the trunk, breathing heavily as Danny's cock softened inside her and he withdrew. Nothing had ever been so intense, so perfect. She glanced behind her at her vampire lover, who had slid down to the floor. His grin was so wide, it lit up the dark corners of the closet.

The floor around him was strewn with their clothing. Her cheeks itched where eye-liner had mixed with sweat and dripped down her face.

She laughed. "It looks like we're going to have to get ready all over again."

Danny's laugh echoed hers, sitting up to cradle her face between her hands and kiss her gently. He pulled her back against him so they were cuddled together under the rack of chaps.

"Worth it. Worth every second."

Robin sank back into his embrace, loving the feel of his arms around her, the peace and perfection of being beside him. *Forever with him is more than I ever dreamed of*, she thought as she breathed in the lush smell of his sweat mixed with tanned leather. *If he hadn't saved me when he did...*

Seyah and the other vampires under Nia's will were all

still there. It was like an itch at the back of her mind. Even as she lay in Danny's arms in perfect harmony, they were trapped there. *How many horrors have they already experienced tonight because we were distracted?*

She tapped Danny's shoulder. "We need to get to work."

He caught the seriousness in her tone and nodded. "Let's go."

HOW A PLACE so lovely could hide such ugliness, Danny would never understand. Even the back door had a certain charm about it, framed with rose bushes. From his crouched position to the left of the door--out of range of the security cameras--he could hear swishes of movement coming from inside. He'd sent a quick text to Margot telling her he was headed to the club to gather intel and her response had been less than encouraging: a series of curses and angry emoticons telling him to wait for the professionals, and stay put until they arrived. But he couldn't stay still. Not when that haunted look came over Robin's face and he knew there were so many others that they'd both left behind at the Blood Oasis. He *had* to help.

Footsteps thumped inside and he froze, the movement tightening his leather getup in ways that were not entirely unpleasant. Danny held his breath as he followed the sound of footsteps growing louder, and then fading away.

He let out a breath and pulled his lock picking tools from one of his boots. Kneeling with the lock at eye level, he selected a long, silver hook, and his smallest torsion wrench. He moved slowly, hoping the enhanced hearing of the vampires inside would be focused on the ecstatic moans of their guests rather than the incriminating sounds of metal scraping against metal.

The soft click of success made him grin, and he slipped inside without a sound. The back areas of the Blood Oasis were less extravagant than the front, but still stunning. The hallways were lined with antique gas lamps which glowed warmer than modern appliances could ever achieve, and the windows' heavy, black, curtains shown with a velvet sheen. The red carpeting would put a movie premiere to shame.

Somewhere out front, Robin was doing her own recon dressed like the best part of every wet dream he'd ever had. The memory of Robin's sated expression after he pounded her into oblivion gave Danny's wild grin some authenticity as he walked down the hallway, providing his best imitation of an excited patron. He counted his steps as he moved, occasionally stretching out wide in a faux yawn to get a feel for the width of the corridor, drawing a map in his mind. The more information he could provide to Christopher's police, the more successful their raid would be.

A vampire with a vacant expression concealed under a thick blanket of makeup giggled and tossed her hair at an older satyr who leaned heavily on her, wobbling on his small, cloven hoofs. They careened back and forth like a pin-ball as the woman struggled to hold the man's drunken, stout form upright.

"You look lovely as ever tonight, my dear," he slurred, his tiny hand gliding down to cup the woman's ass. She couldn't quite hide her wince fast enough and Danny wondered how he had missed these signs the first time he was here.

She giggled. "I wanted to look my best for you, sweetie." Her gaze caught on Danny's and her eyes widened in recognition before quickly turning away.

It was the scared, beseeching look in her eyes that did it, her brown eyes too similar to Robin's. Danny turned back. "Do you need help?" He whispered. "I can get you out of here."

"You picked the wrong night to sneak around," she whispered back as she gave up trying to keep the satyr upright and he slipped down to the floor and began to gently snore. "There's a big event happening, security has been bumped up to keep anyone from escaping once they find their candidates."

"They're making new vampires tonight?" *Robin's out there alone, she doesn't know.* His stomach churned.

"It's a big gala to get the naive and beautiful in here," she whispered fast. The satyr was beginning to come around, blinking and groaning at the light from the candles. "You gotta leave. Now."

"Not until I get what I need."

"They're in the dungeons," she hissed. Louder, to the satyr she cooed, "Oh sweetie face, are you okay? You look like you need another drink." She picked up the satyr like an oversized doll and carried him back in the direction they came, away from the marked bedrooms.

Danny stared after her a long moment. *They're in the dungeons? What does that mean?* It was the best lead he had.

He picked up a dank scent and followed it straight down to the dungeon. It was more decorative than threatening, but solid all the same. Rows of metal doors lined the long, dead-end hallway, each too thick for sound to come through. It was also cold, even for a vampire, and Danny wished he had selected an ensemble that left more to the imagination. The walls were painted a shiny black, with electric candle sconces spaced in intimate alcoves with padded sides, perfect for getting swept up and fucked against the wall.

Danny caught the steady red light of a security camera out of the corner of his eye. Danny knew the model, an ACE-457, consisting of a single steady camera in a small black dome protruding from the ceiling. *Hardly subtle.* He scoffed and rolled to the ground, easily maneuvering into the camera's blind spot as he made his way forward.

The long hallway was separated in to dozens of cells. Each was outfitted with a single sliding window. Danny shrugged. *Some people like to watch.* Danny peeked in a few. Some of the cells were decked out for recreational purposes, filled with a creative array of chains and BDSM paraphernalia. But as Danny made his way towards the cells in the back, he bit back a shudder. Marks that looked like scratches from human fingernails dug along the walls, and splatters of blood that reeked with fear covered the floor. *This isn't just a sex dungeon.*

The ground shook as heavy footsteps approached. *Shit! Just what I need.* Danny ducked into an open cell and froze. He held his breath, and tried to slow the frantic beating of his heart.

Danny quickly peered around the corner of the cell, and cursed himself for getting cornered so easily. The walls, floor, and ceiling were reinforced iron even vampire strength couldn't break. The exit, and only escape, was blocked by a mountain of a vampire, all muscle and no neck. The mountain was glaring into the cells, clearly looking for something. *Has he seen me?*

The answer appeared in the form of a large hand lifting him off the ground and throwing him against the cell wall.

I'll take that as a 'yes'. Danny planted his hands on the floor and kicked the mountainous vampire in the solar plexus with all his might. He used the momentum from the kick to complete his movement into a flip, landing on his feet. Free in the hallway, he sprinted for stairs, pushing at the limit of his vampiric speed so the walls passed in a blur. Shouted curses from the vamp followed at his heels. With a grin, Danny dropped to the ground, slid across the cold floor, and threw open the last iron cell door just in time for his pursuer to slam into it at full speed. The distinctly vampire-shaped dent in the door was comically satisfying.

"Smooth," came a low voice Danny least wanted to hear. He spun to face his only exit. Nia Ashmore glanced over at the dented door and grinned at Danny from several steps up, flanked on either side by axe-wielding vampires. "Just because you dodged the visible security cameras, doesn't mean you weren't picked up on the hidden ones. I know *everything* that goes on here." She tsked. "Prince Dal, I presume? It's too bad you've become so knowledgeable of my organization."

"King Christopher knows of your abuses!" Danny spat. "You're finished."

"Am I?" Nia mockingly brought a thin hand to her chest. "Oh my." She rolled her eyes.

"You will not disrespect the king!" Hot rage flooded Danny's vision.

"That sire of yours is no king of mine. I don't know if he doesn't respect the *hortari,* or is just too pathetic to use it, but..." She crooked her finger forward, and her two guards brought their axes down to Danny's throat. "Let's just say I know how to *deal* with weakness."

Danny braced himself for the killing blow, defiantly staring Nia down. He took a deep breath and readied himself for oblivion.

"Lock him to the dungeons, boys," Nia said. "Since you

like my holding cells so much, you'll get to enjoy the rest of your miserable existence in one. If the king knows about us, then having his sireling as a hostage will be lovely leverage." She wrinkled her nose. "Also I don't need vampire all over my nice floor."

The axes retreated from his neck as thick chains clinked around Danny's wrists. Robin's smile flashed before his eyes, and Danny nearly lost his footing. *No!* Robin was in danger. He'd *led* her to this place. Surely, Nia would spot her in the crowd, especially now that she'd found Danny. Everything was spiraling out of control. A heavy hand pushed him forward, arms clamped around his shoulders dragging him back toward the blood-soaked, back cells.

Robin, my love, he prayed to whoever might be listening. *Please be okay.*

SOMETHING WAS WRONG. Danny should have been back by now. They'd agreed that after he finished his map, they'd meet here. Robin did a third lap of the Blood Oasis, and still no Danny. Being here again, she was struck by how beautiful and amazing this place *could* be. A better DJ, a touch of softer lighting, staff who actually *consented* to work there...it was the little things that could have made this place an empowering retreat of sex and fun.

What would really make it perfect is if she could find Danny.

"Are you here for the Star Mixer?" a cheetah shifter in a pinstripe suit asked, handing her a flyer.

Robin stopped short, remembering her role as casual party-goer and twirled the end of her hair with her finger.

"No. I just came for the fun!" She looked down at the flyer and bit back a gasp.

"I hope we cater to your fantasies!" The man chirped happily before bounding away to approach a woman wearing too much makeup who had just arrived.

Join us for an exciting night full of eternal possibility! Read the front of the flyer in bold letters. The signs she'd passed near the front door made more sense now. The black tie networking affair for aspiring actors and models promised "strength, poise, and the opportunity to proclaim your beauty to the masses." *Nia must be shopping for replacements for the vamps freed when Seth lost his head.* Nothing in the pamphlet mentioned vampires. *Do these people even know what they're being recruited for?*

Robin's stomach churned as she noticed the signage scattered around the Blood Oasis. They had a few hours before the event started, but the staff was already setting up. *No fucking way am I going to let that happen.*

A vampire with a diamond nose ring and a thin-lipped smile leaned against the bar. The woman's eyes widened when she caught Robin's and turned abruptly away. Concerned, Robin came closer.

"I'm under orders to report you to my sire if I see you, Robin," she said fast, stepping back. "But my sire didn't specify *when* I had to report it."

Robin didn't question how the woman knew her name. Danny had killed one of Nia's sirelings for Robin's sake. Both of their names and faces were probably well known by now.

Robin shook her head. "No, but help is coming. I'm here with a friend, we're--"

"Don't tell me anything." The woman looked around quickly, but the folks around them were occupied either dancing or making out. "Look, I'm not allowed to help you. But..." she stopped, considered her words carefully. "Unrelated - did you know that this place has a dungeon? You look like you'd be into our *special* pleasures we offer down there. If you want to check it out, you're going to want to take the second door on the right and..." She rattled off a complex list of directions. Robin grabbed a napkin off the bar and a pen and started to draw a map off of what she described. The woman examined the map and then nodded, her face strained as she skirted the edge of disobeying a *hortari*. Robin kissed the woman's cheek.

"We're going to get you out of here," Robin whispered.

"And I hope we've catered to all your fantasies," the woman replied mechanically.

Robin nodded and slid open the door to the right. There were a few close calls in the hallways, but most of Nia's managers seemed to have better things to do than police the halls. Most of the other vampires she saw turned their heads away and started chatting loudly to whoever they were with about something else. A swelling of pride pushed its way up Robin's chest. No matter what compulsion these poor vampires were under, they found ways to resist.

I'm going to come back for you, she promised silently to their retreating forms.

The smells from the dungeon were overwhelming: sweat, fear, and sex surrounded her to form an impenetrable cloud. She coughed and tried pinching her nose, but it was no use. The sweat and sex smells weren't bad, but the stink of fear made her skin itch.

She slid aside each cell's small, eye-level viewing window as quietly as possible. In one, Robin found a man strapped to a hanging cross groaning in pleasure as a woman encased head to toe in leather whipped him across the ass. In another, a gay couple writhed together in handcuffs.

Where the hell is Danny? There were only two cells left.

Even with enhanced vampire senses, the second-to-last room was so dark, she could barely see the occupants: two men and two women with their arms and legs shackled to the floor in tight balls that barely allowed them to move at all. They were all gagged silent, thick ropes lashed to each of their mouths. *What the hell?* She tried the door, but it was locked shut.

At the sound of her jiggling the latch, the closest man turned to look at her, rage in his narrowed eyes. He pulled at his chains, a muffled scream around the rope echoing around his gag. She recognized him immediately: Seyah.

"Were you one of Seth's vampires?" she whispered through the bars.

He nodded emphatically, hunching over his elbow to point to the others tied up in the cell as well. When Danny killed Seth, his compulsion over his other sirelings was also broken. *My vampire brothers and sisters.* Robin looked around the empty hallway for a key. There was no sign of one and no one around, but that was no guarantee that someone wasn't going to come down at any moment to check on the other guests. Even if she knew how to pick a lock, there was no time to try.

"I will come back for you," she whispered through the door, keeping the eye slot open so they could at least have a little light.

She slid open the window into the last cell. Her heart did a little backflip at the sight of Danny picking a thick padlock using his elongated canine teeth. He was wrapped in so many padlocks and chains, he might as well have been blanketed in them. The locks he'd already unlocked were at least fifty deep on the ground next to him.

"Danny!" She hissed through the door.

He dropped the lock he was currently working on and glared at her.

"What are you doing down here? It's too dangerous!" He immediately dove back for the lock, flicking open the latch with his teeth and going for the next one. It hit its fellow with a low chunk.

"And what are you going to do once you've gotten out of there?" She cocked an eyebrow at him.

"I need to stop tonight's event. Nia's hosting a gala in just a few hours that's going to enslave a *lot* more vampires. We don't have time to wait for Christopher's army to arrive tomorrow." Another lock hit the pile.

"I know. But we don't need to wait for an army." She pointed to the cell next to him. "We have back up right here."

"What?"

"Seth's sirelings are next door," Robin said.

Danny threw another lock against the pile. "So close?" Another lock down. "At least *one* thing is going right with this mission."

Danny worked this way through the locks as she explained to the bound vampires next door about the royal army coming soon to take this place apart.

"You don't have to help. It's going to be risky, but we could use your support."

Seyah and the rest nodded more quickly than she'd hoped. Once Danny got his own door open, he picked open the neighboring door as well, using his lockpicks now that his hands were free until all four of Seth's sirelings were blinking and stretching in their cell.

"How many vampires do Nia and her sirelings control?" Danny asked once they were all free.

"There's twenty here," said the woman closest. She was rubbing her wrists where the shackles had held her down, her expression murderous. "Divided up among Nia's three remaining sireling managers."

"What are we going to do about *Nia*?" asked the other male vampire, saying the woman's name like a curse.

"I can take care of Nia," Danny said. When they all started arguing at once, Danny held up his hands. "I know you all want your revenge, but Nia is older than you, which makes her stronger. You're not going to be a match for her if it comes down to a fight."

There were plenty of grumbles, but eventually they agreed.

"We still have her three guys in charge to take care of," Robin pointed out, which made everybody perk up. "You all know this place better than we do. How do we get twenty compulsion-controlled vamps contained without anybody getting hurt?"

Watching them plan the best approach reminded Robin of the vultrich herding their nestlings to shelter while their mates tore apart snakes with their beaks. She wasn't sure if Danny would appreciate being compared to her birds, but the thought made her smile. The vampires were protecting their nest, no matter what it took.

They split into three groups, each focused on tracking down and either killing or disabling one of Nia's sirelings. One was easy to find: Rick was in a four-way with two female guests and one of his conscripted vamps, a guy with an eyebrow ring and a buzz cut, kneading Rick's shoulders from behind. Rick was thoroughly distracted, but Robin caught the other vamp's eye through the window with ease.

Robin could tell the moment he recognized Seyah and the other of Seth's freed vamps in the hallway behind her. His eyes widened, and he smiled wide, his hands encircling Rick's neck and squeezing hard. Rick passed out before the two guests realized anything was wrong. The vamp said something to them and they smiled, winked at him, and then continued making out with one another. He approached the door and nodded to Seyah.

"Got a knife out here I could borrow? He's only going to be out a few minutes. This asshole needs a beheading."

Seyah started to hand him a weapon he'd picked up from one of the dungeon rooms, but Danny grabbed his hand.

"No, just get them out of there and lock him up." Danny handed the vampire a long length of chain he'd brought up from the dungeon. "The king can put him on trial when he arrives."

"That's not nearly as satisfying," the vampire grumbled, but he bound up the unconscious Rick and hefted him onto his shoulder, giving them all a wink as he headed down to the dungeons.

Two to go.

Robin followed behind as the growing group of liberated vamps searched the hallway for Nia's remaining sirelings, all the while herding guests away into rooms where they could be safely locked away. The second sireling, Jerry, got clubbed over the head and dragged into a room before he recognized Seth's vamps shouldn't be on his floor, while the last, Morty, they found in the middle of the dance floor.

Robin froze, uncertain how to move forward without endangering so many bystanders. One of Seth's vamps, Dulcia, jumped forward to yell, "Sex party in the dungeon!" at the top of her lungs, then motioned for everyone follow her like a scantily-clad pied piper. As the entire dance floor moved downstairs, Morty got swept along in the commotion and was locked in the first cell they could shove him into.

Even with all of Nia's goons taken care of, Danny still looked worried.

Robin touched his arm. "Have you seen any sign of Nia?"

Danny shook his head. "She *has* to be upstairs, it's the only place we haven't looked."

Seyah had found them some blueprints of the building. The upstairs was even more of a maze than the lower floors, purposefully constructed to limit movements and confuse anyone not familiar with the layout.

"Nia's probably in her suite." Seyah pointed to the largest room on the blueprints.

"You're going to need help," Robin said.

He shook his head. "I need you to get everybody out of here. If she makes it past me, I don't want to give her the chance to hurt anybody."

Robin didn't like it, but Danny's logic made sense. Her vampire prince pulled her in for a crushing kiss, his hands cupping her face perfectly. Before she could say anything, he was gone, racing up the stairs.

DANNY FOUGHT against the worry itching at the back of his neck. Robin had proven how remarkably brave and resourceful she was, but she wasn't a warrior. If Nia got away from him, Robin and the other newly-sired vamps would be practically defenseless. He tried to push the thought away so he could focus on the task at hand.

Just don't let her get past you, he told himself, clamping down on any doubts. With a yell, Danny kicked down the gilded door of Nia's suite.

"It's over!" He adjusted his grip on his machete, scanning the room for any sign of the Blood Oasis's evil mistress. Nia's white and gold room was even worse than Danny anticipated. Furs of endangered species covered the floor, and gold-plated statues of Nia's face topped marble columns. One wall was decorated entirely with murals of her face, while another was a giant, floor-to-ceiling mirror. Light danced off the shining blades of two white-handled axes crossed above the fireplace's mantle.

Nia was beside her enormous bed packing a leather duffel bag overflowing with cash and jewels. She stopped short at the sight of Danny.

"You." She spat.

"Me." Danny twirled his machete. "We've subdued your minions." He stepped towards Nia. "The king knows what you've done." He pointed his machete at her. "You're out of options. Come quietly, or in pieces."

"Honey, do you hear that helicopter?" The sounds of whirring blades grew louder with her every word. "I'm *never* out of options." Moving quicker than a blink, Nia dropped her bag, leapt to the mantle, and grabbed the axes off the wall.

"Fuck!" Danny dropped to the ground, one of her axes whizzing past where his throat had been less than a second before.

Nia bellowed as she leapt off the mantle, swinging her other axe overhead with deadly aim at Danny. He rolled fast, avoiding her axe just as the weapon buried deep into the carpeting.

"I so rarely get to do my own dirty work." Nia purred.

She yanked the axe from the floor "I forgot how much fun it can be."

Danny danced back, holding his machete protectively in front of himself, circling her warily.

She was so fast, she had to be old. Really old. The only chance he had to was to keep her distracted, hopefully take her by surprise. "I'm surprised you can do *anything* on your own. Do your minions wipe your ass for you, too?"

Nia smiled and Danny was instantly reminded that gorillas only grinned as a threat. "My minions do whatever I tell them to do. Which is more than I can say for your worthless sire who lets his raggedy mutts disrupt my business."

"Christopher is worth a thousand of you." With a grunt, Danny kicked the massive wooden bed at Nia, the two-hundred pound piece of furniture hurtling through the air toward her. A deafening clatter ripped through the room as the bed exploded, and Nia emerged from the dust between two cleaved halves of the bed, axe-first.

"That bed belonged to Stalin!" she yelled. "Do you know what that thing *cost,* you asshole!"

Danny charged, holding his machete high. He swung his blade in a wide arc, changing the angle at the last second so Nia dodged directly into the path of his weapon. She cried out as the blade sliced across her shoulder, leaving a thin trail of blood behind.

Danny sniffed the air, now pungent with Nia's emotions from her spilled blood. She was *furious.* He grinned. *I can use that.*

Danny dodged back from her rage-fueled axe swing, his chest just out of Nia's reach. "Some master criminal you are."

Nia's blade whipped through the empty air without

making contact, her frustration and rage growing with each swing.

"Fuck this." Nia jumped backward, grabbing one of her golden busts and pitching it with the crack of a fastball directly at his head. Danny swerved to avoid the missile and yelped as her axe swing came down directly into his path.

Oh, shit. Danny moved to block the axe's blow, managing to catch her blade deep into his forearm. The block managed to throw Nia off balance just enough to break her momentum and allow Danny to roll away. He swung his machete at her, driving it into the wooden handle of the axe. With the machete stuck in the axe's shaft, they were caught together. Each struggled against the blade of the each other. For one second, Danny remembered Blagfor, the way his rocklike arms bristled as he pushed against Danny's hand. It hadn't been a fair fight. And Danny didn't have to fight fair.

He kicked Nia hard in the stomach, shooting her across the room and into the wall-length mirror. Sounds of shattering glass echoed around the room as the reflective shards rained down around her, peppering her exposed skin with slices and cuts.

The axe tumbled from her hand and Danny leapt forward to kick it out of her reach.

"Give it up, Nia." Danny approached her slowly, dread growing in his chest. Her blood didn't smell of rage, or even fear, she smelled like anticipation. "Unlike you, I don't enjoy hurting people."

Nia limped towards the fireplace, a red trail of blood following her. "That's why you'll always lose." Nia pressed a panel along the side of the mantel. Gears clicked and the panel, only about a foot wide with a dark hole in the center, slowly slid into the wall.

What now? He braced himself for something terrible:

spikes or flames, maybe even grenade blasts. Danny dove behind the long, white couch, flipping it over him for maximum cover.

Silence.

He peered around the edge of the couch.

Nia was gone, her clothes and jewelry pooled in a pile where she'd been standing.

"Nia?"

Something on the floor hissed and Danny jumped back. A *cobra* lay coiled in Nia's rumpled laundry.

"You slippery sonofabitch! You're a snake shifter?" Danny pulled out his machete and approached cautiously. "You know, machetes were pretty much *designed* for killing snakes."

"Danny!" Robin ran into the room, disheveled but grinning. She held a plastic container of glittering, rainbow-colored worms writhing inside. "I found--" she started to say, but stopped when Nia the snake hissed and swung her diamond-backed head in her direction. "What the fuck?" Robin cried.

"Watch out! It's Nia! She was a shifter before she was a vampire." Danny approached slowly. Just because she was smaller didn't mean she had lost any of her strength or speed.

Nia slithered toward the dark hole in the panel she'd opened and Danny lunged, his machete missing by a hair. He moved to block the escape hatch, seeing only death in her tiny, black gaze.

Out of the corner of his eye, he saw Robin tear the lid off of the container and spring to the window, holding the open box aloft.

Nia slithered toward him, her head waving back and forth. "Little prince, do you really think you can stop me?"

Nia's voice took on a rasping whisper out of her snake's throat. "*Hortari* is part of who we are, and it's good business."

Danny darted forward again but she dodged, laughing, a terrible cackle. Distantly, Danny thought he heard a familiar screeching sound approaching. Robin caught his eye, mouthing,

"Keep her busy."

"Business, huh?" Danny taunted the snake. "You're creating slaves."

The rumbling was getting closer.

Nina chuckled. "We *all* create slaves. I just have the balls to command them."

The screech of birdcalls filled the room, and the walls shook. Robin hurled the container at Nia, showering the snake with worms, and screamed.

"Get back!"

Glass exploded behind them as the windows shattered. Dark shapes crowded and pushed each other to get inside.

Danny dove back behind the couch, pulling Robin with him. The frames of the windows groaned and half the wall broke inward.

Danny pulled Robin closer as sharp, pecking sounds filled the palatial suite.

Robin leaned closer against him. "I found them in the kitchen, some ingredient for a spell Nia was cooking." She touched his face. "I was so worried when I heard all the crashing."

Danny risked a peek over the edge of the couch. The remains of snake dotted the floor in pieces while the vultrich feasted happily on the sky worms and the pieces of snake still stuck to them. The happy flaps of their wings sent showers of discarded feathers into the air.

"Your birds took care of Nia for us." She rested her head on his shoulder.

"I guess they're good at protecting me too."

ROBIN LOVED the feeling of the cold window's glass against her forehead as she looked out at the vultrich chirping and pecking in their new, protected habitat. The gardens of the Blood Oasis had been the perfect biome for a vultrich nesting sanctuary. It was only the first of many that Robin had planned now that she and Danny were the new managers of the club, but she had time. Eternity, in fact.

After the giant birds killed Nia for them, a few of Nia's conscripted vamps had joined Robin on her mission to save the vultriches. Seyah in particular was rabid about opposing construction projects and utility plants which threatened to harm the vultrich's habitat.

Danny fell onto the padded bench beside the window, breathing heavy after his last hour out on the dance floor. After they'd taken down Nia, Danny had called Christopher to stand down his troops. Christopher had come anyway to ensure that his sireling and the others were okay. Christopher had been everything Robin thought a king should be: considerate, commanding, and kind. He also immediately said he would fund Robin's initiative to transport the vultrich nestlings to their new habitat.

"Any word from Samantha about the protection spell?" Danny asked. He hummed a little along with the music.

"It should be up any second now." Robin kissed his cheek. Since the grand reopening, they'd been experimenting with spells to protect their staff and clientele. Robin was overjoyed that her college roommate, Samantha, had gamely agreed to be their new head of magical security to finish working out the bugs.

Robin smiled as a flash of magic surged past her and into the fabric of the building itself. The dancers on the floor all cheered, grinding deeper into their partners.

"Want to test it out?" Danny asked.

Robin shook her head. "No need, I think we're about to see a live demonstration." She nodded toward Kendry at the bar, who was telling a stubby satyr she would not be joining him upstairs. The lovely vampire was one of the few who had decided to stay on as paid staff since she enjoyed most of the work and loved to dance. But a few of her former clients she'd been forced to entertain under the old management couldn't quite seem to understand that she was now able to say "no". The satyr started to make a grab for her, but she pushed him away. He teetered back on his hooves, and then...disappeared.

Robin swiveled to peer out the window, the satisfaction of success like a warm glow suffusing her skin. The misogynist was out past the front gates, jumping up and down and yelling. He banged against the opening of the driveway, but his fists struck against the invisible barrier, which would keep him out until Kendry decided to allow him in. Samantha's spell worked wonders at getting rid of those who weren't respectful of the rules.

"The new security system works perfectly, folks," Robin said into the walkie-talkie at her hip. She leaned forward to brush her lips against Danny's. "We did it!"

"Hmm, yes we did. I never doubted it." He tasted like bourbon and blood. She licked along the inside of his lip and his breath hitched, his hands pulling her closer until she straddled him on the bench.

"Tiger shifter blood?" She kissed him deeper, her tongue

plunging to lick the inside of his cheeks and stroke along his tongue. "Yum. A horny one at that." The taste of the tiger on his lips fed her arousal, the notes of sexual urgency churning in her from even the smallest droplet from his mouth. "My favorite."

Danny's hands massaged her ass, his lips kissing her neck with enough pressure to make her gasp. Her nipples peaked and her hips swayed to the rhythm of the dance floor's music, grinding against him as her heartbeat raced.

"Do you know what's my favorite?" he purred into her mouth.

Her fingers wound into his hair, pulling him closer until his scent surrounded her. "Do you really want me to guess?"

His erect cock was flush with the top of her thighs and she rubbed her clit through her pants along his shaft, loving the friction.

Danny ran his tongue up the side of her neck. "I really don't."

She chuckled and kissed him deeply, pulling down the neck of his shirt to caress the top of his chest. "Then, my sweet, sexy love, what is your favorite?"

"Come see." He grabbed her hand and ran with her through the door, not stopping until they were outside among the trees.

Danny gathered her against his side so they were both leaning against the trunk of an oak tree. The night smelled sweet, the honeysuckle and roses from the garden overlaying the lusher smells of earth, moss, and leaves. Robin relaxed against the bark, the first time she'd taken Danny to see the vultrich nests as well as all those weekends with her parents all layering on top of one another.

"So, are you going to tell me your favorite?" she asked, turning to him. The moonlight hit his face in harsh relief, making his eyes almost glow with luminance and his skin even more smooth and kissable. She'd been so distracted: by the vultriches, by taking down Nia, with setting up the new safe space for the birds and the freed vampires to really think about how perfect her lover was. Danny was more than she'd ever dreamed was possible: funny, loyal, fun, and curious. He ran a finger down the side of her cheek and she bit her lip. He was also pants-wettingly hot.

Danny chuckled. "Well, when I dragged you out here, I had this whole speech planned. I was going to tell you that my favorite thing is you, and that you've brought me more joy in these last months together than in the hundreds of years I lived previously."

His finger caressed from her chin down along her neck to play with the edge of her button-down shirt, teasing her collarbone right inside the fabric. "And I was going to tell you that everything about you is amazing, from your protectiveness, to your daring, to your bravery, to the way your mouth wrinkles when you're annoyed with me and want me to get to the point."

Robin laughed, relaxing her mouth from where she'd been biting the inside of her cheek. Excitement bubbled in the pit of her stomach.

"And I had this whole thing where I was going to talk about everything you told me about your parents, and how nature never seemed to hold any interest to me until you showed me how to look at everything in here with love. And that love for the world is something that I never quite grasped, for all my wandering, until I met you."

He got down on one knee and Robin felt tears form in her eyes.

"Wherever you are is my home, whether it is here or

centuries from now when we want to see how much the world has changed."

She hiccupped, happy sobs building in her chest. "So, you were going to say all that, huh?"

He smiled. "Yeah, but then I thought the better of it." He laughed, pulling a ring from his pocket, the rock inside the classic, gold band: black with veins of green like a vultrich's wing. "I love you more than anything else in this world, and I want to spend every day at your side."

"Yes!" Robin cried, so loud the vultrich down below in the valley called out in response, squawking and running as they tried to find the source of the sound.

"And now we run," Robin said, grabbing his hand.

"Always."

And she smiled as they sprinted back to the house. She knew she'd be running hand in hand with him forever.

Want to know more about Danny's past sireling? Check out what happens to the man he turned in the next installment of Royal Blood: The Vampire's Escape.

THE VAMPIRE'S CHOICE

V alerie Dal ground her teeth as she resisted glancing at her watch for the third time in the past five minutes. The last thing she needed was a last-minute meeting at the palace when she had so much other urgent work to get done. An unprecedented amount of rain was causing major delays on the construction of her latest housing complex, and the stress was starting to get to her. The construction sites were so inundated, even the most grizzled of her crew refused to risk coming to work.

Valerie sighed. Her crews were right, of course, and she wouldn't force for them to work in what was commonly being referred to as a 'monsoon'. But still, Valerie wanted to push forward. This undertaking was much more personal than she'd ever let on.

Her phone buzzed. *Another* pissed-off text from her foreman wanting to know when they'd be able reschedule the meeting with the local coven. Valerie responded that she'd reach out to them as soon as she could, quietly seething as she entered the conference room that was increasingly feeling like a cage.

If the witches pull out of this deal, Christopher is going to owe me. Big time. Being the sireling of the king of the vampires had to have *some* perks. Valerie just needed a little magic to keep moving forward with construction. Their spellwork could maintain an entire hotel downtown made of ice in a climate that rarely dipped below 60 degrees. They could definitely help Valerie manage a little rain. It was even for a good cause: the palace had been harboring victims of *hortari* abuse for months and they were running out of room. For far too many sirelings, inside the castle's walls was the only place they could be safe from their abusive sires. But even the castle had its limits, and Valerie needed to offer them more options.

Valerie took a moment to be grateful her vampire sire--and her king--had called all of his sirelings to the castle that afternoon by request, and not by command.

Valerie bit her lip, concentrating on hiding her impatience. She found a chair near the back of the long, stone room her sire, Christopher, had turned into a conference space. The king and his queen had been doing a lot of redecorating since they took the palace over from his evil brother, Rhys, two years ago. Christopher's brother, and his father before him, had had no use for communal spaces to make collaborative decisions. Their management style tended to involve thick, stone walls and sturdy chains. Christopher was a different kind of leader, one who valued a diversity of opinions and viewpoints before making decisions.

Even if that meant constant meetings for his inner circle.

"You could at least *pretend* to be happy to see us," Valerie's sireling sister Margot said, nudging Valerie with her elbow as she settled into the chair next to hers. "It's been months since we last saw you." Margot studied Valerie's face, her expression growing more concerned the longer she looked at her. Valerie fought the need to squirm in her chair under Margot's penetrating gaze. "You look in need of about a dozen stiff drinks and a pair of muscled masseurs, sweets."

Valerie forced a smile for her sister. The dark-skinned beauty was dressed in a bespoke, black pant suit with enormous beaded jewelry that Valerie guessed was probably designed for Margot by some as-yet-unknown-genius artist Margot was promoting at her art gallery.

Margot threw an arm over Valerie's shoulders, and Valerie fought the urge to lean into her sister's support. It would be so easy to pretend she deserved her sister's unconditional love, to just relax and act like everything was normal. But comfort was for those who deserved it.

"I'm okay," Valerie lied. "I've just got a lot going on. I don't think you guys even really *need* me for this, do you?" Valerie stood to leave.

Margot's elegant eyebrow rose high in an unspoken response and Valerie slumped back into her chair. Christopher wouldn't have asked her there if he didn't need her.

A jolly male voice spoke from the door, "Trying to leave us already?"

"It's not that," Valerie said to her sireling brother, Danny, as he entered, followed closely by his wife, Robin. They were both dressed in black leather that hugged their figures like second skins. Danny's vest opened down the front showing far more skin than Valerie needed to see from a man she considered her brother, and Robin's bustier lifted her breasts with compelling definition out of her lace top. They looked every inch the co-owners of a vampire pleasure palace, and Valerie took a second to push down her envy at the casual confidence they exuded with every step.

"Danny, give her a break," her other sireling brother, Ben, called out from down the table. "I'd rather be in my lab than sitting around discussing *policy*." He gave an exaggerated shudder. His fiancé, Lauren, sitting next to him, giggled and leaned into him. She whispered something into his ear and he chuckled, pulling her closer.

Valerie looked away from the newest couple. Valerie didn't resent her siblings' long-awaited joy, but it sometimes hurt to look at what she would never allow herself to have.

Christopher and Alice entered last. Even after two years together, the king and queen of the vampires couldn't keep their hands off each other.

As was Christopher's way, he didn't sit at the head of the table, instead sitting closer to the middle so that his sirelings were spread out on either side of him. Margot tensed next to Valerie, and she followed Margot's concerned gaze to Christopher's hand holding Alice's on top of the table. A new worry prickled in Valerie's chest. Usually Alice and Christopher held hands lazily, one occasionally stroking the palm of the other. Today, their grips were ironclad, both their knuckles white from clenching.

"Thank you all for coming today. I know you all have other duties that require your attention, so I appreciate your time." Christopher's voice had all its familiar steadiness, but Valerie caught Danny, Ben, and Margot out of the corner of her eye, all leaning toward him. They'd all known Christopher long enough to hear the tension under his calm words.

"I've gathered you all here because we need to devise a permanent solution to a problem which has plagued vampires since our inception. The *hortari*."

"What?" Valerie said, the word escaping her lips in shock. Murmurs of surprise and confusion broke out around the table. The *hortari* was a bane to all vampires, built into their very natures. Anyone who sired a vampire had complete control over whomever they sired. That had always been the way. A sire's voice was an irresistible instrument, which Valerie knew all too well, to her eternal shame. The only example in living memory of a vampire breaking free of the *hortari* was sitting at their table: Alice, Christopher's wife.

Christopher continued. "Since we took power, the court has been bombarded with reports of sires who abuse their control and force their sirelings to commit actions against their will. We have sheltered those few who found ways to report the abuse." He nodded to Valerie. "And investigated their claims, bringing abusive sires to justice." He nodded to Danny, Christopher's lead investigator. "Everyone at this table knows of the horrors of *hortari* abuses, and sought to stop it in whatever way they could."

At the end of the table, Lauren and Ben snuggled close together. Valerie had never heard the full story about what Lauren had been forced to do, but Valerie *did* know that Lauren's sire was buried deep in the castle dungeons, unable to reach her again.

Christopher leaned forward in his chair, his eyes alight with passion. "But it's not enough. There are many vampires who follow the lead set by my brother and father and do whatever they want with the vampires they sire. We thought we would be able to teach more vampires how to break the *hortari*, but..." He looked over at Alice, gesturing for her to jump in.

"We've had no success," Alice said. "I've worked with dozens of vamps, read through thousands of years of lore, and nothing is working. We don't really know how I managed to break my *hortari* bond with Christopher, and it's proving impossible to teach."

Valerie sat forward in her chair. The vampire queen sounded exhausted, and dark shadows haunted her eyes. More than a hundred vampires had escaped their sires in the two years since Christopher had become king. Valerie knew many of the vampires under Christopher's protection from working alongside them to build their new homes. She'd bonded with these people, listened to their stories and dreams for the future. They all looked up to Alice as someone who would help break them all free. If *Alice* was losing hope of a cure... Valerie shook her head. There had to be a way.

Alice pressed her palms hard into the surface of the

table. "In my research, I came across a few interesting theories about the *hortari*. One in particular has promise. What if it isn't just hard coded into our nature? What if it's a curse, or a spell, something that can be undone?"

All around the table, Valerie and the others shifted in their seats. Valerie's head spun. The *hortari* was as much part of being a vampire as drinking blood, shying away from sunlight, and being invincible to everything except fire and beheading.

"But that's impossible--" Valerie started to say.

"Perhaps," Alice said. She reached down into the briefcase at her side and pulled out four thick file folders. "I've come across four different contacts that back up this theory. A few have even reached out to the previous kings, asking for help to break the *hortari* for good." She distributed the folders down the table, one to Ben and Lauren, one to Danny and Robin, one to Margot, and one to Valerie.

Valerie flipped open the inch-thick folder to the profile of a vampire, Mickey Shive, with a blurred, black and white photo of a bearded man in his thirties with long, dirty hair dressed in rags. He looked like he was one aluminum foil hat away from standing on a corner with a "The End is Nigh" sign.

"Seriously?" Valerie asked.

The folder was stuffed thick with official records, printed emails from the last few years, and a stack of handwritten letters going back centuries, all asking for either Christopher or one of his sire line to have an audience with him because Mickey had made an "existence-changing" discovery regarding the *hortari* and needed their help.

"They may look a little crackpot on the surface, but there's a chance that their ideas have *some* credence," Alice said. "We owe it to the vampires we govern--and to any vampires in the future--to at least hear these people out. It will all be worth it if there's a way that we can destroy the *hortari*."

"Any objections?" Christopher asked.

Everybody shook their head, the couples already murmuring plans together as they leafed through their files. Christopher tapped the table to end the meeting, and his family scrambled to their feet.

Valerie closed her file with a snap, her mind whirling with a dozen contradicting thoughts at once. Everybody knew that ending the *hortari* was impossible. It was just how vampires were made.

And yet...

"What do you think?" Margot leaned in close to Valerie as they walked out the door. "Has Christopher finally lost it?"

Valerie shook her head. "We've all lived long enough to know that the world is a complicated place. What if the *hortari* really is a spell? It's not like any other supernaturals have our kind of restraints."

Margot held up her file. "The person I'm going to talk to was last seen in 1867, and her photo's got crazy eyes that even sepia can't soften. Her address is *literally* an insane asylum. If this is considered one of the more reliable leads, I hate to see what the unreliable ones look like."

Indistinct female and male voices trickled down from upstairs. Above was one of the floors Valerie had hastily renovated last month into residences for the stream of *hortari* victims seeking sanctuary. More came in every day as word spread that there was a safe space for them to go.

Valerie shrugged, not trusting her voice to match Margot's disinterested tone. Valerie wanted Alice to be right.

She wanted it to be true so bad, the desire was like a weight in her chest that grew with every step. If they could stop the *hortari* for good... If Valerie could be the one to help make everything right... then perhaps she could begin to forgive herself.

For a second, Valerie felt like she was back in her old office. The memory was as vivid as if she'd awoken back there from a nap. The numbers on her accounting ledgers swam in front of her tired eyes, her staff's quills tapped against the vellum pages. And there was her sireling, Nolan, still alive, smiling down at her, telling her that he just had a few more hours of work to do before he would head to bed. Valerie tensed as she recalled the casual words she'd tossed at him as she walked out the door. And the chilling consequences.

Valerie shook her head, pushing away the memory, and took a deep breath of the night air. The rain which was making soup of her construction site wasn't as bad here. She said her quick goodbyes to her family, pulled up Mickey Shive's address, and hurried toward her car. Mickey's house was a dot in the middle of nowhere, hidden in the mountains, disconnected from civilization.

If there was even the smallest chance that she could stop the *hortari* from harming anyone ever again, she had to try. She owed it to all those seeking asylum at the castle--and to Nolan, burned to death all those centuries ago because of a slip of her tongue--to give it her all.

A few quick texts to her assistant lined up Valerie's construction foreman to take the meeting with the covens. Even if all this trip ended up amounting to was a fool's errand, there wasn't any reason to piss off the witches any further.

. . .

THE HOURS DISAPPEARED under the wheels of Valerie's car as she drove out of the city and onto the single-lane highways toward the last known address of Mickey Shive. She blasted metal music to drown out her thoughts.

Three hours in, text messages from the others started to trickle in.

"Mine's been dead for five years," came the first group text from Danny. "Beheaded by his sirelings after he forced them to lie for centuries that they'd broken the *hortari*."

Valerie turned up the volume and screamed aloud with the music.

The next text came in an hour later from Ben. His lead's sirelings had broken their *hortari* bonds, but didn't know how they'd done it. Ben promised to escort them to the castle to consult with Alice about how she could help duplicate their experience, but it seemed like they weren't any closer to getting rid of the *hortari*.

Four hours turned to six as Valerie drove down the highway, every mile taking her further away from the piles of work she needed to get done back home, and closer to what looked to be a crazy loon.

When she pulled over for a break to drink some blood and stretch her legs, she glanced through his file. Mickey Shive's brief profile did nothing to boost her confidence. Her lip curled when she read who his sire was: Rhys himself. Rhys and Christopher might be brothers sired by the same vampire, but from the moment they were turned, they'd taken to their powers very differently. While Christopher chose his sirelings based on how they could improve the world, and treated them with kindness and respect, Rhys had been a twisted dictator from the beginning. His sirelings tended to be the biggest, baddest minions he could find, neckless meatheads who in turn abused their own sirelings. Mickey had been one of Rhys's first turned, over a millennia ago. The file didn't say anything about what he'd done to get Rhys's attention, but one of the first acts Rhys forced Mickey to do under *hortari* command was to murder his own wife.

A *hortari* victim, one of the Rhys's first if the file was correct. *No wonder he lives out in the middle of nowhere. Poor guy. Nobody deserves that.* Mickey had written letter after letter begging for a member of Christopher's sire line to come meet with him to talk about his discovery regarding the *hortari.* Mickey had escaped from Rhys long before Rhys's rise to power, and spent the last few centuries living in isolation.

Valerie frowned. He apparently paid the bills by working as a remote customer service operative for an IT company. Considering Mickey's age, the fact that he worked a day job at all gave Valerie pause. Most of the vampires she knew worked because they had careers or passions they enjoyed, not because they needed the money. Live long enough and investments eventually paid off, skills grew from apprentice to master-level, and trinkets bought in your youth for pennies were eventually worth millions as antiques. Mickey had to be either wasteful, insane, or broken to be at the point he needed to take a job like that.

Mickey's shack of a home didn't make her feel any better. She'd had to park a few miles away and hike the rest of the way to the house, her GPS her only guide through the unmarked forests. She double-checked the coordinates twice as she approached. Only the well-maintained satellite dish installed next to the house gave any suggestion that anyone lived within the four leaning walls and sagging roof. The structure was ridden with holes, making life hellish for a vampire during the daytime when direct sunlight would stream through, and the roof looked one good wind-storm away from flying off entirely.

Her phone beeped. Margot's lead was a no-go as well. Her vampire was certifiably insane and, in addition to claiming to know the secret of how to destroy the *hortari*, also claimed to have frequent conversations directly with the sun.

Which meant Mickey Shive was their last chance.

Valerie took a deep breath, marshalled her hopes, and called out the greeting of every horror movie protagonist when they first encounter the lunatic inside a crazy hut in the woods.

"Hello?"

∾

THE WOMAN on the phone was one second away from screaming. Mickey recognized the tone well enough he could reliably count down to the explosion.

"Hello? Are you even *listening* to me?"

Mickey knew he should say something to the distraught customer who hadn't figured out her printer wasn't plugged in, but he was having trouble getting a word in edgewise. "Have you tried turning off your computer and turning it back on again?"

His front door creaked, he looked up, and forgot the phone conversation completely. The telephone hung limp in Mickey's hand as he stared at the vision in his doorway.

"Are you Mickey? Mickey Shive? I'm here on behalf of the king." The woman crossed her arms and pursed her lips as she looked him over.

He'd spent decades researching the Dal family, hoping that somebody would finally listen to his pleas. Valerie Dal was more beautiful than her pictures: Latina, petite but strong, her dark brown hair cascading over her perfect amber shoulders. Even in jeans and a long-sleeved t-shirt, her confidence radiated "royalty".

"Yes, I'm..." Mickey swallowed hard. "That's me. I'm here." He pulled the phone closer to his mouth. "Thank you for calling Technical Solutions, all of our operators are currently busy. Please call back another time. Thank you." He slammed his phone down onto the receiver, rattling the pens and empty teacups on his desk.

"I'm Valerie Dal." She approached, holding out her hand for him to shake.

"I know. I'm Mickey. Mickey Shive." Mickey shook her hand, shocked at how natural human contact felt even after all these years. *Squeeze, lift and fall, lift and fall.* He reminded himself how the gesture worked. Mickey built up speed as the memory of the motion came back to him, shaking Valerie's hand with unbridled enthusiasm.

"Okay, that's probably enough." Valerie pulled her hand out of his grip and stepped back. "I saw your letters. You have some information about the *hortari*?"

"Yes!" Mickey jumped out of his chair. "I'm so happy to finally get a response. You have no idea what it's been like." He pulled on a jacket and moved towards the door. "Shall we?"

"Mr. Shive, I'd like to hear what you have to say before following you out into the woods." Valerie's arched eyebrow struck Mickey with unexpected force.

I must look like a maniac right now. Mickey ran his hand through his beard, catching his fingers on tangles, bits of leaves, and the key to his front door, which he had tied in there to keep himself from forgetting it. *I forgot that was in there*, he mused.

"I've been petitioning your sire for ages now. Even got kicked out of the palace a few times last year. Well...dragged out." He rubbed his shoulder at the painful memory. To be fair, he *had* been yelling pretty loudly. "I know how to break the *hortari*. It's a spell. A curse, really. Nobody realized it. It's all some kind of test, stretching over thousands of years, that we've been failing at every day for as long as anyone can remember." He bit his lip. How many times had he practiced explaining this to someone? Thousands of times? Millions? But now, with those amazing brown eyes looking at him, all he could do was spout gibberish. "You have to believe me. I found the source. It's just there." He pointed out the door. Her eyes followed his fingers to look at the woods, and she shifted her weight.

"The queen has a similar theory." She shook her head. "I can't believe I'm doing this. Fine. Where are we going?" Valerie followed Mickey out the door. "My car is parked down by the road."

"We won't be needing that." Mickey nodded up the mountain. "We're going up. The source of the *hortari* is up there."

"And you live next to it?" The skepticism had reappeared on her face.

"It was very hard to find." Mickey heard the defensiveness in his voice and grabbed the duffle bag of supplies he always kept ready by the door for whenever he headed up to the *hortari* cave. The trail was clear and well-traveled from years following the same path. "After so many decades of failing to find it, once I did, here seemed as good a place as any to call home." He didn't look back at the sagging shack as he marched upward. If everything went according to plan, he would never have to see its rotting walls ever again.

Mickey listened to the crack of twigs and rocks under

Valerie's feet behind him. She stayed close at his heels, near enough the breeze blew her scent toward him. She used some kind of flowery shampoo that reminded him of a healthier life he hadn't lived in hundreds of years. Nipping at those memories were the ones he forced himself to never think about. His wife's screams. The feeling of her blood under his fingernails. He increased the pace, concentrating on jumping over the rocks and branches along the nearly-vertical path up the mountain.

"Tell me more about this theory of yours." Valerie's voice startled Mickey so badly, he almost lost his grip on the boulder in front of him. A tumble down three hundred feet of cliff would definitely derail their progress. He took a deep breath, forcing his racing heart to calm.

"When the gods created the first vampires, around two-hundred-thousand years ago, they also created something else. Some of the stories call it a curse, some a necessity, others described it as the price we pay for our immortality."

"The *hortari*." Valerie ducked under a tree branch, her voice tight.

"Yes. It's been with us from the very beginning. The *hortari* is a very powerful spell, forged into a physical object, a statue. The stories say the gods hid the source of the *hortari* deep within the earth, and used their power to protect it from all but the worthy. Many tried to get through, but none were successful and eventually vampires stopped trying. Eventually, the source of the *hortari* was forgotten, and the gods' hiding spot was lost to history. Until I found it." For a second, he was overwhelmed by the memory of finding the ancient text which proved him right; Mickey lost his step and tripped over a raised tree root. He plunged towards the rocky ground, stopped midair by a hand grasping the back of his jacket.

"Be careful." Valerie released her grip on his jacket and Mickey found his footing. She turned her head to the side, her eyes searching Mickey's face. "You think you've located the source of the *hortari*. And it's a statue. Created by the gods." Each short sentence sounded more doubtful than the next. "So why didn't you just end the *hortari* when you found it?"

"If I could have done it on my own, this nightmare would have ended years ago." Mickey sighed. *Do I really have to go over this again?* "I need a member of the Dal family to get near it." *I've written the king thousands of times.* "The *hortari* is hidden in a cave that will only open at the touch of blood from the lines of two brothers at war. Your sire is Christopher and mine is..." Mickey took a deep breath. "My sire is *Rhys*." He spat the word. "I need one of your line to open the cave."

"This sounds like another of Rhys's long cons to get revenge on Christopher. How can I trust that you're not working for your sire?" She didn't seem surprised to hear about his sire, Mickey observed with a sinking heart. He was surprised she agreed to come anywhere near him. *Fucking Rhys.*

"Do you think *you* could hate Rhys more than one of his sirelings?" Mickey kicked at a rock, and watched it roll down the side of the mountain to crash into a lake hundreds of feet below. "Rhys would murder his sirelings and *laugh*." Mickey spat. He leaned against a tree, the rough bark digging into his hand. "You've *heard* the tales of Rhys's horrors, probably saw some when you fought him with your sire." He turned back towards the trail, stomping up the mountain. "I've *lived* it."

Valerie's soft footsteps followed him as they trekked over boulders and through the trees, following the path he'd taken a hundred times before. He hated how much it still wounded him to be tied to Rhys, how he could still lose control at the mere mention of the man's name. So long as Rhys's bond filled Mickey's blood, he would never be free of him. *Unless I can break the* hortari.

The sun had started to rise, and the first rays of light stinging his skin. "We're almost there, don't worry." He turned to reassure Valerie.

Valerie wrapped her scarf over her head, protecting her exposed skin from the sun. "I'm sorry if I was insensitive before, about Rhys." She gave a tiny smile, the first Mickey had spotted from her. It lit up her face in such a burst of unexpected beauty he almost fell again. "I can be kind of an asshole sometimes."

"I'm an asshole every day." Mickey grinned in response. "I really appreciate your trust: coming here, despite who my sire is." *Although if she knew what I've done, she would probably throw me off this mountain.* "It's been a long time since somebody took a risk on my word." He grasped a rock ledge overhead, and pulled himself up with all of his strength. "It means a lot."

With a single leap, Valerie joined him on the stone ledge on the side of the mountain that served as the cave's entrance.

Her smile was grim. "It'll mean a hell of a lot more if we can destroy the *hortari.*"

VALERIE EYED the cave wall in front of them. From far away, the dip in the rock had looked like just another crag of the mountain, but closer up, the alcove was too smooth, created with too much precision to be natural. An archway made of fist-sized rocks was built right against the mountain, a clear sign of 'enter here', if ever she'd seen one. The flat stone inside the archway looked no different than the stones around it, but it buzzed with magic.

Mickey handed her a pocket knife. "Here. You just need to get a drop of blood on this doorway." He gestured at the smooth stone wall in front of them.

Valerie eyed her companion, then the knife. "You want me to...what now?" She didn't know *too* much about magic, but spells involving blood were usually pretty nasty.

"I'll go first." He vibrated with impatience.

Valerie stared. Her first impression of Mickey had evolved during their trek through the wilderness: from probable loon to uncoordinated obsessive. Even with the beard that looked like it hadn't been combed since the Civil War, he had a quality of earnestness about him that was almost charming.

He pressed the knife into the pad of his smallest finger and smeared the blood on the wall, then held it out to her with an expression of desperation. She studied him and the stones. The hope that beat at her chest when Alice first presented her theory had only gotten stronger as they hiked up the mountain. But could redemption really be as easy as breaking a statue?

She shook her head at his offered knife, and bit a small cut along her finger and rubbed her blood next to Mickey's crimson mark. The stones making up the archway began to spin, boring deeper and deeper into the mountain. Valerie jumped back. The buzz of magic from the stones increased a hundredfold, like the mountain was waking up. Words appeared on the entrance to the caves, flashing ancient characters and going through a dozen languages, some Valerie recognized and some she didn't, before landing on English.

THE BLOOD OF TWO WARRING FAMILIES IS ACCEPTED.

"Whoa," Valerie said, glancing at Mickey. His grin, even partially hidden by his beard, was so wide it transformed his face. New words appeared below the first, gold and floating.

YOUR CURSE IS HERE.

Valerie's breath caught in her chest. *It's real.*

"I knew it!" Mickey shouted. He raised his fists in the air, punching toward the sky. "After all those years, I *knew* it!"

New text appeared.

THREE DEADLY CHALLENGES MUST BE OVERCOME:

ONE OF STRENGTH,

ONE OF FORTITUDE,

AND ONE OF SACRIFICE.

Valerie stared at the words. *Deadly challenges? Sacrifice?*

"What do you know about these challenges?" Valerie asked Mickey, not taking her eyes away from the glowing words on the wall.

"Only that nobody's who's tried this before has ever returned." Valerie had expected Mickey to sound scared, but he spoke with a hard determination that boosted her esteem of him by several notches.

The sounds of metal sliding against stone clanged from inside the mountain, and the smooth stone wall ahead of them became filled with darkness. Glowing words appeared to frame the opening.

BEWARE ALL THOSE WHO ENTER.

FREEDOM IS NEVER WITHOUT COST.

AFTER A FAILURE, THIS PATH WILL NOT OPEN FOR ONE HUNDRED YEARS.

Mickey jumped forward toward the dark hole in the wall

and Valerie grabbed his arm. "What are you doing?" she asked.

"The way to break the *hortari* is in there." He pointed toward the door. She strengthened her grip on his arm. "Let me go!"

"No. I am a member of the royal family. It's my responsibility to save our people. You've done your job, finding this place. Now, you should go back to safety. There's no reason why both of us should sacrifice ourselves for this. Those warning signs are pretty clear. This is a one-way trip." Valerie didn't want to die, but after so many centuries of trying to make restitution for a crime that could never be absolved, there was nothing that was going to hold her back.

Mickey fought against her grip. "Everything I have to live for is on the other side of this door. You can't stop me from doing this." She recognized the desperation in his voice as a mirror of her own. "This test was designed for opposing sire lines to work together. This needed both of us to get in; it'll probably take both of us to succeed."

Valerie wasn't convinced how much help a crazy IT consultant was going to be against a magical challenge designed by the gods, but he had a point.

"Fine, but just wait one second." She pulled out her phone. "We need to do this smart." If she wasn't coming back, then Christopher and the other royal sirelings needed to be told. She sent a quick group text to her family.

Track this phone for my location. Shive found the entrance to ancient source of hortari *curse. Going in to break it now. If I don't return, finish the construction I started. I love you all.*

Mickey looked like he was about to explode by the time she hit send and placed the phone in a small alcove in the rock, confirming it had enough signal that her family would be able to track it.

Valerie grabbed his hand, and they ran together through the darkened door before she had a chance to think about how her family would react to that text. The darkness passed over her skin like ice filled with lightning. Freezing magic crackled and pulsed along her skin sending up goosebumps. *If I don't survive this cave, my family is going to kill me.*

Mickey's hand against her palm was the only warmth as the freezing darkness stretched in front of them. Then it disappeared. She stumbled out into an enormous room that appeared all around them. She swore as she caught her balance, scanning the area quickly.

There was no sign of a door behind them; they stood a good twenty feet into the room like they'd been dropped into it from nowhere. Mickey was breathing fast next to her, his eyes also scanning the hundred-foot ceilings that seemed to be carved directly into the mountain, with massive stalactites hanging from the ceiling like jaws about to crunch down on them. Magical orbs floated close to the ceiling, dodging the spikes, illuminating the entire cavern with a day-like brightness that didn't burn their vampiric skin.

The room was a good fifty yards across, with immaculate black and white tiles running the length of the room, and a wooden door on the opposite wall the only break in the stone. The air pulsed with magic, like a heavy fog, waiting and watching.

"The test of strength?" Mickey whispered, his tone puzzled.

Glowing words appeared in the air in front of them.

BE FLIGHT OF FOOT.

FREEDOM AWAITS.

The golden words disappeared and Valerie looked around. "That was helpful." She smirked.

The room was empty. What was there to challenge them? She took a step forward and jumped back as a long-handled scythe whooshed up from the floor and sliced level with her neck.

"Holy shit!" she cursed. All around them, the room surged to life, dozens of scythes whipping up from the ground, slashing at the air, and then coming up again. She ducked, screaming out a warning to Mickey as he stumbled out of the way of a twirling blade. She dove and spun, trying to make out a pattern in the madness. White squares, black squares, no matter how she stepped, the blades still came spinning out and around. Each scythe spun up in a predictable beat, but they weren't synchronized, and waiting to assess the beat of the blade in front of her meant death from the one next to her.

Pain spiked in her shoulder and she jumped out of the way of the scythe that had just missed her neck by inches. Fury blazed along her skin. She was *not* going to die barely making it ten steps into the first challenge. Too much was at stake.

Mickey screamed. He'd been cut badly, a long ribbon of blood along his thigh staining through his pant. He struggled forward, limping on his good leg and barely dodging out of the way of the spinning blades around him.

Movement flashed in the corner of Valerie's eye and, instead of ducking away, she bent and rammed her shoulder forward, breaking the wooden handle of the scythe slicing down at her. She snatched the broken weapon out of the air before it disappeared back into the floor. The weight of the metal blade felt good in her hand, the edge curved like the scimitars she used to wield back when she was much younger.

A scythe came at her and she jumped toward it, slicing

forward with her own blade and chopping the wooden handle in half so the spinning staff continued it's rotating along the floor, but without its deadly blade on the top.

"Yes!" She screamed, leaping ahead toward Mickey's limping figure to behead one scythe after another, leaving a clear and empty trail behind her. She reached Mickey's side, looping his arm around her and taking on his weight. Though the blood seeping through his pant leg stank with fear, Mickey's face was determined.

"We're gonna make it!" she cried, lopping off another scythe-head, pulling him toward the door at the opposite end of the room, chopping them their path. "We're already halfway there."

"Go on! I'm just holding you back," Mickey said.

"Don't you--" She didn't have time to finish when a popping sound, and then a flame burst shot up from the floor in front of their feet. Mickey pulled her backward just in time, the heat stinging her nostrils.

Fire geysers spurted out in front of them at random intervals, a popping sound the only warning before the flames burst up in a twenty-foot column.

Fire and beheading, the only two forces which could kill a vampire, and they were *surrounded* by them.

"Can you run?" Valerie asked Mickey.

He tested his weight on his cut leg. "I'm going to have to," he said through gritted teeth.

"Then run!" It took three steps before she realized he wasn't going to keep up. The cut was already healing-- vampires healed fast--but it had sliced through too many muscles in his thigh. Grabbing hold of his arm, she propped up his bad side with her weight and sprinted forward, their sides pressed together so tightly she could feel his rapid pulse against her rib cage.

A popping sound went off to her right and she dragged him out of the way of another column of fire. Twenty feet remained, and hissing sounded from above their heads. Valerie pushed Mickey to the ground, and they rolled towards the exit together as fireballs began to rain down on top of them, shooting from the tips of the stalactites.

"Flaming tits!" Mickey cursed, and Valerie felt a kind of giddy glee as she laughed and pulled him to their feet. This place was utterly insane. She held the broken scythe blade above her head like a shield and ran them forward.

She didn't wait to use the doorknob, just kicked the door with her full strength, and it flew off its hinges into a darkened corridor beyond.

"Go!" She pushed him through, jumping out of the way of one last scythe that slashed up at her feet. She dove down to the flagstones of the hallway in front of them, clutching her blade with her.

The door behind her closed up into a solid wall, blocking any hope of return.

Mickey planted his palms on his knees and bent double, panting hard. "I should have been training," he wheezed. He examined the wound on his leg. It was already looking better, but it screamed for attention that he didn't have time to give. He glanced down and winced. One of the scythe swings had taken off a huge chunk of beard, leaving a rather sobering cut that was far too close to his neck and chest.

Valerie strode confidently ahead of him, not a single hair out of place. She twirled her wicked-looking scythe easily in her hands, a princess in perpetual motion.

"Flaming tits? Seriously?" Her lips cracked in a wry smile.

Mickey shrugged. "It's an expression."

She looked like she was debating screaming or laughing, deciding on a shrug. "You okay to walk?"

He nodded, forced his spine straight, and pulled his head high. He was *not* going to be a burden during the next challenges. He'd labored for far too many centuries to give up now.

She started walking down the narrow, stone-lined corridor, and Mickey hurried to catch up.

The corridor curved and Mickey tensed, waiting for the next deadly surprise to jump out at them. The corridor opened up into a *forest*, an actual *forest*, complete with cypress and oak trees and gray Spanish moss hanging from the branches like tangled beards, all neatly nestled inside an enormous cavern. It was as if the vegetation from the side of the mountain had simply decided to move indoors, photosynthesis be damned. The trees, moss, even some of the mushrooms Mickey recognized from the forest surrounding his home.

"Holy crap." Valerie stood looking up at the grey rock ceiling extending beyond their line of sight. An enormous ball of light floated in the air high above them, illuminating the entire space. She closed her eyes and grinned, pushing up her shirt sleeves and holding out her bare arms like she was letting the rays seep through her skin. The light highlighted tiny freckles on her nose that Mickey hadn't noticed before.

"This doesn't seem like a test of fortitude." Mickey cautiously stepped out of the shade of the trees. He braced himself for the usual pain of sunlight, squinting as he prepared to jump back to safety. The light was warm and comforting as it danced over his pale skin. There was no pain; no weakness coursed through his body.

"What's happening?" He asked.

"It's a magic cave." Valerie grinned. "It must be a magical sun." She ran her fingers along the bark of a nearby tree. "Can't very well have all this greenery without some light." She looked around "I don't think this is the next test. Shouldn't there be those glowing instructions or something?"

Mickey shrugged. "It's impossible to know for sure. If we survive, though, we should totally come back here and open a vampire resort"

Mickey stopped short. *If we survive*. He heard his own words and remembered: whether or not they succeeded, they were not going to leave this place. He'd spent so many years researching and dreaming about ending the *hortari*, he couldn't afford to delude himself now. There would be no happy ending, no exciting new enterprises with Valerie by his side.

Valerie cleared her throat. "The trees get pretty thick up ahead. Are you sure your leg is okay to go on?" She placed her hand on his arm, gently.

Gods, I hope Valerie makes it out alive. Mickey gave her a nod and headed forward along the neatly-maintained path in front of them. *Valerie will get through this,* he promised himself, even though he knew it was a lie. *She has to.*

"So, your file said you worked in customer service for an IT company," Valerie said.

Mickey cleared his throat. "Yeah, *hortari* research doesn't pay the bills, surprisingly enough." He chose not to mention he'd picked a job which was also the worst punishment he could think of. "Trips to hidden monasteries, bribes to museum guards, and first editions of books don't come cheap. I'm lucky to be able to afford my shack, and I built that by hand."

"That's--" Valerie stopped in her tracks, her eyes scanning the area.

"What's wrong?" Mickey asked. The trees opened up ahead to surround a pool of dark water with a gorgeous, frothing waterfall falling into it. Light sparkled off the edges of the water as still and flat as a mirror.

"We passed this waterfall ten minutes ago." Valerie chewed her lower lip.

"Maybe the gods just weren't very creative when they made this place. Did you ever watch cartoons from the last few decades? They have the same hand-drawn background repeat over and over again."

Valerie threw Mickey a skeptical look. "I don't think that's what's happening here." She hefted her blade over her shoulder and took a mighty swing into one of the trees, leaving a deep cut in the bark.

"Hey! It's not the tree's fault we're lost," he said.

"The tree will be fine. I'm just marking this spot. If we circle around to the waterfall again, we can check this tree. If it's notched, we're going in circles. If not, then your cartoon theory might actually be right. How's your leg?"

Mickey felt along the gash on his thigh. His leg still felt a little stiff, but the wound itself had healed down to the soreness of an old bruise. "I'm good."

Valerie nodded and strode towards the path. "Keep up."

Mickey scrambled after her. Valerie's shoulders were tense.

"Something's bothering you beyond the loop thing. What's wrong?" he asked, jumping over a log to walk at her side.

She glanced at him, and then up at the magical sun

peeking through the leaves. "Just thinking." For a long moment Mickey thought she wasn't going to say anything else, but then she waved an arm around in a wide gesture that seemed to take in the cave, the magic forest, and the trials as a whole. "This place is beautiful. The trees, the waterfall. Even that room with all the scythes and fire was awe-inspiring in its own insane way. For gods who created the *hortari* as some kind of bloody trial, this place has a kind of..." She touched a low-hanging leaf with a finger. "Mercy about it. Everyone who has ever come here has died. And this is the last place they'll ever see." She shook her head. "But I'm glad that of all the leads my siblings followed, that I was the one who came to see you."

She sounded so sad, Mickey wanted to wrap his arms around her and never let go. For all the research Mickey had done about the Dal family, Valerie had always been the most mysterious. Her past was one long blank, her day-to-day utterly dedicated to helping *hortari* victims with no other hobby that he could find. She reminded him of himself, and the thought made him sorry.

"All of your siblings are following leads on how to break the *hortari*?" He asked, hoping to distract her from whatever train of thought had her frowning at the branches.

"Investigating your claim was kind of a last-ditch effort. The king has been fighting the *hortari* with everything he's got, and we're all sick of losing"

"I know I come off as a bit manic sometimes." Mickey smiled. "It means everything to me that Christopher is trying to fight it. Success or no."

Valerie sighed. "His queen, Alice, managed to break the *hortari* for herself. She said it felt like climbing out of an active volcano while carrying cinder blocks." Valerie ducked under a low tree branch. "We still haven't been able to figure out why she succeeded while so many others failed."

Mickey froze. *I could have been free at any time?* Mickey had heard legends of sirelings breaking the *hortari* bond, but he'd always dismissed them as fantasy. *But if hortari commands could really be resisted by a matter of will...* He shuddered. *It's my fault.*

"Are you okay?" Valerie placed her hand on his shoulder. Her warm, brown eyes scanned his face, her forehead furrowed with concern.

"I'm fine." Mickey managed to gasp. Liquid brushed his cheek, and he realized he was crying. "Is that the same waterfall?" Mickey pointed at the clearing up ahead, happy for the distraction. The waterfall and clear, wide pool stood like a glittering jewel through the trees. And there it was: the notch in the tree where Valerie had cut it

"We *are* going in circles! What the fuck?" Valerie hollered in frustration.

"Ooo." A voice tutted from the air above them. "Such language, your highness." A furry, orange man floated on top of a tree branch overhanging the path.

He couldn't have been more than three feet tall, dressed like an old-fashioned banker, complete with a bowler hat and walking stick. His hat was unable to contain the shock of orange hair that trailed down his human-looking face into the bushiest sideburns Mickey had ever seen. The cuffs of his sleeves were overwhelmed by fur.

"Oh gods, what now?" Valerie sighed. "Who are you?"

"Oh *gods*, indeed." The man chuckled for an uncomfortably long time. "I am Elvy, the keeper of these caves." He gave a short bow.

"That's great news!" Mickey attempted a bow in return,

only managing to trip over his own feet. "We're a bit lost. Could you direct us to the next trial?"

"This is a transition area of sorts. And these woods aren't done with you two yet." Elvy pointed to the blade in Valerie's hand. "Do you know how much work it is to upkeep that first test? Sure, it's all run on magic, but *somebody* has to make sure the scythes are sharpened and the fire blasters stay fueled." Elvy snapped his fingers, and Valerie's scythe appeared in his hands. He ran his finger along the blade, pulling back a bleeding digit. "Or would you *prefer* to be hacked to pieces by a dull blade? With strength like yours, it could take days for the job to be done."

"You'll excuse us for not thanking you for trying to kill us." Valerie rolled her eyes.

"The gods make the rules, I just enforce them." He jumped up into the air, bouncing from branch to branch in a rapid dance that made Mickey's head spin. "You two, well, mostly her highness," Elvy nodded at Valerie, "broke twelve of my scythes. Now I have to repair and reset them to perfection, which is a pain in my furry butt. You wrecked my day, so I'm going to ruin yours." The trees swayed as he spoke. "As punishment for destroying twelve scythes, your journey is delayed for twelve hours." He blinked out of sight.

"Now stay there and think about what you did." Elvy's disembodied voice added as the trees stilled.

Valerie frowned at the spot where Elvy had disappeared. "Wait here, and rest your leg. I need to check something." She took off down the path, running at top vampiric speed, so fast she was a blur against the verdant background. Mickey could hear her muttered curses coming from the direction she'd departed, until they suddenly stopped and her footsteps sounded on the other side of him.

"Terrific." Valerie strode over towards the lake, splashing

water on her face. "It really is a damn loop. There's no way out. We're stuck."

Mickey shrugged. "Only for twelve hours." The cool water seemed to call to him. They had the time. *When was the last time I showered?* He wasn't rightly sure. A breeze ruffled the leaves all around them, and Mickey got a good whiff of himself. "Oh, that's not good." He choked on his own stench. "I'm going to take a little bath, if you don't mind." Mickey made his way to the far end of the pond.

"By all means!" Valerie shouted after him, laughing. She sounded so relieved, Mickey blushed. *How bad have I smelled this whole time?*

He stripped down, slid into the water, and dove down to the pond's stone bottom. The submersion was silently peaceful. He scrubbed as best as he could, then surfaced, his long hair and beard plastered to his face, getting in his eyes and sticking to his mouth. *This has got to go.*

Mickey swam over to his clothes, pulling a pocket knife out of his jeans. He waited for the water to still enough to use as a mirror and slowly dragged the blade over his face, removing the beard he'd worn like a mask for all these years. *Ugh, this is what Valerie has been looking at all day? I really should apologize.* Once he was as clean-shaven as could manage with a pocketknife, he took his blade to his dark tangles, chopping off the inches he'd grown in his solitude.

The face looking up from the water's reflection was familiar, like an old friend he'd lost touch with. He smiled, and pulled his clothes on.

Valerie was sitting on the edge of the pond, gazing at the waterfall. Her pant legs were rolled up, and she kicked her feet absentmindedly in the shallow water. She looked magnificent in the light, a slight frown on her face.

Valerie Dal. It still amazed him she was here with him.

Every time he looked at her was a new revelation. Her nose was a little crooked, like it had been broken a few times and not healed right. It wouldn't surprise him. She was remarkably skilled as a warrior for someone who spent most of their time on construction sites. There was no way he would have survived the first test on his own.

I have to do better.

His foot hit a rock and she jerked back, spinning toward him, and then relaxed back into her seat. "I barely recognized you!" She dipped her hand into the pond and splashed water at him. "For a moment there, I thought you were the second trial, coming to get us."

Mickey ran his hand along the stubble on his chin. He shaved as best as he could with the tools at hand, but it was definitely an imperfect job.

"It was time for that beard to go." He shifted uncomfortably, barefoot on the rocks. "The crazy hermit look was getting a bit old."

"I'll say." Valerie's tone was almost saucy. Her eyes roamed his body and newly-exposed face with a fascination that made his blood stir.

Am I reading too much into this? It had been a long while since a woman looked at him like that.

Valerie grinned. "We have eleven and a half hours before we can leave this place. Got any ideas how to pass the time?"

"We should probably rest up," he said.

Valerie's face dropped. "I guess you're right." She sighed, and leaned over to slide her pants down over her hips. "I'm going for a swim." She offered as explanation. She whipped her shirt over her head, making her dark, wavy hair bounce as it was freed from the fabric.

Holy crap. He realized--after he'd already had a nice, long look at her bare abs and freckles that covered most of her chest--that he should probably look away. Clothed only in her matching black bra and panties, Valerie dove into the water, producing the tiniest splash Mickey had ever seen.

Maybe I'm not reading too much into this. Mickey shook off his pants and shirt, waited for her to surface, and then leapt in the air, plummeting into the water in a gloriously splashy cannonball. Even underwater, he could hear Valerie's surprised yelp followed by laughter.

"Very graceful," Valerie said as soon as Mickey surfaced.

Mickey dipped his head in a quick bow. "Only the best for you, my lady."

"Princess Valerie, lady of the construction sites." She stretched her arms out wide in the clear water. "It has a nice ring to it."

"Don't let Elvy hear you say that. He'll put you to work fixing broken scythes." Mickey said. "When I was researching your family, I read about your construction business. For a pencil-pusher, you sure knew your way around flying scythes and plumes of flame."

Valerie blushed. "I wasn't always in construction. When I was first turned, protecting yourself involved a certain familiarity with blade work. But even now, I practice my skills whenever I can. I'll also swing by the construction sites sometimes to help out. You wouldn't believe the number of swinging cranes, dropped hammers, and live wires I've had to dodge."

Mickey swam close to Valerie. "Did I ever say 'thank you' for saving my life back there?"

Valerie wrapped her arms around Mickey's neck, playing with the ends of his hacked-short hair. "As a matter of fact, you did not." She leaned forward, pressing her breasts into his chest as she whispered, "You're welcome to thank me now."

Mickey's heart pounded in his chest as he wound his fingers through her wet hair. He placed his palm against her cheek, gently stroking her face with his thumb. Finally, he brought her lips to his own, devouring their sweetness.

She opened to him and Mickey's tongue danced with hers in ancient rhythms. His hand roamed the planes of her body, feeling hard-earned muscle under her smooth skin. She moaned against him, and he knew they both needed more.

"Valerie, it's been a long time since I--" he started to say, but she cut him off, kissing him hard.

"Me too." She smiled at him, her expression a little shy. "We're all we've got in this place. And I *like* you, Mickey Shive. You believed that all this was real, when nobody else did. And you're brave and..." She ran her hand along his stubbly chin. Her mouth descended on his, her hands caressed down to grab his ass to pull him closer. His cock was achingly hard pressed against her thigh.

With a roar, Mickey lifted Valerie out of the water, laying her down on the smooth boulders lining the banks. He propped himself above her, and drank in the sight of her. Her hair was wild and wet, her skin still slick from the water, and her chest heaved with excitement.

"You're so beautiful," he said. "Strong and clever." Mickey wrapped his arms around her, flicking open the clasp of her bra. "I want to touch all of you."

He slid his hands slowly back around her, trailing the fabric along her skin until she shivered. Mickey moved his mouth to Valerie's neck, kissing and nipping at her sensitive skin. His canines elongated as his passion took hold, the sharp points caressing her. She raked her fingers through his hair as he worked on her, pulling him closer.

Slowly, Mickey moved his way down Valerie's neck,

leaving a trail of kisses that ended at her breasts. He teased Valerie's hardened nipples with his tongue, moving from one globe to the other with excruciating slowness. Valerie gasped as he took her nipple in his mouth and set to work on it with his tongue, flicking and caressing the pink bud.

"Gods, yes." Valerie mewed and bucked under Mickey's touch. A stab of male pride hardened his cock further at the sight of her elongated canines, extended with arousal.

With a wicked grin, Mickey slid down her slick body and positioned his mouth at her core. He massaged her inner thighs with his hands as his lips latched onto her soaking folds. She was warm and soft and open to him as he worked, running lazy laps around her most sensitive area. She cried out when he latched his mouth onto her clit, sucking it and teasing it with his tongue.

Valerie was shaking now, one hand caressing her own breast while the other gently guided Mickey's head. Her cries echoed off the walls of the cavern.

Mickey slid one finger, and then two inside of her, probing and gently stretching her passage before moving inside her in earnest. He pumped his fingers inside her soft core while focusing his oral attention on her clit, moving faster and faster in response to her cries of pleasure.

Valerie's walls shuddered around Mickey's hand as she came. She screamed as she writhed in pleasure, falling back against the shore once her delight had finished coursing through her.

She pulled Mickey towards her, kissing him gently. Her pulse raced under his touch. Her skin shone with a post-orgasmic glow. *I want to make her feel like this forever*, he thought.

Valerie rolled Mickey onto his back, quickly stripping him of his remaining clothes. "Your turn."

She positioned herself above Mickey's throbbing length and slowly lowered her soaking core onto him. Valerie's soft warmth enveloped Mickey, and he resisted the urge to furiously pump into her. She was in charge now.

Once Valerie was in to the hilt, she leaned forward, resting her hands on Mickey's shoulders. Her breasts brushed against his chest as she began to move, slowly at first, and then increasing her pace, sitting up straight now, fully on magnificent display as she fucked him.

Valerie ran her fingers through her long hair, sliding them down her body to cup her breasts, all while bouncing on Mickey's cock. Mickey let out a low groan as he watched, holding back his release as hard as he could. His hand found Valerie's clit and began to rub in time with her thrusts, the two moving faster and faster until they both cried out in pleasure. Valerie shuddered around him, calling his name and he couldn't wait any longer. With a few final thrusts, Mickey spilled himself into her, pulling her close to his chest.

"Mmm." Valerie curled against his side. "That was..." Her fingers danced along Mickey's chest hair. "...amazing."

"You're amazing." Mickey wrapped his arms around her. "You're risking *everything* just to stop the *hortari*, when you're not even in danger of *hortari* abuse. I don't think you know just how incredible that is." He leaned down to kiss the top of her head, but she'd moved.

Valerie leaned back, away from him, her eyes downturned. She sat still, silent, for uncomfortably long.

"I had a sireling once." Her voice was barely a whisper. "I didn't mean to... I'd never..." When her eyes met Mickey's, they were shining with tears. "I knew that being around a sireling, there's always a danger of a *hortari* command accidentally slipping through without meaning to. But I thought I could handle it, that I could be careful, like Christopher was whenever he was around us. But one night, I was tired, distracted, and I gave a *hortari* command that cost my sireling his life. I was so *stupid*."

Mickey sat up and wrapped an arm around her shoulders. "It's not your fault."

Valerie wiped a tear away. "It *was* my fault. I was the one in control, not like you--" She clapped a hand over her mouth.

Holy shit. She knows. Mickey tried to keep his face blank. "Not like me what?" His stomach churned.

"I read up on you before we met. There wasn't a whole lot in your file, but I know about your wife, what Rhys made you do. When the *hortari* takes over, there's no stopping it. There's nothing that you could have done."

"Stop." Mickey croaked. *She knew this whole time? She knew she was traveling with a murderer and didn't say a thing.*

"It's *not* your fault. It's Rhys's fault. And the *hortari*'s fault for giving Rhys that kind of power over you. That's why we're here." She gestured at the cave. "To break free."

"Queen Alice broke free." Mickey was shaking now. "Alice was strong enough to break the *hortari*. Don't you get it?" Mickey ran his hands through his hair, gripping at the shortened ends. "I could have been able to stop it. If I was strong enough, I could have kept Rhys's command at bay." He slumped to the ground. "I could have stopped myself from killing my wife." Mickey stared at his hands, dazed at hearing the words escape his lips.

"No." Valerie took his head in her hands. "You are just as strong as Alice. I think there's more to the *hortari* than just force of will." She wrapped her arms around him. "I know you've been through something terrible, but you must know it was *not* your fault." She gently stroked his hair. "We're going to fix this."

Mickey leaned into Valerie's warmth, and tried to believe her words. *We're going to fix this.* He nodded, trying to collect himself. *We have a job to do.*

"Thanks, I needed that." Mickey grabbed his shirt off the ground. "We've only got a few hours left, we should get our game faces on." He forced a smile onto his face and winked. "There's no way I will be able to concentrate if you're going to be gorgeously naked for the rest of this quest."

"Haha." She splashed him with water, but also grabbed her shirt from a nearby rock and pulled it over her head.

Together, they helped each other find their scattered clothes and get dressed, stealing kisses as they moved around the pond. Finally dressed, they sat on the rocks lining the pond's edge.

"So, what do you think the next trial will be?" Valerie leaned her head against Mickey's shoulder.

"Something easy, I hope," Mickey said.

"With a name like the *test of fortitude*? Probably not." A gurgling sound emerged from the depth of the pond in front of them and Mickey leaned forward.

"What the hell?" Bubbles swam to the surface like the pond was beginning to boil.

Valerie jumped to her feet, grabbing the back of his shirt to pull him away from the pond's edge.

Water surged up from the pond, overflowing its banks and beginning to churn and roll like something huge was awakening under the surface. Mickey and Valerie darted back from the edge.

Ropes of water swung out from the pool, long streams like tentacles that wrapped around both their waists, and yanked them both toward the pool.

Mickey screamed Valerie's name, fighting against the pull of the water that felt like an ice-cold iron band around his middle. He struggled against the water, kicking and squirming, but nothing stopped the pull. For a second he was back there in Rhys's dungeon, his fingers clenched around a knife he couldn't let go of, his mind screaming at his body to stop, his fingers no longer listening to his will as they moved forward at Rhys's command. The pool loomed in front of him, getting closer every second.

"No!" He screamed, but then his mouth was filled with water. A second later, he heard the splash of Valerie's body hitting the surface of the water, the water current churning as she continued to fight. Magical forces sucked him downward, and the water around them swirled in a vortex that churned faster and faster until everything went black.

VALERIE BLINKED HER EYES OPEN, squinting at the sudden bright light. Mickey stood next to her in a massive library, both of them clothed and dry, on their feet beside a stained glass window that took up most of the wall. Through the stained glass, Valerie could see only rock on the other side, like an old university library had been buried intact deep inside the mountain. She massaged her sore ribs, trying to rub some feeling back where the icy tentacles had yanked her into the water.

"Are you okay?" she asked. Mickey was leaning hard against one of the bookshelves, his face ashen.

"Yeah, it just brought up some old memories." His heartbeat under her hand was too fast. Valerie drew him closer until they stood in a tight embrace.

When he'd first emerged from his bath, looking irresistibly scrubbed and scruffy, all Valerie had been able to think about was rubbing her body against his. Adrenaline from the tests, terror of what they still had to face, and the daunting implications if they failed all heightened her need for his touch. But from the moment she'd felt his body against hers, something shifted inside her. It wasn't just about pleasure anymore, it was about *him*. Mickey Shive. Awkward, passionate, earnest, driven Mickey Shive. His tongue on her clit made her squirm, his smoldering eyes on her body made her burn, and his cock fit inside her so perfectly, it hit every sensitive spot at once. She wanted to feel his hot cum inside her every night, feel his hands squeeze her breasts while his lips pressed against hers.

He was shaking, and she ran her fingers soothingly through his hair. "I'm here, we're going to do this together," she said.

He pulled away just far enough to press his lips against hers. "Yes. We've got this. We're going to stop the *hortari* once and for all."

She smiled at the grim determination in his voice. This was her Mickey. He wasn't immune to fear, but he wasn't going to let it stop him. She kept her hand resting on the small of his back as she surveyed the room in front of them.

Books lined the walls not taken up by the windows, stretching up toward the high wooden-buttressed ceiling. The tables and soft chairs Valerie usually associated with libraries were absent, the floor of the room completely bare except for small tiles marked with a strange glyph that lead in a winding path across the floor toward a doorway and landing on the opposite side.

"More scythes do you think?" Mickey asked.

Valerie shook her head. "Only if the gods lack imagination." She glanced at the books, but the spines were all in languages she didn't recognize. "It will probably be a lot more complicated than just having to duck and run."

"Too true, princess!" came a familiar voice from on top of the nearest bookshelf. Elvy sat balanced on the topmost shelf's edge, swinging his feet over the thirty-foot drop. His bowler hat lay on a jaunty angle, and he studied them with far more excitement than the first time they'd met. "You know, you are alright. I like you two."

"Thanks?" Mickey said, glancing at Valerie and then back at Elvy.

"Does that mean you're going to help us get through this challenge?" Valerie asked eagerly.

Elvy frowned, the fur on his face bristling a little and sticking out from his chin at odd angles. "Well, the magical bonds which keep me here stop me from being able to *help* you, you understand. Gods are very specific that way. They want you folks to earn your way through." He winked. "Otherwise, what's the point?"

Valerie peered up at him. *If he's not allowed to help, then what is he doing here?* "Can you at least tell us what this trial is? Surely telling us what needs to be done can't be considered 'helping'?"

Elvy smiled. "This room is a bit treacherous, and the magic that binds it is a bit on the annoying side." He spread his hands and gold lettering appeared written across the air in front of them. He read the words aloud, his high-pitched voice a stark contrast to the ominous words. "*To continue this course, the follower must lead, and the leader must follow blindly.*"

"That makes no sense." Mickey frowned.

Valerie studied the marks on the ground. They were *moving*, the repeating glyph dancing in a winding path across the floor appearing and disappearing every few seconds. She looked around the room. The scores of books lining the walls didn't appear to be much use. But there was one other item: a single crimson blindfold perched on a low shelf.

"Sure it does," she said, picking up the blindfold. "We need to follow the rune trail, but the one who goes first has to be blindfolded so that they can't see, and the person who follows them tells them where to step."

Elvy clapped his hands. "Well done! The last pair took *ages* to figure it out. Perhaps you two aren't as dull as I thought."

"What happens if the person in front steps off the path?" Valerie asked.

"If you stray..." Elvy picked up a book from next to him and tossed it down to the ground, hitting one of the unmarked tiles. The tile fell away, revealing a drop fathoms deep with red lava at the bottom. The smell of sulfur hit Valerie's nostrils and she pushed down her gag reflex. *There's no coming back from that.*

"Oh, and you should know. If you take the blindfold off before you get to the other side, you both die. Good luck!" Elvy blinked away.

Valerie started to bring the blindfold up to her face, but Mickey pulled it out of her hand.

"No, it should be me." He stepped closer until his face was so close, all she would have to do to kiss him would be to raise her head. His transformation from ragged-lunatic-in-a-shack to a rugged hotty still stunned her every time she looked at him. She reached up a hand to cup his cheek, feeling a part of her relax just to feel his skin against hers.

"The instructions were pretty clear. The leader must follow," Valerie said.

Mickey shook his head. "No, it's too dangerous. I trust

you. I should go first. You can lead me through it." His voice, low and sincere, sent little shivers down her spine. She wanted to grab his face and kiss him again, sink into his embrace like they'd done by the waterfall and feel surrounded and filled with him. After so many years denying a connection to anyone, knowing that their end would come soon, every second with him felt more precious.

"I *won't* be the one responsible for your death, don't you understand?" She felt the tears gather in the back of her throat. "Besides, of the two of us, you are *way* more of a 'follower' than I. We have instructions to follow."

Mickey's voice wobbled. "You're right. I just can't..." He turned away. "What if I can't do it?"

"Tough luck. This is the way it's gotta be." She slapped him on the ass. "I know you can do this. I trust you." She pulled the fabric from his fingers and wrapped it three times around her head until she couldn't see. With her eyes blinded, her other senses came alive, the stench of sulfur hitting her nose with greater intensity. Mickey's body heat radiated close to her. His fingers skimmed her arms, leaving goosebumps in his wake, moving up to cradle her face. She leaned forward into his touch as his lips brushed against hers.

"I won't let you fall. We can do this." His voice was steady, but he stood close enough she could hear his heartbeat rocket in his chest.

"I know."

~

VALERIE STOOD BLINDFOLDED in front of him perfectly still, awaiting his command.

"Let's do this." Valerie must have been terrified, but her voice was steady.

She trusts me. Mickey shook his head. *This is too important. Focus.*

The library's stained glass windows and wooden bookcases reminded him of the universities where he'd done so much of his research on the *hortari*. Part of him half-expected to see a grad student with bags under her eyes and a tall coffee attached to her hand rolling a cart of books across the tiles at any moment.

"Mickey?" Valerie tapped her foot with impatience.

"I'm here." He moved to stand behind her, putting both hands on her shoulders so he could steer her with his hands as well as with his voice. She relaxed at his touch, leaning back against him for a second in a movement that reminded him her round ass was quite close to his groin.

The glyph made its winking way across the room, back and forth in no discernable pattern.

Mickey's head swam. He felt like fear had kicked him in the balls. His stomach churned, and he desperately wanted to lie down until the feeling passed. But Valerie needed him. All the other *hortari* victims out there needed him.

"Let's go," Mickey said, to hear the words out loud and make them final.

Valerie nodded. "Point me in the right direction." Her confidence helped his hands stop shaking. He guided her to the beginning of the path. "It's here. Take a step forward and you'll be right on top of it."

Her right foot touched the first glyph and the room shuddered around them, the floor shook, and a deep rumbling sounded above.

"What's happening?" Valerie asked.

"Nothing, we're fine." He bit back a curse before Valerie

realized the depth of shit they were in. The room no longer resembled a library in the slightest. The bookshelves had disappeared, the stained-glass windows as well. All the tiles in the room except for their marked path had fallen away, leaving one winding strip of rock barely the width of a gymnastics beam that curved and twisted over a sheer drop down to boiling lava on either side.

Mother of gods.

"Why is it so much hotter in here?" she asked.

"We're going to be okay. Step forward about three paces," Mickey said, keeping a steady touch on her shoulders. "There's going to be a right turn coming up." He tried to sound confident.

Valerie blindly moved forward, steady on her feet. One step. Two. The next step on the path shimmered.

"Whoa wait!" Mickey yelled, grabbing her and holding her back. *Fuck, fuck, fuck.* The rock directly under her foot faded to translucence before disappearing entirely, reappearing a couple of feet away like a floating island barely wide enough for both of them to stand on.

Mickey struggled to form the words. "The stones are moving!" His brain felt like a stalled out car: heavy and immobile.

"Mickey!" Valerie hollered. "Mickey, focus. I know you can do this. You're in charge now." Rivers of sweat coursed down her body making her shirt stick to her body in a way that would be incredibly sexy if they weren't in mortal danger. "Mickey, you *will* save us."

There was something in her tone that was so matter-of-fact, so confident in the truth of her statement, that it sent Mickey's brain roaring to life. The stone under Valerie's feet shimmered and began to fade. "Jump three feet in front of you, now!"

Valerie leaped just as the rock disappeared beneath their feet. The lava steamed menacingly below them, beckoning and hungry. The path reappeared connected to the rock Valerie stood on, the curving path of rock appearing deceptively stable.

"Okay, three steps forward now." *I got this.* Mickey's heart jumped into his throat as Valerie nearly walked off the edge. "Stop! Smaller steps!"

Valerie put her hands on her hips and turned to Mickey.

"Or I will just adjust my math to your stride." Mickey leaned forward to kiss the back of her neck. "We got this. Okay, take two of your strides, *this* way." He adjusted her shoulders forty-five degrees to the right.

Step after step, they moved along the narrow beam of rock over the lava, Mickey's eyes always on the steps in front of them, wary of the individual rocks moving, vanishing, reappearing. Valerie moved obediently to each of his instructions, her natural grace turning a flee from certain doom into a flowing dance. The heat was so intense, Mickey felt the warmth in his bones like he was being slowly cooked.

They were so close, the end of the path just ten yards away. The door beckoned, a darker spot along the black rocks in front of them. His gaze was so rapt on the door, he almost missed the sudden drop in front of them.

"STOP!" Mickey's voice echoed around the cavern. The stones immediately in front of Valerie's feet had vanished, leaving a ten-yard gap between them and the narrow ledge in front of the door. With vamp strength, a ten-yard jump was possible, but would be tricky to calculate without being able to see the other side, and with such a small landing. *How can I ask her to jump to her doom?*

"Mickey? You okay? What's next?" He hadn't realized

they'd been standing still for almost ten seconds as he stared down at the lava surging far beneath them like a portal to Hell. He glanced down at the stone they stood on. It shimmered, threatening to disappear. *Shit.*

"Remember the width of the pool to the waterfall? It was about ten yards. Picture it in your head. You're going to have to jump exactly that far directly in front of you."

"Are you kidding me?" Valerie's calm confidence had dissipated.

"I'm sorry, it's the only way. You have about ten yards between you and the other side, and there's no stepping stones left." Mickey's heart pounded in his chest, and a shock of adrenaline ran through his body. He clenched his fists before she could feel them trembling on her shoulders. "You need to align perfectly with the other side." He turned Valerie by her shoulders carefully to line her up, taking the opportunity to caress the skin along her neck for possibly the last time.

Valerie turned, her jaw tight with terror. "Can we back up at all?" Her voice wobbled. "Get a running start?"

All of the stones along the floating path had disappeared except the one Valerie and Mickey were standing on, and it was fading fast. They were trapped above a sea of lava, about to be engulfed in flames. Mickey was momentarily grateful that Valerie was spared the sight of it.

"No, we can't back up. You have to jump, Valerie. Right now." Mickey ran his hands reassuringly up and down her arms. "You're jumping for distance, not height. I believe in you."

She pulled her hands high above her head, stretching out her shoulders. "Oh shit. Okay." She bounced on the balls of her feet, psyching herself up.

"Here I go." With a fierce, warrior cry that stung Mickey's

ears, Valerie pushed off of the rock. Mickey followed a split second later. The stone disappeared beneath his feet into the lava, hissing as it melted into oblivion.

Valerie flew, narrowly avoiding hissing spurts of lava that stretched towards her like tentacles. With a sudden thump, she landed, twirling to grab hold of Mickey's arms as he fell nearly on top of her, knocking them both to the ground.

"We're done! We made it."

"Holy shit!" Valerie pulled off the blindfold and looked back at the fiery pit behind her.

Mickey laughed and held her close. "Holy shit is right." He kissed her, unable to let go.

VALERIE HELD MICKEY TIGHT, the solid strength of him reassuring after the last minutes wandering in terrifying, scorching darkness. Making that last leap had been one of the most frightening moments in her long life. She leaned forward, bracing her hands on her knees, unsure whether she was going to vomit.

"That was close as hell. Thanks for getting us through."

Mickey nodded, then looked up over her shoulder. "Well, for what it's worth, this next room looks a lot nicer."

An enormous white stone staircase stretched up in front of them, hundreds of steps which curved out of sight so Valerie couldn't see how far up they went. It could have been stairs to heaven, except that a *true* paradise would have invested in an escalator.

"Didn't we just do the test of fortitude?" she asked to the open air. "What's with the stairs?"

"This can't be the sacrifice, can it?" Mickey eyed the stairs with misgiving. "What do you think? They take something away with every step?"

Valerie's gaze swept up and up. "This is going to suck." She leaned on Mickey's shoulder as she stretched out her calf in anticipation of the climb.

"My, what a load of bright daisies you two are." Elvy appeared about ten steps up, beckoning them forward. "Lighten up. You act as if the gods don't have a sense of justice. Or humor. Picture a puffin. Laugh riot."

The furry, orange man looked happier than any other time they'd seen him, his side-eyed glances at them replaced with a smile that looked almost hopeful.

"It's just stairs," Elvy said. He jumped up and down on one of the steps, then leaped up and down to the stairs on either side. "Stairs. Seriously, you guys. Nothing in here is trying to kill you. The next room, on the other hand...." He waved them forward. "Just follow me."

Mickey sighed, and Valerie smiled, patting his arm. "I think we can trust him," she said.

"What? Not trust me? You *wound* me. I don't know when my feelings were last hurt so horribly!" Elvy's tone dripped with so much sarcasm that Valerie bit back a laugh.

"Yeah, you look devastated," Valerie said. She placed her foot on the stair, relieved that it felt perfectly normal, and started up after Elvy, ten steps turning to twenty as they climbed up impossibly high. The magic man pranced up a few steps in front of them, practically skipping. She was impressed at his stamina until she realized that his feet weren't really touching the stairs, more floating than walking. She glanced over at Mickey to see how he was faring, but--apart from the trickle of sweat beading down his forehead--he looked pensive.

The last challenge was at the top of these stairs. The test

of sacrifice. She wanted to reach out and touch his hand, tell him that everything was going to be okay, that they'd make it through this, but she didn't believe it. Nothing was fair. She'd found the first person in a thousand years she truly wanted to be with, and now they were going to die to save the rest of vampire-kind.

"Hey, if I haven't had the chance to say it, I'm glad we're doing this," she said. "I mean, I'm obviously glad for a chance to stop the *hortari* and all, but what I mean to say is that I'm glad that we're doing it together." She realized she was babbling and stopped.

Mickey's mouth twisted upward into a tight smile. "I know what you mean. I've been trying to get into this cave for so long. I always pictured going in alone, but these tests...there's no way I would have been able to get this far without you. You're," He paused. "Amazing. I wish we could have met sooner." He looked around at the white stone around them. "Under different circumstances."

"When we're not about to die?" she asked.

"Exactly."

Elvy floated down, not even pretending to walk anymore as they continued to trudge up the never-ending stairs. "Buck up! Geeze. You'd think you two would be celebrating. I am. No one has ever made it this far. The pair that made it furthest before you too missed that last jump at the lava pit. I don't usually even bother to clean these stairs, but then you two guys made the leap of faith and...you have an actual shot!" He looked so excited about the prospect, he was practically bouncing in the air like a jiggling, furry balloon.

"Why are you so excited? You're not a vampire. Destroying the *hortari* shouldn't impact you at all," Mickey said.

Elvy flew backward, his hand to his mouth like he'd

been struck. "No impact? This whole place is one big test to ensure that vamps don't break the *hortari* until a pair from warring lines can prove they're ready for the responsibility of free will. When there's no *hortari*, there's no need for this place. And if there's no need for this place, then there's no need for me. And if there's no need for me, then I'm..." He flew upward and started to make curling figure eights in the air. "Freeeeeee!"

Valerie's eyes followed Elvy's happy loops as her feet continued their upward climb. "But why are you even trapped here? Surely *the gods* could have set up some kind of cleaning spell without having to keep a guardian in here with it."

Elvy laughed, then swooped down to float between Valerie and Mickey, leaning in close to their heads like he was confiding a secret. "I *may* have gotten drunk and pissed on the gods' ambrosia garden." He pressed a finger to his lips. "Allegedly."

"And for that, you're stuck polishing scythes and maintaining a lava pit for hundreds of years?" Mickey asked.

"*Thousands*, my boy. Thousands. You vampires have been taking the whole *hortari*-is-inevitable thing for granted for a stupidly long time. But you two," Elvy smiled, turning to look at them. "You seemed different from the start. In fact, you two have given me more hope and entertainment than I've had in a ridiculously long time." He raised a hand and the white stone wall next to them came alive with moving images of forests and mountains like a fifty-foot projector screen. "Any requests? Anything going on out there in the big bad world you'd like to check in on before you, um, check out?"

Before we die, Valerie translated. She was about to ask about whether the witches had set up a spell to get construction going again, but if this was her last glimpse into the outside world, she had to trust that her staff and siblings would take care of the logistics.

"How about our families?" she asked, glancing at Mickey to see if he had a different request.

The images of nature faded away, replaced by enormous projections of Christopher, Alice, and the rest of Christopher's sire line. Valerie's breath caught in her throat. She hadn't thought it was possible to love her family more, but knowing this was probably the last time she would ever see their faces, she wanted to pull them all close to her and never let go.

Her heart ached. They all looked so worried. Alice and Christopher were holding hands, leaning on each other as they sorted through a pile of paperwork. Ben and Lauren were in Ben's lab, five boxes of pizza at their feet. Danny and Robin looked about a minute of foreplay away from fucking away their stress, and Valerie cleared her throat and told Elvy to let their picture disappear for the sake of privacy. Margot was flying a helicopter, the map next to her looking a lot like the map in Mickey's profile. *Good, they got my text.*

"You're very lucky," Mickey said. "I met Christopher and Rhys at about the same time. That was back in the days when sheep herding was the expected career path for just about everybody. I wonder sometimes what would have happened if Christopher had turned me instead."

Valerie stared up at the pictures, then realized something essential was missing. "Wait, I said *our* families. Where's yours?"

Mickey shrugged, pointed to a small image resting near the bottom of the stairs: Rhys, sulking with his arms crossed, manacles heavy on each wrist and ankle, in a dark cell.

"That's all I got," Mickey said.

Valerie's steps slowed as she stared at her sire's murdering, dictator brother she'd helped to overthrow two years before. Even knowing he was locked away in a bunker, she wanted to punch him in the face. She glanced at Mickey and bit back the sarcastic comment hovering on her tongue. Whatever issues she had with Rhys, Mickey's hatred of him ran far deeper.

"Rhys has lots of sirelings. He turned humans all the time. Shouldn't you have far more family than--"

"Yeah, but I don't see any of them as kin," Mickey said. "Rhys is my only family, and that's only because I can't deny the reality that he sired me."

Valerie touched his arm, suddenly wanting to cry. She'd judged him so harshly when she first read his file, assumed the worst because Rhys chose him. She hadn't considered the full weight of the reverse: that he'd been stuck with Rhys forever.

Mickey nodded toward the images of her sireling brothers and sisters. "Not all of us get the chance to have a family like yours."

"If we get out of this..." She didn't finish the sentence. It would be unfair to promise him anything, to dangle a future that wasn't going to happen.

"I know," he said.

She stared at his back as he continued up the steps in front of her, picking up his pace. *If we destroy the hortari and somehow survive this, I'm going to make sure you have a real family.*

Fear raced up her spine. *Fucking hell. When did I fall in love with Mickey?* It was a horrible thought. *Why now?*

Elvy zoomed down to boop them both on the nose. "I swear, I try to do one nice thing for you people. You just *insist* on being gloomy."

"Sorry, Elvy," Valerie said. *Don't piss off the magical guardian of the murder caves.* "The trial of sacrifice is a bit daunting to think about."

"But thank you, we really do appreciate your assistance," Mickey said.

"You should *really* be thanking me for cutting you all off at the waterfall. If you'd just barreled forward into the blindfold challenge, do you think you'd have trusted each other enough to succeed? No, I don't think so." He held his hands outward. "I will accept your praise now."

"Thanks for the help," Valerie said automatically. *Elvy made us stop to help, rather than as punishment for the scythes?* "You are truly a wonderful, wise creature of much benevolence." She looked up at Elvy. "Something like that?"

"That'll do for now." Elvy grinned.

Valerie glanced at Mickey, sadness pulling at her stomach. Elvy's delay had definitely brought them closer together. The touch of Mickey's hands. The softness of his lips against hers. The release and passion of him surging inside her. Unless she pulled him up against the stair's banister right now and fucked him silly, she'd never have a chance to make love to him again.

But they couldn't stop. Every moment they delayed, sirelings continued to be at the mercy of their sires. If Valerie gave into the temptation to pull Mickey into her arms, wrap her fingers into his hair, and fuck him until they both forgot the fate awaiting them, unspeakable horrors could befall a sireling due to their delay. She picked up the pace, forcing her tired legs to take on each step.

"I still think you should lighten up. You're doing the thing you wanted. Life is too short. Especially yours. But fine, have it your way." Elvy tsked with disgust and snapped his fingers.

The steps in front of them abruptly ended, an arching stone gateway appearing in front of them so suddenly Mickey stumbled trying to step onto a stair that was no longer there. Valerie grabbed hold of his waist before he fell, and leaned into his heat for a moment before stepping away.

On the other side of the gateway, a darker, smaller room lurked. Everything about the room screamed that it was *old*, from the decaying temple columns covered with writing so ancient it was unrecognizable to the ancient-looking clay statue of a sexless figure in chains nestled inside an alcove altar on the far side of the cave about thirty yards away.

Elvy looked between them, his expression more grave than Valerie had ever seen him.

"Okay, kids, it's simple." He pointed at the statue. "When the gods created vampires, they stored the magical attributes of the *hortari* curse inside that statue. Break it, and the *hortari* will be destroyed. And, just so you know, breaking it will also shatter the spells which let this place exist. So, heads up." With a tiny smile, he disappeared.

"We just walk over there and break the statue? That seems too--" *easy*. She didn't get a chance to finish the sentence when a torrential wind more powerful than anything she'd ever felt threatened to knock her off her feet. She screamed, digging in her feet and pressing into the gale. Beside her, Mickey wrapped his arms around a column and clung on for dear life.

"Get low!" Mickey shouted, as he slid off the column. He bent down to his knees so he was crawling forward. "We need to lower our center of gravity, keep from getting blown away!"

Valerie fell, slapping the ground and using her arms to pull her way forward. The wind fought her every inch of the way. Her fingers bled from holding on to the rocky surface, cuts marring her hands.

"Valerie, what are you doing?" The male voice was familiar, but she couldn't place it. She looked around the room for the source, but another blast of air made her eyes tear and she couldn't see anyone except for Mickey pressed against the ground five feet away.

"Felicity?" Mickey called out, his head swiveling as he looked around desperately.

"What is it?" Valerie yelled over to him.

"I thought I heard--" he stopped, yelped, and threw himself to the side, struggling to sit up, his eyes wide with terror as he looked at an empty spot on the floor in front of him.

"Mickey!" Valerie screamed, trying to reach him. "Are you okay?"

"He's fine," said the familiar, male voice from the opposite direction.

Valerie turned and stared.

Nolan stood in front of her, blocking her view of the *hortari* statue against the wall. Nolan looked the same as when she last saw him, those precious hours before he died. His tunic and hands were stained with ink from the account books, and his hair was ruffled from how he used to pull at it whenever he concentrated. He stood like the wind didn't impact him at all, his hair floating like he was under water rather than being buffeted by hurricane-level gales.

"Nolan? How are you here? Are you a ghost?"

Nolan shook his head, kneeling down beside her and running a hand across her forehead. He felt real, solid. For a second, she felt like she was back in her old office, Nolan handing her a handkerchief to blot away the ink staining her fingers. She reached up to grab hold of his hand, but her fingers passed through him like he wasn't there.

"I don't understand." She didn't realize she was crying until a tear rolled off her chin and dropped onto her hand. "I'm so sorry! I never meant for you to die."

"I know, I know." Nolan grabbed her hand and pulled her to his feet. For a second, his body seemed to block the wind, and she leaned forward to hug him. Her arms went through him.

"Why can't I touch you when you can touch me?" Valerie asked.

"Because of this." His fist lashed out, his knuckles connecting with her chin in an explosion of unexpected pain that sent her reeling with the shock. She raised her arm to block his next swing, but her arm past through his, allowing his swing to connect solidly with her neck.

"Nolan! Wait! I never meant for you to die! I'm doing all of this for you!" Valerie cried, ducking away from his swinging arm and dodging away, which put her back in the full blast of the wind.

He kicked out the back of her knee, sending her tumbling forward, her leg twisting beneath her. Out of the corner of her eye, she saw Mickey gesturing and yelling toward the empty pocket of air in front of him. *I'm not the only one having to face my demons in here.*

She twisted away from Nolan's foot about to connect with her stomach and rolled, tumbling as far toward the *hortari* statue as she could before she heard the running steps of Nolan beside her and had to dive under his swinging leg. She jumped to her feet and a blast of air nearly knocked her down again.

"Nolan, I'm sorry! What else can I do to make it up to

you? I should have been more careful with my words, with your *life*."

"You think that's why I'm here? Because you told me to *burn the midnight oil*?"

Hearing her thoughtless, stupid words coming from Nolan's mouth were even more painful than remembering saying them. It was back in the decade she worked as a merchant, exploring the seas and commissioning other ships to do the same. It involved a lot of tedious paperwork, and Valerie and Nolan were up against a deadline.

Then, before she finished up for the night, she'd thrown the instructions at him like they didn't matter, "The captain needed this yesterday. Burn the midnight oil until it's done." And she'd left, gone to her office to finish her work until the sun rose, trusting that Nolan would finish up the task.

It wasn't until she smelled the smoke, ran back, and found the entire room flush with flames that ate at all the paper and oil all over the room that she realized the full sickening extent of her words. Nolan's burned and lifeless corpse lay on the ground, far too late to save.

Christopher rarely saw his sirelings, but Valerie had been reckless and cocky, so sure she would always think through the implications of everything she said to the vampires she sired. But one thoughtless idiom--with the weight of the *hortari* curse behind it--had killed a good man, and she had to live with that guilt forever.

"Nolan, I have spent every single day for the last three hundred and eighty years, two weeks, and six days trying to make up for what I did to you." This time she didn't duck, just took the punch Nolan aimed for her chest, embracing the pain and the bruise she knew would blossom if she lived long enough for it to swell. She let the force of it drive her back a few steps, closer to the *hortari* statue.

"That's what I mean!" Nolan's face twisted with a kind of desperate rage. "What happened to me had nothing to do with you!"

"What are you talking about?"

"You've spent all these years so obsessed with how you were responsible for every little thing, and you never once stopped to actually think about what you said. Of course just saying *burn the midnight oil* didn't make me burn up. *Hortari* commands are a *bond* between a sire and a sireling. You didn't mean me harm, and I didn't interpret your command that way. Yeah, I continued to burn a lamp, which I would have done anyway. I just *fell asleep* and knocked it over. It was an idiotic accident."

Valerie blinked at him, uncomprehending, feeling like the room was tilting at an angle as she reevaluated the foundation for every decision she'd made for almost four hundred years.

"You weren't killed because I told you to burn?"

"No!" Nolan grabbed the sides of her face and pulled her forward. "I fell asleep. I was tired, the light those days were fucking candles and oil lamps, and I fell asleep on a pile of papers. I had a bad dream, knocked over the lamp, and *whoosh*."

"Nolan, I'm so sor--"

"Don't you even *think* about apologizing to me again. Stop blaming yourself. Or me. Or any of it. Just do the job you came here to do." He pointed toward the *hortari* statue. Valerie's eyes widened to see how close they'd gotten, the revelations of her rewritten past distracting her from the wind and the pain in her shoulder, knee, and jaw where Nolan had struck her.

She reached for the statue, but an invisible barrier blocked her hands.

"No!" she screamed. Her fingers skimmed over a hard surface--hard and cold as diamond--she couldn't see. She beat at the barrier, the statue so close and just out of reach.

"Like everything else, you can't do this alone," Nolan said, so close his ghostly breath cooled her neck.

Valerie looked at him, then across the room at Mickey, still speaking with his own ghost.

"Mickey! I need you to break the *hortari*!" She yelled over at him. He didn't seem to hear her, trapped in his own conversation, the wind blowing so loud Valerie could barely hear herself. She reached out to Nolan. "Can *you* help me get through this?"

Nolan shook his head. "I would if I could." His voice sounded distant, and he was already starting to fade away.

"You've helped me more than you can ever know," Valerie said.

"You'll want to hurry." Nolan disappeared and Valerie sagged against the wall. She looked around the enclosed room. The door to the stairs had disappeared.

ACROSS THE ROOM, Valerie was fighting and falling against some invisible attacker. Mickey screamed out her name, but she didn't react to his voice. He screamed out to her again, but a hand touched his face and he turned. The chamber blurred as Mickey's eyes filled with tears.

"Felicity." The word was barely a whisper, but the woman standing before him somehow heard over the howling wind and nodded.

The petite blonde wore a bemused expression so familiar it made his chest ache. "Mickey." She sighed. "Of all the husbands I've had, you were always my favorite."

"I was your *only* husband." Mickey's voice trembled.

"That's probably why you landed on top." Felicity stepped forward and ran her hand along Mickey's jawline. Her touch felt warm, alive. "No competition." She grinned.

"How are you here?" Mickey dropped to his knees. "Felicity, I'm so sorry." He reached for her, but when he tried to wrap his arms around her waist and pull her close, he was left grasping at air.

"Sorry?" Felicity yanked Mickey's head up, forcing him to look at her. "For this?" She tilted her head back, and a thin, red line appeared on her neck. The crimson streak spread, stretching wide, and looping around her neck until her head fell to the floor with a thump.

"Oh gods, oh no." Mickey lifted her disembodied head in his hands. *It's happening again.*

The cave disappeared. The curving walls of stone fell away, replaced by the hard lines of an all-too-familiar dungeon. Manacles lined the walls, the floor rank and lick with blood, shit, and sweat under Mickey's knees.

The pain from the wounds along his back, sides, and feet felt as raw as the day Rhys had his men fillet him with their whips. Details he hadn't even recalled until now jumped out with frightening clarity. A moth hung on the bars blocking the windows, its gray wings fluttering in the breeze. A sliver of a moon hung behind the clouds, like it was too ashamed to be a witness.

Rhys, large as life, with a smirk toxic enough to peel paint, paced in front of him where Felicity had been standing a moment before.

"I sired you because you were supposed to be one of the meanest humans around." Rhys ran his tongue against his elongated canines. He stared down at Mickey, his grin sick with delight. "And *now*, only *now* you can't stomach the work. You found a loophole in my *very* specific *hortari* command and let some of my prisoners free. Mickey, Mickey, my sweet boy. That was a mistake."

Rhys's fury was most terrifying when he was the most calm, like the smooth surface of a tar pit. Mickey had been chained away in a sunroom for days, weakened by daylight, unable to feed. But Rhys's prisoners, so young they'd been almost children, were free. Mickey had suffered through the sun, made peace with his own death, and was happy to sacrifice himself so those kids could have a chance. Then Rhys returned. And his smile now promised a fate far worse than death.

Rhys raised his hand, making a come-hither pull with his fingers to someone outside Mickey's cell. Felicity fell sprawling into the cell, her hands and feet bound in heavy chains. Bruises colored her face and hands in purple and red, defensive wounds from one hell of a fight. Mickey's stomach curdled. *How could I be so stupid?* He thought. *Rhys is too cruel to just let me die.*

Mickey shook his head. He knew all this. This already happened. Rhys had given the command and Mickey hadn't been able to stop himself. He'd loved his wife completely, her eyes held more sparkles than the night sky, and her laugh was the music that made his feet dance. But his fingers had still picked up the knife Rhys threw down at his feet. He'd still advanced on his beloved, screaming and crying and fighting with every ounce of will as Rhys repeated his command over and over until it was done.

Mickey blinked and the cave flickered back into focus around him, but the ghost of Rhys's manic laughter remained, flitting through the chamber.

Felicity's head rocked on the ground like a discarded toy. Mickey screamed, his voice lost in the howling wind. "Felicity, it's my fault. I wasn't strong enough. I should have broken the *hortari* to save you." His fingers went through her ghostly head, only air meeting his fingers when he tried to touch her hair.

Felicity's eyes popped open, their blue depths boring into Mickey. "You think you could have broken the *hortari*?" She laughed, and arterial spray splattered from her open neck onto the cold, stone floor.

Mickey screamed and threw himself to the side to avoid the spray, horror shocking him to his soul. "Felicity! No, gods, no. I should have tried harder. I should have done *something* to stop--"

Felicity's body stepped forward and her hands picked up the head, placing it back on Felicity's vacant shoulders. She rotated her neck, the skin along the severed line coming together again like her head and body had never separated. She knelt down until her face was level with Mickey's, and she smiled. All traces of blood and bruises were gone, her smile as bright as their wedding day.

"Oh, you dear, sweet man." Felicity reached forward to gently touch his cheek. "I suppose you couldn't have known. *I* didn't know, not until I died."

"What don't I know?"

"The *hortari* can be broken, this is true. Your queen did it two years ago for your king, her sire. You've been picturing it as a tug-of-war, two parties vying for control, pulling back and forth until it rips apart." She tutted gently. "It takes a cooperative effort, sireling and sire *together* pushing against the *hortari* until it shatters. Christopher and Alice *both* desperately wanted the *hortari* to stop, that's how she broke free. The only way you could have saved me was if Rhys *wanted* you freed from the *hortari*." Felicity's eyes glistened with tears.

"You've spent all this time blaming yourself, haven't you?"

Felicity stepped forward, cradling her hands around Mickey's face like she'd done so many times in life. "I know Rhys killed me, you were his weapon. I'll only be angry if you spend one more instant beating yourself up over this." She gave him a quick peck on the cheek and nodded towards Valerie drumming her fists against an invisible wall blocking her from the *hortari* statue. "You've got a job to do." With a gust of wind, Felicity disappeared.

Mickey staggered to his feet, the wind still threatening to knock him to the ground. And yet, he felt lighter. Centuries of guilt had lifted away. His wife was gone, but it had been Rhys's fault. The *hortari* allowed this to happen, and Mickey was perfectly poised to take vengeance on it.

Valerie clasped his arm, pulling him to her side. "Are you okay?" she asked.

"I will be." Mickey stepped towards the statue, his heart pounding in his chest. Fingers wound through his own, and he turned to see Valerie grinning proudly at him.

"We're actually going to pull this off." She squeezed his hand. She pulled their conjoined hands forward and they passed through a magical barrier as a cold tingling along his skin. Their fingers joined together around the statue. The figure's dead eyes looked ahead, kneeling in manacled chains, the clay tingled with magical currents.

Golden letters appeared in the air in front of their eyes.

THE HORTARI: FREEDOM COMES WITH A DEADLY PRICE

"I'll do it. Maybe if you don't do the actual statue smashing, the cave will spare you," Mickey said, although he expected he knew her answer.

Valerie stepped close, running her fingers through his

hair. "You fool." She kissed him, attacking his mouth with her own, bruising his lips, striking at his tongue. "We're doing to do this like we've done everything else: together."

Mickey took a few deep breaths. "On three," he said. Their clasped hands gripped the statue tighter, Mickey's fingers on the figure's legs, and Valerie's wrapped around the chest.

"One," Valerie chimed in.

"Two." Mickey tensed.

"Three," Valerie bellowed.

They pulled the statue through the barrier and smashed the figure to the ground with all their might, sending shattered fragments in all directions. Valerie pounded her boot into every piece in her sight, and Mickey clenched the larger shards into dust. It took seconds to demolish the statue to nothing.

"We did it!" Valerie yelled. The cave shook, rocking side-to-side like they were at sea.

"We did *something*, all right." Mickey yelled back. The large columns supporting the high ceilings crumbled, shaking the ground as they fell like dominos around them. Mickey screamed out Valerie's name, but it was too late.

With a roar, the cavern fell apart around them, and everything turned to black.

We did it. Mickey thought his last thought with a smile.

VALERIE FOUGHT against the onslaught of sharp edges hitting her face and shoulders as rocks rumbled around her, knocking against her legs and threatening to bury her alive.

"Mickey!" she screamed, running forward, dodging rocks, trying to find him. "Elvy! Are you still here? Mickey!

Where are you?" She could barely hear herself over the deep rumble of rocks and crashing sounds surrounding her. Boulders blocked her everywhere she turned.

She jumped up as high as she could to get away from the onslaught, grabbing hold of hanging stalactites and pulling herself up, kicking away at the rocks that threatened to break her hold and climbing toward the pinpoints of light that promised the outside world.

Rocks bombarded her from all sides, pummeling her head, and she closed her eyes from the grit covering her face. She pulled herself up blind, cursing and screaming Mickey's name, every sense alive for any sound or movement to give her hope that Mickey wasn't already crushed to pieces.

Like I will be if I don't keep climbing. Out there was her family, life, purpose.

"Mickey!" she screamed again.

But Mickey's in here, a traitorous thought reminded her. Valerie's fingertips reached air, breeze flowing over her skin. Her heart flip-flopped in her chest. She blinked open into more darkness, clawing above her, her fingers bloody and torn from the rocks' hard edges.

I'm crawling from my grave. The thought put more power into her limbs, desperation fueling every clawing grasp. The ground here was more soil now than rocks, suffocating her and pushing against her nostrils, pulling at her hair. She fought and pushed, kicked and clawed until she had one whole hand free, then her arm, and she could pull herself upward.

Valerie took a deep breath, cool air hitting her lungs like a gift. She hacked and coughed, dirt and rock fragments from her lungs landing wetly on the grass that waved at her from down the mountainside. The valley where Mickey had lived opened up below her.

The dirt around her was pitted with holes and dips in the ground where the rocks and undergrowth had fallen down the mountain.

"Mickey!" she screamed, carefully making her way across the treacherous ground. She called out his name again. She refused to believe he was gone. *A test of sacrifice.* Surely they'd given up enough. She'd let go of centuries of justifications she'd made for her choices. Nolan had forgiven her. She'd forgiven herself. Surely the gods wouldn't demand she lose Mickey now? They couldn't be that cruel.

Yes, they could. They created the hortari *in the first place.*

A tumble of rocks hit against each other and she spun.

"Mickey! Are you there?" She ran toward the sound, the ground rumbling deep underneath her. A sound almost like a person moaning emerged from one of the holes and she grabbed at the rocks and started tearing them out of the earth, digging as fast as she could, screaming Mickey's name until she heard the sound again.

"Valerie?" The word was so soft, so low, she almost didn't hear it.

She shrieked with joy, throwing away the rocks and clawing at the soil with renewed purpose. Her fingers caught on something that wasn't a rock or a root and she grabbed hold, the smooth flesh of Mickey's hand holding tight to hers.

"I'm going to get you out of there!" She braced her weight and pulled, falling backward as she used all her weight to pull him out of the earth. Mickey rocketed out of the ground, coughing.

He cried out her name and crawled forward until he was next to her on the ground, breathing hard. She pulled him into her arms, not caring about the dirt caked across his skin, and kissed him hard. His arms wrapped around her.

"I thought we were both dead. I thought I'd never see you again," Mickey said, breaking the kiss to move his mouth to her neck. His lips felt incredible pressed against her rapid pulse, his every touch a reminder that they were alive.

"I can't believe we did it. The *hortari* is done." Valerie felt as giddy and full of promise as a first kiss.

"And we're alive." He pulled her even closer, his hands skimming her body like he needed the extra reminder that she was really here, really breathing. His hands pulled at her breasts, clasped her ass. Pleasure followed every place he touched.

"I love you, Mickey Shive." She leaned back slightly so she could see the expression on his face. A grin broke across his face like a shooting star blazing radiance.

"I love you too, Valerie Dal. So much, I never thought it would be possible to love someone so dearly in so short a time."

"I know." She kissed him, her tongue colliding with his as Mickey rolled on top of her, his hands finding the waistband of her pants. He pulled them down so he dived for her pussy, licking her flesh like he was starving for her. Her hips bucked and thrust upward to get closer to his tongue, and her fingers laced through his hair to hold him there. He licked up her seam, his fingers pressing deep into her, finding her most sensitive places, and then thrusting hard so she screamed and surged with pleasure that sparked through her whole body.

"I need you! I need all of you." She panted, her hands shaking from the afterglow of her first orgasm, but desperate to feel him inside her.

"You have me. You have me forever." He pulled down his pants, his hard cock already glistening with pre-cum, and surged into her, lifting up her hips to thrust deep. She cooed and purred at his fullness stretching her insides, feeling connected and whole with him thrusting into her over and over. She was dizzy with pleasure, her fingers clenched around his ass as she urged him onward. He pounded her hard, everything around them disappearing until the world contracted to the smell of him, his touch, and his mouth against hers.

She came hard, his cum filling her a second later as he cried out her name and collapsed onto her. They curled together on the ground, breathing hard. At first she thought the rapid thrumming was his heart against hers, until she looked up and recognized the rhythmic beat of a helicopter headed their way.

"It's Margot!" Valerie jumped to her feet and rearranged her clothing. "My sister is on the way to rescue us."

Mickey quickly pulled up his pants, and got up to stand beside her. "Do you think she'll object to one of Rhys's line becoming part of her family?" He sounded so nervous, it was adorable.

Valerie kissed his cheek. "You were the one who discovered this cave that led to the destruction of the *hortari*. Even if I didn't already love you, they would welcome you."

Margot's helicopter loomed into view. She threw them down a ladder, and they climbed into the helicopter, falling back exhausted into their seats. Margot waved at them from the pilot's chair, yelling, "Am I glad to see you! You have no idea how scared we've been since you sent that text."

"It was worth the worry." Valerie grinned so wide she worried her face might split. "We did it, Margot. We destroyed the *hortari*."

Margot froze. "Holy shit."

"It's true." Mickey bounced with excitement in his seat.

Margot maneuvered the helicopter back in the direction of the castle. "Valerie, text everybody the news. I want the craziest party this kingdom's ever seen to be in full-swing by the time we get there. You changed the world, little sis."

Valerie clutched Mickey's hand. "We both did."

Margot tossed back Valerie's phone, which Valerie was so surprised to see, she nearly dropped it. "A weird guy named Elvy appeared in the copilot's seat, handed this to me, and told me to tell you that he's off on a world-circling bar crawl. He disappeared right before I spotted you two."

Valerie caught Mickey's eye and they smiled. "I'm glad he's finally free," Valerie said. "He helped us a lot." She took a deep breath, kissed Mickey's mouth tenderly. "We really did it." It didn't feel real yet.

He looked as dazed as she did. "No more *hortari*."

Valerie's phone beeped, and she tapped it on to scroll through the photos and videos surging in from everyone she knew. Alice and Christopher were crying with laughter, chorusing "thank you" together while gripping each other's shoulders. Robin and Danny were dancing, grinding up against each other with their arms flung up into the air in wild abandon, surrounded by other dancers jumping up into the air and cheering. Lauren and Danny were at the castle, the two of them laughing amidst a crowd of the castle's resident *hortari* victims, everyone toasting the news with champagne. Warmth filled Valerie's chest. She turned the phone so Mickey could see.

"Looks like happily ever after is real."

Mickey grinned and kissed her. "And not just for us, but for everyone. Forever."

Valerie turned off the phone and snuggled into Mickey's

arms. Through the helicopter's window, the moon smiled down at her. Peace settled like a blanket over her. *This is what love feels like.*

She closed her eyes and breathed in Mickey's scent. "Forever sounds perfect."

THE VAMPIRE'S ESCAPE

Please, *let tonight be the night*, Lauren prayed into the gold-lined bathroom mirror as she dabbed a smudge of lipstick off of her teeth. The dress she was wearing was the same one she wore on her previous date with Trevor, but she'd convinced a seamstress friend to take it apart and make it look new. She winced as a hastily-sewn seam dug into her back. All the expenses and favors to keep up appearances were piling up, and if Trevor didn't come through, she was screwed. *Trevor has to be the one.*

Lauren forced herself not to focus on the lines that had recently appeared around her eyes and mouth. Thirty-eight had not been as kind as thirty-five, and the last three years since Nikolai had died had taken a toll she couldn't afford to show on her face. She padded on some more concealer. It wouldn't do if hot, billionaire Trevor Simm realized she wasn't the twenty-seven-year-old she'd claimed to be.

She adjusted her breasts a little higher into the swooping neckline of her dress, then pushed them down an inch. The trick was to pull off that delicate balance between "lady" and "fuckable", riding both identities convincingly. It made a man recognize he had to *earn* his place in her bed, but also feel confident he would get there eventually. After six months of Trevor's studious and attentive courtship, tonight *had* to be night he'd trade a ring for the honor of having Lauren as his companion for the rest of his life.

You can do this, she told her reflection. *This is what you've trained for your whole life.* Lauren smiled at herself, a well-practiced smile both winning and polite that didn't show teeth--*A lady does not grimace like a chimpanzee*, her mother's words chided in her head—as she soldiered back out into the restaurant.

Chez Fenêtre was still as beautiful as it had been years ago when she was a regular every Tuesday night with Nikolai. Lauren had gently led Trevor into coming up with the idea of inviting her here for their six-month anniversary, calling ahead so the host and staff would know to pretend not to recognize her, but also have her favorite red wine in stock.

Trevor stood as she approached, polite as always, with a tiny, no-teeth smile that Lauren's mother would approve of completely. Detached and charming, like Clark Gable in a black-and-white noir, but with blond hair slicked to the side like a Ken doll, and a slight build. Although he claimed he was thirty, he looked twenty-two at the most.

And Trevor had *money*.

So much money. The kind of money that wore bespoke suits and hand-crafted watches, drove a different Aston Martin every time he picked her up, and flew her on a private jet to Paris for dinner dates.

Her late husband, Nikolai, had been extremely well off, the retired Alpha of a bear shifter clan worth several billion dollars. They'd married as an explicit business arrangement: she provided him companionship and care in return for Nikolai sharing the extravagance of his extremely comfortable lifestyle. Although neither had ever claimed to love the other, over the fifteen years they were together, they developed a real fondness. Every day, Lauren missed the small kindnesses they'd exchanged even to Nikolai's last moments, and the comfort of knowing that she never had to take care of anything except Nikolai's immediate needs.

But when the cancer finally took him, she'd discovered Nikolai's wealth had been his son's all along. The young Alpha granted Lauren a modest stipend to carry her through until she figured out how to support herself, but the money always disappeared faster than she planned.

Trevor pulled out Lauren's chair and motioned for her to

sit down. The waiter was gone, their meal already cleared, but two glasses of champagne stood on the table, with another bottle waiting for them in a silver ice bucket. Her heartbeat quickened.

This is it!

"You look lovely tonight, my dear." Trevor's speech was always a little stilted. But it was all part of his odd charm. He had an old-fashioned nature layered with awkwardness that was cute and endearing, very different from Nikolai's rough confidence.

She smiled, thanking him with an upward glance through her eyebrows to check if his eyes were--*yes, they are*--fixed on her face rather than her breasts. No amount of money would be worth the pawing she got from a few of the men she'd dated soon after Nikolai's passing. Trevor had stood out immediately from the crowd when he never pushed to get physical, agreeing with her insistence that they wait until they were fully committed. The furthest they'd gone was the passionate kissing they'd exchanged on the flight back from their last diving date in the Red Sea.

Trevor had been a great kisser, employing just the right amount of tongue, his hands skimming her breasts with enough delicacy to make her nipples tighten, but avoided being grabby. Even if she'd never mistake it for love, remembering his lips' confident path down her neck and along her chest widened the smile she beamed across the table.

"I'm so happy, Trevor," she said. "Thank you so much for another beautiful night." She indicated the empty, luxurious restaurant around them. He'd bought out the entire place so they could have privacy; only their waiter and the kitchen staff were present, however professionally invisible, during their four-course meal. "I've never been as happy as when I'm with you."

A lie. But it wasn't Trevor's fault she didn't love him yet. He was respectful and sweet. She'd love him eventually.

Trevor smiled. "I am so pleased to hear you say that." He stood up from his chair, took one of the glasses of champagne off of the table, and got down on one knee in front of her.

Yes, yes, yes, yes. Lauren pressed her hands together to keep from clapping in wild glee. *I did it! I did it! At thirty-eight, I still got it!*

"Lauren Vaughan." He slid out a long box from his pocket, far too large for a ring, and flipped it open.

What? She stared at the knife inside the box. It was heavily bejeweled, including a diamond as big as a walnut, the blade only about an inch long, and wickedly sharp.

"Um," she started to say, then stopped. *It's a tiny knife. Let's see how this goes.* But, with her feet hidden under the table's draping tablecloth, she slipped out of her heels, ready to run if the situation called for it.

Trevor smiled at her and pricked the top of his ring finger with the knife, dripping the blood into his champagne. The bubbling liquid turned slowly crimson as the blood mixed with the golden fizz.

"Will you, my love, be my eternal bride of the night?" He raised the glass toward her.

Vampire. It explained so much. His old-fashioned language, how he had so much money without having any sign of an inheritance or job, and his face looked far too young for how he acted. She bit her lip, keeping her face curious as she rapidly thought it through.

Nikolai told her about vampires as part of her introduction to the supernatural world when they were first getting to know each other. She'd never really considered finding someone to turn her--if she had, she'd have done it before the most recent set of wrinkles set in--but why not? She wasn't getting any younger, and Trevor was everything she'd ever looked for in a life companion: rich, kind, and malleable.

"I don't understand. What are you saying?" *Rule one of being a lady: never let a man know what you know.* As far as Trevor was concerned, Lauren was completely oblivious to the supernatural world. She took the glass of red-tinted champagne from his hand and placed it on the table in front of her. He smiled at the gesture and settled back in the chair opposite her.

"I am a vampire, my sweet, just like that masterful character of legend, Dracula. It may be difficult to believe, but witches, werewolves and many other magical beings are all real. *I* am real." He opened his lips and flashed his teeth at her. Even expecting them, Lauren was startled to see his canines elongate down from his mouth until they pressed deep into his lower lip.

"You're a *vampire*?" She made her voice rise in a high note of incredulousness. "You drink *blood*?"

He smiled, that same aloof smirk. "Indeed, I need blood to survive, but I also enjoy the fine foods and lovely meals we've shared. Never fear, I procure my blood from donors. You are safe from my hunger."

She nodded, his answer lining up with what she already knew.

"But, we've been out in the sun together. I thought vampires couldn't go outside during the day." She questioned him, only half listening to his responses, tallying up the answers she knew to be true, playing the part of the ignorant human to give Trevor the opportunity to lie.

"Indeed, we are weakened during the day," he said. "Our

strength and senses are more limited, and direct sunlight can be painful, but I am able to walk in the light."

All true, she nodded to herself. It would have been easy for Trevor to lie about the negative side of vampiric life, but--even though it was clear he wanted Lauren to join him--he didn't.

"That's a relief."

If Trevor was surprised that she was believing him so fast, he certainly didn't show it. Lauren catalogued all the pros and cons Nikolai had told her about vampires: super strength and enhanced senses would be nice (although she wasn't sure when she'd have occasion to use them), and she'd be able to smell the emotions in non-vampires (also, not that useful). Never enjoying the feel of the sun against her skin would be disappointing, but she rarely braved skin-damaging UV rays these days anyway.

She touched her cheek. *I'll never be worried about wrinkles again!* It would be definitely worth it to stop aging, to heal quickly, and to be ultimately invincible to anything but fire or beheading...but then there was the *hortari*. She eyed Trevor. She'd spent the last six months evaluating him as a husband, but as a sire?

Vampire sires had total command over their sirelings' actions; if he chose to employ the hortari, Trevor's will would supersede her own. *That shouldn't be too bad*, she thought, biting the inside of her cheek. In their six months of courtship, he had never raised his voice to her, and been consistently courteous and generous.

"If you turn me into a vampire, what will that mean for *us*?" She worded her question as vaguely as possible, studying his face for any hint that he knew she was dissembling.

He smiled, reaching out across the table to settle his

hand on top of hers. "Since our first glance, I knew you were the one who should spend eternity my side. If I turn you into a vampire, I will be your sire, which means I will have the power of *hortari* over you." Lauren relaxed as soon as he said the word. Trevor brought up the *hortari* when he could easily have lied about it.

"With the *hortari*, I will have the ability to control you with my words, if I choose." Trevor paused, his fingers caressing the top of her hand. "But the *hortari* is only meant to be used in moments of desperate need, to keep new vampires from hurting others as they adjust to their hunger and new abilities. I love you so much, Lauren, I would never command you to do anything you didn't want to."

Lauren's heart soared. He *was* a good man. A good vampire. She'd chosen well. *And I'm going to live forever!* Forever secure. Forever protected. Never having to worry about hiding another wrinkle, or being dumped for someone younger. No more depending on the generosity of her stepson who had never really gotten over the fifty year age difference between her and Nikolai.

She reached across the table to brush her hand along the side of Trevor's face. He was so handsome, he was like an airbrushed movie poster come to life. And he wanted *her*. Thirty-eight year-old, widowed Lauren Vaughan.

"Yes," she said. "I will be your--" *What was that ridiculous way he'd phrased it?* --"bride of the night."

"You breathtaking creature." He threw his head back, his voice deepening. "There are darknesses in life and there are lights, and you are one of the lights, the light of all lights."

Faster even than Nikolai, with all his bear-shifter speed, had ever moved, Trevor tossed the table so it tumbled away from them, champagne and glassware smashing against the opposite wall.

Trevor moved so quickly, Lauren didn't even see him get up, but his hands were on either side of her face and his mouth was on hers, pressing hard with devouring strokes of his tongue. Months of pent-up passion and lust for his hard-cut body flared to life and she pulled him closer until they spilled off of her chair and onto the restaurant's lush carpeting.

His need for her pulled at longings she'd been pushing down for years. He ripped off her dress and Lauren was grateful she'd gone with her sexiest bra and no panties. Trevor's eyes roamed her body and she raised her arms above her head, lifting her breasts up and toward him. She knew she looked hot. She'd worked *hard* to stay this hot. She ran four miles a day, hadn't eaten a carb in ten years, and forced down kale even though it tasted like sour dirt. But it was all worth it for the look in Trevor's eyes.

The man practically drooled at the sight of her, and she squirmed with delight. He tore off his shirt, displaying all the muscles that his perfectly-tailored suits had always hinted lay hidden beneath his posh exterior.

The desperate hunger on his face made arousal pool between Lauren's legs. It had been a *long* three years. She grabbed Trevor's hands, pressing his fingers to her clit as she ravaged his lips. Her hips bucked against his hand, driving her pleasure as the weight of his body pressed on top of hers, building delicious friction against her most sensitive places. She unbuckled his belt, tossing it away. He didn't wait for her to undo the rest of his pants, he simply tore apart the fabric down to his boxers so his erect cock sprang free.

Trevor stroked his cock as his other hand sped up against her clit to a supernatural speed that almost felt like her trusty vibrator at home. Lauren purred at the sensation, kissing his neck and unhooking her bra so she could rub her pointed nipples against his bare chest. His skin was cold, a relief from the warmth building up from between her legs. It was all so fast, she needed his *want*, needed him to not take back his offer of eternal security.

Lauren rolled them over so she was on top, facing away from Trevor. She leaned forward and kissed a trail down Trevor's abs to where she wanted to be. Her lips fastened around his cock, licking up and down his shaft, then kissing downward to take his balls one at a time between her lips as her fingers lavished attention along his dick. He groaned and she pressed Trevor's fingers deeper inside herself so she could fuck his fingers as she licked his cock.

"Oh baby, you're so hot." Trevor groaned. "Your mouth...your fucking mouth." Lauren smiled, power flowing through her like a drug, thrilling at how she broke through Trevor's old-fashioned speech to make him totally lose control. He was always so aloof, his look of helpless abandon as he grabbed the back of her head and fucked her mouth in earnest sent a thrill down to her toes.

He pulled out from her lips at the last moment. "Gods, baby, I need you." He gently pushed her onto her back and she spread open for him, the sweat dripping down his face the highest compliment she'd gotten in ages.

"Come inside me, Trevor." Lauren ground her hips up against his cock, her legs spreading to hook behind his back, pressing her wet core against his tip. "Please, I need more."

"Oh baby, you can have more. You can have everything." He surged deep into her, fucking her fast and hard. She swung her hips up to meet every stroke, her fingers slipping in-between their bodies to finger her clit as his cock pulled out an inch to thrust back in.

He pounded her over and over, words of "harder" and

"faster" and "fuck, yes!" intermingling with each other and then degrading into animal grunts and screams as Trevor's cock moved inside of her. Pleasure built like a surging wave with each touch to her clit until he came inside her, and she followed him over the edge. Just as the orgasm started to subside, Trevor's wrist pressed against her lips and a metallic, salty liquid touched her tongue. She looked up into his eyes, his breathing fast, each exhale of his chest brushing against her nipples.

"Drink, my love. Drink and be mine."

She opened her mouth and sucked on the blood, feeling it roll down her throat. A heavy, languid feeling settled over her and Lauren closed her eyes.

Vampirism, here I come.

THE SUN SET behind Trevor's mansion, blocking the last rays peeking through the blinds of Ben's lab. The small house, set up in the back of Trevor's enormous property behind the pool, was Ben's domain, although it was not without its perils. A dangerous, hiccupping sound came from the table nearest the window, and Ben dove for cover.

His latest invention gurgled like a kangaroo giving birth and whipped around in circles, spurting out liquid before letting out a sad puff of smoke. Ben peeked out from his protective stack of toolboxes and stroked his chin, surprised at the short beard he found. *Didn't I just shave this morning?* He wondered. A glance at his phone. Four days ago. It had been days since he shaved. Or fed.

He scrawled a note in his lab journal and grabbed a bag of blood from the mini-fridge, grateful his nephew, Trevor, remembered to keep it stocked. The blood was donated by an old horse shifter after a day at the spa and tasted of her calm. He let the blood slide smoothly down his throat, and approached his malfunctioning invention with healthy caution.

The gurgling pipes and spinning gears seemed to be in good order, just coated with gas. "Blast and tarnation," Ben cursed. He picked up a rag and gently stroked the sides, wiping off the machine's unfortunate byproduct. The drained blood bag dropped forgotten to his feet.

Ben's latest invention was going to be a game-changer for humanity, if he could just stop it from spraying gasoline everywhere. The desalinator functioned as a component conversion device, turning plastic waste and saltwater into fresh, drinkable water. The only byproduct was gasoline, which Ben couldn't seem to get rid of.

"Hello? Dude?" An unfamiliar voice called out.

"Coming!" Ben wound his way through his lab, turning and inching sideways so his wide shoulders wouldn't topple any of the precarious stacks lining the path down the center of the room. Ben's piles of lab journals, books, beakers, and tools appeared as disorganized chaos to the uneducated eye, but to Ben, his lab's functional disorder was one of his finest feats of engineering.

A gawky human teenager stood just outside the pool house's wide, glass doors. Ben's vampiric nose could smell the teen's boredom and impatience emanating from the boy's blood.

"Pizza delivery." The pizza boy grunted. He shifted his weight, straining under the weight of the seven pizzas stacked almost to his chin.

Ben furrowed his brow. "I didn't order... Nobody here really...*eats*, you see."

From the delivery boy's puzzled expression, it was clear that he did *not* see.

Right. Human. Ben slapped the side of his head, and the boy jumped a little.

"Oops...," Ben chuckled, hoping to set the poor kid at ease. "What I mean is, *of course* we eat. We humans love eating the foods. It's just that..." Ben tried to lean casually on a nearby lab table, and ended up planting his palm in a petri dish of sky worms. He peeled the sticky worms off his hand and deposited them back with their wiggling brothers. The teenager's eyes followed the worms from Ben's hand and back to the dish and he paled.

Ben scooped up a large wrench and began to twirl it between his fingers, but the boy's expression didn't ease.

"Uh, dude? The order said to bring it to the pool house. This *is* the pool house, right?" The teenager resettled the boxes in his arms.

Oh, dear. I'm doing it again. Ben always got a bit flustered when interacting with strangers. He tended to over-articulate, flailing his arms wildly to better ensure he was understood. Once, Ben nearly took a gardener's eye out when chatting about desalination.

"Yes!" Ben cried. "This is my lab, which is situated next to my nephew, Trevor's, pool, which makes it the pool house. Do you see that lovely gothic mansion up the way? That's where he lives with his girlfriend."

The pizza boy had begun to back away slowly from the furious twirling of Ben's wrench. "Cool, dude...cool." He straightened up, suddenly business. "Well you gotta pay for these, man. My boss'll take it out of my check if you don't."

Ben dropped the wrench with a clatter. "Oh, certainly, of course." He patted down his pockets and pulled out a screwdriver and a handful of bolts. He chuckled uncomfortably.

"I'm not great with currency." He rummaged around a cabinet under his lab table, pulling out a rusty coffee can. "I'm sure I have something in here." Ben coughed in the dust as he removed the plastic lid and poured out a fistful of paper and stones. He held it out to the teenager.

"That's like a thousand bucks, and I don't even know how much in..." The delivery boy juggled the stack of boxes slightly to get a closer look. "Are those emeralds?"

"A few emeralds, a ruby or two, and some pirate gold." Ben sighed. "Good times."

"Yeah, man, you owe me $83.95. I don't exactly have change for pirate gold."

"Of course." Ben thought hard for a moment. "Could I ask you to...? Would you be able to just keep all of it, then? That would be very convenient. I could get back to my work and you can use it to buy..." He ventured a guess. "A telescope or whatever you youths are into." He nodded, increasingly pleased at the idea. "Yes. That should work nicely."

"Wow, thanks, man. You're weird, but you're like, *super* nice." The pizza boy grinned and stuffed the lot into his pocket. "Where should I put these?" He nodded at the stack of pizzas.

"Right here." A radiant woman emerged from around the corner of the pool house. *Was she waiting back there?* Ben wondered.

The woman casually tossed her long, blonde hair over one shoulder. She was dressed in a nice dress and pearls that looked a little odd next to Ben's science equipment. In a single motion, she took the seven pizzas out of the delivery boy's arms with ease, holding the heavy stack in one perfectly-manicured hand.

"Bye!" The pizza boy disappeared, running across the wide lawn of Trevor's estate.

"Hello...Susan?" Ben ventured a guess. He thought that was Trevor's girlfriend's name, but hadn't her eyes been a paler blue? This woman's eyes were the dark blue of storms and indigo.

She tucked into the pizza without ceremony, holding the pile of boxes with one hand and the slice in the other while still standing in his doorway. She quickly destroyed the slice topped with bacon and avocado before turning to the other side of the pizza.

"Lauren," she said through a mouthful of food. "We actually haven't met."

"Oh, good. I'm Ben, Benjamin Dal." Ben cleared off two folding chairs, pushing one toward her before slumping into the other. "It's so much easier to meet somebody for the first time. I'm much less likely to have forgotten them."

Lauren nodded thanks for the chair, sitting down gingerly as she took out another slice. "You make a good point." She bit into the pizza and let out a low moan. Ben's eyes widened at the sound.

"So, Lauren." Ben drummed on his knees awkwardly. "What...I mean is, well, I don't want to be rude." He focused his gaze on a drop of grease which dropped from her pizza onto the ground. "Why are you eating pizza in my lab?" Trevor always had a girlfriend: blonde, tall, and lean vampires like Lauren. But they never came out to the pool house. He'd see them around the grounds, sometimes he'd hear them swimming at night, and then they'd leave. And a new one would show up a few months later. It made Ben a little uneasy that Trevor's girlfriends were also his sirelings-- it could certainly make romance more complicated--but such relationships weren't *unheard* of.

"Trevor won't let me eat human food in the house." Lauren said it so matter-of-factly, for a second Ben wasn't sure he'd heard right. *Surely not.* Trevor wasn't letting her eat? That didn't sound reasonable at all.

She smiled and held out the rectangular cardboard box to Ben. "I didn't even know anyone lived out here. I thought the pool house was just filled with junk." Lauren ripped the top off of the box and created a makeshift plate for him, selecting a slice topped with maple bacon and jalapenos. "Give this a try. I bet they didn't make food like this back whenever you were turned."

Ben brought the slice to his lips and took a conservative bite. "I've never really been much of a food person--" He stopped short, the symphony of flavor overwhelming his palate. The taste was like a calm bonfire and a raucous fire-works display all at once. "My, this is delightful!" He chomped down another bite with gusto.

Lauren laughed, a melodic chorus that bubbled out of her, unrestrained. "Oh, we're just getting started. I am dubbing you my new secret pizza buddy." She brought her slice to his, knocking them together. "Clink. Pizza toast."

Ben chewed thoughtfully. "*Secret* pizza buddy, eh?"

Lauren rolled her eyes. "Trevor says since I'm so new to being a vampire, I should push away from my old human ways. As if I could have eaten like this while I was human. He's on a strict, all-blood diet, and thinks I should be, too."

"Surely you're having *some* blood?" Ben asked. Trevor was the sireling of Ben's brother, Danny, and had always been a little strange. But even if Ben's nephew had some weird ideas about how to teach new vampires about their new lives, surely he wasn't *starving* her.

"Of course!" she said and Ben relaxed a little. "But..." She gestured at her lean figure. "I worked my entire life to look a certain way, and that meant saying 'no' to food like this." Lauren grinned madly as she tore into a pepperoni slice.

"Now that these calories don't count, I'm sure as shit going to enjoy it."

"Is that why you became a vampire? Caloric freedom?" Ben held out his makeshift plate, and Lauren slid him another slice.

"That certainly didn't hurt. Neither did the immortality." Lauren laughed. "Can you keep a secret?"

Ben shrugged, pointing around his jumble of a lab. "Who's there to tell?"

Her lips quirked. "Trevor doesn't know I knew all about vampires before we met. My late husband was a bear shifter and he taught me a lot." She brought a finger to her lips. "Don't tell."

"*Late* husband? I'm so sorry." Ben leaned forward to touch her shoulder and she nodded. "You must miss him."

"I'm not even sure why I'm telling you, but I've been living here for a month now and sitting here, I feel..." She looked around like she was searching for the right word. "Comfortable. For the first time in a really long time. I've missed that. I hadn't realized how much until now." Her voice grew faint. "Living with Trevor in his mansion can be a bit intense." She shifted her weight in the chair. "I'm sure you've noticed that he tends to get his way."

Ben nodded. "That certainly appears to be the pattern." He'd met Trevor at his sire, Christopher's coronation, and after just a few minutes of conversation, Trevor arranged to be Ben's patron so Ben could focus on his inventions and not have to worry about logistics. It was all done, with Ben moved in by the pool, in less than a week. That was a year ago, and the time had flown by. "How did you two meet?"

"We met at a museum; they were hosting some sort of gala." Lauren waved her hand dismissively. "Trevor was handsome, charming, rich, and exactly what I was looking for."

Ben raised his eyebrows in surprise.

"I'm not ashamed I'm a career wife," Lauren said. "Some people are really good at building bridges, or flying planes, or doing heart surgery. I just happen to be very good at taking care of a husband." She shrugged her shoulders. "It's just easier for me to do my job if the husband happens to be rich."

"You'll get no judgement from me. For whatever that's worth," Ben said.

"Thanks." Lauren smiled. "Trevor kind of swept me off my feet, to be honest. He was so put-together and smart; he always had the perfect quip at hand, the exact right thing to say in any scenario. We'd go on a date together, and he'd surprise me by flying us to Paris. Lazy weekends on private yachts, private stays at exclusive resorts, helicopter rides over the city..." She sighed. "It was magic. One thing led to another, and now I'm a vampire." She stood up quickly, putting down the pizza and wandering down the center of the room. "What about you? How'd you become a vampire?"

Ben swallowed a bite of pizza quickly so he could speak without peppering Lauren with cheesy spit. "I grew up in Barbados, mid-nineteenth century. Christopher, my sire, found me fixing a broken sugar distiller. You should have seen my face, I was so sure he was going to call down the overseers and have me whipped again." Ben held up his dark-skinned hands. "People who looked like me weren't supposed to be smart, and my owners tended to shoot first and ask questions later." Lauren's mouth hung slightly open in shock, her pizza forgotten for the moment, and Ben hurried on. "But Christopher did no such thing. He offered to sire me, to keep me safe, so I could improve the world with my mechanical knowledge."

"That's quite a debt. No pressure or anything," Lauren said.

"I've come up with a *few* contraptions here and there." He dusted off a blueprint for a self-driving bicycle and showed it to Lauren. "Now I'm trying to focus my work. I'm hoping to do Christopher proud and solve some of the pesky world problems that keep popping up."

Lauren asked, "I imagine a pool house isn't the ideal setup for your work?"

"The conditions aren't ideal, but it's convenient. I can be a bit scatterbrained at times, and I haven't got a head for business at all." Ben pointed at the pneumatic tube running from the east wing of Trevor's house, along the side of the pool held up by spindly columns, and ending at a small station on the lab table closest to the wall. "Trevor takes care of everything: funding, lab supplies, and getting my inventions out to the world so they can be *used*. All I have to do is send him a note like this." Ben scrawled 'beakers' on a scrap of paper and popped it into a plastic cylinder. He placed it into the tube, and with a 'woosh', it flew away towards the mansion.

Lauren watched the paper disappear into the house and her face paled. She looked at her watch and jumped to her feet. "Trevor will be wondering where I've gone. I should be heading back. I'll see you the next time I send a confused pizza guy your way."

He was usually in a rush to get people out of his lab. But, for some reason, he didn't want Lauren to leave. She had a kind face, but he couldn't think of any reason for her to stay.

"Until next time," he said.

"Catch you later, secret pizza buddy." And with a wink, she was gone.

LAUREN SMILED to herself as she pulled open the ridiculously ornate door of Trevor's mansion. If she hadn't needed a safe space to eat pizza, it's possible she would have never investigated the pool house at all. And, whatever she'd expected to be out there, Ben wasn't it. She'd taken for granted that all vampires were like Trevor: pale, aloof, and as timeless as a classic movie. But Ben was *present*, his energy so huge his flailing hands could barely contain it. And yet he also had a calming, grounded quality Lauren associated with personal trainers and manicurists.

And--as much as it embarrassed her to admit it to herself--she hadn't really thought that *of course* there would be black vampires. *And this one has sweet eyes and great hands--*

"Where were you?"

She held her jaw stiff to hide the wince. Trevor's voice grated more than usual after the easiness of being around Ben. Trevor walked down the curving, stone steps, his body framed by the ancient tapestries that lined the wall. The edges of the ancient fabric were frayed, the colors fading from lack of protection from the elements.

"I was walking outside," Lauren said. *Technically* not a lie. She had walked outside from the pool house back to the house. Trevor had never mentioned Ben, just that the pool house was filled with a bunch of his old things. That had been back when she first moved in, getting the grand tour of the Gothic mansion where Trevor insisted she spend all her time. Back then, he'd still been phrasing his words broadly.

The outside world can be dangerous, so don't wander about.
Words which were vague enough to give her the freedom to
go almost anywhere. Lauren was becoming a quick study in
the many interpretations of commands.

"I'm so happy to see you, my love. You looked stressed.
How can I help?" she said quickly, before Trevor asked any
more questions.

"Come here." Trevor pointed to the bottom of the stairs.

Lauren's body locked, the *hortari* taking hold as his
words controlled her body, forcing her steps closer to him.
She resisted, hoping this would be the time her body actually obeyed her, rather than her sire. Her heart hammered
in her chest. Lauren's feet moved on their own accord across
the room, each movement mechanical, making her feel off
balance and a stranger in her own skin.

It was always like this with him, and Lauren choose to
lean into the command, taking long, calming breaths before
letting her legs swing forward one at a time. She'd never
forget the first time the *hortari* locked in on her. She'd only
been a vampire for a day, experimenting with her new abilities. The main hall had called to her, the four-story arched
ceilings giving her plenty of space to see just how high her
newly-strengthened legs could jump.

The feeling had been extraordinary: like flying, each
jump sending her higher. A few more leaps and she was
sure she'd be able to touch the ceiling. Then Trevor had
walked in, told her to stop hopping around like a child and
be still. She plunged to the floor, her feet fusing to the
ground. No matter how she pulled, they wouldn't move until
he gave her permission.

The house was even colder than the night outside; the
gray walls with the narrow windows were placed so high
they barely let in any moonlight, and kept the cold trapped

inside. The enormous fireplaces, built for roaring fires taller than her, lay dark and cold. She knew vampires didn't require warmth, but everything about this place made her shiver, inside and out, and, day by day, it wasn't getting any better.

Her feet carried her across the rest of the room, stopping when they'd arrived at the spot on the floor where Trevor pointed. The moment the order was complete, she relaxed, the *hortari*'s spell broken for the moment. Lauren smiled at her boyfriend and sire.

"Yes, dear?" The endearment sounded a little forced, but she managed to make her smile look genuine. She'd had friends whose husbands had taken a couple of years to manage. She had centuries with Trevor to figure it out. Stick it out long enough, she knew she'd bend him back around her finger.

He spread a handkerchief on top of the wooden banister along the side of the stairs, the white fabric coming away gray with dust. "This house is filthy. You used to love to clean for me."

When was this? Lauren had always tidied up after herself, but she'd never gone out of her way to clean the dozens of rooms in Trevor's palatial mansion. She'd certainly never claimed to *love* cleaning, that's for sure.

In the last month, Lauren had asked him twice about the house's staff, but she had yet to see another soul. This house was *huge*, there had to be people to clean it, maintain the furnishings, and care for the grounds. During the first couple of weeks, she'd heard the sounds of cleaners during the day while she slept, but in the last few weeks, those sounds had stopped, and dust was beginning to show.

"Perhaps, if you'd like, I could make some calls. I'm quite the expert at finding good help." She stepped forward to lay a hand gently on his arm. He liked it when she touched him without being told to. "If the staff you used weren't what you preferred, I know of a great cleaning service. I'd love to look into at least some part-time staff to spruce up the grounds. Perhaps--"

"Lauren." He patted her hand against his arm, leaning forward to cup her face. "I want *you* to be the one to take care of our home."

Oh fuck. That's way too unspecific. Blood drained from her face, but Lauren latched onto her smile and held onto it like a life raft. She could see it like a premonition: her body locked into cleaning this house for the rest of eternity, unable to sleep or eat in a constant fight against dust in this enormous, fucking house. *Take care of* could be interpreted as *hiring staff*. She let out a deep breath. *I can make this work. He just wants to see he's in control.*

"Of course, my love. Where would you like me to start?"

Trevor smiled. "The bookshelf in my bedroom. You could learn a few things from my prize possessions. Dust them, care for them." He grasped her chin, pointing her face upward like he might kiss her. "They deserve your *respect*." Tiny flecks of spittle hit her face. Her smile didn't waver.

"I understand." The words had barely left her lips and her body was already pulling away, forced inexorably upstairs toward Trevor's bedroom. Behind her, Trevor's laugh was high-pitched and shrill.

"That's my good girl."

The relentless drive of the *hortari* eased slightly when she reached Trevor's bedroom. Lauren didn't have the slightest idea where Trevor kept cleaning supplies, so she grabbed one of his shirts from the bottom of his frightening large laundry pile (they *really* needed to hire some help, this was getting ridiculous), and faced his bookshelf.

She hadn't known a lot about Bram Stoker's *Dracula* before she moved in with Trevor, but she now knew far more than she ever wished. Trevor had somehow tracked down a copy of every single of the one thousand, twenty-nine editions. His custom-built bookshelf for his collection was carved with the words,

Listen to them, the children of the night. What music they make!

She picked up the shirt and ran the fabric over the words, partially to block them from view.

When she first moved in, she'd read the book, since it was so clearly one of Trevor's favorites. "Ugh." The small noise of disgust was soft, too soft for anyone to hear, but still satisfying. Horror just wasn't her thing, but she tried to like Trevor's favorite book for his sake.

Dust them, care for them. The dust command was easy. Her hand moved on its own accord, the fabric running in a cursory fashion along the spines, across the top of the books, and the inch of wood in front while barely touching them. She didn't need to dust *well*, just dust enough for the *hortari's* satisfaction. *Care for them* was too vague to require anything specific from her, and thankfully, *hortari* couldn't force her to *feel* anything even as abstract as *caring*. For someone who threw out *hortari* commands as often as Trevor, Lauren thanked the stars every day he was so imprecise with it.

In so many ways, her life could be so much worse, she reminded herself as her hands dusted one row of books, then the next without her guidance. She and Trevor kept separate bedrooms, for one. The sex at the restaurant before he turned her had been great, but then she'd needed a few days for her body to transition to vampire. She'd been laid up in a guest bedroom as every limb felt like it weighed a hundred pounds, and her vision swam in and out like a bad high. Once she was up to full, supernatural strength, able to leap over trees and hear the clicking of every spider crawling along the ceiling, he'd said he would wait until she was ready to move bedrooms.

She gave the top of the books a good, long swipe. *I know you'll beg me for it eventually*, he had said to her, smirking his no-teeth smile. She'd been ready to jump back into some hot vampire sex until he said those words. There was a malice there she hadn't seen before and it scared her. Then his constant commands started up, and she welcomed any excuse to stay away. For all his *eternal bride of the night* line, they weren't married, and it was as good a reason as any to insist she keep Trevor at arms-length as long as she could.

She sighed. *I'm just delaying the inevitable.* Lauren knew how this worked. She lived in his house, drank the blood he provided. An arrangement like that was never free, and without a budget to prove she could adequately run a large home, there was only one thing she would eventually have to do to keep from getting kicked to the curb.

I can do this. With her eyes closed she could imagine it was anyone there with her in the dark. Perhaps someone a little taller, with kind eyes, dark skin, and enormous hands which touched even a wrench with reverence. Perhaps someone who looked at each moment with such wide-eyed wonder and surprise, and talked about a truly horrific past as if it was just a bad dream. It would be so easy to imagine Ben's mouth against her skin, all that huge energy focused on her, his tongue between her legs, sweeping up her slit and sucking on her bud...

Her hand stopped moving. She'd reached the last row of the bookshelf without even noticing. She relaxed, the muscles of her arm sore from moving for so long with no relief. The dusting was complete, the *hortari* broken. She slumped against the wall, leaning her head down to her knees. Imagining being with Ben was pointless. He was a penniless inventor. He was just as dependent on Trevor as she was, and looked at his test tubes with more affection than he looked at her.

"Darling, you don't have to wait for me on the floor," Trevor said as he entered the room. He was all smiles now, dressed in a tuxedo Lauren remembered from one of their fancier dates. She'd thought he looked like James Bond at the time, but now--she blamed her newly-enhanced vampire senses—but he looked like the shifty butler in a murder mystery.

She shook her head. Trevor was her boyfriend, she wanted to like him. She *needed* to like him.

"I bought you something," Trevor said.

"Oh?" The phrase used to make her so happy, why didn't it any more?

He danced back to his closet and emerged with a cerulean, floor-length dress of clinging silk that draped down so low in the back and front it could have been couture overalls.

"Thank you." Lauren got to her feet. The dress would require some high maintenance throughout the night to stay on her body, but she'd been sure to move in with all her specially-designed underwear and body tape in hope of gifts just like this. She ran a hand down the smooth fabric. It was beautiful.

"We're going to the opera tonight. I want you to wear this."

Lauren smiled at him. The *I want* meant it was still her choice, and even if the opera had never been her favorite, an invitation to get out of the house for the first time since she moved in was a delightful new development. Putting in the effort to making it work would be a good first step to getting them back on track.

It took a couple of hours to get her makeup, hair, and cleavage in place and then they were off. Stepping out of his limo and walking hand-in-hand up the red-carpeted staircase into the opera house was like stepping back onto familiar footing.

This was what she knew how to do. She smiled to a couple of witches she'd been friendly with when she was married to Nikolai, and waved across the room to a trio of tiger shifters who regularly and famously would make love in their opera box while the show was going on.

Her smile broadened. Lauren hadn't gone further than the pool house since she'd been turned, but being out among people as a vampire was fascinating. When she was married to Nikolai, she'd have to wait until after introductions for her bear to explain that so-and-so was a cursed Viking or a pixie or a troll, but here she could smell it all in their blood. And so much more. With one inhalation, she knew who was at the show out of forbearance for a loved one, who was keeping up appearances as cultured, and who was genuinely interested in the show (true of more people than she'd anticipated). The tiger shifters' arousal and anticipation of getting under each other's clothes was so palpable she could smell it at thirty feet, but with the way they were eyeing each other, vampire senses weren't necessary to know what they would do once the curtain rose.

"My past love, Felicity, she adored the opera," Trevor said suddenly. He was glancing around the red and gold room, his gaze skimming the chandeliers as big as a car and the modern art which, laid on its size, would be bigger than the layout of the house Lauren grew up in.

"Oh?"

He turned to her, fixing her with one of his pale, blue-eyed stares. "You remind me so much of her. Felicity was breathtaking, so graceful and poised, a true lady through and through, quiet and calm and comforting. Felicity understood true beauty..."

Lauren's attention wandered. He'd mentioned his ex a couple of times, but never waxed on quite so rhapsodically before. *It must be this place.* She'd come to the opera plenty of times with Nikolai when he needed to entertain out of town guests from other shifter clans. Every corner still held memories: of Nikolai bringing her a glass of her favorite wine, of charming his guests when Nikolai accidentally offended someone. The ghost of Nikolai's hand resting as a comfortable weight on the small of her back followed her through the lobby. Trevor's hands were busy with his drink, his fingers caressing his glass as he reminisced, his voice pointed to the walls.

"Felicity was so beautiful in red, you should have seen her--"

"Darling, they're calling us to take our seats," Lauren interrupted. The chimes rang out once more, warning the show was about to start, and Lauren slipped her arm through Trevor's, steering him toward the theater's doors.

"Ah yes, I hadn't realized. Thank you. You really are quite conscientious, Lauren. So like Felicity."

How complementary. She bit back the words from leaving her mouth just in time. Trevor hated sarcasm.

They reached their seats: a private box to the side of the stage with a great view of the entire set as well as the (far more interesting) view into the wings where the sets and actors waited to go on.

Make this work, she reminded herself. She glanced at

Trevor and relaxed a little. He was smiling, leaning back in his chair with one arm draped behind her chair in an intimate gesture.

"Trevor, darling. When I used to come to the opera with friends, there was a game we used to play to help pass the time." Even if he didn't know about Nikolai--*being a widow automatically makes a woman sound old*--there wasn't any reason why they couldn't play. She raised her wine glass to him. "You take a drink whenever there's a trap door, or someone holds a note longer than ten seconds, or--"

"That is unsophisticated." Trevor cut her off. He withdrew his arm from the back of her chair. "You may not play that game."

The *hortari* settled in her hands like an itch against her skin. "But--"

"And you will not talk about it."

Her throat closed up, her words freezing in her throat.

Not good, not good at all.

The curtain lifted, and the attention of the audience shifted toward the stage, but the figures and music were a blur in front of Lauren's eyes. Tears formed and she blinked them back. She missed Nikolai. She missed the solid strength of him, the dry humor he saved just for her during the quiet moments between clan meetings and networking events when it was just the two of them. The opera game hadn't just been because neither of them knew Italian and the histrionics on the stage were repetitive and lasted too long, it was about having something private that they could share together, even in the midst of a crowd.

Ben would understand. She wasn't sure where the thought came from, but she pushed it away.

A trap door on the stage lifted up, raising a woman

wearing a headdress that looked like a cross between a sailboat and bull horns, all painted gold.

Trap door, take a drink, she toasted in her head, then raised her glass to take a sip.

Her hand wouldn't move.

Trevor was glaring at the stage, his arms crossed tight across his chest.

The *hortari* banning her from playing a harmless drinking game wouldn't allow her to raise her glass to her lips. She waited a moment, then took a long gulp of her wine. *Of course, once it's not about the game, then I can drink.*

Lauren sat seething for the rest of the act. She had secreted some blood bags in her clutch, and poured some into her glass once her wine was done. She concentrated on the taste of it sliding down her throat, trying to find some sense of calm. She'd chosen this bag because it was from a giddy dragon shifter who donated it during her honeymoon, and Lauren had hoped the excitement of new love in the blood would help make the evening more enjoyable. But the contrast between her own feeling--wanting to club Trevor over the head--was so extremely different from the dragon's happiness. The taste just made her slump deeper into her chair.

The curtain dropped and the lights turned on signaling intermission. For the first time in her life, Lauren wished the first act had continued a little longer.

Trevor's grip clenched around her hand, hard enough the fine bones of her fingers ground together.

"Darling, you're hurting--" she started to say.

"We're leaving." He pulled her to her feet with a sharp tug, dragging her so fast she missed her footing and fell onto the booth's carpeting. As she fell, she smacked her elbow hard on wooden rail, a shock of pain spiking through her body. Trevor didn't wait for her to get up, sighing exasperatedly as he stalked away, calling over his shoulder for her to "come along, quickly."

The *hortari* kicked in, and there wasn't time to be graceful. Lauren kicked off her shoes, threw aside the front of her skirt to get to her feet as fast as possible. Without her commanding them to, her bare feet dashed after Trevor's rapidly retreating form. Lauren gave one last glance back at their opera box. In the struggle, one of the chairs had knocked over, shattering one of the glasses of blood. Her abandoned shoes were splattered with the red, ruined. She caught up with Trevor halfway down the hallway.

"Felicity would have enjoyed tonight," he muttered, so low she wouldn't have heard it without the enhanced hearing of a vampire. "I've seen this bloody show a million times. I did this for *you*."

They made it through the winding corridors of the old hall, down the stairs, and through the exit of the building before most of the other audience members had gotten out of their seats.

"Are we leaving?" Lauren asked as they passed the front doors. The marble steps out front froze her toes, but she was too scared to complain. "Trevor, talk to me."

"What is there to talk about? You're without any grace, any class. You have no appreciation for the finer things, Felicity, the things that *I* provide for you. Do you know how much I've sacrificed for you? Don't you realize that what I've given you, *all* I've given you, is a gift to show my undying adoration?"

"Trevor, you're scaring me. *I'm* Lauren." She had to run to keep up with him. She touched his arm gently. "Trevor, I'm Lauren."

He glanced at her, then away. He didn't slow until they

reached the parking lot and waved down their driver. Trevor pushed her into the back seat. Fear pulsed at her, quick and hot.

"Shut up, and stay still," Trevor said.

Inside her head, she screamed. Lauren wanted to yell at Trevor for being such an ass, cut him with her words for mortifying her in front of the society she had struggled so hard to join. How many saw her fall in that booth? How many witnessed her fleeing barefoot out to the car? How could she show her face in front of any of them again?

But she couldn't move. Couldn't speak. Only her heart beat fast in her chest, pushing out blood to fuel her body for a screaming match she couldn't speak.

She glanced out the window, at the running lights on the ceiling of the car, anywhere but at the man next to her saying that she looked lovely tonight, and wasn't it nice when they weren't fighting?

I can't do this.

"So... how was your date last night?" Ben asked. He'd seen Trevor and Lauren dressed to the nines as they headed out the night before. He'd never seen anyone look so lovely in blue, even if he thought Lauren looked even more enchanting in her sweater and jeans.

Lauren shook her head. "I don't want to talk about it."

She'd ducked into his pool house lab the second the sun set that night, only relaxing once she'd shut the door behind her. It had taken Ben a few minutes to figure out how to order pizza using his phone, but a half-hour later she was laughing with bits of bacon stuck to the front of her sweater.

Ben let out a slow breath, trying to keep his hands from

shaking as he delicately lowered the final membrane into his device.

"Stay down," he warned as the thin membrane fluttered in the almost non-existent breeze.

"Trust me, I am going nowhere near *that*," Lauren said through a mouthful of spinach and artichoke pizza. She had ducked beneath one of Ben's many lab tables, and had begun to create a small fort out of sheets of metal and boxes of supplies, more to mock Ben's 'mad science' than for actual protection. She peered out of her hiding spot. "Be honest, how many interdimensional portals have you created by accident? Just like, a ballpark."

A chuckle escaped Ben's lips. "Don't make me laugh." He hissed, afraid to speak at a normal volume. Having Lauren in the lab with him made everything more exciting, more *real*. He'd certainly never been in danger of messing up an experiment before due to a case of the giggles. It was odd, but Ben liked it.

Ben gently moved the membrane, made out of a new polymer he invented for the occasion. It had a tendency to burst into flame if introduced to water too quickly, but--if he settled it right--could help increase the rotator's efficiency. He steadied his forceps and inched it downward.

"Ben!" Trevor's voice called out from outside. The pool door swung open hard, banging against the wall.

Ben jumped, losing his grip and dropping the membrane into his latest desalinator. A plume of flame shot into the air, the fire barely missing Ben's face, and he dove for cover.

Lauren's yelp of alarm was hidden by the siren from the sprinkler system creaking to life, erupting water from the overhead taps. Rain soaked the pool house, extinguishing the fire. Ben glanced around noting Lauren was safe under the table, his computer was covered in protective plastic, and anything else of any real value was down in his bedroom in the basement.

"Visiting you is always interesting, old boy." Trevor's long, black cape over a black and silver velvet suit was drenched, along with the stack of paper in his hand. Ben realized he was sopping wet as well, water dripping down his face as Trevor dumped the waterlogged pages into a nearby trash can.

"I *was* bringing you some routine paperwork from the investors, but it appears I will need to recreate these forms for you."

Trevor seemed to be a good mood, Ben was curious to see. Lauren was still hiding out of sight rather than coming out to greet her boyfriend, and Ben wasn't sure what that could imply about his nephew. As Danny's sireling, Trevor was one generation removed from Christopher, but their whole sire line was known for their empathy, creativity, and good-will toward others. It was what made them different from Ben's uncle, Rhys and all of his *hortari*-abusing sirelings. If Trevor wasn't being kind to his sirelings, Ben would certainly have to inform the king. But he needed more evidence than an uneasiness in his gut before he acted. *And yet...*

"Sorry about that." Ben waved vaguely at his charred experiment. "Volatile polymer, you know how it is."

"Actually I don't." Trevor dusted off a wooden stool, sweeping aside his cloak with all the drama of a middle school thespian. Ben smiled. *This* was his awkward, overly-dramatic nephew. Any uneasiness Ben felt was probably just because Trevor was a bit of an odd duck.

Trevor steepled his fingers beneath his chin. "Tell me. How's your latest project going?"

"I'm still perfecting my desalinator." Ben pulled a rolled up blueprint off of a stack of wires and rubber tubing. Out of the corner of his eye, Lauren shrunk further into her hiding spot. *Their relationship isn't my business,* he told himself, pushing aside his unease.

Trevor swiped the blueprints out of Ben's hand, running his fingers down the page and making little comments of 'uh huhs' and 'mmm...interesting'.

"Trevor..." Ben waved around the enormous sheet of paper that was blocking Trevor's view. "That's upside down."

Trevor glared at him, his expression switching from friendly to furious in less than a second.

Whoa. Ben stepped back.

"How dare you hand me upside down blueprints. I give you everything you need to work on your fancies, and you try to make a fool out of me?" Trevor's voice growled.

"But...you took the blueprints *from--*" Ben sputtered.

"Never mind that. Let me see how far you've gotten with my money."

"Right. Um." Ben pulled out his beloved machine, giving the already shining gears a little extra rub for luck. "This one's the most promising model so far. I just put some plastic waste, like this water bottle, into this input here." He pulled open a compartment about the size of a banana and stuffed in a crumpled up bottle. "And add in some ocean water here." He poured from a jug of collected ocean water into a funnel. "And voila!" Ben pressed a big, red button, and the device began to shake, letting out a terrible, grinding sound. The instruments on the lab table all bounced along with the box's vibrations.

"Just another few seconds of this!" Ben shouted above the din.

"Stop that terrible noise!" Trevor screamed, covering his

ears.

A happy "ding!" rang out and the machine stopped. Ben pulled two glass vials from the side of the box.

"Here's our good news and our bad news," Ben said. "We end up with potable drinking water, but also this second vial of waste."

Trevor grabbed the brown byproduct and took a long sniff at the top, then smiled. "Gasoline is *not* waste." Trevor slapped Ben on the shoulder. "You've done it! You've found a way to convert plastics into gasoline!""

Ben frowned. "I found a way to use plastics to convert ocean water into water safe to drink."

"Right, right. This is amazing." Trevor hadn't stopped looking at the gasoline, his longing making Ben increasingly uncomfortable.

Ben gently removed the vial from Trevor's hand. "I'm still working on the prototype. With each version, I'm making it more efficient, maximizing the amount of drinking water that's output while minimizing the gasoline runoff."

Trevor jumped to his feet. "Don't do that. This machine is great just as it is. I predict we'll be able to make this available to investors in just a few weeks. With my business expertise and your science, we will be *unstoppable*. You, me, and my lady are going to go all the way with this one, just you watch."

My lady. Ben knew he was frowning and tried to smooth his expression. The way Trevor said the words sent a chill down Ben's spine.

"So, how are things between you and your newest lady?" Aware that Lauren was within earshot, Ben chose his words carefully.

Trevor grinned. "I think I finally found the one in

Lauren."

"That's wonderful. But it's not the first time I've heard you say that about a girlfriend." *At least the last three*, Ben didn't say.

"Those cows I courted before Lauren didn't know how to really take care of a man. Lauren has enormous potential. I'm certain I'll be able to mold her into what I need." Trevor sneered.

A sneer isn't evidence that something is wrong, Ben reminded himself. He was a scientist. He needed *proof*. "Your last girlfriend, Susan, I think, was nice. She'd sing by the pool sometimes. Whatever happened with her?" Ben cautiously probed.

Trevor shifted his weight, looking at the ground. "You could say I gave her some flowers and sent her on her way." He nodded, making steely eye contact with Ben. "Yes. That's exactly what I did."

Trevor's words were innocent enough, but his tone made the hairs on the back of Ben's neck stick up. Each second of silence that passed was exponentially more awkward than the one before it.

"Speaking of business." Ben nodded at his wet, ash-covered workbench.

"Right. I'll leave you to it, then." Trevor moved towards the door. "I'll be back with a drier version of that paperwork for you to sign. Standard stuff." With a sweep of his cape, he was gone.

"Thanks for not ratting me out." Lauren's voice was small and low from under the table.

"No problem, but..." Ben fiddled with some clear pipettes, twirling them between his fingers. "Why were you hiding from Trevor? He's your sire *and* your boyfriend. Aren't you two getting along?" Ben asked.

"I think I made a mistake." Lauren fixed her hair, looking everywhere but at Ben. "I thought I knew what I was getting myself into when I let Trevor turn me." She straightened up. "Being with him is...complicated." She laughed nervously. "Ugh. If I was human, I would so need a drink right now."

Ben beamed, excited to have the solution so easily at hand. "I know just the place. AUDREY'S. You'll love it." He moved towards the door, his wet shoes squishing against the floor.

"I would absolutely love to, but I can't." Lauren slumped. "I'm not allowed to. Trevor's used the *hortari* to prevent me from leaving the grounds unsupervised." She shrugged. "I'm stuck here."

"Hardly." Ben guided her to the door. "I'll keep an eye on you. Surely the *hortari* would consider me a responsible adult?"

"Oh, absolutely," Lauren said solemnly. Her eyes twinkled, and the hint of a smile grew on her lips.

"Good. Then come with me, I'll keep you safe." Ben desperately hoped it was true.

LAUREN HADN'T BEEN in a dive bar since high school when she used to sneak into the college bars with a fake ID. The off-balance stools and stained tables she passed reassured Lauren this was a place where she could relax, and vying for status here wouldn't matter. She'd been to a few places that catered to the supernatural set--Nikolai's favorite cocktail lounge was in a glitzy ice hotel owned by a bear shifter and a witch--but she'd never been anywhere quite so *enthusiastic* about embracing what most humans considered impossible.

"What is this place?" she asked Ben as they made their way to a cozy booth in the back. Her hand clamped tightly around his arm, even if the cramped space made it difficult to walk arm in arm.

"This is AUDREY'S. It's a bar for people like us. It was opened by the witch grandmother of the current owner, Audrey." He nodded toward a red-haired witch standing next to the bartender, scanning through an enormous, ancient-looking tome behind the bar.

"It's, um--"

Ben smiled, handing her a flyer of that week's events. "Careful. Rumor is, this place is a little bit alive, so you wouldn't want to insult it."

"I wasn't!" What she'd intended to say was *interesting*, which probably wasn't the best move if the bar was sensitive. "It's *lovely*. Everyone seems to be having a lot of fun."

A horse shifter brayed with joy as she wheeled out an old karaoke machine and quickly set it up in the center of the bar.

Looking around, Lauren had never seen so many supernaturals in one place. The place was packed with pixies, yetis, dragon shifters, werewolves, bear shifters, and witches, all together in mixed groups around the rickety tables. There was even a woman whose body was entirely made of intertwining swamp grasses and sticks wearing a lab coat, glasses, and nothing else.

Cheers rang out (with a few interspersed, good-natured groans) as the karaoke machine sprang to life and folks handed forward pieces of paper to sign-up to sing.

Lauren gave Ben a speculative glance and he laughed, holding up his hands. "Trust me, you don't want to hear me sing. I'm an off-key fog horn."

A very pale hand slid forward to deposit two drinks on

their table. "Oh sweetie, you think there is actually going to be singing? Just you watch." Lola the bartender--a pale woman with disarmingly red lips, a rose tattoo across her entire chest, and hundreds of small braids surrounding her head--grinned into Lauren's eyes. Lauren's shoulders relaxed a little just being near her. The woman wasn't a vampire, but Lauren couldn't identify what Lola was even when Lauren leaned unnecessarily close to shake the woman's hand. Something old and odd, but that was all she could smell.

Lola nodded to the glass in front of Lauren. "That's my patented calm down juice. Just don't ask what's in it."

Lauren glanced down at her drink. It definitely had blood in it, she could smell a sense of the donor's calm and wellbeing, but the drink was bright purple and steamed a little.

Ben looked at his glass. "Am I allowed to ask?" He held it up to the light, and gave an experimental sniff.

Lola laughed. "Don't worry, you have your usual. Blood donated by a science fair winner, your favorite. With just a splash of tequila."

"Thanks!" He replied with such enthusiasm, Lauren giggled.

"Everyone! Tonight I will be your Master of Karaoke!" The bar's owner, Audrey, stood at the microphone, her arms raised above her head. The room cheered. She held up a clear bowl filled with the dozen or so cards which had already been filled out. "You all know the rules, but a quick reminder: pass up your cards if you want a turn and *don't* be the asshole who volunteers your friends without their okay." She smiled broadly to the room and dug her hand deep into the bowl, withdrawing a card. "And our first up is Shelby Meyer, singing 'Niveis Incantamentum'!"

The whole room cheered and made good natured cat calls as a tiger shifter wearing tight, black leather came to the front of the room.

Lauren leaned forward to whisper to Ben, "I've never heard of that song. What language is that?"

Ben smiled and tapped his nose. "You'll see."

The tiger shifter pressed play on the tablet at the front of the small stage and words that looked like a mix of Latin and esoteric symbols projected onto the wall behind her. Music swelled through the speakers, a fast drum beat with soaring violins playing a tune that Lauren didn't recognize, but knew she'd be humming for the next week. A bouncing ball on the screen beat out a countdown to when the words started. Lauren felt herself being drawn forward toward the words. The air tasted thicker, with strange currents moving along her skin that tickled and cooled all at once. She glanced at Ben, who was already grinning with delight.

The woman started to sing, her voice not entirely on key, but following the words with perfect ease and a confidence that made it easy not to notice that her tune didn't quite line up with the violins. Lauren couldn't understand the words, but as the tiger shifter sang, the room dropped in temperature and all around the bar, couples cuddled closer together and grinned, looking up and around in anticipation of something.

Lauren eyed Ben. He was so big, looked so warm. Would he welcome it if she just slid a little closer to soak in some of his heat? Every time she'd gone by the pool house, he'd always worn that oversized lab coat which completely hid his body. But before they left to come to the bar, he'd changed into a clean t-shirt right there in front of her: whipping off his lab coat, removing the grease-stained shirt he'd been wearing underneath, and revealing an incredible set of washboard abs, surprisingly ripped arms, and a beautifully-muscled back which narrowed down at his waist in a delectable triangle. She'd barely been able to breathe, and now that she knew the glory hidden beneath his lab coats, the temptation to snuggle up a little beckoned like an itch.

The music swelled and the tiger shifter swayed her hips, her fingers twirling like she was playing a piano in the air to the song's beat.

Something small and white hit Lauren's nose and she looked up.

Snow! Snow was falling from the ceiling in perfect, crystalline flakes. It swirled around the room in spiraling eddies that danced to the tune of the music.

"This is amazing!" Lauren cried, her voice lost in the cheers and applause from around the room.

Ben grinned and slid his chair over next to her with a look of pure bliss on his face. It took just the smallest movement and Lauren's head rested on his shoulder, her side lightly brushing his side.

"*This* is how magic is supposed to be," he said.

Lauren nodded, his shoulder brushing the side of her face as her head moved. *This is how love is supposed to be*. The thought came, sudden and unwelcome. She pushed it down, sitting up straight. Ben wasn't an option. He was her friend, and she was with Trevor.

The song slowed, the tempo calming, and the tiger lowered her arms, her singing growing soft. The room warmed, the snowflakes vanished one by one like tiny stars winking out, and the music lulled to silence. As the song ended, Lauren clapped enthusiastically, joined by everyone else in the room. She didn't look at Ben, hoping her face wasn't blushing as furiously as she thought it was.

I cannot be falling in love with Ben.

The tiger shifter made her way back to her table, getting high-fives, thumbs up, and slaps on the back all the way to her chair, and Audrey jumped back onto the stage. The red-haired witch pulled another card from the bowl and the swamp-grass woman swayed up to the mic when her name was called. Lauren took a sip of her purple drink, feeling calm and a deep joy settle in her bones. The comfort reminded her of pizza, of her folding chair at the pool house, and Ben's eyes.

"This is a lullaby of my people." The woman's voice was rasping and low like the sound of the wind through tall grasses. When she pressed play on the tablet, calming plinks of harps and a plonking ring of what Lauren guessed was some kind of xylophone emerged from the speakers. As the woman sang, ghostlike images emerged to hang in the air above their heads. Grassy hills and trees against brilliant sunsets floated and bumped together like they were suspended in enormous bubbles.

"Thank you for bringing me here," Lauren said in a low voice to Ben. "I thought I knew everything there was to know about the supernatural world after all those years being the wife of a bear shifter, but there's *so* much."

Ben nodded. "More than can be seen or experienced in a hundred lifetimes. My brother, Danny, was an explorer for a few centuries, and tried to see everything in the world. He found that by the time he'd gotten all the way around the world, where he'd been had already changed. There's always new things to see. Now he's running a club with his fiancé, but does investigations for our sire, the king, that take him all over the world."

She wanted to ask about what an investigator did. Traveling around the world discovering new things sounded great. But she latched onto the most important piece of information. "Your sire is the *king*? You're a *prince*?"

Ben shrugged. A floating image of a mountainside crowned with clouds bounced against his head like a balloon before joining its fellows dancing around the rafters. "Christopher turned me long before he was king. He's always had a sense of responsibility towards all living things, and makes a point of only turning folks who he thinks will help the world in some way. It's a lot to live up to, but it really fuels me." He sipped thoughtfully at his drink. "I've invented my fair share of gizmos, but the machine I'm working on will do some *real* good. Once we can safely purify water from the oceans as drinkable water, then all drought could be eliminated. Diseases that spread from unclean water will disappear." He was so excited, he practically vibrated in his seat.

"You put me to shame," Lauren said, smiling at him. "You became a vampire to really make a difference. I just did it because..." Her voice trailed off.

"Because why?" His smile was kind, his arm going around her shoulder to pull her close. She relaxed against his arm, feeling the smooth edges of his muscles through her sweater. Lauren wanted to curl even closer, but she held back, keeping what she hoped would only be construed as a companionable cuddle, if such a thing existed.

"Well, I didn't exactly grow up being encouraged to make the world a better place. It's not an excuse, but it's true. As soon as I was walking, my parents squeezed me into puffy dresses and took me on the pageant circuit. I was no better than the prized pig at a state fair."

Lauren's lip curled at a particularly hateful memory of having her scalp burned by curling irons. The pain lingered for days, but no matter how much she cried, her mother just told her to suck it up, since none of the injuries were visible beneath her hair.

"Judges would assess how cute I was, how brightly I could hold a smile, and if my costume walked the right line between jailbait and pedophilia." She could hear the bitterness in her own voice and took a deep breath. The soothing voice of the swamp lady at the mic calmed her until even her toes relaxed. "When I was seven or eight, I got cast in a few commercials for cereal and toothpaste and such, but I never saw any of that money. My parents told friends and family that everything I was earning was going into a college fund, but the cash never made it out of the liquor store. Every time the debts racked up, I got trotted out to earn money. Our survival relied on how pretty I was."

Ben's eyes were bright as he studied her face. He gave her hand a comforting squeeze. "You have so much more than that to offer."

Lauren shrugged. "I wish I'd heard that years ago. When I was nineteen, my parents died in a skiing accident, and I didn't know how to take care of myself. So I guess I just fell back into what I was trained to do." She smiled wanly.

Audrey was back at the podium announcing the next singer, and Lauren startled in her chair. She'd been so focused on her memories, she hadn't even noticed that the swamp lady's song had finished, the image bubbles vanished like they never existed. Next up to the stage was an enormous troll whose head brushed the ceiling. He led the room in a rousing drinking song that seemed to be mostly grunts and "yahoo!" sung at regular intervals. No magical images or spells took shape in the air, but once the whole room got into the song, the entire bar shook and swayed along with the stomping feet.

Ben touched her shoulder. "Want to go outside? Escape this rowdy crew for a bit?"

Lauren nodded. The music had knocked her from the worst of her memories, but she didn't feel up to singing along just yet.

The night was quiet. A long field stretched out back to a line of trees. Scorch marks in the grass and random holes in the ground signaled that AUDREY's backyard was used for a different purpose during the day, but it was abandoned now. The moon was as bright as day to her vampiric vision, and Lauren breathed deep in the safety of the open space.

Ben held out a hand and she took it, walking in companionable silence to the middle of the field and lying beside him flat on her back, looking up at the stars. She felt like a teenager again, sneaking out of her bedroom to meet up with a boy, the stillness of the night full of possibility. Ben's presence was solid next to her, his usually bursting energy contained.

"I know it's not my place to say..." He started to say.

"What?"

"Well, your parents were a bit awful."

Lauren laughed, a highly unladylike snort her mother would have hated. "A bit." She let out a long breath. "They taught me what they believed. My mother would go out of her way to tell me how she pitied women who 'let themselves down' by not wearing makeup to the grocery store. Father taught me to spot a degenerate by jeans worn too low or if a guy sported a tattoo." That hadn't stopped Lauren from dating as many 'degenerate' low-jeans-wearing-tattooed boys in high school as she could find, but that was a story for another day. "It was constantly stated as fact that if I wasn't skinny and pretty and happy and popular, I'd be starving and degraded by the end of the day."

Even now, knowing that she would never age, her fingers itched to check her skin in the mirror for new wrinkles. She'd effectively done what her mother had tried to achieve through all those facelifts and Botox sessions: Lauren had managed to maintain her body forever in a perfect state of almost-youth. The knowledge made her less pleased than she thought it would.

Ben shook his head. "I know a thing or two about being judged based on appearances. I've been black in America for the last few hundred years, after all, but at least I've always been surrounded by people who appreciated what else I could offer."

Lauren gave him a pained smile. "I know my story doesn't really compare. I never suffered any *real* hardship. Nikolai, my first husband, was really sweet. He was a friend of my parents' who I had met a few times when I was younger. His son was already grown and out of the house when my parents died and Nikolai offered me the protection of his income and a home in exchange for being his wife. I said yes. And he was true to his word: he took care of everything. He bought our house, I used his credit cards. We grew to be comfortable with each other, and those were some of my happiest years. But after he died, I felt just...lost. Those three years before I met Trevor were the first time I'd ever really lived on my own. It terrified me to be under my own control."

"Well, tonight's the night. Nobody's telling you what to do right now. What do you wanna do?" Ben asked.

The back door of the bar swung open and music from inside streamed out into the night. The wafting strains of a slow, swinging beat stole out in the darkness, a man's voice smooth and smoky intertwining with the notes.

Lauren stood up and held out her hand to help Ben to his feet. He stood up next to her in one, flowing motion.

"Dance with me." Her parents only let her dance tap routines for her pageant recitals. Nikolai had a bad hip and would just hold her hand as he bobbed his head to the music. She was never free to dance the way she wanted to.

"I'd love to," Ben said. His hands brushed her hand and her hip, his touch light, letting her lead.

The music grew louder, and twinkling lights that changed color as they floated along streamed out of the bar's back door. The lights turned into a flood of rainbow pinpricks of light that shimmered and surged until they blanketed the sky. The music was now coming *from* the lights, surrounding the two of them and lighting up Ben's face in planes of blue and gold that complemented the pink of his lips and the brightness of his eyes.

Lauren smiled up at the lights, then closed her eyes, feeling the music flow through her from her head down to her toes. The beat pulsed deep in her chest, pumping down to her legs and arms, the surge of the music modulating and caressing her as she moved. Her arms floated up above her head, her hips swayed, her feet lifted and twirled in steps she had never learned, but that felt *right*. Her hair tossed, wild and free, with the beat, one hand pressing against Ben's, while she twirled away from him and then back until she could feel his heat, and then twirling away. She kicked out, felt the movement of the air as Ben danced away, moving behind her, but staying close, his hands touching for the comfort of contact, but not guiding.

For once, she didn't care what she looked like, if her movements were graceful or awkward, if Ben was following or staring. It didn't matter. It was her dance, just her and the music, and every note was sweet.

The song continued on, each verse increasing in intensity until the drums hammered into her bones and her feet flew so fast she kicked off the ground and felt it fall away beneath her. She jumped higher and higher, pushing her vampire strength until her head met the twinkling light and, for a moment, they surrounded her face like old friends.

Ben clapped and whooped, and she stopped jumping to take a look at him. His arms were flung in the air alongside her, kicking and jumping with wild abandon, no technique, just joy. She laughed, copying his movements and feeling warmth down to her toes when he twirled, an echo of how she'd been dancing a moment before. They didn't touch, but she sensed his movements like electricity binding their bodies together, the music connecting their hands, their feet, their hips together as one laughing, flapping creature under the twinkling lights above their heads.

The music slowed, the lights dimmed, until they were once again alone under the stars. She moved closer to Ben. His steps mirrored hers until they stood so close, their chests brushed with each breath.

Nobody's telling you what to do right now. What do you wanna do?

Ben's words echoed in her head like a dare. She stared into his face, which locked on hers with an expression of such bare longing and hunger, her breath hitched. She licked her lips to moisten them, her hands moving up to stroke his shoulders and squeeze the muscles gently. The currents between them felt like living things drawing them closer, and she leaned into it, longing for his embrace, wanting to press her lips to the eyelids of his calm eyes, run her fingers along the sides of his smiling lips, feel his hands on her, covering her skin, entering her everywhere.

The crash of a bottle breaking from inside the bar made

her jump.

She stepped back, stumbling a little over the grass. *I'm with Trevor. This is wrong.*

Ben leaned forward to steady her, but she put up her hands to brush away his help.

"We can't," she said.

Ben nodded. "I'll drive us back."

THEY DIDN'T SPEAK on the way home, just a quick, "bye," before Lauren slipped into the house. What was there to say? *Thank you for possibly the best night of my life.* It sounded trite, false, like the sort of thing she used to say to Trevor. *I think I'm falling in love with you.* It was too much, too true, and she couldn't say it. Under all those words was a thought she wasn't entirely sure how to voice. She leaned her head against the glass door of the porch and listened to the click of Ben's lab door on the opposite side of the pool.

I'm afraid what Trevor will do to us if he knows.

I SHOULD HAVE KISSED HER. I shouldn't want to kiss her at all. Ben's thoughts dueled with each other as he entered his lab. He seethed at her late parents, even her late husband, everyone who had ever had a hand in convincing her that her looks dictated her worth. Ben wanted to protect her, to hold her, to keep her safe not just from everything out in the world, but from the poison installed in her mind. *She's spectacular.*

Ben was halfway through the lab when he stopped short and frowned. Books that were once arranged in a neat stack were scattered on the ground. His blueprints, usually rolled into a pyramid-shaped pile in the corner, were flung all over the place. His pipettes had been moved, and even his lab notebook was missing.

Someone's been sciencing in my lab.

The familiar sound of a glass test tube being crushed under a boot made Ben spin towards the source. Trevor had made it as far as the door, one hand on the handle and the other cradling a stack of blueprints. Ben could see the outline of his lab journal sticking out the back of Trevor's pants. *Is nothing sacred?*

Ben cleared his throat. "Is there something I can help you with?"

Trevor spun, his grip tightening on the blueprints. "I was just going to make digital backups of your work. That fire the other day made me realize you have everything on *paper* in here. Of course, I was going to discuss it with you, I just..." Trevor stammered. "You weren't here. So I figured, since I pay for everything anyway, I'd..." He shrugged.

Ben wanted to believe him. If it wasn't for Trevor's nervously bobbing Adam's apple, or the bead of sweat that was currently making its way down Trevor's temple, he might have.

"That's not the kind of thing you need to sneak around to do." Ben's voice was a low growl.

Trevor paused, nodded. "Quite right. Quite right." Ben wanted to laugh. Trevor assembling thought was like a train struggling to make it up too steep a hill. Ben could almost see the steam coming out of the man's ears from the effort. "Anyway... since I have you here..."

Trevor desperately looked around until his eye fell on the stack of paper he'd brought with him the day before. He picked them out of the trash, smoothing out the top pages, which had since dried and were mostly readable.

"I still need you to sign these. It's nothing important, but if you could..." He flipped to the back page and pointed to a blank signature line. "That would be great."

Ben slid the stack of papers closer, pulling it out of Trevor's grip so he could read the pages hidden by Trevor's hand. As Ben scanned the words, his eyes widened, and his jaw went slack.

"What is this, Trevor? This says that I relinquish *all ownership* of my desalination device. It puts you in complete control of how this machine is used, all the profits from any potential sales, and lists you as the *official owner of this patent*." Ben clenched his fist, balling up the incriminating document. "*What is this*?" He shouted.

Trevor let out an aggravated sigh. "*This* is business. I'm the one who can figure out how to make money from your gadgets. Do you realize how much certain nations and nation-sized corporations would pay for this machine to never see the light of day?" Trevor paced a short distance, back and forth, a manic smile growing on his face. "*Trillions.* The answer is trillions of dollars." He flipped back to the signature page. "Sign this and we'll be wealthy beyond our wildest dreams."

"No." Ben's voice was quiet, but firm. "We talked about this. You were going to help me *distribute* my gadgets. My machine will provide clean water to those who need it." He ripped the heavy stack of papers in half in a single tear, dropping them into a metal bucket at his feet. "I will *not* allow you to whore out my invention to a bunch of oil companies." Ben grabbed his jar of polymer scraps and threw them into the bucket. "This will be open-source. Available online to anybody who needs it."

Trevor shook his head and sneered, not paying attention. Ben grabbed the jug of ocean water and poured it into the bucket, the polymer igniting in a whoosh of flames that had Trevor scrambling for the door.

"You're insane, you know that?" Trevor ran outside, Ben close on his heels. Ben was older, faster, and snatched the blueprints from under Trevor's arm. The sprinkler system switched on inside the pool house, but Ben ignored it. He held out his hand.

"My lab journal, if you please." Ben gestured meaningfully at the rectangular bulge in the back of Trevor's pants.

"Fine." Trevor pulled the lab journal out of the back of his pants and handed it to Ben. "*I'm* already fabulously wealthy. I'm not the one living off of charity, leeching off of family like some pathetic idealist."

"You're a worm, Trevor. I'll never know why Danny sired you. You're selfish and devious, and you treat Lauren like garbage."

"Hey!" Trevor cut Ben off, the single word slicing through the air. "I only put up with you and your absent-minded professor act since you're my uncle and I don't need Danny on my case. But Lauren is *my* girlfriend." He took a step closer to Ben. "I'm not a fool, you know. She goes on her little walks and comes home reeking of pizza and seawater. You don't trust me around your little toys? Well, I don't trust you around my woman. Stay away from Lauren, and I'll stay away from your gadgets. Deal?" The door slammed behind Trevor as he stomped back up to the main house.

Ben's gaze followed him, his eyes seeking out some sign of Lauren in the house until he realized what he was doing. Trevor was a little shit, but he had a point. Lauren was with Trevor. And she'd made her choice.

He sighed. "Deal."

∼

LAUREN COULD STILL HEAR the music from the twinkling lights in her head as she pushed the outfit she'd worn to AUDREY'S as far down into her laundry hamper as possible and changed into a flowing, lace nightgown that looked like something out of a Gothic novel. Picking up a rag, she pranced over on light feet to Trevor's book case. Dusting was easy enough, didn't require any attention, and was as good an activity as any to appease Trevor's demands.

She hummed bars of music softly to herself, letting her feet dance a little to the beat, her hips swaying as she reached up to move the rag along the top shelves. If she closed her eyes, she could almost picture herself back there now: the coolness of the night sky playing against her skin, and Ben's beloved presence supportive at her side.

A chill ran through her and she knew she was being watched. She stopped moving, the hum dying in her throat. She knew who was standing at the door before she finished turning, his lurking stare so oppressive she could feel it across the room.

"I just had an *interesting* conversation with Ben." Trevor leaned against his bedroom's door frame, his arms crossed. A shiver of fear ran down her spine. His face was so closed, so cold. The way he stood in the shadow, his eyes looked like black holes.

"Oh?" she tried to sound disinterested as her heart hammered in her chest. She was impressed her hand didn't shake, but continued to slide across the book spines.

"He seemed to think that I wasn't treating you well." His voice was a low growl.

"I can't imagine why he'd think something so ridiculous," she said, her voice smooth. "You have a very comfortable home. I have everything I could possibly need, and most importantly, I have *you*. I'm hardly mistreated." She grabbed at one of the sturdier hardback copies of *Dracula* and spun around to face him. "I hadn't even read *Dracula* before I came here. Imagine that. It's such a *great* book, and you introduced me to it, my sweet."

Trevor walked forward, plucked the book from her hand, and slid it back into the bookshelf, flush with its fellows.

"*Dracula* is one of the most beautiful love stories of all time." His voice was harsh, his breathing quick. "His wife was *murdered* by the treachery of his foul enemies and, rather than exist without her, he chose an immortal life, having faith that their love was so strong, she would be born again to be with him." He leaned in closer. "Even her engagement to another man could not keep her from her *real* love, her *eternal* love with the man who had waited hundreds of years to be with her." Trevor leaned closer and closer with each word.

"I thought..." She swallowed hard. "The immortal love part, is that in the book?" It wasn't. It was created for the 1990's movie version and repeated as canon ever since. All those hours on the internet researching Dracula to please her new boyfriend now fell flat. The vampire in the original *Dracula* was simply a monster. He didn't love, he didn't long for connection. He just killed and fed and controlled.

"What do you know?" Trevor stepped away from her. "You know nothing of vampires, nothing of love."

Ben's face flashed in front of her eyes. Even Nikolai for a second, although a love of a different kind. *I know love. It's just not with you.* She bit her tongue.

"Perhaps not. Perhaps I still need to learn about love." She kept her voice calm, but her jaw was so tense, the words barely scraped by her clenched teeth. "But perhaps we can learn together. Part of love is talking with each other, trying to understand each other."

Trevor eyed her, pacing back and forth between her and the bed like a caged beast.

"Communication can be hard. Here, I'll start." Lauren took a deep breath. "The *hortari* commands. *I feel...*" She put extra emphasis on the *I feel* statement lauded by marriage gurus everywhere. "...that the *hortari* is being used to command me to do things that I would happily do if asked politely." She stepped forward to place a hand on his arm. "I really wish you would stop, it's unkind."

"*Unkind?* I am your sire!" Trevor shouted, stepping away from her. "It is my *right* to shape you, to teach you to be who you are supposed to be!"

"And who am I *supposed* to be?" she asked. *Not good, not good, not good.* Her heart hammered in her chest.

"My love!" He pulled at his hair, his pacing speeding up to an intense prowl back and forth across the room. "You *are* my Felicity, don't you see? Your gracefulness, your voice, your hair. You are her. Born again to be with me!"

Lauren stepped back, found the bookshelf too close, and inched to the side, trying to edge herself closer to the door. "What are you talking about?"

"You are the one! You were born to love me! To obey me! This time you will do as I say!"

"No. We're done, Trevor. I don't know who this Felicity was, or what happened between the two of you, but I'm not her. I'm me. And if you can't see that using the *hortari* to completely control my life is wrong, then we are *really* done." She made a break for the door, sprinting at top speed.

Trevor was faster. "You bitch!" His arm clenched around her midsection, lifting her off the ground. She screamed and kicked.

"Let me down! Stop this!"

"You are my love!" He threw her across the room and she landed hard against the wall, sending a painting of a Romanian castle crashing to the floor in a shower of glass. Lauren bounced off the hard surface, landing on her side amidst glass shards on the carpeting.

"You should *burn* for me." Trevor growled.

Everything hurt. The window had cracked from the force of her hitting the wall, glass imbedded in the palms of her hands. She groaned, pushing herself up and pulling the glass out of her hand. The wound closed immediately, but the pain remained, deep bruises forming where her ribs were cracked, and her leg twisted uncomfortably beneath her.

Lauren glared at him from the floor. "You're a monster."

If he heard, he ignored her, stalking forward until he put two fingers under her chin and dragged her upward until she stood on shaking legs. He leaned close. "You'll learn your lesson. You *will* burn for me. Burn through the night, my love."

The *hortari* took control and Lauren screamed. More pain than she'd ever experienced in her life blazed along her skin. She burned like she was on fire; every part of her skin felt raw and inflamed.

Burn through the night, he'd said. The night still had hours to go. *No!*

Desperation gave her strength. She pushed Trevor away, spinning to leap through the cracked window and plummeted two stories down to the backyard. Glass rained down around her, but the cuts were meaningless compared to the imaginary fire which consumed her. She stumbled across the property, screaming and crying, and dove into the pool.

The water closed around her in comforting coolness, but

the burning didn't stop. Her nightgown pooled around her, even the soft lace too much pressure on her raw skin. She tossed the fabric away and sank down to the bottom of the pool. Vampires couldn't drown. The water was quiet.

A splash sounded above her head and she knew she wasn't alone. Filled with an animalistic panic, she kicked off the bottom, wrenched the pool's ladder from its mooring, and spun, searching for Trevor's inevitable attack.

There was no Trevor, only Ben standing in front of her wearing only pajama bottoms with train sets printed on them. His hands rose in front of him in surrender. "Lauren, it's me."

"Ben." She dropped the ladder with a splash, leaping forward until she was in his arms. His touch against her skin didn't hurt, but also didn't decrease the pain. "Trevor's insane!" She pulled him in closer, pushing her bare breasts to his chest, wrapping her legs around his waist.

"Lauren--" His voice was hesitant, a warning that only a few hours ago they'd stepped back from each other rather than betray their loyalties to Trevor.

She cut him off by pressing her lips to his. "Trevor and I are through." He stiffened in surprise and then melted into her, his hands roaming her bare back and resting on her ass, pulling her hips closer as his cock hardened against her inner thighs through the thin fabric of his pants.

"I've wanted this since we met." She tightened her legs around his waist and grabbed his hands from her ass to firmly plant them on her breasts. He groaned and did as she bid, massaging and stroking her erect nipples. She slipped her fingers down to the elastic waistband of his pajamas and pulled them down until she could stroke his cock in the water.

"Oooo, gods. Yes, don't stop." He groaned, his hips thrusting.

"I dumped Trevor, and he's burning me for it." But was he? Her skin wasn't on fire with pain anymore. It tingled with arousal and lust, burning figuratively with *passion*.

Oh hortari, *you clever curse. It's all about the interpretation.* "Ben, I burn for you. I have since we met. Make love to me. I need you." She sighed and nibbled his earlobe, arousal surging in her core. The movements of their bodies made the water lap playfully against her naked skin.

"Lauren, my love, I burn for you too." His tongue surged into her mouth as his hand slipped down between them and stroked down her slit, finding her clit and massaging it in delicate circles. She flexed her hips to give him better access, her hand pumping his cock in time with his movements. His hard body against hers felt perfect, her torso lining up with his so she could lean forward to kiss him as his fingers worked their magic along her clit and then plunged inside her, never stopping their urgent dance along her most sensitive spot.

Distantly, Lauren heard Trevor blasting OneRepublic and Timbaland's "Apologize" like a moping teenager from the top floor, but Trevor didn't matter any more. Ben's breath in her ear made her tingle, everything enhanced. The scent of his skin made her want to lick all of him she could touch. His intense gaze never left her face as he assessed her pleasure and made small adjustments to his caress along her breast, soaring her to higher heights. Her chest heaved as arousal built in waves, the water lapping at her legs up to her breasts pushing her to such intense pleasure she came screaming, biting hard into Ben's shoulder to muffle the sound.

"That's it, my love." His hand moved in calm strokes

along her spine as his cock jumped in her hand. "I love seeing joy on your face."

Lauren kissed his sweet mouth, pulling him close and reaching down to slip his cock inside her--he was so thick, he stretched her walls with a glorious soreness, perfect and lush--then flexed her hips to ride him.

He groaned. "Oh gods, that's amazing." He held her close as he carried her to the wall of the pool, pressing her back up against the side so he could have better leverage to thrust into her warmth, his cock pushing deep into her over and over, withdrawing almost all the way to surge back in again.

She held on so tight, she feared her nails were hurting him, but he just grinned with wild abandon and pounded her harder. She loved it, knowing she was making him lose control, that her clever and kind lover was losing his mind fucking her.

Ben pulled her to the shallowest part of the pool and set her down on the gentle incline, changing the angle of her hips so his cock brushed her clit with each slide inside of her. Pleasure built again, even more intense than the first time, her toes curling as she threw her head back, letting her orgasm take her over and over. His cock stiffened, expanding just as he came inside her.

They lay side by side in the water for a long moment, her skin still pulsing with need. *Burn through the night. Oh, lord.* She looked up at the moon. Still a few hours to go. "Ben...I need..."

"Don't worry. I've got you." He picked her up and carried her into the pool house, both of them dripping water all the way in the door. The lab was too cluttered to carry her, but he took her hand and led her toward the back of his lab. The lab smelled like ocean water and singed paper, but the slight, lingering smell of pizza made her smile. She stroked

Ben's bare back, loving the closeness of him. She trusted him more than anyone she'd ever known. He made her feel safe, loved, just as she loved him.

He kicked aside a carpet and opened up a hidden door in the floor. He flicked on a light next to the door and led the way down a short ladder into his bedroom. It was exactly what she would expect of Ben: utilitarian, with a double bed that had clearly never been made, but smelled clean. A small chest of clothes and a poster of the Periodic Table were the only decorations.

"I'm sorry. It's not exactly luxurious. If you...um...stick around, I can definitely jazz up the place a bit. One of my sireling sisters is a designer and she can--"

Lauren stopped his babbling with a swift kiss. "It's great," she said. "I'm with you. I don't care what the room looks like."

He grinned his beautiful grin and swooped in for a longer kiss, his mouth hot and needy against hers. She pushed them both toward the bed, the two tumbling back onto the unmade covers. Their legs tangled together, their hands trying to touch everything at once. Ben's lips found her neck, kissing a trail down past her breasts and her stomach to settle with his mouth latched firmly to her clit. Lauren cried out, her hands automatically reaching down to curl around his hair and keep him firmly planted there as he licked and kissed her core.

"You taste so good." He licked at her. "I want to always taste my cum on you," he muttered into her pussy.

She arched her back, pressing her flesh closer to his tongue. "Oooo, don't stop. Don't you dare stop."

"Darling, I'm going to eat you out until the sun rises."

She didn't think it was possible to cum so many times. After the fifth, she lost count. An hour later, he recovered enough to fuck her again and she rode him for as long as they could stand, switching positions so he could pound her from behind, and she refused to let him cum again until he was inside her mouth, his salty cum dribbling down her lips and she swallowed deep. She felt addicted to his touch, kissing and stroking everything she could reach. Even after the sun rose and the incessant burning of the *hortari* died away, she couldn't stop kissing him. It was mid-morning before she collapsed into sleep, curled up against Ben's side, his hand even in sleep curled around her breast.

Time was shaky at best in Ben's basement, but she guessed it was at least afternoon, from the way her stomach gurgled, when she woke up. She rolled to her side to see Ben was already awake, looking down at her with an expression of wonder.

"I keep thinking I'll blink and realize I'm dreaming," he said.

"I'm not going to be able to stay here," she said. "Trevor's still my sire, and he won't just let me go."

Ben nodded, his fingers caressing back and forth along her hip in tiny circles. Lauren smiled. Ben couldn't stop moving, even when still in bed. "I know. There are safe places for you to go. My sire, Christopher, has been trying to track down instances of *hortari* abuse, bring the abusers to justice. I can get you to the castle if that's where you want to go."

Lauren laughed, since the alternative was to cry. *There's been a way out all along?* She could have left after that disaster of an opera date. She could have left after the first time his command locked her into doing his will. Sure, he had commanded she couldn't leave the house without supervision, but she could have found a way around it. She *had* found a way around it to go to AUDREY'S with Ben.

"Come with me." She grabbed his hand, held it to her chest cradled between her breasts. "Trevor is a monster. He'll use you just as surely as he used me. Be with me." She'd survived her parents' degradation. She'd survived Trevor's violence. She'd survived her flesh feeling like it was on fire. She had proven she could survive anything on her own. But she didn't *want* to do it alone.

She looked deep into Ben's beautiful eyes. "I love you, Benjamin Dal."

His hands cupped her face. "And I love you, Lauren Vaughan, with everything I am. Wherever you want to go, whatever you want to do, I will follow."

The rest of the day passed in a blur of endearments, remembered moments together eating pizza and chatting about when each realized that they loved the other. Ben said it was the first time she'd pressed bacon pizza into his hand; Lauren admitted she hadn't realized her feelings were love until AUDREY'S. They made love again until Lauren chased them both into the shower to clean up, where they made love again, which meant getting cleaned up again.

Ben slid open the trap door to his lab as the sun slipped over the horizon, glancing about to confirm that Trevor wasn't about. From the sound of the break-up playlist still blasting from the top floor, he hadn't even noticed the noises they were making in the pool the night before.

Not my problem anymore.

She'd borrowed a set of pants and a shirt from Ben's closet, lashing it across her lean body with a belt. The clothes were hopelessly oversized and made her look fat, but she didn't care.

They were getting out of here. Together, they crept out of the pool house, sticking to the shadows along the fence. Ben pulled out a device and pointed it at his home. It shimmered for a second before shrinking down to the size of a quarter.

Lauren stared. She'd been *inside* that house. She'd *slept* in that house. She glanced at the device in Ben's hand. *Fucking hell.* Only the pneumatic tube which led from the side of the pool house into the mansion remained, a reaching hand to nowhere. Ben jogged over to pick up the button-sized home and pop it into a plastic bag he pulled from his pocket.

"You have no idea how many times I've dropped this and flooded my house." He winked at her and tapped at the bag. "This helps."

Lauren giggled and rolled her eyes. "Let's just get out of here."

BRANCHES CRUNCHED under Ben's boots as they ran along the forest trail, super vampiric speed making short work of their progress along the back of Trevor's estate. Ben resisted the urge to laugh, to jump for joy.

Lauren turned towards Ben and smiled, her face lighting up the night more brightly than the full moon. They had come to a point where they didn't need to speak words to be understood. *I love you*, her face beamed at him. *I love you back*, Ben indicated with a squeeze of her hand. Everything was perfect. Almost.

They just had to get away before Trevor realized they weren't coming back. Lauren didn't need to face whatever that jerk tossed her way if they encountered him.

Following a different path than they'd taken to get out when they went to AUDREY'S in case Trevor was on the lookout for them, they hurried through the trees to get to the less-security-covered back door of the garage.

Lauren slowed their run to a stroll, guiding Ben to match her pace. "I think the well...everything took it out of me." She panted. "Let's just walk." Lauren wrapped her arm around Ben's back and leaned into him as they strolled along.

"This is nice." Ben sighed. "I've been living in that pool house for so long, only leaving when Christopher summoned me for something. I was so focused on my work, I never took the time to explore the grounds. I almost missed seeing how much beauty there is in the world." He never took his eyes off of Lauren.

Lauren blushed, looking down. "I wouldn't have pegged Trevor for the gardening type."

She was changing the subject and it made Ben sad. Could she really not accept how much he cared for her? *It's a good thing I have all the time in the world to convince her.*

Lauren knelt down next to a wide patch of yellow flowers with purple spots. "Can you picture him, rooting in the dirt with a trowel and a big, floppy hat?" She leaned in to give one of the flowers a sniff.

"No!" Ben jumped forward and lifted Lauren into his arms.

He'd been so focused on Lauren's beautiful face, he hadn't taken a good look at the flowers. Horror crept up Ben's spine as he stared down at the flowers he'd only ever seen once before.

"Keep back from those. They're harmful to our kind."

"Really?" Lauren took a step back, her eyes narrowed as she studied the flowers at her feet. "I've never heard of anything like that. Beheading and fire, those both make sense for taking down us vamps. But flower power?"

"These are kkot. They're incredibly rare. They take a certain amount of *effort* to grow." He swallowed down rising bile. "They won't kill you, but contact with a kkot puts vampires in a deep sleep. Ingesting, touching, or even smelling the flower can knock one of us out cold."

She studied his face, her eyebrows puckered in worry. "There's more to this, isn't there? Why would Trevor grow a flower that could harm him?"

Ben shook his head, stepping back further from the flowers, holding Lauren's hand tight. *There are so many. So very many.*

Lauren squeezed Ben's hand. "Tell me." She nodded firmly. "I want to know."

"I've only seen this once before: my uncle, Rhys, had a mass grave of all of his enemies." Ben swallowed hard and turned to Lauren. "Kkot only grows in the soil where *a lot* of vampires have been buried together." The words came slowly as the full implication of what Trevor had done, of what his nephew had become while Ben wasn't paying attention, chilled him to his core. "These are trophies. The flowers. For kkot clusters like this to grow, he has to be dumping the bodies all together, so the flowers would remind him of what he did."

I should have noticed a long time ago. All those girlfriends. *I should have stopped him. I should have told Danny, told Christopher, told anyone.* "Underneath our feet lay dozens of dead vampires."

Lauren gasped, her hand going to her throat and she swallowed loud. "Oh, gods." She paced back and forth in a small circle behind Ben. "I *knew* Trevor could be a sadistic asshole, but this is insane. Murder?" She turned to Ben.

Ben wished he could say something comforting, tell her that it was all some silly misunderstanding and they weren't presently standing over a mass grave. He wanted to pull her into his arms and assure her that everything was going to be okay.

I've been living alongside a serial killer, collaborating in business with a serial killer. Ben closed his eyes, then forced himself to open them and really look at the flowers. He wasn't responsible for Trevor becoming a monster, but he was responsible for ignoring his doubts.

"I can't let Trevor keep doing this to people. Gods, you could have been next..." The mere thought of Trevor harming Lauren, that she might have soon disappeared under the cold earth, was like taking a punch to the gut. Ben staggered backwards.

"*We* have to stop him." Lauren's fists clenched tight. "He can't just use women up and dispose of them like broken dolls."

Ben nodded. "I have to stop him. I'm older, and therefore stronger, than he is. I'll contact his sire, Danny, and the king, but we can't risk Trevor realizing we're both gone and escaping. I need to go back." He took Lauren's hand in his own. "You're newly-turned, and still under his command. You should walk away, hide out someplace, and wait for me to find you. If I take Trevor down, nothing will get in our way. We can be together, and we can be safe."

He knew Lauren's answer before she spoke the words. She was strong in so many ways. She wasn't going to take a back seat.

"Don't be stupid." She pulled Ben close for a deep kiss, her tongue running a quick, delicious lap around his mouth. "I'm coming with you. We're going to take this bastard down together."

Ben held Lauren close. His eyes swept over the graves,

the kkot flowers the only markers of the lives that had been extinguished. "I have an idea."

LAUREN'S FEET softly padded through the grass as she made a quick loop around the perimeter of the house, peering into each window. She found Trevor's shadow prowling around the top floor of his bedroom. Just seeing his outline made her feet still like a deer caught in the fatal head beams of a truck.

We have to stop him. Her words to Ben got her moving again. She crept around to the entrance of the east wing, her palms sweating before she even slipped inside.

Trevor's house had always been creepy, but knowing that it was the home of a serial killer made the oppressive darkness of the place even more skin-crawling. The lines of stone arches embedded in the ceiling reminded her of rib caves, and the high, dark windows were like too many eyes peering down at her.

The pneumatic tube ran into the east wing, half of which was taken up by a gym. She wondered if the exercise area had come with the house, since it wasn't like anyone living here actually needed to work out. When he was first showing her around, Trevor had even discouraged her from using any of the equipment. At the time, she'd thought he was just explaining another advantage of being a vampire, but could there have been more to it than that? *Was he ensuring I'd stay weaker, unable to fight back?*

Lauren pushed the thought down. She couldn't think about how she had *sex* with a serial killer. Those memories of pleasure on the restaurant floor promising a future of security were as tainted as kkot-planted soil. Bile rose and she choked it down before the smell told Trevor where she was.

Think of Ben, think of goodness, think about how we're going to get the rat bastard.

She almost tripped over Trevor's SCUBA tanks lining the mirrored wall of the gym. They'd worn those SCUBA tanks when on a spectacular trip to Sharm el Sheikh outside Cairo, back when he'd been pretending to be human and that he actually needed to breathe under water.

How couldn't I see he was such a monster? There had to have been signs. Long talks about art, history, music, and where they were going to go next for six months. Trevor would do most of the talking and Lauren would smile and nod, every few minutes asking a question to let Trevor keep talking about his interests. But never about himself. They'd never talked about past relationships, and she'd avoided bringing it up for fear she'd let slip about her previous marriage over too many glasses of wine.

I wanted him to be my savior, so I ignored the warning signs.

She rubbed between her eyes, forcing her gaze away from the tanks and their reminder of how deeply--in her desperation to find someone to provide for her--she'd failed herself.

Lauren found the lever for the pneumatic tube exactly where Ben said it was going to be: a red handle hidden behind a box of what looked like costumes from a Shakespeare play. She triumphantly flipped a switch on the panel from Auto to Manual. The clock in the east wing's tower chimed it was eight and Lauren slipped on her gas mask before the chimes stopped. A sound of hissing air came from the long tube. She smiled.

Back in the re-sized pool house, Ben had ground up the kkot flowers they'd spent the last few hours carefully harvesting, and he'd used one of his gadgets to convert their petals into a gas. He had the expertise to pump the gas through the pneumatic tube into the house, but someone on the other side had to open up the hatch and ensure that the gas made it all the way in to knock out Trevor.

By Ben's calculations, the gas would hit Trevor's room quickly, filling it in under thirty seconds and then moving out to the rest of house. Kkot was brutal: one whiff and he'd be unconscious for hours. Lauren smiled grimly at the thought. It would be a small revenge for those who were gone, but Lauren liked the thought that the flowers which marked Trevor's victims would be part of what took him down.

After she engaged the pneumatic tube, the plan was for Lauren to get out as quickly as possible. Once Ben filled the house with gas, he'd stop the pump, and come collect Trevor for transport to the castle for judgment.

Lauren made it all the way to the back door before she stopped, her hand shying away from the door knob. She looked back at the stairs, memories haunting her of her feet being commanded to cross that room, of standing at Trevor's mercy.

She *needed* to see Trevor unconscious. Before Ben came in and took control of the situation, she wanted to see Trevor helpless at her feet, done in by their plan.

Before she lost her nerve, she ran up the stairs to Trevor's room, scanning the ground for any sign of his motionless body. He wasn't in his bedroom, or the library, or her room, or any of the bathrooms. She even pulled back the shower curtains, her heart hammering in her chest, old horror movie instincts kicking in as she braced for what might be behind.

But nothing. Every room was empty.

Did he escape? If he'd slipped out onto the grounds, then Ben might be in trouble. She ran as fast as she could, doing one last sweep of all the rooms to make sure. The gas had to have permeated every room of the house by now--Ben had rigged the pneumatic tube to connect with the vents once it got inside for maximum coverage.

Lauren made it halfway through the last storage room before she realized that something was wrong. She backtracked, chasing a feeling that she was missing something crucial. She stopped short at the gym, scanning the rows of SCUBA gear until she counted.

One was missing, an outline of dust on the floor marking where it had sat until recently.

Oh shit.

A flash of movement in the corner of her eye was the only warning she got. Lauren dropped to the ground ducking under the wild swing of a SCUBA tank.

Trevor swung fast at her face and she rolled out of the way, jumping to her feet as the clash of metal against hardwood shook the floor. She dove over the steps of a stair climber and grabbed four kettlebells from the rack by the wall. Adrenaline surged.

Trevor's face contorted in a grimace and memories of being humiliated at the opera, of getting hurtled into his bedroom wall, feeling like she was burning to death plucked at the corner of her mind, fueling her rage. The weights felt as light as pebbles to her vampire strength and she flung them as fast as she could at Trevor's oncoming form. One hit his shoulder, the other his chest, but two missed, flying harmlessly over his shoulder to embed in the opposite wall.

He howled and ran toward her. She ducked and rolled under his outstretched hands, punching him hard in the groin as she slid beneath him. He doubled over, but recovered quickly, jumping away from her attempts to pull off the gas mask which protected him from the kkot.

Inside his SCUBA gear, Trevor's mouth moved in what Lauren guessed from the confident sneer on his face were commands.

Lauren laughed, pointing to her earplugs, firmly in place. "I can't hear you, you asshole!"

His second of shock was all she needed. Lauren leapt forward and yanked away Trevor's face mask. He grabbed his nose with one hand, closing his mouth. His triumphant glare communicated what he couldn't dare open his mouth to voice: *vampires don't need to breathe, you fool.*

Lauren picked up the SCUBA tank and swung with all of her might. It connected with Trevor's skull with a clang that reverberated through the room and shook the mirrors on the wall. Trevor gasped in shock at the blow, taking in a deep breath of kkot. He fell over to the ground, and lay still. Lauren stood over him.

She almost kicked him in the face, but stopped herself. *I'm better than him.* She used chains pulled from the exercise equipment to hogtie his hands and feet together behind his back. With a happy sigh, she pulled out her earplugs.

Ben ran through the door a second later, his face also covered with a gas mask.

"I heard the sounds of banging. Are you all right?" he asked, running forward to pull her into his arms and study Trevor's slow breathing.

"I'm more than all right." Lauren smiled wide, showing every tooth. "I won."

◠

"GUILTY ON ALL COUNTS!" The judge's voice echoed through the royal courthouse; it was quickly overcome by cheers.

Ben pulled Lauren into his arms and spun her in a tight circle. She laughed and held tightly onto him.

"Trevor will never be able to hurt you or anyone else ever again." Ben brought her back to the ground and held her close.

"Damn straight," Lauren joked, wrapping her arms around Ben's neck and pulling him in for a long, lingering kiss. Her hair, which she had down and wild, tickled his nose, and her overjoyed smile warmed him to his toes.

"Hey, no making out in the court!" A voice interrupted them.

Ben turned to see Danny Dal, hand-in-hand with his fiancé Robin, striding towards Ben and Lauren down the hallway.

"It's good to see you." Danny shook Ben's hand. "I can't believe things with Trevor got so out of hand." He sighed. "I knew he had some weird ideas about Dracula and all, but this..." He pointed at the evidence still tacked up on a bulletin board: the faces of the fifty six women Trevor had killed over the centuries.

Trevor had admitted everything during the trial. Ben suspected the egomaniacal pipsqueak had been longing to talk about his "dark romance" as he called it, for a long time. Back when he was still human, Trevor had a crush on a woman named Felicity. She was disgusted by him, so Trevor begged Danny to turn him, in hopes that Felicity would find Trevor more appealing as a 'creature of the night'. When that didn't work, Trevor spent centuries turning women who looked like Felicity, controlling them to fulfill the delusional fantasies he'd envisioned for his life with his "true love". Whenever one of his sirelings deviated from the script in his head, Trevor killed her and turned another.

"I'm beyond grateful that you were able to bring him to justice," Danny said, his expression grave. "I should have never turned him, or at least I should have kept a better eye on him."

"I didn't stop him alone." Ben wrapped his arm around Lauren's waist. "This is Lauren, the *real* brains behind our operation." He rested his index finger on his chin. "And the brawn, too, now that I think about it."

Robin nudged Danny with her elbow, her laugh bringing a smile to Danny's dour face. "I believe it. It's such hard work keeping these dashing men in line, isn't it?"

"Non-stop toil, really." Lauren's tone was somber, but she was grinning wildly.

"So what's next for you two?" Danny asked. "Trevor's mansion is in my name. It's yours if you want it. You can move out of the pool house and live large for a change."

"We're sticking with the pool house," Lauren said.

Ben pulled a clear plastic bag out of his pocket and held it at eye level. "We'll just be taking it with us." The miniaturized pool house was inside, but now closer to the size of a baseball than a button. He'd added a few new rooms to his home while it was still miniaturized--much easier and cost-effective to do it that way--and Lauren had been completely enchanted by what he'd built for her.

"That'll explain the outfit, then." Danny failed to stifle a laugh.

"What?" Ben looked down at his head-to-toe khaki ensemble. He'd bought what he had been assured by centuries of reading fiction was the exact correct thing to wear. The wide-brimmed hat was a bit large for his head, and the binoculars he had tucked into one of the overly-large pockets weighed him down a bit, but he'd never been more excited.

"I think he looks adorable." Lauren squeezed his arm. "We're going on a world tour, starting with a safari. Ben's desalinator has helped so many people in so many countries, I think it's only fair that he gets to see how much good he's done in person. And I'm looking forward to roaming free for a change. With our house in a bag, we can go anywhere we want at any time."

Ben's chest swelled with pride. Once his desalination machine was finished, Lauren had helped him load up the specs online so people all over the globe could build their own. Clean drinking water was now easily available in places where it was once seen as a luxury.

Lauren twined her fingers through Ben's and whispered in his ear. "I love you, you know."

"I love you, too." Ben pulled her close. He had an idea for proposing once they reached Kenya, but he wasn't sure he'd be able to wait that long.

They walked out of the courtroom, away from Trevor and the van taking him to the hole in the ground he was going to live in for the foreseeable future. The only thing that mattered was Lauren and Ben moving forward together.

"Let's go dancing" Ben said.

Lauren kissed him. "With you? Always."

Our vampire adventures conclude in the action-packed final installment of the *Royal Blood* series, *The Vampire's Choice*.

Dear Reader,

We hoped you enjoyed **Royal Blood**. We really love this world and creating more places and people to inhabit it. Many readers wrote asking; "What's up with Lola?" Well, stay tuned for more of Lola's mysterious meddling because the adventures at AUDREY'S (and the paranormal romantic interludes) aren't over.

When we first published this series, we got a lot of emails from fans thanking us for these books. Some liked certain series and sets of characters more than others. As authors, we love feedback. Your appreciation for this world is the reason why we keep writing books in this world.

Reviews are increasingly tough to come by these days. You, the reader, have the power now to make or break a book. So, tell us what you like, what you loved, even what you hated. We'd love to hear from you.

Thank you so much for reading **Royal Blood** and for spending time with our wacky brains.

Have fun, everybody

Annie & Jess ("AJ") Tipton

MEET AJ TIPTON

AJ Tipton is the pseudonym of a writing team: Annie and Jess (Get it? "AJ." You get it). Corporate drones by day, we spend our evenings writing fantasies to astound, arouse, and amuse. Located in Brooklyn, we are total dorks and love it.

Want more stories of the bizarre and wondrous? Sign up for the new publications subscription list and you'll be the first to know when new books become available. There might also be other surprises along the way. Or just contact us directly at a.j.tipton.author@gmail.com

Our ideas for future books--everything from sex robots to ghost brothels--will keep us busy for many years to come, so follow along for the fun and let us know what series you like best. We love to hear from readers.

ajtiptonauthor.wordpress.com
ajtiptonauthor@gmail.com

www.ingramcontent.com/pod-product-compliance
Lightning Source LLC
Chambersburg PA
CBHW030605180626
46816CB00005B/1681